The
OFF-LIMITS
RULE

The

OFF-LIMITS RULE

A NOVEL

SARAH ADAMS

DELL BOOKS

NEW YORK

2024 Dell Trade Paperback Edition

Copyright © 2021 by Sarah Adams
Excerpt from *The Temporary Roomie* by Sarah Adams
copyright © 2021 by Sarah Adams

Published in the United States by Dell, an imprint of Random House, a division of Penguin Random House LLC, New York.

Originally self-published in the United States by the author in 2021.

DELL and the D colophon are registered trademarks of Penguin Random House LLC.

LIBRARY OF CONGRESS CATALOGING-IN-PUBLICATION DATA
Names: Adams, Sarah, 1991– author.
Title: The off-limits rule: a novel / Sarah Adams.
Description: 2024 Dell trade paperback edition. | New York: Dell Books, 2024.
Identifiers: LCCN 2024001749 (print) | LCCN 2024001750 (ebook) |
ISBN 9780593871751 (paperback) | ISBN 9780593871768 (ebook)
Subjects: LCGFT: Romance fiction. | Novels.
Classification: LCC PS3601.D3947 O34 2024 (print) |
LCC PS3601.D3947 (ebook) | DDC 813/.6—dc23/eng/20240117
LC record available at https://lccn.loc.gov/2024001749
LC ebook record available at https://lccn.loc.gov/2024001750

Printed in the United States of America on acid-free paper

This book contains an excerpt from the forthcoming book
The Temporary Roomie by Sarah Adams. This excerpt has been set for this
edition only and may not reflect the final content of the forthcoming edition.

randomhousebooks.com

2   4   6   8   9   7   5   3   1

Title page art by Radiocat © Adobe Stock Photos

Book design by Sara Bereta

To the real hero of my books: sugary cereal

A NOTE FROM SARAH

Hello, reader! Although this book is very much a romcom and written in a way to uplift and leave you feeling nothing but happy and hopeful, it does contain heavier elements. For those who need a little extra assurance before they begin reading, I have provided a content warning below. However, please be aware that the content warning *does* include spoilers.

XO Sarah

Content warning: Please be advised that The Off-Limits Rule *features a woman who, in the past, had an unplanned pregnancy she chose to keep and a side character who is currently walking the same path. Themes of body image after having children are also explored delicately and positively. The story also contains light swearing and implied intimacy.*

The
OFF-LIMITS
RULE

CHAPTER 1

Lucy

I'm splayed out like a starfish ripped from the ocean and dried up on the carpet of my new bedroom. I've been here for an hour, watching the fan blades go round and round, thinking I could have turned on a show by now, but what's the point anyway? My fan friends are just as entertaining as anything on TV these days. Besides, fan blades don't fill you with romantic illusions about this crappy, *crappy* world and make you feel that you will get everything you've always wanted. No, Fanny, Fandrick, Fantasia, and Fandall don't tell me I'll get my happy ending in this life. They just—

"Oh my gosh." The sound of my older brother's voice pulls me out of my fan entertainment, and I roll my head to the side, squinting at his blurry figure filling my doorframe. "This is next-level pitiful, Luce." Drew strides into my room, steps over my useless body covered in candy wrappers, and mercilessly rips back the curtains.

I hiss like a vampire that's just been easily beaten in an over-complicated plot when the light falls onto my body. *Light was the key the whole time!* My muscles are too puny and wasted away from my forty-eight-hour feeling-sorry-for-myself binge to even throw my hand over my eyes. "Stop it, jerk. Close those and leave me be!"

He towers over me and shakes his head of brown hair like he can't believe the pitiful excuse of a human I am. I peek up through my melancholy just enough to register that I should trim his hair soon. "Look at you. Your face is covered in chocolate, and you smell."

"Rude. I never stink. I can go weeks without deodorant and still—" I lift my arm and wince when I get a whiff of myself. "Oh yeah, shit, that's bad."

His eyebrows are lifted, and he's nodding with a humorless smile. "You need to get out of this room. I gave you a few days to pout that things didn't turn out like you wanted, but now it's time to get up and get moving."

"I don't *pout*."

"Your lip is actually jutting out."

I suck the offending lip back into my mouth and bite it. Drew extends his hand, and I take it, but only because I really have to pee and not at all because I secretly know he's right and I've wallowed long enough. When my world went south a few days ago, the first thing I did was call Drew to come get me and my son, Levi—not like, come get us from the restaurant but come get us from Atlanta, Georgia, where I was paving my own way, making my life happen for myself, living the dream, and failing miserably at all of it.

Drew didn't even bat an eye when I asked him to come help me pack up my dignity and haul it back home. From the beginning, he wasn't thrilled about my decision to move out of Tennessee and away from our family, so without hesitating he said, "Be there tomorrow, Luce. I'll bring a truck." And he did. He spent the whole next day helping me pack everything in that dinky (very smelly) apartment, and then he drove me back to his house in Nashville, where my son and I will be living (rent-free, *bless him*) for the foreseeable future.

The only reason I've been able to spend the past few days interviewing my fan blades is because my amazing parents took my four-year-old for a few days while I get unpacked and settled. I don't think they meant for me to settle my butt into the carpet and lie here for the entire weekend making excellent fan friends, but it's what I've done, and no one is allowed to judge me because judging isn't nice.

Once I'm standing, Drew sizes me up, and let me tell you, he does *not* like what he sees. "I think you have a bird's nest in your hair. Go take a shower."

"I don't feel like showering. I'll just spray some dry shampoo to kill the stink. And maybe the birds."

He catches my arm when I try to turn away. "As your older brother, I'm telling you . . . get in that shower or I will put you in it, clothes and all, because honestly they could use a wash too."

I narrow my eyes and stand up on my tiptoes to look more frightening—I think the effect would be better if I didn't feel chocolate smeared across the side of my face. "I'm a grown, adult woman with a child, so your older-brother threats aren't effective anymore."

He tilts his head down slowly—making a point that he's, like, nineteen million feet taller than me—and makes direct eye contact. "You're wearing dinosaur PJ pants. And as long as you call me, pulling that *baby-sister* card when you need my help with something, the older-brother threats count."

I raise an indignant chin. "I never do that." *I definitely do it all the time.*

"Take a shower, then put on a swimsuit."

I make a disgusted *ugh* sound. "I am *not* going swimming with you. All I want to do is eat disgusting takeout, fill my body to the brim with MSG, and then crawl under the covers until next year rolls around with shiny new promises of happiness."

He's not listening. He's turning me around and pushing me toward the bathroom. "Get to it, stinky. Like it or not, you're putting on a swimsuit and coming with me. It's been too long since you've seen the sun, and you look like a cadaver." I feel blessed that he didn't mention I smell like one too.

"I hate the pool." I'm a cartoon now, and my arms are long droopy noodles, dragging across the floor as I'm pushed toward the bathroom.

"Lucky we're not going to one then. My buddy and I are taking the boat out to wakeboard for the afternoon. You're coming too."

I'm standing motionless in the bathroom now, eyebrows-deep in my sullen mood as Drew pulls back the shower curtain and starts the water. He digs under the sink and pulls out a fluffy towel, tossing it onto the counter. He's giving me tough love right now, but I know underneath all this dominance is a soft, squishy middle. Drew has one tender spot in life, and it's me. The tenderness also extends to Levi by association and because my son's cheeks are so chunky and round you can't help but dissolve into a pool of wobbly Jell-O when he smiles at you.

"Isn't it, like . . . frowned upon to skip work on a Wednesday?" I ask, trying to needle him so he'll leave me alone with my candy bars and sadness.

"Yes, but it's *Sunday*." The judgment in his voice is thick. "And unless one of my patients goes into labor, I have Sundays off."

I blow air out through my mouth, making a motorboat sound because I'm too lethargic and wasted on chocolate from my pity party for snappy comebacks. Which is sad because snappy comebacks are my thing.

"Lucy," Drew says, bending to catch my eye like he knows my thoughts were starting to wander back down the dark tunnel to mopey-land. He points behind him to the steaming water. "Lather, rinse, and repeat. You'll feel better. Promise." He leans forward and gives a dramatic sniff. "Maybe even repeat a few times. Then move on to the toothbrush, because I think something crawled into your mouth and died." *Siblings are so sweet.*

I punch him hard in the arm, and he just smiles like he's happy to see me showing some signs of life. "But seriously, thank you," I say quietly. "Thanks for taking me in too. You're always rescuing me."

The day I realized I was a week late for my period, Drew was the one who drove to the store and bought my pregnancy test. He's the one who held me when I cried and told me that if I wanted to keep the baby, I wouldn't have to go it alone because I'd have him (and then my parents quickly hip-checked him out of the way and reminded me I'd have them too). This is part of the reason I moved to Atlanta a year ago—not because I wanted to get away from them but because I wanted to prove to myself I could stand on my own two feet and support my son.

Spoiler alert: I can't.

I'm a twenty-nine-year-old single mom and unemployed hairdresser (I got fired from the salon I was working at) who's having to live with my older brother because I don't have a penny in savings. Turns out, kids are mega-expensive. And when you choose to live away from your support system as a single parent, you have to put your child in daycare (which costs your arm) and hire babysitters when you want to go out on the weekend (which costs your leg), or hire a full-time nanny (which costs your soul).

Although Levi's dad, Brent, pays child support, it's just not quite enough to help me get ahead of bills and debt. Brent is not a bad guy or anything, and he's even offered to pay extra to help give me a financial cushion, but for some reason I'd rather start wearing tennis shoes without socks and selling them to people on the internet who want them *extra sweaty* before I take more money from Brent. He's always had too much emotional pull in my life. At one point I might have dreamed of us actually becoming a family one day—but not anymore. Those dreams have long since evaporated, and now, anytime he texts me after midnight saying something like, *Why don't we ever get together, just the two of us?*, I know better than to respond.

Drew gives me a soft smile and really doesn't have to say anything because we have that sibling telepathy thing that lets me see inside his head. He speaks anyway. "You'd do the same for me."

"Yeah. Of course I would." But I'll never need to because Drew has his life together one hundred percent of the time.

He pulls me in for a hug. "I'm sorry you're bummed, but I'm glad you're home and you and that jackass broke up."

And just like that, our sibling comradery vanishes and I'd like to kick him in the shins. I settle for pushing out of his hug. "He wasn't a jackass!"

"Yeah, he was. You just need some space from him to see it."

"No, *Andrew*, he just wasn't smooth and *super cool* like you assume you are, and that's why you didn't like him. But he wasn't a jackass."

I really don't know why I'm defending Tim so much. I wasn't in love with him or anything. In fact, that's why we broke up. There was no spark, and we were basically friends who kissed (and not all that often). I'd never even introduced him to Levi because somewhere in the back of my mind I always knew our relationship wasn't going anywhere.

I'm a little ashamed to admit it, but I only dated him because he was *there* and available. I was new to Atlanta, having taken an open position at a new salon, and he was one of my first clients. We hit it off, started dating (if you can even call it that since we barely saw each other due to me not having any friends or family around to help babysit), and, for a few months, fell into a comfortable pattern of going out on Saturday nights when I could afford to hire the sixteen-year-old down the street. She had a more active dating life than me, though, so I had to book her weeks out and pay her a fortune.

Then the roommate I moved to Atlanta with got engaged to her boyfriend and asked to break our lease agreement early so she could move in with him. I, being a woman deeply afraid of confrontation, agreed wholeheartedly before remembering that I didn't trust anyone else to live with me and my son. I tried to make it work financially on my own for a while, but then the burden just got too heavy. I was two months behind on rent, and then I lost my job at the salon because I canceled on too many clients.

Did I mention it's super hard to be a single parent without a nearby support system? Turns out, most bosses really don't give a crap about your child at home with a stomach bug and unable to go into daycare. They really only care that you didn't show up to work and earn them the money they were counting on.

So I got fired, and then the next week Tim and I broke up, and *then* I got the official eviction notice from my landlord. I didn't need any time to think about what to do. I called Drew and told him to come get me, and then I cut Atlanta off like a bad split end.

Now I'm sad, but not because I miss Tim. I'm sad because I

don't miss Tim and my life feels like way more of a mess than it should at age twenty-nine. It's like I'm mourning something I hoped could happen but didn't.

"No," says Drew, "I didn't like him because when I came to visit and the three of us went to dinner, he said he was cold and accepted your sweater when you took it off and gave it to him."

I feel a familiar defensiveness boil in my chest. "He has a *thyroid problem* and gets cold easily. And I told you, I wasn't even cold!"

"Then why'd you take my sweatshirt after he took yours?"

"Because . . ." I drop my gaze, hoping he doesn't catch my defeated look. "It had been six months since I'd seen you and I missed you?" I can't let Drew know I also found Tim annoying at times or else he'll add it to his ongoing list titled Drew Knows Better Than Lucy. *It is a solid list, though.*

He doesn't comment on my blatant lie, just lifts an eyebrow and points to the running water. "Stop stalling and take your shower. But make it quick or we're gonna be late."

Well, joke's on him because I don't even want to go out with him and his *buddy,* and I don't care one bit if we're late. In fact, I feel like teaching my brother a lesson, so I turn on some music and take an extra-long time, reenacting every sad shower scene I've ever witnessed, letting the spray of the water rush over my face as depressing songs play on the speaker in my bedroom.

Bang, bang, bang.

I jump out of my sopping-wet skin and press myself back against the tile, certain I'm about to be murdered by a polite killer who likes to knock before he enters, but then Drew's voice booms through the door. "I swear to God, Lucy, I will cut off the hot water if you don't get out soon. Also, that's enough Sarah McLachlan." He turns off my Super Sad Mix and blares "Ice Ice Baby" as an overt threat.

Ah—so nice living together again.

I want to be furious with Drew, but instead I'm using all my willpower to not laugh.

I'm a whiny baby all the way to the boat dock. *The sun is too bright. My head hurts. There's nothing good on the radio.* Honestly, I'm surprised Drew didn't unlock the doors, pull the handle, and push me out onto the interstate. That's what I would have done if the roles were reversed, because even I don't want to hang out with me right now. Even so, he took my annoyance in stride, turning off the radio, giving me his sunglasses, offering to stop for Advil. Really, it's suspicious how syrupy sweet my brother is being.

At the last minute, I even asked him if we could make a pit stop at our mom and dad's house so I could check on Levi. Let's be honest, Levi is with his two favorite people in the world, so he's not missing me. My mom has probably fed him so many sugary treats he's completely forgotten my name.

When the door opens and I see my little cutie, blond hair all askew in various cowlicks, eyes bright with sugar overdose, and white powder mysteriously coating his lips, my suspicions are confirmed.

I glance down at my child and then up at his grandparents standing at attention behind him, mischief written all over their faces. "This is a surprise drop-by . . . you know, to make sure everyone's following the rules," I say, drawling out the last word like I'm a detective tilting her aviators down, completely on to their tricks.

Both grandparents make a show of gulping nervously, and I abruptly drop down to get eye level with Levi. I reach out and run a finger across his top lip, bringing the powdered sugar close to my eye for inspection. "Mm-hmm . . . just what I thought. Donut residue." He giggles and licks his lip nearly up to his nose to get every particle of sugar he can. *I taught him well.*

My mom puts her hand on Levi's shoulder and squeezes. "Stay strong, buddy."

I narrow my eyes up at my mother (also my favorite person in the world) and shoot to my feet, getting in her face like a drill sergeant. "How many?" My voice growls menacingly. Levi giggles again, and I glance down at him. "Do you think this is funny, little man?"

"Mom, you're so silly."

"How many?" I repeat to my mom, undeterred by the adorable chunky-cheeked boy. She lifts her chin and makes a show of pressing her lips closed. "I see . . . that's how it's going to be? Fine. I know who to go to when I want the truth."

"Luce, come on, we gotta go," Drew says, sounding a little impatient behind me. *Someone has lost his funny bone.*

I hold up my finger behind me in his direction and shush him before taking a slow step directly in front of my dad. His eyes widen, and I know he'll be an easy crack. "So, Mr. Marshall, are you going to talk, or are we going to have to do this the hard way—"

"*Three!*" he blurts, and my mom shoots him the stink eye.

I grin and push my imaginary glasses back up the bridge of my nose. "Thought so. Sir, ma'am, do you happen to know the effects too much sugar have on—"

I don't get to finish my sentence because Drew picks me up, tosses me over his shoulder, and starts carrying me away. "Bye, guys," he says with a smile and wave. "We'll have our phones if you need us."

"*Wait!* Let me at least kiss my child goodbye, you oaf."

He pauses and backs up a few steps, bending down so I'm lowered to lip level with Levi. He laughs and laughs at the sight of me on "Uncle Drew's" shoulder, so much so that I'm barely able to plant a kiss on his sugary cheek from all his giggling.

"Love you, baby. Be good for Grammy and Grandad," I tell him, feeling my heart squeeze a little painfully at the thought of leaving him again. Other than the times I had to work, Levi and I haven't spent much time apart this last year. Although I'm happy to see him reunited with family, I also have this strong desire to stay close to him. Plus, stuffing my face with donuts sounds infinitely better than going out with Drew and his buddy on the boat.

"Have fun, you two," say my parents, breaking character to wrap an arm around each other and wave as Drew walks us away and deposits me in the front seat of his car.

After our twenty-minute drive, we pull into the marina, and I take my sweet time getting out of the car. Maybe if I move slow enough, he'll leave me behind and just let me curl up in a depressed ball under a tree somewhere.

He can see right through my shenanigans. "Dammit, Lucy, do I have to drag you onto the boat too? You're going on the lake, because you need this whether you can see it or not. Quit being a pain in the butt and get moving."

"What happened to Mr. Congeniality from the car ride?" I ask, getting out and slamming my door shut.

He pulls a cooler from the trunk and grins at me—his eyes a darker blue than mine, filled with sibling exasperation. "I was hoping you'd get it all out of your system so Johnny Raincloud wouldn't follow us out on the water."

"You didn't have to bring me, you know. If you wanted a happy companion, you could have just invited some of those fun women who love you."

"I didn't want to bring a fun woman. I wanted to bring you. My annoying little sister."

I narrow my eyes and cross my arms.

He jerks his head toward the back seat. "Grab the towels and let's get on the water."

"One hour," I say, following behind him with the towels like a stubborn puppy that doesn't want to walk on a leash but knows it doesn't have a choice. "I'm staying for one hour and that's it. Then I'm going back to my candy bar babies."

"Just get in the boat, Eeyore," says Drew, fighting a smile as he extends his hand to help me over the railing.

Once in the boat, I run my palms along the bright-white upholstery. It's hot to the touch, and I can't help but smile at my brother's dream come true. He's always wanted a boat, and he finally made it happen. He's been working his butt off the past several years, completing medical school and then enduring his residency and whatever else doctors have to go through. Now he is an ob-gyn in a small private practice, and this was his official "doctor" present to himself.

Other than a partner feeling slightly uncomfortable with him working closely with women's bodies all day, I can't help but wonder why he's still single. He's good-looking, funny, and outgoing. Most women love him, yet he won't have it. He dates (a lot) but has never been interested in settling down.

Taking my towel, I lay it across the boiling-hot leather before sitting so I don't sear my butt cheeks. I settle in, begrudgingly feeling like Drew was right; it really does feel good to be outside with the sun tickling my skin. "So, which buddy is coming out with us? Farty Marty or Sweaty Steven?" Oddly, all of Drew's friends have terrible flaws, so much so that I'm beginning to wonder if he has a beauty complex and refuses to associate with anyone prettier than him.

"Cooper," he says while shoving the cooler into a little side compartment.

Ah, yes, the recently moved-out roommate. I haven't met this one yet. He moved in with Drew about a year ago, right after I left town, and they apparently became besties right away. Drew won't let me refer to them as that, though, so I make sure to do it as often as I can.

"Hmm . . . Cooper Pooper."

"Don't do that."

"I have to. How will I remember his name otherwise?"

Drew doesn't look at me as he secures the boat canopy. "Repeat it to yourself five times."

"Cooper Pooper. Cooper Pooper. Cooper Poo—"

"Not what I meant, and you know it," Drew says, looking over his shoulder with the same look the actors on *SNL* get when they try not to let the audience see them laugh. *He missed me.*

I shut my eyes and lean my head back, feeling the sun singe my eyelids and trying to imagine what terrible flaw of Cooper's I will have to endure all day. Bad BO? Snaggleteeth? Greasy hair? Probably a heavy combination of everything.

I don't know, and it doesn't matter anyway. I'm just going to lean back against the warm leather and sleep the day away. Drew forced me out here, but he can't force me to smile or pretend I'm enjoying life with Pooper Scooper Cooper. *See?* I'll never forget his name now. My method works.

I hear footsteps approaching on the dock, but my eyes feel too heavy to open. Probably all that MSG really settling into my bloodstream and trying to embalm my body.

"Hey, Coop," says Drew, and I can feel my whole body stiffen with dread. He's here. What's it going to be? My money is on the BO. "Just throw your stuff over there by Lucy. Oh, by the way, that's my sister."

I guess that's my cue to open my eyes and try to act like I don't see the nasty hair-sprouting mole on the tip of this guy's nose.

CHAPTER 2

Lucy

I open my eyes to sudden blinding light and the shape of a man; it's hard to see him with the sun blazing over his head like he just beamed down from heaven. I lift my hand to shield my eyes and—*oh my gosh, stop it right now!* This can't be one of Drew's friends. Cooper Pooper is hot. My brain is short-circuiting looking at the miles and miles of lean, tan, toned, *tempting* muscles. I'm sure I look feral staring at him. All my words are drying up and getting stuck in my throat like I've never seen a man before. But the truth is, I've never seen a man like *him*—not outside of the movies, at least.

His tousled blond hair hangs in styled yet effortlessly beachy waves, just long enough to swoop over one eyebrow and curl up at the nape of his neck like it *has* to be rebellious. His eyes are bright, kick-you-in-the-stomach, crystal-clear-Tahiti-water blue, and his smile is all blinding-white teeth against bronze tanned skin. Someone give me a piece of glass—I think I could cut it using his jaw. All he needs is a wet suit and a surfboard and he would be Surfing Ken.

Maybe I already have sun poisoning and I'm just hallucinating. He's too gorgeous to be real.

"Nice to finally meet you, Lucy." *The hallucination speaks!*

And that means I have to speak too. He holds out his hand for me to shake, and suddenly I'm a weirdo who should never leave her house. My brain has never needed to act under this kind of pressure before and can't handle the sight of his large hand waiting for my skin to brush against his, and *wow,* my mind is making this way more sensual than it needs to be.

Because my thoughts are all tripping over themselves, I extend my *left* hand (not my right, like a normal person would for a handshake) to receive his greeting. Yep, it's true, and it's painfully awkward as I wrap my fingers around his like I'm a dainty little English crumpet and then just kind of jiggle his hand side to side like it's a fish.

Yeah, it's cool, I'll just jump off the boat now.

"Hhhhhhi," I say, and then abruptly let go of his hand. I'm now a robot that's just been doused in water and is malfunctioning.

His dirty-blond eyebrows climb up his forehead and mingle with his wavy locks. Then he gives me an amused, tilted smile, and my whole world flips on end. I'd bet he's not fazed or all that surprised by my oddness because this is most likely a normal reaction when someone is faced with his masculine beauty. He just assumes this is how the world around him behaves.

Drew pops into existence beside Cooper and does that man-friend, slap-on-the-back thing. "Believe it or not, Lucy has given a handshake before, but she's a little out of sorts from the move. And possibly an MSG overdose." *I'm going to kill him.*

"It's cool," says Cooper with a melting smile that makes me

want to giggle like a freak. "And a breakup with your boyfriend, right? Drew filled me in."

"Boyfriend?"

Drew scoffs with a smile. "Yeah. *Tim*—remember him? The reason you had melted chocolate smeared all over your face about an hour ago?"

I'm absolutely going to put laxatives in his coffee tomorrow.

My brother has never been less of a wingman. Clearly this is the hottest guy I've ever seen, so how about let's not tell him I've been stuffing my face with candy and am a complete loser, *yeah*?

"Oh, yes. Him. *Tim*. Yeah, we broke up." I make a slicing motion with my thumb across my throat, and now my statement seems slightly more vicious than intended. "Donezo. We're over— totally over."

He gets it. Stop talking, Lucy.

This is not okay or fair. I'm not prepared for this. I shouldn't be faced with a man of this caliber so soon after a breakup with a completely lukewarm guy. If this were a video game, I'd have just somehow stumbled over a cheat code and would now be facing the final boss to defeat. Level 100: Brother's Hot Best Friend.

Drew is seriously looking at me like I've lost my mind, and guess what? I have. "Luce, I think you need some sleep."

No, I need to make out with Cooper.

"I definitely do," I say with a breathy laugh that's uncomfortable for everyone. I hop up from my seat and go dig in the cooler for a water just to have a reason to look away from Cooper and gather my senses. "I think I'm dehydrated too. It's hot out here, right?"

No one answers, but both men look a little stunned as I guzzle my water.

Finally, Drew shakes his head and steps closer to me so he can drop his voice. "Hey, you okay?" He's surprisingly tender right now, misreading my actions as those of a woman who's about to break down into a heartbroken sob rather than cackling nervous laughter.

That's fine. I'd rather him think I'm losing it over Tim than salivating at the sight of the perfect male specimen at the front of the boat. "Yeah. Sorry. Just . . . processing everything still."

If he's not buying it, Drew doesn't let on. He gives me a quick nod, then turns to sit in the captain's seat and start the engine.

"All right, let's get out of here before the marina gets too busy. Cooper, will you untie us?"

He does. But first, Cooper rakes his hand through his hair and settles a flat-bill hat backward on his head, taking his sexiness up to an unhealthy range. I watch from the corner of my eye like a stealthy assassin.

Once we're slowly gliding through the marina, Cooper plops down onto one of the bench seats at the front and extends his long legs in front of him, staring out at the lake. Drew looks over his shoulder at me still standing in the far back corner of the boat and eyes me like he's afraid I might need to be life-flighted to the hospital. "You gonna sit down? I'm about to take off."

"Oh. Sure." Would it be weird if I just sat down right here on the floor?

I think Drew knows I'm contemplating it because he jerks his head toward the front and lowers his voice. "Go sit up there with Cooper. He's a nice guy. I wouldn't have invited him out here if I thought he would be rude to you."

Ha! He thinks I'm afraid to go sit by Cooper because I'm worried he's going to hit on me or something. The absurdity of this makes me want to double over with laughter.

I don't want to go sit by Cooper because I wasn't expecting the sexiest man alive to be joining us on this boating adventure today, and so I have the legs of a woolly mammoth. Also, I had every intention of scaring off whatever horrid, sweaty, greasy, snaggly friend Drew brought out with us, so I wore the most wholesome and frumpy one-piece the world has ever seen. *It's bad, friends. Real bad.*

The swimsuit in question is left over from my senior year swim meet a thousand years ago. It's one of those special swim team brands that looks sort of tie-dye but in the worst colors imaginable, and the fabric is no longer sleek and smooth. It's ratty, and rough, and a little saggy in all the wrong places.

Luckily, I had the forethought to wear a cover-up, a garment that will not be leaving my body the entire day.

I swallow and try to force my legs to stop wobbling as I stumble my way out to the bow. I take my seat like we're playing musical chairs and someone just cut the music so my seat is about to disappear. *Why am I like this?*

Sitting down, I tuck my legs tightly up under me so Cooper doesn't get a peek at my one-inch-long leg hairs and keep my eyes set firmly to *anywhere but at the man sitting to my right.*

Drew throttles up, and the engine roars as the boat takes off, whipping my hair around my face. The wind is such a punk, trying to lift my cover-up just to embarrass me. I lock it down with my hands and wish to high heaven I were one of those women who looks effortlessly sexy all the time with her hair twirling around her face like a Disney princess. You know, the ones who never have to worry about shaving their legs because they go for routine waxes? The ones who would never hold on to a swimsuit from their high school years and only own little next-to-nothing numbers that show off their cute boobs.

My boobs are cute in a one-is-slightly-bigger-than-the-other kind of way. The size and shape of my breasts are irrelevant though, given no one will notice them today because of how they are completely mashed down in this soul-sucking one-piece. My butt, however, is dimply. There's no way around it. Honestly, I'm fine with my dimples, but one look at a man like Cooper tells me he would not be. I put him solidly in the *Pilates instructors only* category.

Trying to be stealthy, I sneak a sidelong peek, nearly jumping out of my skin and over the side of the motoring boat when I catch him looking at me too. Our eyes collide for one pounding heartbeat, and I think I see a glimmer of something in his before I rip my gaze from him and back out over the water. *No looking at his glimmer, Lucy.*

I bite my lips together and try to hold back an embarrassed smile. How am I going to make it through this day with him? I'm used to comfortable, snuggle-up-and-read-a-book Tim—not sensual, eye-glimmering Cooper.

Thinking of Tim gives me an idea, though! When we pull into a cove and Drew cuts the engine, I reach for my tote bag and pull out a book. Just the feel of the warm matte cover between my fingers helps me relax. *Yes, this is good.* I can bury my nose in the pages like I normally do and let the story carry me to a different place.

A different place where Cooper isn't rising from his seat, reaching for the back of his tank top, and yanking it off over his head. A place far, *far* away from the defined, rock-hard abdomen hovering perfectly in my line of sight. Oh gosh, it's getting worse. Cooper pulls out a can of spray sunscreen and starts dousing his body in a nice, muscle-enhancing sheen, then rubs it in, his large biceps and shoulders bunching and tensing as he moves.

I didn't even realize seeing an Adonis V in real life was on my bucket list, but here we are, and I'm checking it off.

"Good book?" Cooper's voice rumbles at me, making me shamefully peel my eyes away from his six-pack up to his amused grin.

Busted.

My cheeks are lava, and all I can do is blink and turn my gaze back down to my book, begging it to magically transport me into its world. Because in this one, I have no idea how to interact with a man who looks like that. He's all muscles and charisma, and right now I'm ninety-seven percent candy bars and MSG.

CHAPTER 3

Cooper

Well, this is the worst.

Come out on the boat with me and my sister, Cooper. It'll be fun, Cooper.

Guess what, Drew—it's not fun. His sister is supposed to be burly looking, the female version of *him*. She's supposed to have a deep, husky voice, and if I squint, I would get her and Drew mixed up. That's what every guy hopes his best friend's little sister will look like.

Lucy, however, is freaking gorgeous.

She looks absolutely nothing like Drew. The only thing these two have in common is their eyes. Except, on Drew, they are just plain blue. Dude has blue eyes, end of story. On Lucy, they are *deep*-indigo irises framed by long, dark lashes. Her skin is a soft milky white, and her hair is dark auburn, almost brown but not quite.

The worst part of all? She's got that girl-next-door vibe to her. The kind that's so shy she can't make eye contact with me while my shirt is off. The kind that makes her cheeks go pink every time I talk to her. It's rare to run into someone who genuinely blushes these days, and here she is, yanking down the hem of her cover-up and darting secret glances at me when she thinks I'm not looking.

I'm looking, though.

I've had my peripherals trained on her from the moment I stepped onto the boat. Which brings me to my next problem and, actually, the *real* worst part of it all. She's off-limits. Lucy might as well have a neon flashing DO NOT TOUCH marquee above her head. Not only is she Drew's sister, but she is fresh out of a breakup and, if I remember correctly, has a little boy. I know about the breakup not only because Drew overstated it like a dipshit when I first got in the boat, but also because he borrowed my truck to go move her back from Georgia. Now I'm wishing I would have offered to go get her in his place.

He wouldn't have let me, though, because he's super protective of her. He's expressed his hatred for her ex-boyfriend, Tim, since they met. He never even had a really good reason for his dislike, just that the guy didn't deserve her. I have to agree now. Only a few minutes in Lucy's company proves she's different—special.

"Cooper! We should go cliff jumping!" A woman named Bailey pulls me from my thoughts with a splash of water to my face.

About ten minutes after we put down the anchor, a boat full of Drew's and my friends pulled up. They tied up with us, cranked up their music, and tossed floats out into the water. Everyone jumped in almost immediately, soaking up the sun and enjoying the water. But not Lucy.

She took one look at our new companions and hunkered down in the front of the boat with a book. No one pressed her to join us, and since I have no idea how I'm supposed to act around her, I didn't either. I'm just trying to follow Drew's lead, but it feels wrong to leave her up there in the boat alone. Then again, he did say she was pretty heartbroken. Maybe she's just not feeling it today and wants to be alone.

"Cooper?" Bailey asks. "Helllllooo, did you hear me?"

I blink and turn my head to her. She's smiling a megawatt smile, perched on her bright-yellow pineapple float, and I know she's flirting. She always flirts with me because we've had sort of an on-again, off-again thing for a while now that never amounts to anything and, honestly, never will.

"Sorry, cliff jumping—yeah, sounds good." I turn my eyes back up toward the boat, even though I can't actually see Lucy from down here. "Let's go in a few minutes. I'll be right back." I swim over to the ladder and have to pass Drew on the way.

He sticks out the hand holding his beer in front of me so I can't pass because, apparently, he's a bouncer now. "Where are you going?"

"Grabbing a water." *And going to see your sister.*

His eyes narrow a little, but he withdraws his arm. "Okay. Just don't go bug Lucy, okay? She's going through some stuff."

My head kicks back. "I resent the implication that I would ever go *bug* a woman."

"You know what I mean." Yeah, unfortunately I do. He's telling me to leave her alone. The warning is there in his eyes, and it's threatening as hell. I've never been on this end of Drew's ire, and I don't particularly like it.

It was about a year ago that I moved away from Charlotte, North Carolina, in favor of somewhere a lot less . . . near my ex. I put in applications with a few top-tier marketing firms around the country, and Hampton Creative was the first interview I got. It was a great fit right away and a huge promotion (and pay raise) from my last position. Everything fell into place quickly, and I found out through a friend of a friend about a guy named Drew Marshall needing a roommate. We had a brief phone call where we both determined the other sounded somewhat normal, and then the next thing I knew, I was living in Nashville (blissfully far away from Janie) with a great job and a great roommate. It was the perfect place to reinvent myself—and reinvent myself I did.

For the last year, my motto has been *nothing but fun*. I date a lot, I go out a lot, and I've become that guy you call when you want to have a good time. I think every date I've been on has been a subconscious middle finger to my ex. *She didn't want me, so I'll prove just how wanted I can be.* Problem is, she isn't watching me. She's been too busy falling in love with someone else, getting married, and starting a family.

I guess you could say I've diverted from my usual path this past year, and I'm just now realizing, in this moment when I find myself wanting to go spend time with Lucy Marshall, that Drew only knows *this* Cooper—the one who's so freaking jaded from having his heart torn up that he's made the word *commitment* sound like a swear word.

Drew doesn't know anything about the person I was back in Charlotte. This blip in my life is the whole picture to him. And sure, he's liked this version as his wingman, but he doesn't want me anywhere near his sister because of it.

"I get it, and it's all good, man."

He nods, and I nod, and it's all settled now. I'll stay away from Lucy.

Except I don't.

I step into the boat and wrap a towel around my waist before my feet carry me directly to the bow where she's sitting. My eyes immediately snag on Lucy's bare legs stretched out in front of her. She's so engrossed in her book that, at first, she doesn't even realize I'm standing here. But then she looks to the side, makes direct eye contact with my navel, and scrambles to tuck her legs under her so fast she nearly dumps her book into the lake.

She's yet to actually talk to me other than the soft "Hi" she gave me earlier along with the weirdest handshake of my life. Somehow, though, it went down as my favorite too. She's awkward, and I'm drawn to her in a way that kind of scares me—scares me because if Drew knew, he'd castrate me.

"Hey. Hi," she says, shifting in her seat, eyes bouncing everywhere to keep from having to look at my face too long. I make her nervous. "What's up?" She aggressively pushes a lock of hair out of her eyes and then finally really looks at my face.

She freezes like she wasn't expecting me to be smiling down at her.

"Can I sit with you?"

Those long, dark lashes blink. "Yeah, of course." She gestures to where I was sitting earlier, but I don't take that seat. I sit right beside Lucy (a little too close) and look at her over my shoulder, noting another blush on her cheeks.

"Are you having fun?" I ask.

"Mm-hmm. Yeah, lots of fun." Her voice is a little squeaky.

I grin and nod toward her book. "Really? Because it kinda looks like you've just been up here reading all day instead of having a good time."

She looks at me over her book with a mischievous sort of smile. The expression makes my stomach coil up tight—which is odd because it hasn't done that in a long time. "Who says reading can't be fun?"

"You sound like my third grade teacher." I notice Lucy's smile fade a little, and she scrunches her nose, eyes dropping down to her lap because she thinks I've just insulted her. Only because this is an emergency, I ignore the DO NOT TOUCH sign and bump her shoulder with mine. "I had a major crush on her, though. You should have seen how many stars I got on my reading chart."

This makes Lucy laugh, dimples popping beside her mouth, and suddenly making her laugh is all I want to do. You know, as a friend. Because even though I find her ridiculously attractive, I'm also not going to try to start anything up with a woman who's just come out of a breakup. She's vulnerable, and I'm not a vulture, so I'll just make her smile for purely friendly reasons. Also, the whole Drew-death-glare situation was a little scary.

"So, you're a big flirt, huh? Like, is it tough for you to talk to a woman and not try to seduce her?"

A laugh bursts from my mouth because I kind of can't believe she had the guts to call me out like that. "Maybe a little less creepy than you make it sound, but yeah, I guess you could call me a flirt."

"Well . . ." She wiggles her finger in my direction. "You don't have to do all that here with me. I don't need the pity hangout."

"Why do you think I'm giving you a pity hangout?"

She tips a shoulder and pretends to be interested in her book. "Because you saw Drew's bookish little sister up here on the boat and felt bad that I was alone, and as the token flirt guy, you felt it was your job to entertain me." She looks up. "I'm saying I release you of your responsibility."

An incredulous smile pulls over my mouth because I really like her. I like that she says what she thinks and is not afraid to call it like she sees it from the start. Except, she's not seeing it right this time. "I'm not up here talking to you because you're Drew's sister, believe me." In fact, her being Drew's sister is the only reason I *haven't* asked her out already. "And you know, I think I'm offended that you've so easily diminished me to nothing but the *token flirt*."

"Are you actually offended?"

"Maybe."

She narrows her eyes. "Okay, I give you one minute to convince me I have you pegged wrong."

I lift an amused eyebrow. "You're serious?"

She looks down at her phone and swipes across the screen until a one-minute timer appears. "Clock's ticking," she says.

Well, shit. Suddenly, this is important for reasons I don't quite understand. I sit up straight and clear my throat. "Okay. I work in marketing. I'm from Charlotte—"

She grimaces. "Those tidbits aren't going to help you. Dive deeper. Forty seconds left."

"Ah—damn, okay. I like to play solitaire on my computer. I'm really close with my parents; we talk almost every day, though it's mainly to help them figure out how to change the input on their TV again. I like to bake, but I'm terrible at it. And I own a rescue shelter for abused animals."

The alarm chimes on her phone, and her mouth falls open. "Do you really?"

"No," I say with a chuckle. "But I felt like I wasn't making a very good case for myself and needed some extra points."

She laughs and shakes her head in mock reprimand. "Like I said, token flirt for sure."

I guess she's not wrong. I turned myself into this guy on purpose. So why does it feel so uncomfortable to own it now? Maybe I'm a little tired of it. Maybe I'm ready to start veering back toward my old path.

"And what about you?"

"Oh, I'm squarely in the bookish category. I never even attempt to flirt because it always ends badly." Her face is so serious right now. She really means this from the bottom of her heart. "I see you looking at me skeptically, but it's true. I'm exactly the opposite of you and Drew."

Ah—speaking of Drew, I should really be getting up now and leaving Lucy the hell alone. She's smiling, so my mission is accomplished. (*Hurrah for the token flirt doing his duty!*) For some reason, though, I can't. I don't want to go back down in the water with everyone else. I want to sit here and watch this beautiful woman blush and continue having odd conversations with her that make me want to smile more than I've smiled since Janie. So, I do the wrong thing and stretch my arm out across the bench seat (not the arm closest to Lucy, because I don't have a death wish) and settle in.

"You two do seem pretty different. And you definitely look nothing alike." Why did I add that last part?

Her nose crinkles again with an uncomfortable smile. "Well, most people think he's pretty hot, so I don't quite know how to take that."

I squint one eye. "Trying to get me to flirt with you again?"

Her smile drops, and now she has owl eyes. The blush is back. "What? No! I was just saying a fact, not at all trying to get you to flirt with me. I don't even really like compliments because I never know what to do with them, and—"

"Lucy, relax," I say with a chuckle. "I was just messing with you." I want to bump her shoulder again but refrain because I'm a saint and a very good friend.

"Oh." She sinks back against the bench again and laughs at herself. "I'm sorry. I— This is why I prefer reading to actually talking to people. Less chance of humiliating myself." She tucks her nose back down into her book like she's intending to jump inside it *Reading Rainbow* style.

I'm not ready to lose her to that book yet.

"Well, now that you've admitted you're only using that book to hide"—I pluck it from her hand and toss it onto the bench across from us—"you have no choice but to put it down and come hang out with us."

She looks from the water, where everyone is floating, back to her lap. "I'm good up here. Thanks, though."

What? She's not going to come out to the water at all? Maybe Drew was right and Lucy really is having a hard time after breaking up with Tim. "All right, well, I won't push you to come out there with us. Breakups are hard, so I understand wanting to just chill by yourself."

She lets out a sharp *ha,* and then her hand immediately flies up to cover her mouth. "I didn't mean to laugh," she says from behind her hand. "It's just . . ." She shakes her head. "Never mind."

Okay, that was definitely not the reaction of a woman aching with a broken heart. My spirits lift. *Tim Shmim.* "You can't bait me like that and then leave me hanging." I lower her hand away from her mouth. "What were you going to say?"

Lucy stares at where my hand is covering hers. I let it go, realizing I've already touched her twice in five minutes when I'm supposed to touch her *never in my entire life.* "It's not the breakup. Don't tell Drew, because it will go straight to his head, but I never liked Tim all that much. The reason I don't want to swim has nothing to do with my breakup."

She gives me a look that's sort of shy and reserved but loaded with meaning, and now I'm worried Drew was right. For the first time in quite a while, I feel unsure of myself. Am I . . . *bugging* her?

I'm a pretty straightforward guy, so instead of lying awake to-night, wondering, I ask, "Is it me? Am I making you uncomfort-able? Just say the word, and I'll totally leave you al—"

"I didn't shave my legs," she says suddenly, eyes snapping back to me like she didn't mean to cave on her secret so quickly.

I, however, am fighting a smile, relieved that I'm not com-pletely unappealing to her—not that I want to be appealing to her. Because, you know . . . I can't. "Is that supposed to be a big deal?"

"No, I don't think you get it. I haven't shaved my legs in, like . . . *weeks*. It's bad." My eyes unconsciously begin to drift down toward her legs, but she reaches out quickly and grabs my chin, keeping it lifted. "Don't look! What are you doing?! It's em-barrassing!"

I'm laughing now; I can't help it. "Well, what do you expect me to do? You've just put a red button in front of me and told me not to press it. Of course I'm going to." Something in my mind alerts me to the realization that I'm not just talking about looking at her hairy legs. My eyes drift toward the edge of the boat, expecting to find Drew pointing a sword in my direction, threatening a duel.

Except, no. I don't think the pull I'm feeling toward Lucy has anything to do with the red-button principle, and, instead, has ev-erything to do with the way I genuinely enjoy talking to her, feel-ing like I have no idea what she'll say next and loving that nothing comes out of her mouth unless it is absolutely true.

Right away, she seems like someone who doesn't play games. And guess what? I'm tired of games.

Lucy tucks her legs tighter under her and gives me a warning side-eye.

"Come on." I wiggle my fingers in front of me. She gives me a quizzical look. "Show me."

"No! I will not *show* you. I'm going to stay snuggled up with my book and let you and Drew enjoy your time with your friends." She makes a *shoo* gesture, like she's completely done with me.

"Lucy. I don't give a shit about the hair on your legs, and no one else will either. Look, I'll prove it."

I reach out and grab her foot, pulling it and her leg out from under her. Before she can protest, I run my hand gently from her ankle up her shin to her knee, and I can tell you one thing, I really *don't* give a shit about the hair. I meant for the gesture to be playful and funny and break the ice between us, but instead I feel sparks flying off my fingertips. *Not good to have that strong of a reaction to a woman I need to stay away from.*

I slide my eyes up to her face, and her mouth is open, eyes wide, cheeks crimson red. "I. Can't. Believe. You. Just. Did. That." She blinks at me and then at the place where I haven't moved my hand from her knee yet. I need to move it. I *should* move it. But I don't want to. Her skin is warm beneath my palm, and touching her feels different than I've felt with anyone else. "Goodness, you really are a flirt."

Her words act like a bucket of cold water. She doesn't think I'm being genuine, and also . . . *Drew's sister.* I can't act this way with her.

I smile and pull my hand back. "Sorry. Not trying to *seduce* you, I swear," I say, emphasizing the word to remind her of her earlier ridiculous statement. Time to tug us back into the friend zone—probably my least favorite of all the zones. "But now that I've not only seen but also touched your hairy legs and you don't see me running away screaming, you have no choice but to come cliff jumping with us."

"Cliff jumping?! No." She's vehemently shaking her head. "No, no, no. I don't do that kind of thing."

"By 'that kind of thing' you mean exhilarating fun?"

"Don't make me remind you about my book. I go on all kinds of exhilarating adventures in those."

I scoot a little closer without meaning to. "I would argue that books give the illusion of fun. But believe me, there's nothing like the real thing."

She lifts an eyebrow, and I could swear she scoots closer too. "I'll argue that you're wrong. Studies show that reading a book actually increases dopamine in your brain and reduces stress."

"You know what else releases dopamine and reduces stress?" I watch Lucy swallow, and her eyes dip to my mouth. "Cliff jumping," I whisper with a smug smile.

The corners of her lips curve up softly as she continues staring at mine, making this moment feel oddly intimate and charged. I wonder if she's feeling the same pull I'm feeling.

"Cooper!" Bailey and her friend Jessica both singsong at me from in the water. "Come on! Let's go to the cliffs."

"Yeah, *Cooper.*" That's Drew now, mocking their flirtatious voices. "*Let's go! I need you to hold my hand while we jump!*" His voice sounds ridiculous, and it's followed up by an *oof.* I imagine Bailey and Jessica both hitting him in the stomach.

I look back at Lucy, and her new closed-off expression pokes at me. "You guys go without me," I say.

Her eyebrows furrow tightly together, like she can't fathom that I would want to stay on this boat with her rather than go off with the others to the cliffs. "Why aren't you going?"

I shrug. "Because I don't want to leave you here alone."

"But . . . I'll be fine here. I've got my—"

"*Book.* Yes, I know. But just imagine how much fun we'll have talking and flirting back here on the boat while they go cliff jump for a while." I raise and lower my eyebrows once. "You can have me all to yourself. Endless flirting opportunities. You won't even have a minute to waste on your book, we'll be so deep in conversation. I've got an entire list of questions I'm dying to ask the second they're all gone."

Her eyebrows sink low. "I see what you're doing."

"What's that?"

"Trying to make cliff jumping seem more appealing than staying behind and being forced to talk."

"Absolutely. Is it working?"

Her smile pulls up in one corner. "Yes." She rolls her eyes when she sees my smile grow. "Fine, I'm in. Let's go."

CHAPTER 4

Lucy

I'm *not* in. So very not in. In fact, I'd say I'm pretty solidly out.

With every single step I climb up this cliffside, I question my mental stability more and more. Obviously, there are some cylinders not firing correctly in my head to have so easily succumbed to reverse psychology. One minute I'm blissfully reading on the boat. The next Cooper is beside me, sending electrical currents through my body with a single look, and then he's threatening to unleash his full flirtatious abilities on me, and I panicked. There's no way I wouldn't humiliate myself if left alone with Cooper for more than ten minutes.

Now I'm almost to the top of the cliff, and all I want to do is drop to the ground and spread my body out to grip the earth as much as possible. This is terrifying. And so high up! Worst part of all, I'm up here alone, with everyone down below, floating in the water and chanting my name. *Super.* I love when people chant my name to get me to jump off fifty-foot cliffs.

I should have stayed home.

I reach the top, and my legs wobble when I look over the edge. Ohhhhh no. I can't do this. Did I mention I'm deathly afraid of heights? So afraid that I even avoid the glass railings on the second floor of the mall. I'm a spineless jellyfish for agreeing to this—for letting Cooper's hypnotic aqua eyes coax me into adventure. I *hate* adventure. If there were a shirt with that saying, I'd buy it and wear it every day with a matching hat.

"You okay up there, Luce?" Drew yells from the water. He knows my fear of heights and was skeptical when I said I'd jump. I was offended at his look of disbelief at the time, but now I want to go back in time and strap myself into his Jeep and tell him to gun it all the way home.

My ego will never allow it though.

"Super!" I yell from the edge with a double thumbs-up. "Just savoring the view!"

I hear Bailey and her friends shout *You can do it!* from the water, but Drew yells the exact opposite. "You don't have to jump, Lucy. Just come back down."

Come back down? That sounds great. I actually really like that option. Is there an elevator around here I'm not seeing?

"Don't listen to him, Lucy." That's Cooper's voice now. He sounds like the devil on my shoulder, and I want to tell him to shut his beautiful mouth. "You can do this. Just jump."

I take another peek over the edge, and my vision does that thing where it starts to tunnel, making it look like the water is growing farther away. My gaze shifts to Cooper, and I take in his encouraging smile and wet hair. It strikes me how odd it is that I'm even up here in the first place. I've never been this girl . . . the girl who feels the need to impress anyone—especially not a guy.

But I don't know. I feel differently around Cooper. I *want* to impress him. Maybe I'm just emotionally unstable? Maybe this is a terrible rebound crush? Maybe I'm making a fool of myself because there's no way a guy like him would ever be interested in me? All of the above, I think, but no matter the reason, looking down at him makes me want to jump for the first time in my life. I can't explain it.

Too bad I can't because my legs are backing up, and I can't stop them. My body is on autopilot preservation mode now, and all I can think about is that I have a son I really want to stay alive for. I shift myself all the way back until I'm flush with the rock wall behind me. Sharp ridges press into my shoulder blades, but I like it because it means I'm safely in contact with Mother Earth.

"I can't do it!" I shut my eyes and yell, prepared to endure all the ridicule and roasting the group wants to throw at me. It's fine; I'll never see them again anyway, and Drew looked like he'd rather I didn't jump in the first place. I should have listened. Drew is always right.

"Yes, you can." Cooper's soft voice close to my face makes me jump (but not off the cliff).

I open my eyes to find him standing right beside me, barechested with sparkling eyes. Do they ever stop doing that? His blond hair looks darker wet, water dripping off his waves and rolling down his muscular shoulders, pecs, smooth abs . . . and now I have to stop tracking that water droplet's path before he catches me being a perv.

My heart is frantic as he steps a little closer. Has it ever raced like this before? I don't think I was ever physically aware of my BPM with Tim. I felt cozy with him, like I could take a pleasant nap at any time and wake up fully rested.

Cooper looks like adrenaline in the flesh as his grin tilts and he takes my hand. "You won't regret it," he says, and suddenly, even though I'm firmly planted on this cliff, my stomach feels like I'm in a free fall.

I swallow. "It's a bigger drop than I thought."

"Just means it'll be more fun."

I grunt. "You and I think differently."

He squeezes my hand, and I tell my little palpitating heart to knock it off. Cooper is a flirt; he would probably hold my mom's hand too, if she were scared to jump. It's what he does. He's just that guy, you know? The one who's confident enough to show affection to everyone he meets. Could charm the pants off an angry troll. This—holding my hand—means nothing to him.

Which is why it makes me so mad that it means something to me.

"Think more like me then, just this once. If you hate it, I'll never make you do it again."

My eyes tiptoe to the edge of the cliff, and my stomach does a barrel roll. "If I hate it, I'm going to take your cellphone and throw it in the water."

He laughs. "Seems fair to me. Let's go." He hitches his head toward the edge, and I take a deep breath.

I barely get the word *okay* out before Cooper is tugging me with him, running full steam ahead toward the edge. My feet leave the warmth of the rocks, and my stomach jumps into my throat as we drop. I scream like a tiny little girl, and Cooper's hand is locked on mine so tight, promising he's with me the whole time. Butterflies soar through my body for only a split second before we crash into the water and it swallows us up.

Darkness surrounds me for a heartbeat before I feel Cooper's hand tug me up to the surface, and to my surprise I come up laughing. I open my eyes and find him pushing his hair back from his face and smiling in a way that flips my stomach even more than jumping off that cliff did.

"I did it!" I squeal, feeling a surge of pride, and relief, and . . . yep, dopamine rushing through me.

Before I even realize it, I'm laughing and swimming to him, intending to wrap my arms around his neck to celebrate. When I get closer, though, Cooper's eyes catch over my shoulder, then his hand shoots up out of the water to give me a high five.

A high five.

Right.

Reality swallows me up much like the water did, and I remember that Cooper is the kind of guy who could probably have anyone he wanted. I'm just Drew's sister. He doesn't want me like *that*. All that flirting up on the cliff was only his way of getting me to feel more comfortable to jump. It was nothing but a friendly service he offered me.

"That was awesome, Lucy. Way to go. How do you feel?" he asks, but some of the glimmer seems to have left his eyes. I guess now that he got his adrenaline fix, he's all good.

I muster up my best I'm-totally-fine-with-this-I-love-high-fives smile and slap his hand. "I think your cellphone will live to see another day."

He grins and holds my gaze. Honestly, he's so attractive I have to turn away, because looking at him and knowing I'll never have a man like that is hurting more than breaking up with Tim ever did. It's only after I make it back to the ladder that I let my smile slip.

It felt good to jump.

It felt good to be looked at the way Cooper looked at me up on that cliff.

I feel something inside me shift, new fault lines cracking

their way through my heart, and I have a feeling they're not going away.

After climbing up the ladder, I look down at the sopping-wet shirt I've been wearing over my swimsuit all day and attempt to wring it out. This is ridiculous. Who cares if I'm wearing an ugly swimsuit? Who cares if I look a little frumpy? Who cares if my legs are hairy? Those two seconds of heart-in-my-throat free fall made me realize something: I don't push myself enough. Somewhere along the line in my life, I stopped jumping. It's time to start again.

I grab the hem of my shirt and whip it off over my head. *World, meet my tie-dye one-piece! Isn't she glorious?!* The sun feels good on my skin, and it feels wonderful not to care what anyone else is thinking of me.

But when I reach for a towel, my skin prickles with awareness. I glance over my shoulder and find Cooper, gaze searing into me with not a hint of a teasing smile on his lips. In fact, his eyes are kindling, and though they never dip below my face, I know he's already looked. He's looked, and I somehow get the sense that maybe my swimsuit isn't quite as frumpy as I thought. I feel my cheeks turn into candy apples, and ever so slowly, a grin spreads over Cooper's face.

I press my lips together and try to hide an embarrassed smile of my own.

Then Bailey jumps onto Cooper's back and laughs as she tries to get him to wrestle her in the water.

Right. Happy bubble popped. Moment over.

I wrap a towel around me and head to the front of the boat to find my book, but unfortunately, it doesn't hold my attention like it did before.

———

Drew and I have been quiet for most of the drive home. We're both zapped from the sun, a little crispy, and dehydrated. He has one hand on the steering wheel and the other resting on the console between us. He's never afraid to take up too much space. By contrast, my feet are up on the seat and I'm hugging my knees, wearing an oversized sweatshirt and staring out the window.

He taps the steering wheel a few times. "Glad you came out today. Sorry if it was a little much for you."

I keep my eyes trained out the window, remembering what it felt like to have Cooper's hand laced with mine. "It wasn't too much."

He's quiet for a minute, and then I see from the corner of my eye that he glances at me again. "So you're feeling better than you were this morning?"

"Yeah. Actually, I am. Thanks for inviting me. I feel like going out on the lake was exactly what I needed."

"Good . . . great." He *tap, tap, taps* the steering wheel again. "That's good."

Well, that's a weird tone.

I meet his intense look with a furrowed brow. "What is it?"

"Nothing."

"Spit it out, or I'll frog your leg." I'm good at it too. Leaves a nice bruise.

His head tilts to the side a little, then he looks down at the wheel and back to the road. "It's nothing really. Just . . . I guess I've been wondering why you jumped off the cliff today."

"Huh?" I'm a little confused by his odd comment.

We pull up to a stoplight, and Drew turns the full weight of his gaze to me. "You hate heights, Luce. Why'd you do it?"

I shrug, suddenly feeling defensive. "Because I wanted to."

"No," he says, voice more clipped than I've ever heard from

him before. "You did it because *Cooper* wanted you to." I suck in a breath and hold it because I'm not at all sure how to respond to that. Drew looks so stern and protective right now, like I'm fifteen again and he's showing up to my date, interrupting our make-out session and about to tattle to Mom.

"Look, I get it," he continues. "He's a smooth dude and one of my best friends. But because he and I are so close, I've seen too much to be comfortable with the idea of you dating him. So . . . I guess . . ."

"You guess what?"

He sighs like it pains him to say this. "I want you to stay away from him." After a beat, he adds, "Romantically, I mean."

This is the second time I have felt like laughing in my brother's face today. It's hilarious that he thinks there would be a need for him to ask me to stay away from his friend. Did he see the beautiful, fun women who were hanging all over Cooper today? Ha! Yeah . . . he's got nothing to worry about from me and my momness.

"Drew," I say with a chuckle, "you're being ridiculous. Nothing romantic will happen between Cooper and me."

And that night, I'm still laughing about our conversation as I shower, pull on an old T-shirt, and slip into bed. I flip off the light and turn over to bury my head into my pillow when my phone lights up with a text.

I blink at the screen, registering the name *Cooper James,* and wonder if maybe I've already fallen asleep and this is going to turn into the best dream of my life. It has to be a dream because Cooper and I didn't exchange numbers today. I would remember typing his name into my phone. Also, *Cooper* would have been spelled wrong because my hands would have been shaking terribly.

Okay, so I'll just play along with this dream and read what "Cooper" texted me. When I do, I see a text from earlier in the day, sent from my phone to his.

> LUCY: This is Cooper. I'm texting myself from your phone so you can have my number. You know . . . token flirt and all that. 😊

I jolt up in bed and stare down at the screen. He stole my phone and texted himself?! So I could have his number?! I instinctively look to my closed door like Drew might be receiving sibling vibes and will burst in at any moment. When he doesn't, I scoot down, reenacting my teen years by reading the text under my comforter.

> COOPER: It was fun hanging out today. Thanks for jumping with me.

And then a video comes through that I had no idea he took. Apparently, he left his phone recording on the boat. I hit Play and smile at the sight of Cooper and me, hand in hand, running and jumping off the cliff. My screams are more than a little embarrassing, but when I zoom in I'm shocked to see how big my smile is— and I'm not looking at the water.

I'm looking at Cooper . . . and he's looking at me.

CHAPTER 5

Lucy

It's been two weeks since my cliff-jumping adventure. A lot has happened in that time.

I got a job! Well, not so much me as my mom who called in a favor with one of her friends who called her friend who called her cousin who got me a chair at Honeysuckle Salon. Nashville may be a big-time town now, but if you grew up here those roots run deep, and everybody's mama knows everybody's mama. It's always good to be on the mamas' side, because they are the ones running this town.

I actually really like Honeysuckle Salon. The stylists are all sweet ladies who seem pretty down to earth and not the kind to get catty or stir up drama, and the aesthetic is beautiful. The floors are a cream marble, and all the salon chairs are upholstered in expensive light-brown leather. The fixtures are either gold or brushed brass, and there's some sort of lemon oil diffusing in the room. It's definitely not *Steel Magnolias* in here. Best part is, I don't even have to put Levi in daycare because my mom retired last year and has been able to stay home with him every day for me. It's like an enormous boulder has rolled off my back, and I'm able to breathe again for the first time in a year.

Yep, everything is great being back home. Drew and I have been hanging out after Levi goes to bed, watching movies, and— *Okay, yeah, I'm freaking out a little because Cooper hasn't texted at all!* And I've been racking my brain every day for these past two weeks, wondering why he never responded to my text. It was a nice text, a heartfelt message that went something like this: *Aw, great video! Super fun day.*

Good, right? If only I'd left it at that. But then I just had to go and text him again because I'm not a normal human and should just hide in a hole for the rest of my life.

LUCY: Seriously. Just want to say thank you for today. Jumping off that cliff was the most fun I've had in a long time, and it helped me realize I need to be more adventurous and step out of my safe box more often. It was nice being challenged by you, and I think you're a really great guy. Maybe you could challenge me again sometime :)

I know . . . it's bad. Painful even. Cringe-worthy. *Desperate.* No wonder he never responded. He's probably been too busy packing up his house and moving across the country so his new stalker, Lucy, can't find him and cut a lock of his hair to keep under her pillow.

I don't even know why I did it. I'm not normally the type to spill my guts to a guy like that, but something about Cooper makes me temporarily lose my mind. As such, it's probably a good thing he hasn't texted or come around at all. Who knows what I would do in person? Best to just focus on my work, which is where

I am now, sweeping up a pile of hair from my last client and preparing to clock out for the day.

Jessie, the salon owner, my new best friend, and an all-around sweetheart, walks up to my station. "Hey, Lucy, do you have time to squeeze in a last-minute cut?"

To be honest, my feet are killing me and I'd like to go home, but I'm also trying to save every penny I have to get my own place sooner rather than later. Drew is amazing, and I know he doesn't mind having me, but still . . . a single guy doesn't want his baby sister staying with him forever. And I get tired of having to wear a bra around the house.

"Anything for you, sunshine." I'm not even sucking up. Jessie and I sort of hit it off from the moment we met last week. After my interview, she and I went out for margaritas (hers a virgin because she's four months pregnant) and talked until the restaurant had to kick us out. I learned over dinner that Jessie is not married or in a relationship, so there is a story there with her pregnancy, but I figure she'll tell me when she feels comfortable.

"Thank you!" she says, looking relieved. "It's a men's cut, so it shouldn't take too long, and your shirt is kind of see-through in this light, so you'll probably get a great tip."

I gasp and look down. "What! It is not!" Shoot, it is. You can see my pink bra right through my black-and-white-striped tee. "Why didn't you tell me that earlier?!"

She laughs. "Why are you freaking out? Look around this room—you're the most modestly dressed woman in here."

She's right. Another stylist is wearing high-waisted dress pants and one of those fashionable sports bras. Another is wearing a sundress with a plunging neckline and has killer boobs. And me . . . I'm wearing distressed jeans and a striped T-shirt. I've come to terms with the fact that in a room full of designer brands,

I'll always be a Target. I love Target. Let's see a designer brand try to sell delicious soft pretzels in their store.

The door of the salon chimes, and Jessie and I both swivel our heads to see who entered. I kid you not, life turns to slow motion, and "SexyBack" by Justin Timberlake starts playing over the speakers as Cooper James steps through the door. The sudden burst of air tosses his wavy locks around his attractive-as-sin face, and he pulls his sunglasses off, making his arm muscles flex under the rolled-up sleeves of his crisp white button-down. Every single woman in the salon notices. Our jaws are collectively hitting the floor, and I'm sure he can count each of my fillings, because as good as Cooper looked without a shirt, he almost looks more in- credible wearing one—and nicely tailored business attire at that. I think it's because the fabric strains against his chest and biceps, whispering a tantalizing secret of what's underneath, daring you to find out if it's true or not.

He pauses in front of the reception desk, and his aqua eyes rise, cutting across the salon.

I drop to the floor.

Not in a swoon but more of a hit-the-deck sort of way. I hun- ker down, rolling up into a tiny pathetic ball behind my rolling cart of hair products because *he cannot see me.*

Jessie looks down at me with wide, disbelieving eyes. She's never met an animal like me in the wild. "*What* are you doing?"

"Shhhh, don't draw attention to me! Look over there. No! Stop. You're still looking at me!"

"Yeah, 'cause I'm worried I might need to throw you in my car and drop you off at the closest mental health facility for an evalu- ation."

"Mental health is not something to joke about."

"Who says I'm joking!" she says in a loud whisper.

I rise up slightly to peek over the hairsprays. "What is *he* doing here?"

"Hmm . . . getting his oil changed?" When I look up at her with hope in my eyes, she looks like she's going to smack me upside the head. "What do you think he's doing here?! Getting his damn hair cut! And he's probably the guy who called and requested you."

"Me?" I ask, like maybe someone else is standing right behind me that I don't see.

"Yes, you. Do you know him?"

"No. Yes. No. I mean, kind of. He's my brother's best friend, and I sent him a humiliating text message the other day that he never responded to, so now I can never show my face around him again."

"Like a nude photo text?"

I give her a face that says, *Do you really think I'm the type to send a nude photo?* and then I gesture toward my childish position on the floor just to really drive the point home.

She chuckles and waves me off. "Yeah, never mind, don't know why I asked that. So, let me see it."

"What?"

"The text. I'll tell you if it's actually bad or just in your head. And if it's all in your head, you can go cut his hair without having to worry about it."

I think about it for a split second before reaching into my back pocket and pulling out my phone. I swipe it open and hand it over to her. At this point, I can see that the receptionist has asked Cooper to take a seat in the waiting area and is beginning to walk toward me. Her eyes catch me squatting down on the ground, and I give her a *Keep it moving, Melissa* gesture. With only a slight falter to her steps, she walks past me toward the break room.

I look back up in time to see Jessie stifle a laugh with the back of her hand while reading my text.

I quietly moan and lean my head back against the cart. "It's that bad, isn't it?"

"Oh yeah. You might want to just have your mail forwarded to this little corner you're in from now on." She hands me back my phone, looking like this is the most amusing thing she's ever encountered. "It's even worse seeing him in person. He's superhot. Definitely used to smooth women."

"Ughhh, you're the worst friend."

"Technically, I'm your boss."

"Oh great. Now I'm doubly embarrassed."

She laughs and nudges me with her sneaker. "I'm kidding! Okay, look, it's bad, but it's not horrendous. There's a chance he thought it was sweet and endearing."

"He would have responded."

"Yeah . . . but I'm trying to make you feel better because he's seen me talking to you now and is headed over here."

"*No!*" I say, feeling panic race through my veins. I look left and right for an escape and then up, directly into Cooper's smirking eyes. I shoot up from the ground like a bottle rocket, pretending to clutch something in my hand and holding it over my head. "Found it, Jessie! It just rolled under the cart. *Oh,* hi, Cooper! How long have you been here?" My voice would match a high C on the piano.

He knows I'm full of crap. He ignores my question and looks cool as a cucumber as he grins and asks, "What'd you lose down there?"

"Huh?" I'm trying to buy some time. Maybe I'll suddenly find out I'm a magician and can pull something incredible from my back pocket. Like a bunny.

"You said you lost something—just wondering what it was." He crosses his arms, eyes glinting—challenging.

"Oh, you know . . . just a . . . *flafflehem*." I say that last word while coughing into the crook of my arm. "So anyway! You here for a haircut?"

Out of nowhere, the other stylists materialize beside Cooper. Their eyes are extra wide and blinky. One says, "You were just getting ready to head out though, right, Lucy? I'd be happy to take him for you if you want."

Oh, really, *Tiffany,* would you be happy to take him for me?

Cooper looks over to her and smiles politely—or is it flirtatiously? Does he think she's sexy in her business sports bra? That thought suddenly makes me stomp the ground, making one loud BAM so that Cooper looks back at me. Honestly, I'm just as startled by my actions as they are. I don't know what happened; I just know I felt the overwhelming need for him to *not* be looking at her. *When did I become this person?* Looks like I'm going to be the one to bring a little drama to this salon.

Cooper's eyebrows rise, and I smile sweetly and stomp lightly a few more times, also rubbing my leg. "Foot fell asleep. I hate when that happens."

Jessie is behind Cooper, shaking her head and trying not to dissolve into a fit of laughter because she can't believe someone is truly as awkward as I am. Little does she know, this only scrapes the surface.

"Well, thanks for all the concern, everyone, but I'm good. I have plenty of time to cut his hair, so there's no issue! Thanks, yeah, bye-bye," I say, trying to shoo them out of my space, but really I want to whack them with a stick. *Go on now, get out of here! There's nothing here for you!* Oof, I've got to get a handle on my jealousy.

I turn to face Cooper and nearly fall over when I realize his eyes were on me that whole time, a soft grin tilting the side of his mouth, an indiscernible look in his eyes. Reserved and intrigued. Sort of like he either wants to pin me against the wall and kiss me into oblivion or help me do my taxes.

More than likely, whatever attraction I think I'm seeing is just wishful thinking.

CHAPTER 6

Cooper

One thing is for certain: I shouldn't be here.

I was doing so good staying away, minding my own business like Drew wants me to, but then he and I met for lunch today and he casually mentioned that Lucy got a job in a salon that just so happens to be about two miles from my office downtown.

Suddenly, it was like someone would have to chain me to my desk to keep me there. I've got a good poker face, so I don't think Drew suspected I completely tuned out the rest of our conversation and was instead mapping the quickest route to her salon in my head.

So, basically, I'm not sure what I'm doing here. I don't even need a haircut, but I just wanted to be near her again, and the idea of being near her without Drew *also* being near her was too much temptation to resist. Plus, when I talked to my mom on the phone earlier and told her my predicament, she practically screamed at me to go see Lucy. Actually, her exact words were, "*I want grandkids, Cooper.* Go see that woman!"

So here I am.

"Okay, so, do you want to sit down?" Lucy asks with a quivering smile, gesturing toward the chair.

I run my hand through my hair and look down at the chair, really hoping she's good at what she does. To be honest, though, I think I'd let her buzz my head if it meant I got to talk to her uninterrupted for thirty minutes. "Yeah. Thanks for fitting me in so last minute." I sit down and run my hands along my pants, realizing my palms are sweating. *Weird.* When's the last time they did that?

"No problem."

She's stiff as a board and absolutely will not make eye contact with me. I'm guessing it has something to do with that paragraph-long text she sent me—the one I've literally read thirty times because it's so freaking cute I can't stand it. It's a painfully awkward message, one that most people would have probably spent an hour concocting and cutting down until it read *me too* with no hint of their feelings whatsoever. But I'm pretty sure Lucy just typed those words out and mashed Send without giving it a moment's thought. I love that. Her honesty and vulnerability were on display; she didn't cut a single bit of it. Which makes me a complete jerk for not responding.

But I couldn't. Everything I typed in response either let on how into her I am or sounded completely weak and apathetic in comparison. I'll be honest, the last time I let a woman know how wild I was about her, it didn't end in my favor. I realize I need to get over it, though. I know I can't keep licking this wound forever.

I start to ask how she's doing at the exact same time she asks if I've been here before. Our sentences collide in one awkward game of Twister, and we both make eye contact and laugh like gangly teens.

"You first," I say with a weird chuckle I've definitely never done before.

"I was just going to ask if you've been in here before," she says as she turns and bends to retrieve a cape from her station. In this moment, I'm given the perfect glimpse of her butt (and I don't mean to look, but it's just right there in front of me), and all I can think about is how nicely those jeans fit her curves. This does nothing to help me put coherent thoughts together.

She stands back up and turns to look at me, maybe catching me checking her out because her cheeks flush when she comes to drape the cape around my neck. "Oh yeah. Totally," I say.

"You have? Who's your usual stylist?"

Then I realize what she asked. "*What?* I mean no."

She's just as confused as I am. Her dark eyebrows furrow over her deep-blue eyes. "Huh?"

"I'm not . . . sure. What was the question again?" Ohhhh gosh, what the hell is happening to me? Are *my* cheeks flushing now? That's definitely never happened before. And man, is this cape hot or what, 'cause I'm sweating. *Get it together, Cooper.*

I feel like I'm back in junior high, trying to talk to a girl. Or no, I definitely had more game back then, unlike this pathetic attempt. Lucy is doing something strange to my insides. And now she's smiling with her dimples over my shoulder because she can tell I'm completely losing it, and I wonder if I leave now, could I somehow convince her she was in a car accident and everything that just transpired between us only happened in her coma?

I shake my head, determined to get my act together. "Sorry. This is why I don't have caffeine after three o'clock." *Shut up, shut up, shut up! You don't tell women you're interested in that you can't have caffeine after three like you're a million years old.*

"Wow. Okay. So, to answer your original question, yes, this is my first time in this salon."

Her smile is still bright and in place. I'm glad she's enjoying watching me drown like this. I guess it serves me right for not responding to her text. My mom, however, will be so ashamed when she calls later asking for all the details. "How did you know I work here?"

"Drew told me, over lunch this afternoon. So I thought I'd come by and . . ." My words trail off when she starts running her fingers through the back of my hair. She begins at the nape of my neck, then runs them up the entire curve of my head—over and over. I think there's a purpose to this other than to turn me on, but at the moment I can't tell what it would be.

She shifts her gaze from my hair to the mirror, where our eyes meet, and she smiles softly. "Go ahead, I'm listening. Just checking the angle of your cut to see what your stylist normally does."

If by *stylist* she means the burly dude covered in tattoos at the barbershop who slaps a cape on me too tight and then tells me to sit down and shut up while he trims my hair, then yeah, I have one of those. He provides nowhere near as pleasant an experience as Lucy, though.

She finally releases her fingers from my hair, and as she busies herself preparing her scissors, comb, and spray bottle, I attempt a few other awkward conversation topics—all of which Lucy promptly shuts down with short, single-syllable answers, and I realize she's giving me the cold shoulder because of my text freeze-out. I only know her from our afternoon on the boat together and our brief text exchange, but that's enough to understand that a quiet Lucy is not a happy Lucy.

As much as I don't want to, I have to bring up the elephant in the room. "Listen, about your text a couple weeks ago . . ."

She freezes, scissors hovering frighteningly above my ear—*please don't chop it off*—and grimaces. "Oh no. Please, let's just forget I ever sent it. Okay? Okay. Good." Pink is clawing up her neck now, and I'd be lying if I said I didn't like it.

"You have nothing to be embarrassed about. I'm the one who should be embarrassed."

Lucy grabs a spray bottle and starts dousing me. Less on the hair, more on the face. I feel like a troublemaking cat that's just been reprimanded. "Oh, oops. Here, let me wipe that off." She smooshes a plush towel into my face, patting over and over again, seemingly trying to absorb all my words (or smother me to death).

"It's dry, Lucy." She keeps patting, so I finally reach up and grab the towel, tossing it onto the workstation.

Quick as lightning, she brandishes a hairdryer and turns it on full blast. "YOUR HAIR WAS TOO WET. GOTTA DRY IT A BIT," she yells above the noise.

I can do nothing but sit stunned, watching my hair twist and fly around my head, wondering how long she's going to make me sit here like this. She lifts both her eyebrows at me with an overly bright smile, and I'm certain she will go to terrifying lengths to avoid talking to me about this.

Sitting forward, I grab the cord of the hairdryer and yank it out of the wall. Consuming silence follows, and Lucy's eyes dart to the spray bottle again. Oh geez, we're going to be here all day repeating this cycle.

Before her fingers can touch the spray bottle, I wrap my hand gently around her wrist, bringing her to a stop and forcing her to look at me. "Lucy, will you listen to me? I'm sorry about not responding, and I really regret it. I'm not very good at heartfelt, honest texts, so I wasn't sure how to respond to you. But I had fun jumping off the cliff with you, and I definitely want to do it again."

Her eyebrows are still pinched together in discomfort, but her shoulders ease a little. "Okay," she says quietly, then says it again one more time as she releases the last bit of stress from her body. "But now can we just forget I ever sent it?"

"No," I say, daring to run my thumb across the side of her wrist. "Why?"

I smile. "Because I liked it."

She swallows and looks skeptical. "You did?"

"Yeah . . . I did."

I like that Lucy wears her thoughts and emotions on her face so openly that I can always know what's going through her head. I like that she was so nervous to see me again that she ducked down and hid behind a cart. *Who does that?* And I *love* that she smiles when she runs her fingers through my hair. The list of reasons why I like Lucy Marshall seems to grow every time I'm around her.

Basically, I'm in so much trouble.

Our spell is broken when Lucy's phone starts buzzing on her station. She peeks at it, then looks at me with a sheepish smile. "It's my son FaceTiming me. Do you mind if I answer really quick? I haven't gotten to talk to him all day."

"Of course not. Go right ahead."

Lucy positions her phone in front of her face, pulls a wide smile over her pink lips, and then swipes to answer the call. I can tell the moment the picture connects, because her face beams. "Hi, baby!"

"Hi, Mom!" That must be Levi. "Grammy wants to know if you're coming to get me soooooooon."

Lucy laughs. "Honey, you've got to pull the phone away from your nose so I can see you. There! Wait. Ah—no, don't spin!"

I can hear her little boy cackling like a villain as he, apparently, spins with the phone. Lucy contorts her face to look as if she's on the world's most intense ride and the g-force is too much to handle. I'm mesmerized. I don't want to look away for even a second. I haven't been ready to pursue a serious relationship again since Janie, and honestly, commitment has been all too easy to avoid. Every woman I've met lately seems nice but completely forgettable to me.

That is, until Lucy. She's incredible, and seeing her here, talking to her son and making him laugh with her ridiculous faces, not giving a crap about what anyone else in this salon thinks . . . it's taking me from attraction to full-blown *crush*. Like I might leave here and research cheesy putt-putt golf places because, somehow, I get the feeling she'd actually enjoy going and wouldn't pretend to be too cool for it. She might even want to bring Levi—and I'd want her to because I think it would be really fun to see her with him.

Gosh, I need to have a conversation with Drew. Man to man, complete intentions laid out on the table between us. That's the only way I would ever pursue something with his sister. The problem is, I don't know if she's ready for that yet after her breakup and move. And she has a son, which means I need to proceed with even more caution and know my own feelings are for sure before I approach Lucy about it. A woman like her comes along once in a lifetime, though, so I don't plan on dragging my feet.

So what do you do when you're not in love with someone yet, but you can feel the potential for it, but you also can't date her because she's definitely commitment material and her brother might murder you?

Friends.

I hate that word. But it's my only option right now.

CHAPTER 7

Lucy

"Honey, I'm home!" I shout into the house the moment I step inside.

I kick off my shoes and groan because I feel like Cinderella's evil stepsister if she had actually shoved her big fat feet into those glass slippers, then wore them all day while hairdressing. Note to self: work shoes should not be found on the five-dollar sale rack. Lesson learned. Moving on.

"Hey! I'm in here," Drew calls from the living room.

I make my way down the little entry hall and peek my head around the corner. He's sitting on the edge of the couch, playing a video game. How is it even fair that grown men are allowed to still play video games (and a doctor no less), but if he walked in on me playing with my old Barbies he would send me to therapy?

"Did you get off work early today?"

"Yeah, my last patient canceled. Where's Levi?"

"He's at Mom and Dad's tonight. I was planning on getting him after work, but when I called to say I was on my way, he asked if he could spend the night instead." The poor kid missed his grandparents so much while we were in Georgia, and I think he's trying to make up for lost time by spending every waking moment with them, which is honestly okay with me. I've barely had any help over the past year, so even though I've been working full-time at the salon for the past week, I feel like a shriveled-up, half-dead plant that's being watered and fertilized. Well . . . watered at least. Still single over here, so no fertilizing happening yet.

"Okay, well, have fun playing that little twelve-year-old boy's game. I'm going to go grab a shower because I basically cut a mop off someone's head today, and I think ninety percent of it is somehow stuck in my underwear."

"Do you overshare like this with everyone or just me?"

"I save it all up just for you, big brother!" I say, heading toward the stairs with the intent to shower, dress myself in my comfiest PJs, and then crash into my pillow for the rest of the night.

Drew calls out before I leave the room, "Hey, you want to get a pizza and rent a movie tonight?"

I smile to myself because if teenage me—the one whose older brother was embarrassed to be seen with her and always put up a fuss if asked to drive her anywhere—could see grown-up me now, best friends with that same brother, she'd never believe it. "I want to, but I'm so tired I don't think I can. I plan on getting under my covers and finding a way to have Chinese food delivered right to my bed."

His eyes leave the screen for the first time to shoot me a reprimanding look. "Not really, right? That's super unsafe."

I take off my smelly sock and throw it at him. "No, I'm not serious! Geez, what do you think I am? Five years old?"

He chuckles and turns his eyes back to the TV. "Says the

woman who just threw a sock at me and has her toenails painted in a rainbow pattern."

"Thank you for noticing my nails. Now, leave me alone. I'm going to take my shower."

"Wait. Want me to order a pizza? I'll even deliver it to your bed."

"Awww, now I see why other people like you. Pepperoni please," I call back to him as I make my way up the stairs.

When I lay my phone on the bathroom counter, it lights up with a text, which effectively lights up my whole body.

COOPER: What are you doing tonight?

Did I mention this is part of the reason I'm so exhausted today? After Cooper left the salon yesterday (with a fantastic new haircut, I might add), he texted me about how much he liked the cut, then we continued to text until 1:30 in the morning. I kept expecting to get one of those awful ending-the-conversation texts, like *Well, it's been nice chatting!* but it never came. We texted until I accidentally fell asleep and woke up to my cheek mashed against my phone's screen, the letter *P* typed at least two hundred times into the text box.

It was a great talk with Cooper, though. He told me about his job (he works as the senior brand manager at a marketing agency called Hampton Creative) and how he moved here from Charlotte last year to take the position he has now. I asked him if doing what he does in marketing is his passion and if that's why he was willing to move for the job, but he just replied, *Eh. It's a job. I like it, but it's never going to be what fulfills me. It was just a convenient reason to leave town.*

There was so much loaded into that last sentence, but I didn't dive into it because I felt like he would have offered up the can of worms if he felt like it. Still, as someone who knows all too well what it's like to need a convenient reason to leave town, I can spot a tragic life story from a mile away. I also know what it's like to not want to talk about it.

So, I moved on and told him about how my mom was a hairdresser before she retired, and how she let me help her put in a full foil highlight on her friend's hair in our kitchen when I was only ten. Hairdressing always seemed like the logical path to take since it was something I knew I was good at, and thankfully, I've enjoyed it more and more every year. I feel sort of similar to Cooper—it's a job I like, but it will never be what fills me up, and I'm okay with that. I don't think everyone is meant to have a career that changes the world. Sometimes you've just gotta pay the bills and then clock out so you can get to the life you love the most, which, for me, is being with Levi.

After our night of back-and-forth texts, Cooper and I feel like friends. Friends who talk about TV shows and hobbies and crack jokes. I know things about him, beyond the shade of his eyes and what he wears to work, and somehow that makes me feel powerful. It also lets me see that I misjudged him slightly when I first met him. It's not so much that Cooper's a flirt as he is just fun and engaging. Drew had talked him up as a real player, someone who should not be trusted, but I don't get those vibes from him—especially not when he texts me pictures of watching *Wheel of Fortune* and brags about how quickly he can solve the puzzle.

I bite the corner of my lip and reread Cooper's message, wondering what a sexy woman of the world would reply. Probably something like *Wouldn't you like to know* ... with a winky-face emoji and fireworks or something else equally elusive that leads you to believe it's an innuendo. But we all know I can't pull off a text like that, nor would anyone believe I'm up to anything innuendo-related, so I just respond honestly.

LUCY: Putting on comfy pjs and being lazy at home. You?

I turn on the shower and wait for it to heat up while I stare at my phone, willing his response to come through quickly. Almost instantly, I see that wonderful little dot-dot-dot icon appear, and I bounce on the balls of my feet, waiting for the text. But then the dots disappear. And then reappear. And then disappear again. This time, they don't reappear, and my heart drops. He must have gotten busy . . .

My shoulders slump, and I set my phone face down, trying to convince myself that I don't even care if he texts me back or not. But that's not true, is it? Because now I'm placing my palms on the countertop and staring at myself in the mirror, wondering what Cooper sees when he looks at me. I'm wearing a loose side braid and a light-pink jersey knit dress. I have bronzer on my cheeks and mascara on my lashes, but that's it. Does he think I look like a child compared to the women he's used to? I saw Bailey—and I could tell they've had a history—and she and I have *nothing* in common.

I put my hands on my boobs and squish them up, looking at myself from every angle, and then let them drop again with a sigh. The only words that come to mind are *plain* and *mediocre*. If I were a color, I'd be beige. There's nothing exciting about beige. If everything Drew implies about Cooper is true, I'm sure he's used to red, turquoise, and chartreuse.

When I start to feel antsy about Cooper still not texting me back, I decide to suspend my self-scrutinizing and shed my clothes. I shower off, exfoliating and scrubbing other people's gross hair off my body until I smell like a Hawaiian flower. I pull on a pair of gray joggers, a sports bra, and a black tank top, and that's that. I've officially completed my not-going-anywhere-for-the-night look.

I check my phone, registering that there are no new notifications because Cooper never bothered to text me back. That's fine. I'm fine. I don't care. This is me officially giving up on anything concerning Cooper James. He's probably getting showered (*Do not think about Cooper in the shower . . . or . . . on second thought, yes, let's do*) and dressing himself to the nines so he can go clubbing with a beautiful woman in a slinky little dress right now. She'll be all coy smiles and tantalizing hair flips and brushing her fingers across his biceps, and Cooper will lavish her with flirts and attention all night. They'll be a beautiful pair full of charm and charisma.

And now I'm the most jealous human being on the face of the earth. I'm almost certain my skin is turning green.

I throw my head over and wind my hair up in a towel, deciding I need to get out of my head before I do something weird, like track Cooper down and stalk him with binoculars all night. What I need is some music.

Going to my room, I put in my earbuds and turn on one of Ariana Grande's old albums. I like to think I'm a great dancer, which is exactly why I never dance anywhere besides alone in my room where no one can point out the falseness of that statement.

For three whole minutes, I tune out the rest of the world and move. I twerk. I shimmy. I throw my hands over my head and roll my body, pretending I'm Beyoncé and have just stepped into a club to give everyone a surprise performance. *I know all this fierceness is a lot to handle, boys, but you're going to have to try to contain yourselves.*

Saying it feels great to let loose is an understatement. I feel free. I feel like laughing at myself . . . I feel someone watching me.

Whipping around, I find Cooper (*Cooper!*) leaning against my doorframe, the top two buttons of his dress shirt undone, grinning devilishly with a pizza box in his hands.

I rip out my earbuds and chuck them to the other side of the room like maybe that will convince him I wasn't just doing what he saw me doing. His smile only grows, and he gently lifts the box a little higher. "Someone order a pizza?"

My cheeks are melting off my face. "What . . . what are you doing here?!"

He ignores my question (mainly because the answer is clearly in his hands; he moonlights as a pizza delivery man) and, instead, nods toward me, his eyes grazing from my head to my toes and back up again. "I like that move you did."

"Which move?" I ask, sounding pained and definitely like I'm dreading his answer, but also hopeful that maybe I looked like Shakira that whole time and not a member of the Wiggles like I suspect.

"Where you kinda shook your butt but also did that jumping thing. And I like your twisty towel up there too." *Oh good god, someone please push me out of my window.*

I groan and shove my face into my hands, contemplating if I'd rather move to Mexico or Alaska. Both would accomplish the goal of never having to face Cooper again. "No! Why do embarrassing things keep happening to me around you? Please forget you ever saw *any* of that."

He's chuckling now, so pleased with himself for witnessing this moment. "Why? I don't want to forget it—it was cute."

Cute?! I'm a twenty-nine-year-old woman! I'm not supposed to be *cute* when dancing to sexy music in my room.

"Just stop," I say, crossing the room, planting my hands on his chest, and pushing him out. Except, this is making it worse because I can feel his hard muscles under his crisp button-down shirt, taunting me. "Go. Out. Now."

Cooper's laugh tickles every nerve ending in my body as he half-heartedly resists my attempted shoving. "Why? I was liking the show."

"Well, the *cute show* is over now, so you'll have to go watch some bunnies in sunglasses or something to get your fix." I mean to say it as a joke, but my words come out with a little too much acid slathered in an extra helping of bitterness.

His smile fades, and he hits the brakes, letting me know the only reason he was budging before was because he was allowing it. Now he's a stone statue, staring down at me with searching eyes. "Wait, did I upset you?"

I fix my gaze on his chest and continue my attempt to move this mountain so I don't have to look him in the eye. "No. Of course not. I don't get upset. Ever."

"I did. I totally did. I'm sorry, Lucy. I didn't mean to embarrass you. Like I said, I thought it was—"

"*Ohmygosh,* if you say 'cute' one more time, I'm going to shove your face into that pizza." *And someone please get this obnoxious towel off my head!*

I tear it off in one swooping movement and spin around to retreat into my room. I will barricade this door and fashion a makeshift delivery basket out my window for sustenance and supplies. Mark my words, I will never look at Cooper again.

Except, he shifts the pizza to one hand and catches hold of my hand with the other. He tugs me back in a sort of *Dancing with the Stars* move, and I bump into his chest. I'm so close to him now I can smell the mint gum on his breath when he asks, "Is that what made you mad? That I called you cute?" His dark-blond eyebrows are pulled together, and I'm surprised to see the happy-go-lucky beach boy can look stern . . . severe . . . heart-palpitatingly masculine.

My only response is a shrug and forced swallow.

I watch his Adam's apple go up and down, and suddenly this hallway feels like a teeny-tiny thimble. "See, the problem is, I can't take it back, because it *was* cute." *Yeah, yeah, I get it. You think I'm a cutie patootie.* But then his voice drops to a husky whisper, and his thumb rubs a subtle path across the back of my hand. "*So* damn cute."

Oh.

Okay.

I've definitely never heard the word *cute* sound quite like that before—with a rumble and such delicious undertones it makes me think he has a different definition of the word than I do. I swallow and raise my gaze to meet his. Those Tahitian-water eyes are smoldering, like blue fire when the flame is so hot it's lethal.

"Lucy . . ."

"Coop!" Drew yells from somewhere downstairs, making us both startle. "Did you find Lucy?"

Cooper holds my gaze, ignoring my brother. "Why don't you want to be called cute?"

I look down the hall, afraid Drew will surface at any moment and see Cooper tenderly holding my wrist—and then chop it off with a samurai sword. "It's nothing."

"It's something, and I want to know what it is." The decisive punctuation of each word tells me he will stay here all night holding me like this if I don't tell him the truth.

"Cooper!" Drew calls again, and my heart starts doing jumping jacks.

My gaze bounces between the hallway and Cooper, and I know I have no choice. "Cute is what I've always been called, and lately I've been tired of it. Somehow, Drew gets to be exciting and adventurous and successful, and I'm usually just tired with a patch of something sticky on my shirt from my four-year-old." I shake my head, feeling like I'm not really explaining it right. I'm only starting to grasp the way I feel myself, so it's hard to put it into words. "I mean . . . I'm only twenty-nine years old, for goodness' sake, and sometimes I feel . . . ugh. I don't know. I just haven't wanted to feel cute."

"What do you want to feel?"

Dare I say it? I know once I do, I won't be able to put the words back in my mouth. Speaking of mouths, I think I might be staring at Cooper's when I say, "Exciting . . . vibrant . . . I don't know—dangerous?" Gosh that sounded ridiculous. "Just the opposite of cute, okay?"

Wonderful. Now I've not only completed my word vomit, I've taken it up a notch by adding in a layer of deep-seated emotions that probably should have been worked out in a therapist's office a long time ago. I can't meet his eyes. I'm terrified to see a patronizing look in them.

Drew yells once again. "Seriously, did you have a stroke up there or something?"

His voice sounds closer, like maybe he's about to come up the stairs.

"Sorry! I found her! We're coming down!" Cooper yells without looking away from me. He squeezes my wrist lightly then leans in a little to whisper, "We're going to talk more about this later."

"I'd rather not."

"Tough." I look up and can't help but smile when I see Cooper's soft smiling eyes, no hints of patronizing anywhere to be found.

"I thought you were super tired and going straight to bed," Drew says around his slice of pizza. I love my brother, but I seriously want to smack him sometimes. It's like he's intentionally trying to kill any game I might have in front of Cooper. *Actually, I bet that's exactly what he's doing.*

I swallow my bite. "Yeah, well, the shower helped."

God, this is awkward. We're all sitting in the living room on Drew's sectional. Cooper and I keep stealing looks at each other, but my brother is sitting between us, completely oblivious to the sparks flying in the air. At least, there are sparks on my end— freaking fireworks shooting off from the top of my head. I think Cooper might be shooting fireworks too, but it's hard to tell with my brother constantly leaning forward and blocking my view.

"So what movie are we watching?" Drew asks.

"Whatever you want." Cooper's voice sounds a little clipped. Annoyed? I think I'm reading too much into everything. It's like Cooper's touch in the hallway flipped a new switch in my mind, and suddenly I can hear colors. I'm a genius now. Someone could ask me what the square root of pi is, and . . . nah, I still wouldn't know it. But I *am* more aware that the walls are more gray than blue.

Drew wolfs down another big bite. "How about *The Big Sick* or something?"

"That's a romance," I say a little too sharply.

His gaze swings to me with amused eyebrows pulling together. "Just because you hate romance doesn't mean I have to."

My mouth falls open. "I do not *hate* romance."

"My bad. I just thought since you were in a romance-less relationship for so long, you weren't into it." He's clearly being playful and trying to get a rise out of me. Well, he won't get it.

"That's just rude," I say with my arms crossed, studiously avoiding Cooper's gaze so my face doesn't burst into flames. "I could be heartbroken over here, and you're just driving the knife right through my heart."

He waves me off. "Yeah, but you're not. It took you all of forty-eight hours to realize you don't want a guy who borrows your sweaters."

"Will you knock it off about the sweater?! That happened one time, dummy." I hit him in the head with a pillow, and he rocks over onto his side, laughing.

"You guys are very grown up," Cooper deadpans. "It's intimidating, really."

"We know," we both say at the same time, then Drew reaches for another slice of pizza.

"Actually, you know what, if you're over Grim Tim, I could set you up with someone." *Look who suddenly likes nicknames!*

My eyes shoot to Cooper of their own accord. He, however, is frowning severely at Drew. Question is, what kind of frown is that? A don't-you-dare-try-to-set-her-up-with-me frown, or an I'm-super-jealous-please-don't-set-her-up-with-anyone-other-than-me frown? The thought that it's probably the first of those two options makes my heart sink and my mouth spit out the word *sure* before I can think better of it.

"Really?" both men ask me at the same time.

"I thought it was going to be more difficult to convince you than that," says Drew.

"Yeah . . . me too." I don't know what to make of Cooper's expression, but I do know the watch wrapped around his wrist is somehow the sexiest thing I've ever seen. His skin is so tan the blond hairs on his arms stand out, and hunter green is definitely his color. When his strong jaw twitches like it is now, I want to sit in his lap and trail kisses all the way down his neck.

And now I'm staring . . .

I swallow and clear my throat. "Well, call me crazy, but I thought it might be fun to see if there are single men out there who won't need my sweater in restaurants."

Drew's eyes light up, and he points at me. "So you admit it! Tim *was* annoying."

I roll my eyes. "Gloating doesn't look good on you."

"Gosh, you should have met this guy," Drew says to Cooper. "He was the worst. So particular about everything. Like when the hostess sat us by the kitchen, he made us move because—"

"Okay!" I cut in. "This is not going to turn into a night of pointing out how ridiculous Lucy's ex-boyfriend was, thank you very much." My face is flaming because I can't stand the thought of Cooper knowing I've never been able to snag a good guy, knowing the good catches never seem to want to come anywhere near me.

I wasn't even Brent's first choice the night he turned me into a mom. The place was dimly lit, he was bored, and I was one of the few single females there. I'm pretty sure he still only talks to me when he's bored and there are no other women nearby to pay attention to. That's the only reason I can think of to explain why he would think it's acceptable to break plans with me at the last second, saying something came up, but then hours later, on Instagram, post pictures of his date making an annoying flirty face at the camera.

Really, Brent? You didn't even have the decency to try to hide it from me that you were canceling on me for another woman?

But it's not like I ever thought any time he and I spent together would constitute a date—I know better than that. He made it clear I wasn't his type from day one, but I think a very sad, pathetic part of me always hoped I could weasel my way into his heart and change his mind if he ever gave me the chance. Not anymore, though. I'm blissfully over him, out from under his spell. Even so, I do think all those years of pining after a man who didn't want me back scarred me in a deeper way than I realized at the time. Because now, no matter how hard I try to believe in myself, there's still a voice that whispers, *You don't have anything to offer.*

Drew bumps my knee with his and tries to catch my eye like he knows exactly where my mind went and is trying to pull me out of it. "Don't worry. We'll find you a good guy, Lucy. One who actually gives you his jacket for a change."

"I'm skeptical such an incredible hero exists." I laugh lightheartedly, but it promptly dies out when my eyes lock with Cooper's.

Cyan blue mixed with his stern expression hits me like a tidal wave, and I'm momentarily knocked breathless. He makes no move to look away or soften his features. Instead, I get the feeling he's trying to tell me something without words. My skin prickles, and each of my nerve endings urges me to pay attention. I can't, though, because Drew is here, and he's going on and on about potential men he works with and a guy he plays basketball with, and I just really want to duct-tape his mouth and push him out of the room so I can explore what Cooper's gaze is communicating.

After a few very intense moments, Cooper's mouth softens ever so slightly into a crooked grin, and his eyes fall down to the water glass in his hand. The charged moment tears in two, and Drew's voice seeps back into my consciousness.

". . . so you're good with me giving him your number?"

I blink a few times and take in a breath like I've just surfaced from the depths of the ocean. "Oh. Yeah. That's okay with me."

CHAPTER 8

Cooper

COOPER: You still up?

LUCY: Isn't this how every single booty call starts?

LUCY: Ha ha.

LUCY: Can you just forget I said that please? I know this isn't a booty call.

LUCY: What I mean is, YEP, I'm up.

COOPER: Come outside. Don't let Drew hear you.

LUCY: What? Why?

COOPER: Just do it.

LUCY: What are you? Nike? Tell me why. This feels like a prank.

COOPER: Did you have really traumatic teen years or something?

LUCY: I'd rather not answer that question.

COOPER: Lucy, this is not a prank. I'm taking you on a late-night adventure.

LUCY: But it's like 10:00!

COOPER: No excuses. Let's go.

keep my truck lights off, and I'm parked a few houses down from Lucy's. It's odd how much this makes me feel sixteen again, trying to sneak her out of her house without her parents finding out. Except she is the parent this time, and we're playing a game of Get Past the Brother—which honestly feels riskier, because I really like Drew a lot. I don't get the same thrill I used to get from sneaking around, because Drew has been a great friend, and whether he knows it or not, he helped me out of a really gloomy time in my life.

But then I see Lucy slip out the door and I completely forget everything I just felt. This is absolutely thrilling.

She looks side to side and folds her arms tightly around her, clearly worried I'm going to pop out of a bush. I flash my lights twice, and even from this far away I can see her beaming smile. She looks back toward the darkened house, then hurries down the path toward my truck. The interior glows in warm light when she opens the door, making her soft features look like velvet.

"Hi," she says, sliding up into the leather seat.

"Hi."

Her eyes scan around the cab and then up to me. "*This* is your truck?"

I'm not sure what that inflection is supposed to mean. "Yes?"

I've always been proud of this vehicle. It's my dad's old 1972 Ford F250, but it's fully restored, painted in a matte hunter green with blacked-out rims and baseball leather interior. This truck turned me into that guy who, when asked if he has any children, pulls out a picture of what he drives. That is, until two seconds ago when Lucy added a strange inflection and made me want to park it in my garage, cover it with a sheet, and pretend I've never heard of it.

She chuckles. "Sorry. I think I emphasized the wrong word. I just meant I've already ridden in this truck before, but I didn't realize it was yours."

"Oh," I say, letting out a breath of relief that I don't have to disown my favorite possession now. "Yeah, when Drew helped you move home, right?"

"Yep." She gives a private smile, and I want to know what it means more than anything, but she keeps it to herself. "I like it." Her fingers go to the glove box, and she unashamedly opens it, takes a peek, and closes it again. And now she's dropping down the visor and flicking it back up. She plucks the change from my cup holder, counts it, and drops it back in. I'm mesmerized. How long will she go on like this if I let her?

"Lucy . . ." I say on a chuckle, and she whips her head up, tosses her hands in the air, and lets them fall dramatically against her lap.

"I know, okay?! But I'm a ball of nerves. Why am I in here? What are we doing?"

Earlier tonight, I called this woman "cute" and she looked like she was going to break down in tears. Then, when she admitted she felt boxed in and set aside, I couldn't take it. I might not be able to do anything about making her feel anything more than *cute* without having her brother remove any dangly parts of my body, but I can do something about her needing excitement.

My grin slants. "We're doing something dangerous tonight."

Her smile drops, and her eyes do that wide owl thing that is uniquely *Lucy*. It's adorable, but I don't dare tell her because I know she'll take it like I'm saying, *You should start wearing oversized bows in your hair* rather than *You're so adorable I want to kiss every inch of your skin.*

"Dangerous?" Her voice quivers a little.

"Yep." I hold out my hand for a low five. "You in?"

She bites her lips together and looks down at my hand. "I'm in." And then, because she's Lucy, she takes my hand and wiggles it.

"No, no, no. Are you insane? I'm a mom, Cooper—I can't freaking go to jail."

I grin and cut the engine to my truck. "You're not going to go to jail."

Even in the dark, I can tell her eyes are wide. "TRESPASSING IS A CRIME!"

"Shhhh," I say, chuckling and covering her mouth with my hand. Now all I can see are her big blue eyes sparkling. "It's going to be fine. I know the owner."

She pulls my hand away from her mouth but, as I notice with great pleasure, doesn't let go of it. "Then why don't you use that handy little device there called a cellphone to call the owner and ask him or her for permission first?"

I run my thumb across hers. "Because what fun would that be? I thought you wanted to do something dangerous."

She growls a little. "I was thinking something more along the lines of trying to eat a whole gallon of ice cream in one night and not throw up."

"Wild woman."

My taunt gets me a sideways glare. "Cooper. I *can't* be wild anymore. I'm responsible for more than just me. If I go to jail, I have a four-year-old who will really miss his mama and, frankly, be startled to see how ugly she looks in orange."

I squeeze her hand. "Lucy, trust me. I won't let you go to jail. We're going to jump in and jump out, then hit the road."

She groans and gently bangs her head back against the headrest a few times. "This is not a smart decision. You're a bad influence."

"That's my tagline. Now come on. Get out and shut your door quietly."

"Because if I don't . . . I'LL GO TO JAIL!"

"I'm going to personally drive you to jail and drop you off myself if you don't quit yelling that."

We both get out and stealthily shut our doors. I should say I shut *my* door quietly. Lucy tries to shut hers slowly, but it isn't hard enough to latch. She presses it a few times, but it still doesn't seal, so she has to throw her hip into it, making it shut with the absolute loudest *WHAM* I've ever heard.

She hisses and bares her teeth in an awkward expression. "Oops. Sorry."

I shake my head and hold out my hand before I even realize what I'm doing. Lucy takes it without a moment's hesitation, and I pull her down the sidewalk. Again, I parked a few houses down from our destination—because you can't exactly park in the driveway of the property you're about to trespass on.

It seems like everyone is asleep in the surrounding houses because the street is basically dark. I don't think anyone will see us and call the cops, but if they do it'll make this night a whole lot more interesting.

"I can't believe you're making me do this!" Lucy says as we trudge across the lawn, rounding the corner of the house and heading for the back gate.

"Relax, we're just having some fun." I let go of her hand to reach over the gate and unlatch it.

"I can't relax!" She's whisper-hissing at me. "I have a terrible feeling you're recruiting me into your felon gang or something, and to initiate me you're going to send me into this house to steal their big-screen TV."

Now that's a funny mental image: Lucy trying to lift a massive television out of a house on her own. I'm almost tempted to make her do it just so I can take pictures and always have something to make me laugh on rainy days.

"What's a felon gang?" I ask, tugging her through the gate with me. "Is that like a special subcategory of gangs?"

"You know . . . like a group of felons who gang up together to steal."

"You basically just restated the original title with more non-descriptive words. Here, stay close so we don't trip the light sensors."

"Ohgoshohgoshohgosh," she says, staying close to my back as we hug the outer perimeter of the yard, heading toward the pool. It feels good to have her this close to me. She smells sweet. I can't pinpoint the scent; it's just soft and sweet. Maybe even a little fruity. "I'm going to jail. I am *going* to jail. I, Lucy, will be going to jail."

"What do I have to do to get you to stop chanting that?" We're at the pool gate now; I unlatch it and step inside, holding it open for her.

"Buckle me back into your truck and take me home safely."

I level her with a loaded look. "Is that really what you want?"

She knows what I mean. This moment is more than just *this* moment. This is Lucy's chance to choose to live. She told me in her long-winded first text that she wished she were challenged more. Well, here it is—her first challenge.

She holds my gaze, taking in a long deep breath through her nose. She looks toward the darkened house, and when her eyes turn back to me I see worry. "Lucy, I think you need this. Tomorrow morning you'll wake up, and go get your son, and have break-fast, and be a mom with all the bells and whistles—"

"I don't wear bells and whistles on Thursdays."

"—but tonight . . . you are just Lucy, a woman who deserves to let loose and have fun. What do you say?" I'm only about thirty percent sure she'll do it. She doesn't really have a good reason to trust me. Like she said, for all she knows, I'm a terrible guy and am actually leading her into trouble.

But when a slow smile starts to spread over her mouth, warm blood rushes through my veins, pumping and reviving my old familiar heart until it's three sizes bigger. *No more stealing Christmas for me.* "Let's do this." But she quickly amends her declaration: "As long as *this* is only jumping in the pool and not actually destroying or stealing any property."

I smile. "None of those things." I step toward her to put a hand on her lower back and urge her through the gate. "Just swimming."

CHAPTER 9

Lucy

"Wait—I didn't bring my swimsuit," I say, blinking down at the gorgeous pool. It's all lit up with warm lights and the reflection of the moon. It's calling to me like I'm a little hobbit. *Luuucccyyyy . . .*

But that doesn't change the fact that I don't have my swimsuit. Cooper is standing close to me, his arm nearly brushing mine, and suddenly I remember every teen movie I've ever seen. Maybe he wasn't expecting a swimsuit—just a *birthday* suit.

I blink up at him. "Oh no. Were you . . . ? Are we supposed to skinny-dip?" My face flames just thinking about it. There's no way the lights projecting up from the bottom of the pool will be at all flattering on my pasty body. "I don't think I'm up for that."

His low chuckle rolls down my spine. "No, we're jumping in just like this." Then his grin tilts. "But if you have your heart set on skinny-dipping, don't let me get in the way."

"You're so selfless."

His smile is full and bright now. And then—*and then*—he reaches to the back of his shirt and peels it off over his head. He tosses it aside, and every single one of his fantastic muscles winks at me. They have the same voice as Joey Tribbiani: *How you doin'?* I take a mental picture so later, when I can't sleep, I'll push all those sheep aside and count each of his muscles instead.

"I thought you said we weren't taking off our clothes?" Oh my gosh, he looks so good standing there shirtless in gym shorts with the nighttime sky at his back. I want to shove him in that pool just out of anger for being this sexy. My ovaries are screaming, *HIM! WE PICK HIM!!!* But their opinion no longer matters ever since they got me knocked up by a man who didn't want a relationship with me, so I tell them to shut it.

"You're overthinking this. Come on, ready?" Cooper wraps his big manly hand around mine, and my heart slams against my chest. "ONE!"

"Shhh, don't yell—they'll hear you!"

"TWO!"

"Oh my gosh, we're going to jail!"

"THREE!"

"Don't make a big splash or—" I don't get to finish.

Cooper jumps off the ledge, taking me with him in one big, glorious splash.

Cooper and I both emerge from the water, sputtering laughs and pushing water out of our faces. It feels a lot like that day at the lake, but different. Because it's dark, and we're alone, and I'm buzzing off of a different high than adrenaline. Cooper planned this. He wanted me to experience something thrilling tonight.

The water is warm, and surprisingly, the lights on the bottom of the pool *are* flattering. At least they are for him. His skin looks softer, more taut and inviting, as we swim from the deep end to the shallow, laughing like goons the entire way. Cooper keeps looking over his large shoulder with such a big smile and twinkle in his eyes it feels like a dream. I expect to wake up any minute, realizing I dreamed about the pool only because I've peed myself. Don't judge—pregnancy was not kind to my bladder.

"How do you feel?" he asks after we've made it to the shallow end and are both standing. He pushes his hand through his hair, and water droplets glisten all over his body. He is a sight to behold, and all I can think is how incredible it would feel to have his arms wrap around me and hold me in a straitjacket of love.

"Amazing." I lie back in the water to swim a backstroke to the side of the pool. My T-shirt and shorts drag like weights as I make my way over and rest my elbows against the edge. The stars are bright and twinkly, only adding to the feeling that this is all a figment of my imagination. This is something I wouldn't normally, in a million years, do. I don't go out late at night—certainly not with a man, and definitely not to break into someone's pool and enjoy a little dip.

Cooper's smile is tilted, and he starts walking across the pool to my side. Seeing him move toward me with his tan muscular chest, that damp tousled hair, and the inky sky as a backdrop . . . it makes me think I need to separate our ends of the pool with some sort of net. To protect him from me, obviously—not the reverse. Because Cooper thinks I'm *cute,* and I think he is a Greek god of fertility.

"What are you doing?" I ask, sounding nervous and unsure as he gets closer. Is this pool heated? I think it's getting hotter somehow.

I step back, pressing myself fully against the scratchy concrete side so I don't accidentally jump the man stopping a mere three inches away. He smiles down at me and then raises both hands to cup my face. *IT'S REALLY HAPPENING?!* That's my uterus screaming this time, and I really hope he can't hear it. It sounds like a desperate old hag.

His hands are warm as he smiles and runs his thumbs over both of my cheekbones. "You have mascara streaks."

I shut my eyes tight so he doesn't see the embarrassment shining through them. Is it actually completely impossible for me to be cool around this guy? How long have I been standing here looking like a bride left on her wedding day?

Cooper chuckles but doesn't remove his hands. "You blush so easily."

"Ugh. Stop. That makes it worse!" I open my eyes to find him smiling.

"But I like it when you blush."

My stomach twists into knots. He's still holding my face, and his large body is right there in front of me, and I want nothing more than to plant both of my hands on his chest and see . . . just *see* what his skin feels like beneath my fingers. But Drew's warning springs back to my mind like that annoying Whac-A-Mole game where the mole keeps popping its head up and you can never hit it with the hammer. If I give in to temptation and kiss Cooper, it would mean something to me—a big something. I'm already having to treat my heart like a cartoon and grab it by the back of its shirt, holding it in place while it tries to run away from me. If what Drew says about Cooper is right, for him it would just be another kiss, a regular Wednesday-night activity.

He's a flirt—maybe even a player. His ocean eyes tell me to dive in and enjoy the water. They promise he'd give me the best kiss of my entire life. Actually, no. They say a kiss won't be enough. They say they'll need all night to do the work they want to complete.

Which is exactly why I can't. *Nope.*

Not. Gonna. Happen.

Must stay strong.

I swallow and look over his shoulder, not noticing the way the water pools in the little area between his collarbone and shoulder muscle. "We need to go. This has been fun, but I *really* don't want to get caught."

"Too late." His hands drop away, but his eyes are definitely still holding me.

"What do you mean?"

His grin makes my chest tighten. "You're caught." He tilts his head toward the house, but I still don't understand. "That's my house, Lucy. You're in my pool."

What?! I'm in Cooper's pool right now? I blink at the beautiful house behind him, and my brain feels like it's full of molasses with how slowly it's processing this new information. Then, when everything snaps into place, my eyes toss grenades at him, and I lunge forward to splash him. "You big liar!" *Splash. Splash. Splash.* He laughs and turns his face away to avoid my attacks. "Why did you make me think we were trespassing?!" I don't give him a chance to respond. I lurch forward and wrap my arm around his neck, trying to drag him under and drown him.

He's actually pretty pliable and easy to drown because he's laughing so hard his muscles are momentarily incapacitated. Why does it feel so amazing to be stronger than Superman? I dunk his head under the water and pull it back up. "You're"—*dunk*—"SO"—*dunk*—"mean!"—*dunk*.

This time, when I pull him up out of the water, his muscles

revive themselves and he stands to his full height, towering over me like a monster that's just been made stronger from all the torture. I turn to scramble away, but—oh yeah—I'm in water and bogged down by, like, fifteen pounds of extra weight from my clothes. Cooper easily catches me and swoops me up in his arms. He's cradling me, and I'm fully pressed up against his fantastic body now. I don't want to acknowledge how good it feels . . . but, oh boy, do I. Every inch of me feels like it's sparking and reacting.

Do you know what happens when you mix water and electricity?

Electrocution.

"You're gonna pay for all that waterboarding," he says, carrying me up the steps of the pool like I weigh no more than a wet towel.

I squirm and kick, but he just keeps walking until we're out of the water. He goes to the deep end, then flashes me one last sizzling, torturous grin before launching me in the air, tossing me right back into the pool. I scream in midair, then the water engulfs me. No sooner do I surface and catch my breath than I feel his arms come around me and start hauling me to the stairs again. Yes, he laughs like a wicked villain and chucks me in a second time.

I'm laughing so hard at the absurdity of this night that I don't even try to fight back. I can't remember the last time I felt like laughing this hard. After the third time I get sent airborne, he gives up, letting me surface and float on my back, staring up at the sky. I feel Cooper's hands around my body once more, but this time he doesn't take me out of the pool. He holds me, and his fingertips wipe what I'm sure are more mascara stains off my cheeks, but I don't feel as embarrassed about it this time.

He swims us back to the shallow end and sets me on the little wading ledge in the water, and then he sits down right beside me, our shoulders pressed together like he *has* to be touching me in some way. Why? Because it's normal for him? Because he's hoping to turn this into more?

I squint up at the sky again, feeling his eyes on my face. "Are you trying to get me to sleep with you?" I ask boldly, because sometimes I can't help but say what's in my head. It's my super-power and my curse.

If he's shocked by my question, he doesn't act like it. "No."

I can't decide if I'm comforted or let down by his answer. "Okay. Then what was the point of tonight? Bringing me here . . . letting me think we were doing something illegal? It feels like this might be your signature move or something."

"My move?" His voice is full of amusement.

"Yeah, you know, like you have this whole scene worked out perfectly to where women are putty in your hands."

"Are you putty in my hands right now?" His words make chill bumps erupt across my skin.

I can't answer that question. "How many?" I ask, turning things back around on him because I'm too scared he'll be able to see the answer to his question written on my face in highlighter. I probably look like I've broken out in heart-shaped chickenpox.

He shakes his head, a soft smile on his lips. "This is not a move. You're the first woman I've even had in this pool."

Oh.

My shoulders relax a little, but then, when I lean a little more into his shoulder, realization zaps through me. "Wait! That's your move, isn't it?! Taking women to do special things for the first time!" I point an accusing finger at him.

He grabs my finger and lowers it like I had the barrel of a gun aimed at his chest. "Will you stop it? I don't have a *move*." His grin curves into something wolfish. "Never needed one."

I roll my eyes and make a *blehhhhhh* sound.

He laughs. "Lucy, I brought you here because I wanted to cheer you up. You seemed so down earlier when I called you cute—like I meant cute in a tiny-purring-kitten way."

"Actually, I thought you meant it in an awwww-look-at-that-adorable-mom-letting-loose kind of way."

"And that's worse?" he asks with a crooked brow.

"Much."

"Why's that?"

"Because . . ." I shrug. "I don't know exactly. I think there's a stigma that comes along with being a mom, and when you're young like me, it's confusing. I should be in my prime, thriving, and . . . attractive. Instead, at least three times a day, I have to re-move a stain from my shirt that Levi left behind. It's like earning the title of *Mom* immediately zapped all the attractiveness right out of me." Why did I just tell him all of that? I can't help but al-ways spill my guts around him for some terrible reason.

"I can tell you right now that's not true. No one sees you that way." He pauses briefly, then turns his eyes to me. "I definitely don't see you like that. In fact . . . I'm sort of envious of you."

My mouth falls open. "No way."

"Yes way."

"What does my life have that could possibly make you envi-ous?"

He turns his blue eyes to me, and I see a hint of sadness. "My life hasn't exactly turned out the way I hoped." *Well, that's mysteri-ous.* I keep waiting for him to expound and tell me what it is that's lacking, but he doesn't. Instead, he changes the subject. "Can I ask you a personal question?"

"Sure."

"Levi's dad . . . what's the deal there?"

I scrunch my nose and groan, tilting my head back. "I thought you were going to ask what my star sign is or something."

"That's not even close to a personal question. Plus, I know nothing about star signs." He bumps my shoulder. "But if you don't want to tell me about Levi's dad, I understand."

For some reason, I *do* want to tell him. I want to tell him everything all the time. "It's okay. It's not exactly classified information. Ask almost anyone around this town and they'll tell you the truth: Lucy aimed too high."

Cooper frowns, and his head jerks back a little. "Why in the world would you think that?"

"I don't know. I mean, I'm generally liked by most people, but I've always been sort of . . . overlooked." I shrug to downplay the heaviness of that word. "People seem to think I make a better *friend* than girlfriend. So, when I met Brent, Levi's dad, at a party and he paid me the slightest bit of attention, I was a goner. He was in med school, really good-looking, and definitely what most people would consider a ladies' man." *Sort of like you.*

"Anyway, that entire night was a mistake—one I greatly regretted when those pink lines popped up." Even almost five years later, I can still remember exactly how it felt seeing that test verify that I was going to have a baby. The way my stomach twisted and my lungs squeezed. And yet—even though I knew I had options, my decision formed immediately in my heart as solid as bones. "It was so terrifying at the time, and although I regret that Brent is Levi's dad, I don't regret my son at all. As cliché as it sounds, he's the best thing that has ever happened to me."

Cooper's smile is tender. "I could see that yesterday even just from that short conversation you had with him over FaceTime."

I laugh. "I don't think you can call him torturing me with dizzying circles a conversation."

"I liked getting to see you talk to him." I don't know how to respond to that, so I stay quiet. Cooper's eyes glance down to where he cups water in his hand and pours it back out in a repetitive motion. Finally, he asks, "So you and Brent? How long were you together?"

My gaze shoots up to his face, realizing he doesn't get it. Apparently, Drew hasn't told him the whole story. A nervous, slightly self-deprecating chuckle falls from my mouth as I attempt to muster up the dignity for this story. "Never. We have never been a couple. That night after the party—and maybe a few more here and there over the years—was it for us. He was . . . Well, he was never interested in me, just didn't want to be alone that night I guess, and I was . . . there." I wince at how terrible my own words make me feel. "When I told him I was pregnant, he was really quick to extinguish any idea that we would be a couple in any way, shape, or form."

"Wow . . . what a . . ." He trails off.

"A what?"

"A dick. He's a freaking dick."

I sputter a laugh because it feels way too good to hear someone else think and say that same thing about Brent. "Yeah. He kind of is. I mean, I don't want to paint too bad of a picture, because he really is a good dad to Levi, which I think is why I held out hope for so long that we'd be a couple one day. Well, that and because he would, every now and then, say subtle little things that would make me think he was coming around to the idea and he'd like to be a family one day too. But then, in the next moment, he'd start dating someone new, and I finally realized his words were all just hot air."

He nods and hums a quiet understanding sound. "Do you still hope you'll get together one day?"

I don't have to consider this for even a second. In fact, my words probably come out with a little too much force. "God, no. That's actually why I moved away. I needed some space from Brent, and honestly, even though it was the hardest thing being away from my family and having to manage everything on my own, it was the best thing for me. I needed a new start, a town far enough away that if Brent asked me to go to dinner, I wouldn't drop everything and say yes, only to have him stand me up when someone else became available."

"Did that happen?"

"More times than I'd like to admit."

I don't want to, but I peek at Cooper, admiring the way his broad shoulders glisten as they hover above the surface of the water. This moment feels so intimate, and I can't help but wonder why he's asking all of this. Friendship? Intrigue? Something more? I swirl my finger on the surface of the water and dare another glance at him, taking note of his pinched eyebrows and mouth pressed into a line.

"Do you think less of me now . . . after hearing all that?"

My words seem to snap him out of his thoughts. His brow clears, and his eyes catch on mine. "No, not at all." A soft, sad chuckle rolls through his chest, and I watch his Adam's apple move up and down. "I was just thinking how similar our stories are, actually."

"Really? Which part?" Suddenly, I'm nervous he's going to tell me he has a son somewhere, which is so hypocritical of me to feel nervous about, but here I am, asking anyway. "Do you . . . have a child?"

"No, but I do have an ex-girlfriend I eagerly left behind in another state."

Why does that make my heart sink a little lower? Is he contemplating going home? Going back to her? I have to ask. "I see. So this is your temporary stop? Will you go back when you find closure?" *Like I did.*

Although . . . I also had to come back because I lost my job and was evicted. Cooper doesn't seem to have monetary issues, judging by this incredible house and pool.

He lifts an eyebrow, looking slightly mischievous. "Is that a little dejection I hear in your voice? A hint of jealousy maybe?"

I sputter a laugh and shove him because, for some reason, that smile tugging the corner of his mouth up makes me feel flirty and light. And yes, it was most definitely a flirty shove. The kind where my hand lingers a little too long on his biceps, liking the way his muscle flexes under my touch.

One thing is certain: there's some kind of chemistry between Cooper and me. I just don't know if he feels it with whichever woman he's with at the moment or if this is something different.

"Not in the least. I was just wondering if I should save all my moving boxes for you or not."

He smiles at me over his shoulder. "I'm not going anywhere."

And then my eyes take in the very moment he runs his teeth across his bottom lip. I track the motion, feeling mesmerized and buzzed even though I haven't had anything to drink. In this dream, it feels like real life is far away—unreachable. Cooper is thrilling, sweet, inviting, and a little dangerous. Just looking at his lips makes mine tingle. They know he would be the most devastating kisser. Suddenly, I have to know. My heart pounds almost painfully, trying to remind me with obnoxious thuds that this is probably not something I should be doing. But I'm already living dangerously tonight, so what's one more tiny bit of adventure?

I'm staring at his lips and, before I realize it, leaning in. Because my eyes have not left his lips, I see when he releases them from his teeth and they part, his chest expanding with air. My insides are burning, and all I want is to kiss him and be kissed by him.

I press forward, and he stays perfectly still . . . until I get about an inch from his mouth, then he pulls back. He doesn't turn away, but he leans back from me ever so slightly, enough to get the message across that this kiss of mine is not going to be received. It takes my mind a second to fully register what is happening.

But when it does, realization crashes into me like I jumped out of a plane without a parachute.

He's turning me down. Embarrassment slaps me in the face, and I'm afraid to give rejection a name. So instead, I play it off like I don't care one bit that he doesn't want to kiss me and shoot up to my feet. Water sloshes down my legs and cascades from my shirt, making it sound as if I'm peeing a waterfall. It only serves to remind me that I'm not like the exciting women in movies, who, when placed in this situation, would have taken off their clothes and had a delicious night of skinny-dipping with this hot man. No, I had to stay fully clothed and bare my entire soul to him instead. Wonderful. *Such a cute look, Lucy.*

Drew will be happy to hear that he has nothing to worry about with Cooper. He's just like Levi's dad—in other words, interested in everyone besides me.

I need to get away from him.

I turn and step up onto the ledge, but Cooper reaches out and wraps his hand around my calf. It's warm and possessive and makes me want to cry because I know he doesn't mean the gesture the way it's coming across. "Lucy, wait. Let me explain—"

"You don't have to explain anything, Cooper. We're good. All good! I'm fine. Really fine. Awesome, even."

He squeezes my calf. "Just listen to me—"

I shut my eyes tight and smile tensely. "Seriously, please, I'm begging you—can we not talk about it? Will you just take me home, please?" I'm so close to crying, which makes this even worse.

He hears the plea (and wobble) in my voice, sighs, and lets go of me so he can stand. "All right, fine." He looks away and whispers a curse under his breath, then looks back at me. "Let's at least go inside first so I can get you a towel."

Inside? His house? Ugh. I'd rather die of hypothermia right about now than have to endure any more awkwardness with Cooper.

CHAPTER 10

Cooper

I rejected Lucy, and I've never ever felt like a worse human being. I wish someone would punch me. Just right in the freaking face. Knock some teeth out, make my nose bleed—the works. Instead, Lucy trails behind me like the most heart-wrenching sight of a wounded puppy you've ever seen. I want to scoop her up and snuggle her into oblivion so her tail will wag again.

I can hear her clothes sloshing dramatically with every step toward my back door. I try to slow my pace to walk side by side with her, but she's not having it. She slows down too, and now we look like we're both moving in slow motion, the most ridiculous scene of two adults anyone has ever witnessed. I hate that she's embarrassed, and I hate that I'm the one who made her feel that way. But what can I say? I panicked.

Normally, a kiss wouldn't be a big deal, and I'd be happy to oblige her need for physical contact. I guess that's the point. Lately, I've been that guy you go to for a fun time. No strings attached; no commitment needed. I once let a complete stranger kiss me in a bar without us ever saying a single word to each other. She was eyeing me from a few stools down, and we were trading flirtatious glances back and forth, and the next thing I know, she's spinning my chair around and making out with me right there in front of everyone. My only thought at the time was, *Why not? I'm not in a relationship anymore.*

But when Lucy leaned forward time stopped, and I had a hundred thoughts flood my mind at once. Most of those thoughts were how much I really wanted to kiss her, how good she'd feel against my lips, but then I thought about how much I'd like to have a relationship with her. I don't want something no-strings-attached with her. I don't want to be just a fun time for her—the one who floats around aimlessly like a twenty-year-old with nothing but time ahead of him. Actually, I didn't even act that way in my early twenties. I've always wanted a family and a steady relationship. But after Janie, I freaked out for a second. Lucy's bringing me back, reminding me of old dreams I forgot I had, reminding me what it's like to want to see someone day in and day out, to plan for the holidays together and have inside jokes no one else will get. I feel some of my wounds seal up, and I realize I might be ready for all that again.

But then I remembered Drew and his look of warning, because he has no idea I am capable of or desire any sort of a long-term relationship. I never told him about Janie. I just wanted to leave her back in Charlotte along with my humiliation. So basically, he thinks I will certainly, one hundred percent, without fail, break Lucy's heart, and that's a fair assumption since that's the only side of me he's ever seen.

All of this, coupled with the fact that Lucy is so much more to me than the possibility of a fun random hookup. And I get the impression she feels a connection between us too. Maybe she was

just trying to continue the theme of the evening and live sponta-
neously, but I don't think so. I think she *likes* me.

So yeah, I cut off any chance of a kiss because I feel like if we're
going to do this, we need to do it right. I have to talk to Drew first
and make sure he knows my intention before I try to start anything up with her, and I have to make sure Lucy knows what she's
getting into with me. She's special. Loving, and full of heart, and
has a child. I don't intend to make her life any more difficult than
it already is, so I want to get this right from the get-go.

Although, I realize, as I open the door for Lucy and she won't
meet my eye, that I might have just sabotaged any chance of a
good start. She thinks I'm not interested in her. Maybe even that
I'm not attracted to her, which makes me want to groan because
just looking into that woman's eyes makes my pulse skitter. She's
breathtaking, even soaked to the bone and hair turning into wild,
frizzy curls. It's taking everything in me not to say *forget it* and
wrap my arms around her.

But nope . . . nope, nope, nope. Can't do that. Not to a best
friend's sister. The repercussions would be too great.

When I shut the door behind us, it's quiet, and alone in the
dark like this, I still feel the possibility of what could be with her.
Which is why I flip on the bright overhead kitchen light. We both
squint at the sudden dose of reality. The charged, magical pool
moment is over, and Lucy looks like she's torn between anger and
mortification, arms tightly crossed and shoulders bunched up.

"The bathroom is this way," I say, nodding and walking through
the kitchen toward the main hall.

"I'm good here," she says, and when I look back she adds,
"Don't want to drip on your floor."

Riiiiight. What she means is, *How about you drop dead, Cooper?*

I leave Lucy with her back superglued to the door and head to my master bathroom to change out of my wet clothes and grab her a towel. When I come back into the kitchen, I see Lucy curiously peeking her head around the corner to the living room. She hears me approach and springs back to her spot at the door.

I smile at the guilty expression on her face. "Here, I went ahead and brought you some of my clothes so you don't have to be cold on the way home." She looks down at the sweatpants and T-shirt like maybe they're full of frogs and I'm trying to trick her into wearing them. "I know they'll be a little big, but I figured it would be more comfortable than what you've got on."

She swallows and gives me a tight smile. "Thanks."

I step forward and wrap the towel around her shoulders. I'm conscious of every tiny moment, every breath, every blink of her eyes as I look down at her with my hands lingering on her shoulders. Her long lashes are cast down to the lump of clothing in her hands, and I feel the need to clarify what happened, even if she doesn't want to hear it. "Lucy—"

"Your house is empty," she says in a rush, cutting me off.

I frown and look around, momentarily jarred by her change of subject. "Oh. Yeah. I just moved in a month ago."

She pulls away, forcing my hands to drop, and steps farther into the kitchen. It's clear she's not going to let me address why I turned her down. "Or maybe you're really just a squatter." She tosses a mischievous smirk over her shoulder, and the fact that she's joking again makes me relax slightly.

"You caught me. Only a few more months before squatter's rights kick in." It actually does look like that, though.

I bought this place because I liked that it was modern and also homey. The kitchen has slate-gray cabinets and white marble countertops, and although it's not huge, it's open concept, making it feel spacious. The floors are a light hardwood throughout, and it has that new-build-house smell. But the rest is bare, minus a gray midcentury couch in the living room and my bed in the master. I've tried looking for furniture online, but every time I get ready to click Buy, I can't commit.

Lucy delicately runs her fingers across the countertop and looks toward the empty breakfast nook. It's surrounded by windows that overlook the pool. "It's a really pretty house. It'll look amazing when you get moved in."

"I am moved in."

Her eyes fly to me and then to the space around her with a new realization. "But there's nothing in here."

"Not true." I point toward the sink. "There's a bowl in the sink."

She gives a short laugh and looks at me like she still can't fully believe I'm telling the truth. "How long did you say you've lived here?"

"A month, give or take."

Her eyes widen, and she spins on her heels, charging into the living room. She flips on the light and takes in the pathetic couch sitting in the middle of the room facing a large empty wall where a TV should be.

"Before you picture me sitting in here in the dark, staring at that wall like a psycho, just know I watch movies on my laptop."

Now Lucy is making herself at home as she buzzes through the living room and down the hallway. There's a new energy about her that I like, something determined and comfortable. After flipping on a switch in the guest bathroom, frowning at it, and then doing the same with two more rooms, she goes all the way down the hall to my bedroom.

There, she turns on the light but just hovers at the edge. Her eyes make one quick sweep over my king-sized bed and then move up to me, where I am looking over her shoulder. "You own two pieces of furniture, Cooper. *Two*. What is this house, like, two thousand square feet? And you own *two* pieces of furniture?" She says this like maybe I hadn't already realized it and this should be some great epiphany for me.

"Don't forget about the bowl."

"Why?"

"Because bowls are important too."

She looks like she wants to laugh but holds back. "I mean . . . why do you not have any furniture?"

I shrug and lean against the doorframe. We're both lingering outside my bedroom, like maybe if we accidentally stepped in there at the same time, the bed would suck us into its vortex. "I can't decide on anything. It all feels so permanent. It's a big decision, and I guess . . ." Oh, I regret tacking on that *I guess* immediately.

"You guess what?"

I narrow an eye and smile at her sudden eagerness to find out my dirty secret. Well, it's the least I can do to be honest with her after all she's told me tonight, right? "You can't make fun of me. It's pretty sappy. But . . . I guess some part of me knows I'll have a girlfriend or wife in here with me one day because this is my *settling-down* house. Puts a little more pressure on picking something another person would enjoy too."

She looks up at me, and her lips part like there are words hovering in her mouth, but she doesn't want to let them out.

"What?" I ask, being the pushy one now. My eyes sweep over her face, and I can't believe how striking she is even in soggy wet clothes and no makeup. I've never met another woman I thought looked truly beautiful in a state like this.

"I'm just surprised to hear that you have thoughts like that . . . about marriage and women sharing your house and all."

"It'll probably just be one woman." She nudges my arm with a playful laugh, and I'm thankful she's not hiding anymore. "But I get why you're surprised. I do tend to put off serious *short-term-relationship-only* vibes, but I haven't always been like that. I—uh—sort of went through a bad breakup back in Charlotte."

"The ex-girlfriend you mentioned in the pool?"

I nod slowly, not excited to unpack all these memories. "Janie. She and I were together for a few years, and I was wild about her—like, head over heels. She always said she loved me too, so I thought we were on the same page. Spoiler: we weren't. I finally set up this whole big proposal with tons of string lights, and flowers, and a musician, and . . . gosh, it's so embarrassing, thinking back on it. I looked like an absolute loser when I got down on my knee in front of all our friends and popped the question only for her to say no. We broke up right after that—about a year and a half ago."

Lucy sucks in a sharp breath, and the pity I see on her face is almost as excruciating to see now as it was back then, painted on the faces of all our friends. "Cooper, I'm so sorry."

I shake my head and shrug, eager to be done with this conversation. "It's in the past. Janie's married now, and they just announced they're pregnant, so you know, it all worked out and all that." *Worked out for her, at least.*

"But that's why you needed to get away." Lucy speaks with so much empathy, like she completely understands that need to start over away from the person who caused you so much pain. And that's because she does know.

"Yeah. I've never even told Drew about . . . Janie. As far as he knows, I'm not capable of a commitment, because when I got here to Nashville, I just sort of threw myself headfirst into wiping her out of my memory and avoiding anything close to a relationship." *Until now.* "Anyway, that's what I meant earlier by feeling envious of you. I did want to be married—have kids, the whole nine yards." I should feel more embarrassed after admitting all of this to Lucy, but I don't. I feel lighter.

"Hmm," she says softly, leaning her shoulder against the doorframe. "And you still do."

I quirk an eyebrow at her. "I do?"

"Yeah, you can't fool me. I can read you like a book." She grins. "And you literally already told me you haven't furnished it yet because you want to pick out things a wife or girlfriend would like. I might suggest starting with a TV. Most people enjoy those. Or if you want to get really wild, a house plant."

"A house plant? Damn. Those choices are endless. Do you think a woman would like a Ficus?"

She rolls her eyes dramatically. "If a Ficus is your first choice, it's clear you're not ready for this step yet, pal."

"Pal?" I ask with a laugh.

She laughs too before her smile sobers. We both stand in a kind of awkward, heavy silence for a minute before she surprises me with a turn in conversation I'm not expecting. "Listen, it was a mistake that I tried to kiss you earlier. I was just caught up in the moment, and the stars, and the water . . . and well, anyway, I didn't mean to do it. Can we please just forget about it?"

I feel like we should talk about it more, like I should tell her exactly why I turned away and make sure she knows her trying to kiss me did not feel like a mistake to me. But I know I can't explain it without telling her the whole truth—that I like her and can see myself wanting *more* with her. I have to wait until I've talked to Drew. I need to do this the right way, as much for myself as for Lucy.

I inhale a deep breath and narrow my eyes down at the fragile expression painted on her face. Finally, I release my breath and nod. "If you say so. I won't bring it up anymore."

She looks considerably more relieved and holds out her hand for me to shake, like this is an official business deal we've just made. It'll hold up in court as far as she's concerned.

I reach out and take Lucy's hand . . . and wiggle it because she's already rubbing off on me.

Lucy doesn't give me any time to say anything further on the subject before she smiles and turns, disappearing into the guest bathroom to change her clothes. I remain motionless in the hallway, wondering if Drew would be pissed if I woke him up right now to get his permission to date Lucy. Even better question: Was she being honest about only being caught up in the moment?

I hope not.

CHAPTER 11

Lucy

Waking up in Cooper's clothes is a heady feeling. His shirt smells rugged and handsome, just like him, and for some reason I can't bring myself to take it off. *Just one more quick minute,* I tell myself like a freak as I bring the cotton to my nose and drag in a deep breath. So good. He's the only man I've ever known to smell as good as he looks.

Being rejected last night was definitely one of the worst moments of my life. But then, after we talked more and he shared everything about his ex, it was clear that Cooper's heart is good, and even if he is a bit of a flirt, he's not the type of guy to string me along for no reason. It was good he didn't kiss me since he's obviously not into me. It's a tiny bit (read: massively) disheartening that he doesn't feel the same way about me that I feel about him, but it's better that he is up-front about it and not playing with my emotions and treating me like a passing encounter he never intends to follow through on (*ahem,* Brent).

Also, I don't think I have anything to be embarrassed about, because I'm pretty sure Cooper is used to most people trying to kiss him. I bet it's a very regular occurrence. If he made out with every person who ever tried to lock lips with him, it would turn into his full-time job. So, it's fine. I'm going to choose not to freak out about it or dive into a hole of closed-off mortification in typical Lucy style and, instead, go about my day. I also might have decided to take that memory and shove it somewhere deep down where I can never reach it again and pretend it never happened. *Denial is healthy, right?*

Cooper's sweatpants are loose around my waist, and I have to roll them three times before leaving my room to make breakfast. My mom said she could keep Levi as long as I needed, but since I don't have any appointments today (still building my clientele), I took the day off and am anxious to be reunited. I decide to get my day going early so I can pick him up this morning instead of later. Being a mom is kind of weird. One minute, you're begging a sitter to take your terrible/snotty/sleepless kid off your hands, then five minutes after they're gone, you find yourself misty-eyed, staring at pictures you took yesterday of that darling/angelic/precious child and wondering if it's too soon to go pick them up.

"Where'd you get those clothes?" My brother's voice booms from behind me, making me startle and launch the cereal I was pouring into the air. It's raining hearts, stars, horseshoes, clovers, and balloons.

I put my hand over my heart and let out a breathy laugh. "Gosh. You scared me."

He's not deterred. Drew's eyes are like lasers on Cooper's shirt draping my body like a tent. "Whose shirt? It looks familiar."

Oh shoot, oh shoot, oh shoot. What am I going to say? Lie?

Tell the truth? Drop my bowl of cereal and run out the door? Actually, yeah, that make-a-break-for-it option sounds pretty good.

I swallow and tiptoe around the truth. "Just from a guy."

"Which guy?"

Which guy . . . ? Good question. "Why does it matter?" My pitch is too high. It sounds like a siren alerting him to danger.

Drew's eyes narrow on my shirt like he's trying to place it. Why did I have to parade around the house in this like a lovesick shmuck? "Looks like one of Cooper's T-shirts."

I laugh a booming HA-HA-HA and throw my head back like no real person ever does when they are laughing because I'm a terrible liar. "Cooper's shirt! Now that's funny!"

His face is devoid of amusement. We look like an illustration of opposites. "Not really. What's wrong with you?"

I wipe an imaginary laughter tear. "Nothing. It's just a funny thought. *Me,* wearing one of *your* friend's shirts. How would I have even gotten it? Broken into his house and stolen it without him knowing so I could wear it and smell it forever?"

He sighs. "Tell me right now—did you do that, Lucy?"

"Oh my gosh! No!" I pick up my bowl of cereal to carry it to my room and escape the brother inquisition. "I can't believe you even asked me that."

The moment my back is to him, I widen my eyes and puff out a relieved breath, then hightail it to my room. Pretending to be angry at his lack of faith in me works, and Drew doesn't bug me the rest of the morning about the clothes. I then try to concoct a believable story about the origin of these garments so I can wear them around the house for the rest of my life. Cooper is never getting them back.

"Helllloooo, anyone home?" I yell into my parents' house.

"Up here, honey!" says my mom from upstairs.

I take the stairs two at a time like I've done forever, then follow the sound of laughter all the way into their bonus room. I stop on the threshold and smile at the sight of what looks like a room struck by a hurricane of fun. All around, there are pillows forming various paths to end tables covered in blankets. There are plastic laundry hampers turned upside down and a long blanket tied to the running ceiling fan. My mom is standing like a flamingo, perched on the arm of the couch, and my dad is lying face down, acting like a human bridge with his feet on the couch and chest on the coffee table. Levi is walking, arms outstretched like wings, using my dad as a balance beam.

"Hi, hon! How's your day?" asks my mom like this is the most normal situation to find them in.

I laugh and step in farther, ready to ask her what they're up to, when the room collectively erupts in one giant *NOOOO!*, making me jump back and nearly fall onto my butt.

"What!" I ask, clutching my heart and wondering if it's possible to die of fright.

"Mom, that's lava!" Levi says, eyes wide and pointing to the floor where I was about to step.

"Ohhhh, I see now." Suddenly, all the bridges and pillows make sense. "How do I get over there to you, then?"

"You have to take the fluffy golden road, over to the reading rainbow, and up the super slipper mountain."

My mom raises her hand. "I made it up the slipper mountain, but I had a casualty." She points to her foot. Apparently, if you touch the lava, you lose that extremity for the remainder of the game.

"And that," says Levi, pointing to the blanket swirling in the middle of the room, "is the tornado. Don't get near it or it will suck you up!" Levi's eyes are shining as he relays the rest of the rules to me. His cheeks are rosy and bright, and my heart stretches painfully.

I felt like a failure having to come home and move in with Drew after leaving to make a fresh start in a new town. It wasn't even that there was anything wrong with Nashville or my family or friends. I just felt this overwhelming need to try something new. Make a change. And yeah, maybe get away from all the tourists thinking cowboy boots and hats are the proper attire for our city. Believe me, there is no faster way to be hated by Nashville natives than to dress up like you're going to a honky-tonk for brunch.

But no matter how hard I tried to make Georgia feel like home, it never worked. There was always a gaping hole that Levi and I could both feel. And now, being here and seeing my kid happy and reunited with my parents, I know coming home was the right thing to do.

"How was your night?" Mom asks after I've made it down the fluffy golden road, over the reading rainbow, and up the slipper mountain to stand on the armrest with her.

My mom and I look remarkably similar, which, honestly, I'm grateful for. I've always looked young for my age, and even now people assume I'm Levi's nanny most of the time, but I don't hate it because it just means I'll age as gracefully as her.

"It was great," I say as we hug while trying not to topple off the armrest.

Suddenly, I hear her take in a sharp sniff, and she pulls back to look at me. "*You spent the night with a man!*"

My eyes widen, and my mouth falls open. How did she know that?!

"You did what, young lady?" asks my dad. It's so hard to take him seriously while he's planking across the furniture.

"Oh, hush, Scott. Your daughter is not a baby anymore. She's allowed to spend the night with a man."

"Not unless she has a ring on her finger and I've handed her off in front of God and a preacher."

Mom rolls her eyes. "So old-fashioned. You do know how we got our precious grandson, right?"

Levi's head suddenly pops up and swivels in our direction. "How *did* you get me?"

"The stork," we all say in practiced unison, and luckily, Levi accepts our answer for now.

Mom's eyes whip back to me, and she jumps to the ground, yanking me down with her. "Now, come on, I'm putting on a pot of coffee and you're gonna tell me all about him."

"*La, la, la.* I don't want to hear any of that heathen talk!" my dad yells at our retreating figures, but I can hear the amusement in his voice.

"Then plug your ears, old man." Mom drags me down the hall, nearly pulling my arm out of its socket.

"Levi!" I bellow over my shoulder. "Come save me from your grammy! I'm going to need a rescue mission!"

Mom keeps tugging me. "Levi, if you stay out of the kitchen for fifteen minutes, I'll bake you chocolate chip cookies and let you eat them for lunch."

"Oooh, you're ruthless."

Once we're in the kitchen, she turns to face me and cocks a sassy eyebrow. "You're gonna have to up your ante if you want to play with the big kids, darlin'. Now, sit and tell me all about him."

I pull out a kitchen chair and do as I'm told. "How do you even know I spent the night with a man?"

"Unless you've changed your perfume to Old Spice, it was beyond obvious. You smell like the men's body wash aisle, and I do mean that in the best way."

I smell like Cooper? Why does that thought make me feel all tingly and hot?

"Well, you're right. I did hang out with a man last night, but not in the way you're thinking. We're just friends."

"Pumpkin, I'm not ignorant. You don't come away smelling like your *friend* when you're just hanging out." I wish she wouldn't do that—plant ideas in my head that shouldn't be there. It's every parent's responsibility to think their child poops rainbows, but she shouldn't be trying to make me think that about myself too. I tried going after someone above my level before . . . It didn't work out for me, and I don't care to do it again. Cooper had a chance to prove me wrong last night, and he didn't. He pulled away from my kiss, and that told me everything I needed to know.

"I only smell like him because after we got done swimming, he let me wear his clothes."

Her eyebrow rises another centimeter into the smug-mother-who-knows-everything zone.

"Mom, I'm serious. Please don't make this something it's not. I've embarrassed myself in front of him more times than I can count, and it's clear that he is *not* interested in me like I am in him. I need to get him out of my head, and your meddling is not helping."

"But—"

"Mom."

"I just—"

I cut her off with a *zip it up* gesture and matching sound.

Her shoulders slump over adorably, and she rolls her eyes like she's the teen and I'm sucking all of her fun. "Fine, I'll zip it up. But are you *sure* he's not interested and you're not maybe projecting your own insecurities onto the situation?" Clearly, she doesn't know the meaning of *zip it up.*

"Unfortunately, yes . . . I'm positive he's not interested."

CHAPTER 12

Cooper

"I'm interested in your sister," I say to Drew after he takes the last sip of his second beer. It's Friday night, a couple days after my pool adventure with Lucy; and yep, I did bring Drew out for drinks, buy him wings to butter him up, and then get him a little bit buzzed in hopes that he would not knock my teeth out when I announced I had feelings for Lucy. I also brought him to a crowded sports bar so there would be witnesses.

He blinks with wide eyes, reminding me of Lucy a little, then slowly sets down his empty glass. "Now the large basket of wings makes sense. You probably should have thrown in some jalapeño poppers too."

I tap my finger on the table, debating flagging down the waitress. By the slightly grim look marring Drew's brow, though, I get the feeling cheese-filled peppers aren't going to be my saving grace tonight.

I wait for him to speak, to acknowledge what I said about Lucy, but instead he turns his eyes up to the TV and is suddenly so engrossed in a hockey game you'd think he was an actual fan. Which he's not. Drew is not into sports, but apparently tonight he's the biggest Preds fan you've ever seen.

He throws his hands up and groans when they miss a shot, and I blink at him. "You don't even know what the little black thing they're fighting over on the ice is called," I say, narrowing my eyes and daring to call his bluff.

He swings his gaze to me and smirks. "*Puck* off, Cooper."

Sport puns—this is bad. Uncharted territory, even. "Okay, can we stop pretending we like hockey and just have it out? You're pissed I like your sister. Just say it."

Drew's jaw tics, but he shakes his head. "Not pissed." He says it in the same tone a woman uses when she says *I'm fine*. She's never fine, men, and you're going to sleep on the couch that night.

I stare at Drew, waiting for more, but he just seals up his lips and leans back in his chair to aim his attention at the TV again. I'm going to buy him a shirt that says *World's Biggest Hockey Fan*.

"That's it? You're not going to talk about it with me? Just going to pout and watch your new favorite sport?"

He cuts his eyes to me. "Really? You think it's a good idea to poke me until I fight you?"

"Yeah. I'd rather you fight me than ignore me for sports. I never thought I'd sympathize with a married woman so much, but tonight has changed me."

Drew looks like he wants to smile but has already set his face to frown mode and won't budge. "Look, I'm not upset, because I know I can trust you . . ."

I let out a breath I've been holding all night. I gotta say, I didn't see him—

". . . to ignore your feelings and stay away from Lucy like we discussed." *Oh. Well, that was a letdown.* "I appreciate you owning up to it, though, telling it to me straight. You're a good friend, Coop."

If that isn't some manipulative crap, I don't know what is.

He reaches across the table and slaps me on the back. It jars my body a little, and I feel lost. He's just masterfully steered this conversation in exactly the direction he wants it to go, leaving no room for argument. He's brilliant, actually, because he almost managed to make me think I'm on his side on this, like I really never intended to go after Lucy. This way, we both get to be the good guy and leave here as jolly best friends. *So jolly.*

Drew shifts the conversation and tells me that, this Monday, he'll be headed to Costa Rica for three weeks on a volunteer medical trip. He's been doing these once a year since he graduated med school, and he spends grueling hours providing obstetric and gynecological care to women who otherwise might not receive it. It's amazing and yet another reason why I like Drew and care about his opinion. He's a good guy.

I shift in my chair, deciding to press the subject one more time. "Right. I hope it's a good trip. But . . . just for the sake of conversation . . . it wouldn't be *so* terrible if I dated Lucy, right?"

He scoffs and looks past me to flag down our waitress, holding up his empty glass. "It would be the absolute worst thing in the world for her."

My eyebrows rise. "The worst? Wow. That's . . . bad."

The waitress walks up, and Drew orders another beer, asking me if I want one too, but I decline because I have a policy to only drink when I'm happy. And I don't feel very happy anymore.

Once the waitress walks away, Drew leans his elbows onto the table and looks at me. "Listen, even though it makes us sound like kids to admit it, we're best friends. I'd braid you a bracelet if I knew how. But really, all that means is I've seen too much to be comfortable with you dating my sister. You and I both know you're incapable of a committed relationship, and Lucy needs someone who is going to commit to her and Levi for the rest of their lives. She deserves that."

Drew is looking at me like we're on the same team, like I'm going to nod and adamantly agree that I'm a player and will never be the family man Lucy needs. Well, guess what? I'm not nodding, because I don't agree. In fact, I feel a little angry.

Problem is, I don't have a right to be angry at Drew. I mean, I do in that he's being a shitty friend to me by shutting me down right away, but it's not entirely his fault. I was never honest with him, never told him about how long I was with Janie before. He has no idea that I'm capable of caring for someone long-term. Most likely he thinks I'll sleep with Lucy once and forget her because that's how I've operated most recently.

But now I'm tired of dating around. It's not as much fun as it used to be. It was a phase I grew out of quickly, and now I just feel lonely. I could tell Drew all of this, but it's not how we normally do things. We always keep our conversations pretty surface level, and that fact is annoying me in this moment when he isn't even willing to talk this out with me. Ask me any questions. Nothing.

If he did, I'd tell him everything—about Janie, and how much I missed her at first, and why I had to move away. I'd even tell him about how, a few weeks ago (before Lucy even came into town), our friend Molly called me up at ten o'clock, seeing if I wanted to come over to her place. I told her I wasn't up for a hookup that night because I was pretty tired from work and just wanted to chill. I invited her over to watch a movie with me though, and she declined, so I watched *The Holiday* by myself.

I want to tell Drew all of this. I want to tell him I want to watch *The Holiday* with Lucy. Explain that I don't know how to interact with kids, but I'm ready to learn. I would never string Lucy along, especially given her circumstances in life. I wouldn't be bringing this up tonight if I wasn't serious about my intentions.

But I don't tell him any of that, because at this point it will sound like I'm being defensive, and no one wants to have to convince another person of their good qualities. If he doesn't think I'm good enough for Lucy, maybe I'm not . . . or maybe I just need to convince him I can be.

I'm not ready to tell Drew everything about me yet, but I think I should start to be more honest, at least little by little.

"I get it," I say, leaning back in my chair and trying to find the right words. "Maybe I'm not right for Lucy, but I do think I'm ready to change some stuff in my life . . . pursue a serious relationship with someone."

"That's great, man. Just don't let Lucy be your test subject."

Test subject. Those words feel like acid on my tongue as I repeat them to myself on my drive home from the bar. *Test subject.* Is that really what he thinks I would do? It's clear that Drew has a different opinion of me than I've had of myself. I don't know; part of me wants to be ticked at him, but another part wonders if I'd react any differently if I had a sister and the roles were reversed. *Nope.* I'd probably be giving him crap too.

Lucy is officially off-limits. I know I need to get her out of my head, but I can't.

And as I pull up to my house and park in the driveway, a queasy feeling settles into my stomach at the thought of not seeing her again. She's unlike any other woman I've ever known, and I feel a pull to her that I don't know how to deny. What if Drew is wrong and Lucy is the one for me that everyone talks about? My soul mate or whatever.

Shoot, even worse, my body is having a physical reaction to the thought of not seeing her again. I suddenly feel sick, and achy, and . . . okay, so maybe this is not entirely due to Lucy? What are the odds the burger I had at the bar gave me food poisoning?

Pretty high, considering the way I spend the next hour of my life. And because no one should be judged harshly for decisions they make on their deathbed, I don't want to hear any crap about the fact that I call Lucy, hoping she'll come over and take care of me.

CHAPTER 13

Lucy

I've just finished singing Levi a song and scratching his back until he falls asleep when Cooper calls. It's a little strange that he's actually calling me instead of texting, but we're friends, right? Friends call friends.

"Cooper. Hey," I say in my totally-cool-I-have-cute-guys-calling-me-all-the-time tone.

"Hi, Lucy," he says in a gritty voice that immediately makes alarms blare in my head.

"Why do you sound like you're knocking on death's door?" I ask while shutting my door so Drew doesn't overhear.

He sounds like a lifelong smoker when he says, "Because I am, in fact, dying."

"What?! What's wrong?" *Okay, Luce, let's take it down just a bit.*

"I have food poisoning. I can't keep anything down."

"Oh, Cooper. Where are you right now?"

He breathes deeply for two seconds before answering. "In my hallway. On the floor. I can't make it to my room." He sounds so pitiful and miserable that I can't think of anything other than going straight over there and helping.

But I don't know if I should. It's not really my place to go nurse him back to health, and given the other night, when I tried to kiss him and he rejected me, it seems a little strange for him to be calling me. Isn't that the kind of thing you call a girlfriend for? "Do . . . you have anyone who can come take care of you?" I chicken out at the last second and add, "Like your mom?"

"I'm sure she would if I asked, but she and my dad live in a retirement community about seven hours away."

Right. "So you don't have anyone? Like . . . Bailey maybe?" I press the palm of my hand to my head, feeling like such a corn nut for asking. What am I trying to get him to say here? The man is clearly miserable, and I'm trying to get him to DTR when we don't even have one! I've totally lost my mind.

"Uh—no. Bailey . . . I don't want to call Bailey."

My heart soars on the back of a tiny magical hummingbird. I feel weightless. I don't know what it means yet, but Cooper is calling me, hoping I will come take care of him. And I refuse to think so poorly of myself to believe he's only chosen me because I'm a mom and have excellent bedside manner. There's something here. I just don't know what it is yet.

"Cooper . . ." I say, unable to keep the smile from my voice, "are you calling because you want me to come over and take care of you?"

There's a tiny pause, and I hear him swallow. "Yeah. It's embarrassing."

Light bursts from my cheeks like I have just harnessed my superpowers for the first time. I feel invincible. "I'll be right over."

After I hang up, I carry the baby monitor out to Drew, who is watching TV in the living room, and tell him one of my friends is sick and needs my help. I purposely avoid any pronoun usage because I am an evil genius, and thankfully, hearing the urgency in my voice, Drew spares me the third degree. Tomorrow is Saturday, so he tells me he doesn't have to go into the office, and he'll take care of breakfast for Levi if I'm late.

Guilt over lying to Drew tries to claw its way across my skin, but I refuse to let it, because I'm lying to him with noble intentions, right?

I'm standing at Cooper's door, waiting for him to answer and feeling too excited for someone who's about to aid a sick man. This is when I realize my crush might be getting a little out of control.

When he doesn't answer the door after I knock, I pull out my phone and call him.

He just grunts when it connects.

"Hey, I'm here."

"Is the door not unlocked?" he asks, sounding way worse than earlier.

I try the handle. "Nope. Sorry."

He lets out a curse that makes me smile for some reason. "Okay. I'm coming. I'll see you in a year when I make it to the door."

A minute later it opens, and Cooper stands before me with alarmingly pale skin, a big comforter draped over his head and around his shoulders, no shirt, jeans sitting low and showing off the waistband of his black boxer briefs.

"Lucy." He says my name like a plea, and it tears me right in half.

"Oh, Cooper. You don't look good."

He gives me the most pitiful smile I've ever seen. "That's 'cause I'm dying, remember?" Apparently it's true what they say, and men are big babies when they're sick. I once had to go to work with a fever of a hundred and one and mastitis, but a little stomach trouble has completely taken out this six-foot man. It's sort of adorable, and I love it.

Cooper looks down at me through half-lidded eyes. The flirtatious spark and cool-guy demeanor that are usually present with him are nowhere to be found, and instead he looks a little fragile. Unable to stop myself, I step forward and rest my hand against his cheek and then his forehead.

"You don't have a fever, so that's good."

His eyes shut as my hand slides from his forehead down his temple. He turns his face toward it and sort of presses his cheek against my palm again. Did he just nuzzle me? Like a little love nuzzle? It's a tiny gesture, but it makes my stomach jump into my throat. His face rests lightly against my hand before he groans, pulling away. "Come in. I have to go finish dying."

I watch Cooper and his blanket cape disappear down a hallway, and then I turn my eyes to the empty house. I remember everything I have tucked underneath my arm and decide to start the task of making this place more comfortable while trying to ignore the horrific sounds coming from down the hall.

First, I make my way into Cooper's kitchen, admire the double oven and wonder if he ever uses it, and then fill up a glass with ice and ginger ale. I didn't know if he had any straws, so I bought a pack because it's a fact that no one wants to drink out of a wide-rimmed glass when they've been puking.

Next, I go into the living room and unpack the hamper. Cooper's couch gets a comfy new blanket, and his mantel gets a soft vanilla-scented candle and a cute faux succulent that adds a tiny bit of color to the room. Don't get me wrong, the place still looks pathetic but at least slightly more like someone lives here.

Once I'm finished, I'm not sure what to do. Should I sit down and wait for him? Go check on him and make sure he hasn't passed out in the bathroom? A moment ago, in the doorway, things felt different between us. A little less friend-like, a little more *something* . . . but then I remember my rejected kiss and feel even more confused.

Still . . . he called me over here because he was desperate, right? I should go check on him.

Tiptoeing my way down the hall, I make it to his bedroom and eye his rumpled king-sized bed that makes my stomach flutter. The room smells like him, and a strong part of me wants to dive onto his mattress and make blanket angels in the covers, absorbing all of his scent so I can take it home with me.

Cooper isn't in here, but I notice a cracked door inside his room with light peeking out. I'm just about to go open it when I hear the shower faucet turn on and catch the tiniest glimpse of skin, just enough to know there's a human in there with no clothes on, and I bolt from the room, run into the living room, and leap onto the couch, deciding it's best to await further instructions from Cooper rather than barging into his bathroom and seeing him naked in the shower.

Ten minutes and a whole lot of daydreams later, I'm still sitting stiff as a board, trying to figure out what my purpose is here, when I hear footsteps coming down the hall. My breath catches when Cooper turns the corner. He's barefoot, wearing gray cotton joggers and a white T-shirt. His wet hair is slightly unruly, and he has a five-o'clock shadow, making him look like a walking ad for men's shower gel. Whatever scent it is, I'm buying a whole case. The warm, clean, masculine smell precedes him as he approaches, and I drag in a deep breath, thankful he doesn't smell like a sick person. His blue eyes snag on me sitting on his couch, and I stiffen again.

"Oh. Sorry. Is it okay that I'm still here?" I shake my head and pull my feet out from under me. "I wasn't sure . . . I mean . . . maybe you want me to go? I should have just left the ginger ale. I just—" Before I can fully slip my feet back into my sandals and stand, Cooper comes over and collapses onto the couch, spreading out over the entire length of it and resting his head in my lap.

My breath freezes in my lungs, and I sit stunned for a solid minute with my hands in the air. Cooper doesn't say a single word. He shuts his eyes and snuggles his head back against my stomach like this is something we do every single night. *I guess he doesn't want the ginger ale . . . ?*

Another small groan rumbles from his chest and breaks my heart. I may be enjoying this moment immensely, but he clearly feels terrible. Without really thinking, my hands lower, and my fingers thread through his hair. I barely touch him at first, worried that maybe I'm crossing some invisible boundary since we're not in the salon and he's not my client right now. But then he snuggles in further and makes a contented noise that empowers me to apply more pressure. For several minutes, I rake my fingers over Cooper's scalp, wondering what the hell is happening. I try to stay emotionally detached from this moment, assuring myself that it's only occurring because he feels terrible and can sense the motherliness in me, but it's no use. I love the way his wavy hair feels slipping through my fingers and how comfortable and docile he looks curled up in my lap.

I think Cooper is asleep, because his breathing has been deep and steady, but with his eyes shut he says, "I like the stuff you brought."

My fingers stop their caress. "Consider it a housewarming gift."

Suddenly, Cooper's big shoulders shift and bunch under his shirt as he lifts up slightly to reach something on the cushion beside me. He lays his head back down in my lap and hands a remote up to me. "Here. Rent whatever you want to watch."

That's when I notice the TV mounted on the wall for the first time. "Hey, you got a TV."

"Yeah. You inspired me to start adding a few things."

I *refuse* to let those words go to my heart. He means inspired in that I brought it to his attention, not that I made him want to start filling his house with homey things because he's desperately in love with me.

"What do you want to watch?" I ask, turning on the TV, then looking down when Cooper doesn't answer. His eyes are closed, and he looks passed out. I smile, running my hand through his hair one more time while scrolling through his queue and settling on a movie I haven't seen in way too long. "I hope you don't mind watching *The Holiday.*"

He doesn't answer, but I do see the corner of his mouth quirk up before he takes in a deep breath and wraps one of his arms tightly around my thighs like he's holding on to a pillow. He's *snuggling* me. I look around, briefly waiting for the *Punk'd* camera crew to burst out from a closet.

When they don't, I look back down at Cooper. "Do—do you want a pillow?"

He grunts a negative answer and holds on to me tighter. "You're perfect," he mumbles into my legs.

"You mean perfectly squishy like a pillow?" I ask, not really enjoying that answer.

"No," he answers matter-of-factly. "Just perfect." But that's all he says.

I can't help the smile tugging at my mouth as I watch Cooper fall asleep snuggling my legs. It strikes me that this is exactly how Levi lies down when he's sick, because I'm the most important thing to him, and when someone feels horrible, they want to keep the most important thing in their life nearby for comfort.

So why is Cooper holding on to me like this?

CHAPTER 14

Lucy

My feet are killing me, and I swap all of my weight to my left foot, hoping to give my right a break as I place the two hundredth foil in my client's hair. She and her bestie popped in here an hour ago, right at closing time, and begged Jessie and me to squeeze them in for last-minute highlight appointments. I wanted to laugh in their faces, but then she tucked some hair behind her ear, and her SUV-sized diamond ring raised its eyebrows suggestively at me. Jessie also saw the dollar signs hovering over these ladies' heads, and we both became the world's most accommodating stylists. *Would you like a glass of wine? A foot rub? Need me to do your grocery shopping? Socks mended? SURE! Don't forget to tip, and no, I don't have change for a hundred.*

But believe me, we are more than working for this money. They wanted highlights, lowlights, dark roots, and to talk non-stop until my ears bleed and my brain oozes out of my nose. You'd think they'd want to talk to each other, but no.

"How far along are you?" the girl named Sasha asks Jessie—which is honestly a bold move because Jessie's baby bump is still small enough to potentially be an undigested burger.

"I'm in my second trimester."

"Cute. Who's your baby daddy?"

Jessie falters with her foil, though I doubt anyone noticed it but me. It's an invasive question (one I've never had the guts to ask) and I'm sure not one Jessie appreciates. "Like, his name? You wouldn't know him."

"You never know," the girl says with a cheeky grin that no one appreciates. "I get around." Just for that, Sasha is going to leave with slightly brassier highlights than she'd like. "I'm kidding, girl! So, did he bail? I noticed you don't have a ring on."

Jessie gives a tight smile in the mirror. "Yep. Bailed."

My heart tugs. I know exactly what that feels like. I know how it feels to have to answer those prodding questions, and I know what it feels like to not be wanted. If it wasn't weird, I'd go wrap my arms around Jessie, snuggle her right here in the middle of the salon, and tell her she *will* get through it.

"Ugh, too bad. Men suck," says Sasha's friend Carrie. "They *never* do what they say they're going to."

This triggers something in Sasha, and her jaw drops as she sharply turns her head to Carrie. "Did he seriously still not add you on Snapchat?!"

Carrie abruptly whips her head toward Sasha, ripping a foil from my hand that I had just perfectly placed. *Yeah, don't mind me, I'm not doing anything important back here.* "No! And he, like, *promised* he would before he left town today." She plops back heavily against the chair again and pouts at her reflection. "Why is it so difficult for men to follow through and contact us like they say they will?"

"You're telling me!" I say, shocking myself that I said that out loud.

Jessie looks even more shocked. She paints a little lightener onto a strand of Sasha's hair, then slowly moves her gaze up to me with sassy lifted eyebrows. "Is this about Cooper? Do tell."

Carrie gasps with joy and completely turns around in her seat, knees tucked up to her chest and clapping with excitement. "*Tell us!*"

It makes me laugh how eager these women are to jump into my drama, but I also kind of love them for it. Besides, who else am I going to talk to about this? My only other friend is Drew, and I definitely can't discuss it with him.

"Okay, well, yeah. So, there's this guy . . . my brother's best friend—" The girls *oooooh* collectively, and Jessie just gives a guttural laugh. "Anyway. He's the best-looking man I've ever seen and definitely has women fawning over him at every turn. I thought there was no way he would be interested in me, but then . . ."

"Yeah?!" They are way too excited to hear this story.

"Well, he sort of started flirting with me. And texting me. And . . . sneaking me off on secret late-night pool adventures."

"Shut up. I'm so jealous of you right now. Keep going."

"And then . . . I tried to kiss him. And he rejected me."

"Ouch," says the choir of women.

"Yeah. But here's the really confusing part: he was still super touchy-feely with me the rest of that night, even sent me a sweet good night text. *And then,* about two weeks ago, he came down with food poisoning and called me to come over and take care of him."

"Did you?"

"Yes, of course I did. And he was so adorable and sweet and laid his head in my lap and slept the entire night snuggling my thighs like they were his favorite stuffed animal from childhood."

"And then?"

"And then nothing." My eyes catch on the droopy, wilted bouquet of flowers on my station that I refuse to throw away despite the mold now creeping up the stems, and I correct myself. "Well, not *nothing.* The next morning we had a stilted goodbye where he almost seemed to regret the night, so I hightailed it out of there, ready to write him off forever, until this gorgeous—well, it *was* gorgeous—bouquet showed up here at work with a thank-you card for taking care of him. The card also mentioned that he'd be happy to return the favor next time I'm feeling bad."

"You said all of this happened two weeks ago?" asks Sasha. I think she's about to pull out a notepad and pen. Before the night is up, there will be pictures and maps and red strands of twine connecting clues all across the salon walls.

I sigh and wince a little. "Yeah. That's bad, right? That means he's not interested?"

Carrie pipes up. "Not necessarily. You said he's your brother's best friend?"

"Yeah."

Both women look at each other and give one affirming nod before saying in perfect harmony, "Bro code."

"Bro code?"

"Yes, grandma. Even I know what they're talking about." Jessie wants to act like she's not into this gossip, but she's just as invested as I am. One minute ago, we thought these girls were ridiculous and an insult to women everywhere, and now we are sitting at their feet, begging to be inducted into their super-special club. "Part of the bro code is not dating a friend's sister, and I'm pretty sure if she's a baby sister, it's doubly enforced."

My shoulders sag because, somehow, I know they are right. Drew even told me to stay away from Cooper. Did he tell Cooper the same thing? That makes me feel both thankful that I'm so loved and like I want to dismember my brother for thinking he has any sort of say over my life.

"How do I know for sure?"

"You text him."

"And ask him?"

"No. That will make you look desperate, especially if that's not the real reason he's ghosting you." I take back everything I ever said about this woman. She's brilliant. Scholarly. Should be teaching a course at a university, because what she's explaining right now is a way better life skill than algebra. "Instead, text him first—something flirty but innocuous."

Now I'm the one who needs a notepad. *Someone get me a notepad!* "Okay, flirty and innocuous. Got it." I don't got it—and Sasha suspects as much.

"Just say *Hi* with a little smiley face."

"That's it?" I ask with wide, frantic eyes. My chest is constricting. My breath is too short. How do I know if I'm having a heart attack?

Carrie laughs and takes over. "Yes. That's it. And then if he responds, go from there. Keep the conversation short and minimal. Don't give away too much that you're interested in him. And whatever you do, do not respond right away. Oh, also, it's best to ghost him after four texts, especially if he asks what you're up to, so you can leave him wanting more. Don't respond for two days."

"Two?!"

"Two. Don't mess it up," Sasha warns, turning back to sit properly in her seat.

————

Thirty minutes after we close the door behind my new BFFs, Sasha and Carrie, I stare down at my phone and type out exactly what I was instructed to send.

Jessie hovers over my shoulder, breathing on my neck and making me even more nervous. But there's no going back. I've decided in my head that Cooper is worth it. Plus, I've already embarrassed myself in front of him several times. Really, I've got nothing to lose.

LUCY: Hi:)

"Oh gosh, I did it!" I say, dropping my phone onto the counter like it suddenly morphed into molten lava.

"Yep. Now we wait." Jessie puts her hands on her lower back to ease the ache. It's hard enough being a hairdresser when you're not pregnant, but with the added weight in the front, it's total death to your back. Even so, I know Jessie is touchy about this subject, and she would rip my head off if I asked if she's feeling okay because, for some reason, she doesn't like to show any signs of weakness.

I swallow down the lump of regret in my throat as I stare at my phone again. *What if he doesn't respond?* "I guess we don't have to hover over my phone like the Grim Reaper until he responds. I'm going to go sweep up."

I get two steps away and then hear it ping. I race back and snatch it from the counter before Jessie gets the chance.

COOPER: Hi back:)

"*Ughhhh.* Hi back?! Sasha didn't prepare me for that reply!" Of course he would respond like that—with way more game than anyone should ever have. Why didn't I get Sasha's number?!

Jessie's eyes are wide too, and she puts her hands out in front of her in the classic *settle down* gesture. "Okay, let's just take a breath. She said not to respond right away anyway. Let's harness our inner rich goddess and see what reply pops into our heads."

"I don't have enough self-tanner in my bloodstream to fully harness mine."

"*Oooh, I know!*" she nearly shouts. "Say . . . *Sup?*"

I gawk at her. "*Sup?!* What am I, a frat guy in a salmon shirt and little shorts with anchors printed on them?"

"Well, do you have any better ideas?"

"Yes. I'm going to the cellphone store and changing my number. Problem solved."

Jessie is about to tell me I'm off my rocker when another text comes through, and we both scream like someone just jumped out of a closet and yelled *BOO!*

COOPER: What have you been up to?

"Okay, okay, okay, that's good. He's interested. He's keeping the conversation going. Now, do exactly what Sasha said and ghost him."

"Too late. I sent a reply while you were talking," I say, trying to angle my phone away so she can't judge.

"You didn't."

"I did."

She shakes her head, looking exasperated. "What did you say?"

I reluctantly show her my text.

LUCY: Nothing. Been super bored.

Her face is so disapproving. She thinks my response is garbage. "Oh great. Now he knows you're pathetic and desperate."

I gasp. "Hey! I'm not pathetic and desperate." But I totally am, and now I'm itching to correct myself. Jessie sees the look in my eyes and turns her head to the side so she can shoot me an effective side glare.

"Don't text anything else—"

She doesn't get to finish before I've shot off another gem.

LUCY: But not like super bored. I mean I've been doing stuff.

Not just sitting around thinking about you.

The second after I hit Send, I feel in my bones that it was a mistake. Yep, so bad. I groan. "What have I done! I'm a disgrace to single women everywhere! I have to fix this."

"No! Lucy, don't you dare text one more thing. Hand over the phone." Now she's looking at me like I'm holding my thumb over the trigger of a bomb detonator. She's inching forward, and I'm inching away, fingers poised to fly across the keyboard at record speed. "*Luuuuuucy,*" she says in warning.

I hold her gaze and whisper, "I'm sorry, Jessie. I have to." And then I bolt across the salon, pregnant Jessie hot on my heels. My thumbs mash the screen in ungraceful movements as I zigzag around furniture, trying to outsmart Jessie by doing a spin move when she corners me. "HA! PREGNANT SUCKER!" I yell while pressing Send on the best text I've ever concocted.

Jessie slumps over into a chair, trying to catch her breath. "You're beyond help. If Cooper doesn't ghost you after whatever terrible thing you sent him, marry that man."

I look down and reread what I wrote. The moment the tag

under the text moves from *delivered* to *read*, I want to enter the witness protection program.

LUCY: What I'm trying to say is, I have done the appropriate amount of things since we last saw each other. Not too much, not too little. And I have thought about you. But also an appropriate amount. Some might even say a friendly amount.

Cooper surprises me and doesn't ghost me. He doesn't even make me wait for a response.

COOPER: That's too bad. I liked it better when I thought you were pining for me.

"Wow, those are some top-notch flirting skills," Jessie says, appearing over my shoulder like the blond genie in that old TV show.

Seeing his name on my screen has done something to me, further ignited the same flame I usually feel in his presence, but intensified it. For some reason, I'm willing to risk my dignity for this man, because I miss him. And I can't remember ever caring about a man enough to miss him this much when he's not around.

I take a deep breath and type out a message. Jessie doesn't fight me this time.

LUCY: Hey, so, Drew left two weeks ago for his medical trip, and I was planning on taking Levi to the park in the morning to fly his kite. Drew usually goes with us, but since he's not around, I was wondering if you'd want to come? I know it probably doesn't sound very exciting, but if you're free, we'd love to have some company. I mean . . . if you don't have any hot dates to go on. If you do, no worries, I totally understand.

I try to swallow my heart back down from my throat while I wait for a response. I also decide that if Cooper says no to this, I'll be done. I will find a way to force this crush out of my heart because it would be nothing but a waste of time to pursue a man who doesn't want to fly a kite with me and Levi. My son and I are a package deal, and I will *always* choose Levi over a man.

Levi is the reason I picked up my pride and carried it back home with me to live with Drew after I failed to pave my own way in Georgia. He's why I've sat through unbearable meals with Brent and every single one of his girlfriends over the years so I can get to know the women who will be a presence in my son's life. He's why my favorite jeans will never fit me again but I still refuse to throw them away.

So, if he doesn't want me *and* Levi, I'll let any hopes I have of Cooper falling for someone like me go.

But . . . maybe I won't have to.

COOPER: Pick you guys up at 9?

CHAPTER 15

Lucy

Okay, don't panic, Lucy. Don't panic.
    Ding dong.

I'm panicking! I'm panicking so hard. Red-flashing-lights, alarms-sounding, someone-give-this-woman-a-sedative panicking!

Cooper is here to take Levi and me to the park, and not only do I suddenly not know how to walk normally anymore, but my mouth is all dried up and devoid of the moisture necessary to speak. I've never introduced my son to a boyfriend before—not that Cooper is a boyfriend, or anything even resembling one. But I think we can comfortably state that he's a crush . . . a crush like I haven't had since high school when I cut out too many pictures of Orlando Bloom and pasted them to my wall. Yeah, that's right, glued—not taped. I was serious.

I haven't resorted to that level of crushing with Cooper yet, but mostly because he doesn't have a social media account, so there's nowhere to download and print photos of his gorgeous face. Ha ha, kidding. I'd never do that.

Never . . .

"He's here!" Levi shouts, acting as an unnecessary second doorbell.

"Oh, great!" Does my voice sound high-pitched to you? "Go get your shoes on, and I'll answer the door."

"K!" Levi runs off, a blur of blond hair as he dashes to the mudroom for his shoes.

I take that opportunity to full-on madwoman-sprint to the door and fling it open. I spring out at Cooper like a jack-in-the-box, and he responds appropriately. His shoulders jump, and he takes a quick step back before realizing I'm not a psycho murderer and relaxing his shoulders.

I shut the door behind me and lean back against it with my hands on the doorknob. Cooper takes one deep breath and shakes his head, smiling. "Geez, woman. I thought I was about to have a heart attack at thirty-two."

My eyebrows pull together. "Have you had your blood pressure checked lately?"

He's wearing a baseball hat, but since I'm so short I can still see his eyes—his confused eyes. "Huh?"

"Just saying . . . it's not uncommon for men to have heart attacks at thirty. You should have your—" And then I realize I'm being a weirdo again and give myself a mental slap. "Never mind. I just wanted to get to you before Levi so you can know a few things."

He crosses his toned arms and assumes a serious expression. "Okay, shoot."

"He's never been introduced to any of my male friends before, so be prepared for any uncomfortable question under the sun, and just know that I have zero control over what comes out of his mouth."

"Like, what are we talking? Is Santa Claus real, or where do babies come from?"

"Probably some combination of both. Defer to me on both accounts."

"Got it. Go on."

I grip the handle harder, using it as an anchor so I don't go wrapping my arms around his tempting shoulders. This casual cotton tee is really working for him. Let's be real, though—everything works for him. "He's a four-year-old. He's going to get super upset with the kite sometimes, and he might throw a tantrum when it's time to leave. When we're in the car, he likes to listen to 'Wheels on the Bus' on repeat. And he almost always—"

"Lucy . . ." Cooper says, cutting me off with a heart-melting smile. He steps forward, and I watch his hands rise up to rest on my hips. I'm a human circuit board now. Electrical currents zing through me, and I'm pretty sure if his index finger touched the tip of my nose, my entire body would light up like a rainbow strobe light.

Cooper's hands squeeze my hips as he pries me away from the door to inch up closer to him. I'm silent because obviously *I have no idea what's happening*. Are we at this level of touching now? Can I get in on this action too?

He pulls me up close to him, and it takes me an embarrassing amount of time to realize he's hugging me. His arms are wrapped around my shoulders and flexing as he presses me up firmly against him. I tentatively raise my arms and settle them properly on his back—light as a feather, afraid that if I give those hands too much power, they'll take over and suddenly be under his shirt, squeezing every ridge I find. And there are many, people.

Because my face is pressed against his pectoral muscles, I feel his words more than hear them. "Stop freaking out. I've met children before, and I liked almost half of them." I feel empowered by his joke and pinch his side. He jolts a little and chuckles. "Seriously. It's going to be a fun day, so stop worrying."

"I can't help but worry. I'm a mom—it's what we do."

"You don't have to, though."

Wait, did he just . . . ? Yeah. Cooper just kissed the top of my head. It was so soft it was almost undetectable. Like he didn't mean to but couldn't help himself at the same time. Suddenly, the bro code theory holds a little more weight. I want to come right out and ask Cooper, but I'm not quite ready yet. I need to gather more supporting evidence, and when I'm seventy-five percent sure, I'll ask him.

"So . . . I'm your only man-friend to ever meet Levi? Is there a reason for that?" I can hear the smug amusement in his voice.

"Yeah, but don't go getting a big head," I say, realizing we're still hugging in a very *not-just-friends* sort of way. "You're also my *only* man-friend."

In the next moment, the front door flies open. Cooper not only releases me in record time but also manages to somehow roll me away from him like I'm a leper in biblical times. I stare at him with wide eyes and laughter building in my throat. Cooper's embarrassed smile is probably the sexiest thing I've seen.

He looks at me and stage-whispers, "You got in my head."

"Can we go now, Mom?" Levi asks, blue sneakers Velcroed on, tall Buzz Lightyear sock game on point, and completely unfazed by the giant man who was just snuggling his mama.

"Yeah, babe, we can." I hold my hand out and wiggle my fingers for Levi to step out and take. "I want you to meet Mr. Cooper. He's . . . one of Uncle Drew's friends."

Levi takes my hand and squints up at Cooper. "Hi," he says with a little wave.

I don't know what I was expecting Cooper to do with Levi. Actually, yes, I do. I thought he would be kind, but probably try to shake his hand and say something either a little too old for Levi like *How's algebra going this year?* or swing too far the other way and talk to him in a baby voice.

I didn't expect him to squat down to Levi's level and hold out his fist. "What's up, buddy? You can just call me Cooper—or Coop, like your uncle does. Cool if I come fly a kite with you today?"

Levi's face lights up as he pounds his fist into Cooper's, looking so proud of himself for already knowing what to do because this is what he always does with Uncle Drew.

"Yeah! You can come! Do you like my socks?" Levi sticks a leg out.

Cooper makes a big show of studying the sock. "Dude, I am so jealous of these socks. I don't care what anyone says—Buzz Lightyear is cooler than Woody."

And just like that, Levi lets Cooper into his super-secret favorite-people-in-the-world-only club. It's very elite and prestigious, and I don't mean to brag, but I'm definitely in it. I think it's time we make T-shirts.

Cooper stands back up with a soft smile aimed down at me. I think he knows he's in Levi's club now, and I think he likes it. "Ready to go have some fun?" he asks, glittering aqua eyes showing off almost a little too much.

CHAPTER 16

Lucy

"I 'll drive," Cooper says, dead serious as we all walk out to my little white Honda Civic. He holds out his hand as if it's nothing out of the ordinary.

I hold my keys a little closer to my chest. "Why? You don't trust my driving?"

"My mom is a very good driver," Levi says, stepping in between us.

"Thank you, babe," I say, ruffling his hair.

He turns his face up to Cooper. "She only hits the curb sometimes now."

My smile falls, and Cooper's lips press together suspiciously. He extends his hand for the keys again. "I trust you, Lucy. I just want to drive you around today so you can relax."

Right. I shouldn't feel a surge of emotions at that tiny statement, and the fact that I am feeling them probably means I've set my bar way too low in the past. Either way, I hold out my keys with the ring pinched tightly between my thumb and index finger, as if they open the locks to a kingdom rather than my little Honda Civic.

"I don't trust many people to drive when Levi is going to be in the car," I say when he looks to where his open palm is waiting beneath the keys that I'm reluctant to drop.

"Do you trust me? It's okay if the answer is no. I'll ride shot-gun."

I narrow my eyes. "Depends. How's your driving record?"

"Two tickets. No wrecks."

"How fast were you going?"

"Ten over the speed limit both times."

I drop the keys into his hand and give him the sternest look I can muster. "No speeding with us in the car."

His grin pops. "Yes, ma'am."

After helping Levi get buckled into the car, I climb into my passenger seat and then stop short, covering my mouth to smother a laugh. Cooper—sweet Cooper—is situated in the driver's seat and barely fitting inside the vehicle. His long legs are scrunched up so his bent knee is pretty much beside the wheel, and he has the window down so he can hang his elbow out.

"Something funny?" he asks with raised eyebrows.

And yes, the sight is hilarious, but it's also something else. It's . . . hot. Don't ask me how it's possible, but the fact is, seeing this huge man packed like a sardine into my tiny old car, with his hand draped over the steering wheel like it's the most normal thing in the world, is doing things to my body. Good things. Delicious things. Things that make me want Cooper to do things to me too. But not before he takes off his shirt and turns his hat around backward and drives me around town with a trunk loaded down with groceries. Do I need better fantasies?

"Do you maybe want to scoot your seat back a little, Cooper?"

"I already did," he says gravely.

"You look like you're heading to the circus." The sexy circus, but still.

"He doesn't have a clown nose, though," Levi says pragmatically.

Cooper looks over his shoulder to Levi and then shrugs. "You're right. I guess we'll just have to go on to the park like we planned. Everyone buckled?"

After confirming we're all safely secured, Cooper puts his hand on the back of my seat, biceps and forearm muscles on full display as he looks over his shoulder and reverses. I've never been more turned on in my life.

I didn't think it was possible to feel more attracted to Cooper after the car reversing situation, but it turns out my desire for this man knows no bounds. Because here at the park, as I lie on the blanket spread over the grass watching this ridiculously attractive man chase my son and his kite across the lawn, my ovaries turn into unruly hellions, bent on making sure I lust after this man in every possible way.

The grass is green and crunchy, a perfect contrast to the soft blue sky overhead. And although the sun is on full blast today, there's a constant breeze pushing through, making the heat more bearable. It's a perfect day for flying a kite. So perfect that everything feels surreal at this moment. Like how Cooper is smiling from ear to ear as he hoists Levi onto his shoulders so they can work together to retrieve the kite they just got stuck in a tree. Or a few minutes ago when Levi finally got the kite in the air. He had several failed attempts before, so when it finally started flying behind him, he was so excited he ran all the way to Cooper, who was cheering so enthusiastically that Levi forgot about the kite completely, dropping the string to run straight into Cooper's arms for a big bear hug.

My heart quakes at the sight, and a nonstop bubbling sensation has been filtering through it ever since. After a minute, Levi frees the kite, and Cooper carefully sets him back on the ground. I see him point in my direction while telling Levi something.

Levi takes off toward me in a full sprint, the kite dragging behind him and getting snagged on several sticks along the way until he reaches the blanket and barrels into me with a huge hug. "Can we get ice cream?!" he asks, his little face hovering over mine with big fluffy clouds in the sky behind his head. "I asked Cooper, but he told me I had to ask you. Can we?"

Levi's joy is contagious. "Okay, we can get ice cream," I say and then start gently poking him in the ribs, making him laugh and squirm. "But you have to promise me you'll eat all your veggies with dinner. Promise?"

I hold up my pinky, and Levi locks his around mine, a look so eager and solemn you'd think he was pledging to save the world. "Yes. Promise."

"What are we pinky promising?" Cooper asks, crashing down on the picnic blanket beside us. His eyes are sparkling, and his skin is flushed from the sun. God, I could easily get used to more days like this. And that thought terrifies me.

"To eat all our veggies with dinner! Are you going to eat yours?"

"I never skip my veggies," Cooper says, matching Levi's enthusiasm. He then makes a big dorky show of lifting his arm and flexing his biceps. "That's how you get muscles like these."

Levi is all spellbound wonder, and I'm trying not to die laughing at Cooper's cheesiness.

"Mom!" Levi suddenly yells, as if I'm clear across the park and not sitting directly beside him. "You know what Cooper told me? Airplanes feel like roller coasters! Do you think it feels like one?" He asks, not shocking me in the least by the abrupt change in subject but clearly leaving a stunned Cooper in the wake of his topic shift. *Welcome to life with a four-year-old.*

I grin lightly at Cooper over Levi's shoulder. "A little bit. The airplane goes really fast at takeoff and sometimes makes my stomach have butterflies. But that part doesn't last long."

"Well, I think it sounds fun! Can we go on one? And maybe we can bring Cooper with us!" he says, like it's just as simple as getting ice cream. It's sweet how quickly Levi has taken to Cooper, but I'd be lying if I said it didn't worry me a little too. Because there's a possibility that Cooper will disappear by tomorrow, and we'll never see him again. And this is exactly why I don't usually introduce men I'm dating to Levi. I don't want him to get attached when there's no reason for him to.

I notice Cooper watching me with furrowed eyebrows and realize I've taken a long time to respond to Levi's question. Suspiciously long. "Uh, yeah, I'm sure we'll go on an airplane sometime soon, buddy!"

"But can Cooper come too?" Levi is relentless, clearly not deterred by my attempt to sidestep his question. And by the stubborn look in his eyes, he's not going to quit asking unless I address it.

But I've been a mom for four years now—so that means I've got a couple of tricks up my sleeve.

"Tell you what," I say with sparkling eyes. "Why don't we take an airplane ride with Cooper right now?"

I lay down on my back, hearing the sharp blades of grass crunch under the blanket, and then tell Levi to stand at my feet. My four-year-old looks at me like I've lost all sense but eventually stands. I then lift my feet up in the air and extend my arms toward the sky. "Here, take my hands and then lean your stomach against my feet."

He does but looks skeptical, like this might be one big prank. I can't bring myself to look at Cooper and see what he thinks of me. Maybe he'll take one look at me like this and the fact that I'm a mom will really hit home for the first time. I'm not sure if there actually is anything between us to lose in the first place, but if this is the thing to turn Cooper off from me, then good riddance, because I'll never stop being a goof for my kid.

Once Levi is in place, I begin the entertainment. "Hello, ladies and gentlemen, this is your captain speaking. Please buckle up and remain seated until the aircraft is at a cruising altitude and the seatbelt sign is turned off. On behalf of Mom Airlines, we hope you enjoy your flight."

Levi laughs, and in the next moment, I'm hoisting him up in the air by my feet and whooshing him in circles. A wide sparkling smile beams across his face as he laughs and laughs and laughs. This is the kind of smile from my son that I live for.

I'm laughing too, letting joy overtake me as I tell myself to let loose with my son and not worry about what the man beside me thinks. And after a few minutes, when my leg muscles are burning and my lungs are exhausted from laughing, I set Levi back down and brave a glance at Cooper James.

He's sitting back, long legs stretched out in front of him, with one ankle over the other, and staring at me with a smile so warm and content it makes my insides melt.

"Lucy, stand up," Cooper says suddenly, making my smile drop and a wave of self-consciousness roll over me. I thought it was a nice smile he was giving me, but maybe it was pitying instead?

But no . . . that can't be.

My heart races, waiting for any hints that he's about to say something rude, and I'm going to have to ask Levi to look away while I dropkick Cooper in the crotch. But then a playful smile splits his mouth, and he lays back, lifting his feet in the air just like I did with Levi.

"What are you doing?" I ask, mystified and chuckling.

"Climb on," he says, gesturing toward his feet, but my stomach swoops as it interprets his statement in a completely different way that is not at all park appropriate. I shove that thought away and watch silently as this man who I once thought was nothing but a token flirt raises his hands up in the air, waiting for me to stand and take them.

"You're kidding," I say, darting a nervous glance around the park at anyone who might be watching. Not to mention my little boy, who is chanting for me to do it.

"Don't look around. Look at me. I'm not kidding." He wiggles his big fingers at me. *Wiggles them!* I didn't even know a man like Cooper was capable of such a silly movement. "Don't tell me you're scared of airplanes too?" he asks, a small, teasing grin on his mouth.

I can't help but chuckle at this whole situation. "I love flying in airplanes."

"Okay then, hop on. You shouldn't have to miss out on all the fun."

Again, that emotional fizziness hits my heart because I'm so used to providing everything for everyone around me that I do miss out on a lot. And it's in this moment that I know Cooper would never be the type of man to take the sweater from my back to keep himself warm.

"Go, Mom!" Levi urges, looking at me like he'll disown me if I don't do this.

Cooper kicks off his shoes and then shoots his socked feet up in the air once again. I want to snap a picture and post it on social media. I'm willing to bet no one would believe this sight.

And then, because I want to experience fun too, I do it. I go over to Cooper, intertwine my fingers with his, palm to palm, and situate my abdomen against his feet. I get one delicious smile from Cooper, his head half on the blanket and half in the grass, before he tenses his abdominal muscles and flies me into the air.

I'm hovering above Cooper, squealing like a little baby girl and cackling with laughter. Cooper holds me up there until my stomach is aching and he tells me to let go of his hands and balance. I don't even hesitate this time. I let go and do as he says, because I'm high on dopamine. Because I trust him.

I'm sure we look like the most ridiculous, annoying people in the world, but I don't care. I'm having the time of my life, and Levi is enjoying the sight of me being silly so much that he rolls onto the ground, laughing so hard I wouldn't be surprised if he pees his pants. It's the best sound I've ever heard. A close second, however, is the sound of Cooper's full deep laugh filtering through the breeze. I turn my gaze down and take in the sight of the most attractive man I've ever seen. His mouth is creased on either side from his deep smile, and his bright white teeth shine up at me, not a hint of the smooth flirty guy with lines from the boat in sight.

And somehow I know, this is the real Cooper James. This is him at his absolute happiest. It's right there in his eyes. And as he sets my feet back on the ground but doesn't immediately let go of my hand, I feel it in his touch too.

CHAPTER 17

Lucy

After ice cream, Levi invited Cooper back to the house for lunch (PB&J sandwiches). I told him Cooper was probably way too busy, giving Cooper more than enough chances to politely excuse himself, but he just gave me a dramatic *pshhhh* and said he never turns down a good PB&J.

On the way home, Cooper noticed my check oil light was on and asked how long it had been since the oil had been changed. I replied with, "What's an oil change?" so he stopped in at the auto supply shop and bought me a few bottles of oil.

At home, I made sandwiches while the men got to work on the car, and when I walked outside with a tray of lunch, I nearly passed out. In another life, I dropped the tray and it clanged dramatically on the ground. Because when Cooper slid out from under my vehicle, his shirt was off, and I couldn't keep my eyes from sliding down every single one of his tanned, cut muscles. Cooper's body is all large shoulders and defined pecs, tapering down to a six-pack and rippling obliques, with just the tiniest sprinkle of hair in the center of his chest. Somehow, seeing him standing there in jeans, no shirt, and a backward baseball cap, it felt downright dirty. I almost suggested he donate his body to science, because when they finally get the cloning thing figured out, he needs to be the one they replicate.

As if that wasn't enough of a sight to behold, he helped Levi out from under the car, and *he too* had his shirt off. The two of them stood there, hands on their hips, a lovely example of opposites. One was all hard body and sun-kissed skin, the other the little dough boy with an adorable round stomach pooching out over his Spiderman underwear waistband. It was too much. And honestly, my heart ached at the sight of it. Partly because Levi looked so proud and happy, but also because there's a very real chance that all of this wonderfulness will go poof and disappear as quickly as it arrived.

Cooper and I are not a couple, and he's the most desirable, sought-after bachelor in town (I'm assuming, because . . . look at him). It might be fun for him to play house with me today, but the day in and day out of being a parent is not all kicks and giggles like this. I just can't picture a man like him, one who has everything to offer, choosing to settle down and jump right into a *family man* role.

Which is why now, as I'm standing in the kitchen, rinsing the plates, I try to avoid replaying any memories of this day. And I certainly try to ignore Cooper when he walks in (still shirtless) and leans back against the counter directly beside me. I wish I found his confidence repellent. I wish the cocky grin he flashes me because he *knows* he looks good in this pose, with his arms crossed and biceps bulging, didn't make my stomach twist into a salty little pretzel.

"You're busy in here," he says, and I only allow myself one tiny glance at him before focusing my attention back on the dishes.

"Yep. Busy, busy. Lots of work for us moms."

He reaches over and cuts the water off, gaze burning into my face. He doesn't say anything, just stares, waiting for me to make eye contact with him.

I finally do with a dramatic what-do-you-want-now face, and he grins. "You can see your reflection in that plate you've been polishing for the last ten minutes. Why don't you put it down and come build Legos with us?"

Because I don't want to. I can't. It's too domestic, and I'm starting to see that inviting Cooper into our life like this was a *very* bad idea. He fits too well but won't want to stay, and now I will judge every other man against this perfect specimen, and it's just not fair.

Thankfully, I don't have to tell him anything because I'm saved by my phone buzzing on the counter. Cooper looks over his shoulder and picks it up, unashamedly reading the caller ID before handing it to me. "Unknown number. Probably just a tele-marketer."

Probably, but I will buy fifty of whatever they are selling just to be able to avoid this conversation with Cooper, so I answer with an exuberant "Hello!"

"Hey, is this Lucy?" a man asks.

"Yep, it's me."

He gives a slightly nervous-sounding chuckle before saying, "Hey. My name is Ethan Townsing, and I'm friends with your brother. I'm a PA, and I work at the same hospital where Drew delivers."

"Oh. Hi," I say, slightly at a loss, because this conversation feels odd. Cooper sees my speculative frown, and his eyebrows pinch together as he shrugs and mouths, *Who is it?*

I wave him off and keep listening. "I hope this is okay, but he gave me your number and said you might be up for going out sometime. I realize this is super weird because we've never met, but I'm hoping you trust your brother to play matchmaker as much as I do . . ." I'm slightly distracted at this point because Cooper has moved to press himself up beside me and lean his ear in toward the phone. He smells so freaking good. Like his body-wash, man musk, and motor oil. *Focus, Lucy.* ". . . anyway, I know this is last minute, but I was wondering if you'd like to go to dinner tonight?"

Cooper pulls a disgusted face mixed with a who-does-this-guy-think-he-is headshake.

"Oh . . . well . . ."

"Before you say no, I'm texting you a picture of myself right now so you can see I'm a normal-looking guy and not covered in warts or anything else that would be considered gross. I'm a PA in the pediatrics wing, and I have a seven-year-old daughter."

My phone pings with a text, and sure enough, he is pretty normal looking. He's wearing a button-down shirt, midthirties maybe, nice brown hair, and glasses.

"Got it, and your word holds up—you're very normal looking." Oops. Did that sound rude? Cooper stifles a laugh, so I think it did. "Oh, shoot. What I meant was—"

He laughs. "Don't worry about it. I know what you meant, and I'm the one who said *normal* first, so I have no reason to be offended, remember? Also, I realize this is awkward, and you probably feel a little blindsided, so feel free to hang up and think it over before giving me your answer."

But the whole time he's talking, I'm staring at Cooper. Perfect, swoony, funny, hot Cooper. And I realize I have to say yes to this guy. Cooper is out of my league. He knows it. I know it. Levi probably even knows it. And Drew *definitely* knows it, otherwise he wouldn't have warned me to stay away from him. More than that, Ethan is actually asking me out, whereas, so far, Cooper ghosted me until I was the one to start things up.

Ethan is exactly the reality check I need.

Cooper is watching me closely as I respond. "Actually, I don't need time to think it over. If Drew trusts you, I do too. If my parents can watch my son, I'd love to go out tonight!"

Cooper's smile drops into a full grimace that makes my heart tremor with hope. Hope that he's jealous? *Ridiculous, Lucy.*

"Great. I'll see what reservations I can get on such short notice, and then I'll text you an address and time. Want to meet at the restaurant, or should I pick you up?"

"Let's meet."

"Sounds good. Looking forward to it, Lucy."

"Me too," I say, trying to force some joy into my tone.

I hang up, and Cooper sinks back against the counter again, looking less confident and more thunderous now as he crosses his arms and studies me. "Tonight, huh? Didn't want to play it cool and tell him you were busy tonight?"

I mimic his pose, leaning against the adjacent counter. "Nope. I've never been cool before—why pretend I am now? Do you have a problem with me going out with him tonight?" Oh, I really wish I'd left off that last part. I might as well have laid my feelings out on a silver platter in front of him and said *Dig in!*

His eyes narrow slightly, and because he is shirtless, I can see his big chest fill up with air and hold it for three beats before letting it out in a rush. "No. You deserve to go out and have fun."

I resist the urge to melt into a depressed puddle on the floor.

A second later, my phone pings with a text from Ethan, giving me the name of the restaurant and saying our reservation is for seven o'clock. My first thought is that, on a normal night, I would have already eaten a full meal plus whatever Levi refused to eat by that time *and* snuck Skittles in the pantry when he wasn't looking. My second thought is . . . "Oh, shoot. Thistle is a fancy restaurant, isn't it?" I ask Cooper, looking up with wide, frightened eyes.

He chuckles softly and nods like I'm the cutest thing he's ever seen—and I don't mean *cute* in a sexy way. "Yeah. What's wrong with that?"

I shake my head, feeling the weight of my bad, *bad* decision settling over me. "I don't have fancy clothes! I have mom clothes. Appropriate for crouching down on the ground and playing leapfrog with Levi without showing my butt crack kind of clothes."

His grin widens, and honestly, I want to jump him. He holds out his hand for me, and I hesitate a moment before taking it. He starts tugging me out of the kitchen toward my bedroom. "Come on. Let's see what you've got."

I giggle like a silly little schoolgirl who just learned about innuendos and my brain definitely assumed that was one, and also because seeing his fantastic back as he pulls me toward my bedroom has carbonated my nerves, making them foam up through my body. "You're going to help me pick out my clothes?"

"Yep."

"Well, that's nice of you."

"Mm-hmm. I'm a stand-up guy." Does anyone else think he sounds a little more gruff than normal? It's probably all in my head. What jealous man would help a woman pick out the perfect outfit for a date?

We step into my explosion of a room, and I pull Cooper to a stop, my face flaming with embarrassment. "Wait! Close your eyes. I need to pick up a few things."

He doesn't obey, just smiles. "Too late—already saw the pink underwear on the floor by the dresser. It was literally the first thing my eyes made contact with." He's so full of smug delight, and I race across the room, rip the offending article from the ground, and toss it into my hamper.

Cooper sits down on the edge of my bed and bounces a little before turning a daring grin at me. His thoughts are projecting from his eyes as he makes a show of checking how springy my mattress is.

I point a threatening finger at him. "Stop that!"

"Stop what?" he asks, all innocence.

"I know you're just trying to get a rise out of me by doing suggestive things on my bed. Knock it off."

He leans back onto his elbows and—*will someone please get this man a shirt?!* "I told you, I like seeing you blush."

Great, now this is the image of Cooper that's going to be burned into my mind all night as I have to go stare at a mediocre man and pretend I find him half as attractive as the Calvin Klein model lying across my mattress.

"You need to put on a shirt."

He grins because he can completely read my thoughts. "Yes, ma'am."

CHAPTER 18

Cooper

Levi strolls into the room and sits down beside me on the bed. Together, we stare at the closed bathroom door, waiting for Lucy to come out.

"We're waiting to see if we like your mom's outfit," I tell him, even though he wasn't asking.

"I like her dinosaur pants. She should wear those," he says, offering up his suggestion.

I nod, ready to suggest it to Lucy, when the door opens and she steps out. Her face says she'd rather be serving jury duty than modeling outfits for me. "Okay, first of all, the dinosaur pants he's talking about are PJs. It's completely acceptable to wear a T-rex on your clothes when you're sleeping."

I grin and hold up my hands. "I wasn't judging, just wondering where I could find a pair."

"I have some that match. Wanna see?" Levi is already darting off the bed and racing out of the room. I love this kid's commitment to everything. I've yet to see him walk anywhere.

I turn my eyes back to Lucy and take in her outfit from head to toe. She squirms under my gaze and tucks some hair back behind her ear. "Well? Do you like this outfit?"

I pop my eyes back up to her face. "Oh. Was I supposed to be looking at the clothes?"

Lucy's cheeks flush, and she tries to hold back a smile as she picks up a house shoe and chucks it at me. It hits my chest and falls pathetically to the ground, wounding me none. "Come on. Be serious." *I was being serious.* "Do you like it or not?"

"Okay," I say, focusing this time and situating myself with better posture—perfect for focusing. I let my eyes scan her body again, but this time only paying attention to the clothes. She's wearing black dress pants that look as if they've seen better days and a fancy blouse that, personally, I'd only consider pulling out if the queen suddenly showed up for tea. "That's quite a few ruffles on the neckline." I wiggle my fingers at my own neck, signifying the problem area.

Her shoulders drop in defeat. "Ugh. I know. I hate this shirt. I only wear it to funerals."

"Maybe not the best vibe to bring with you into a date, then." I think that shirt should have been buried along with the casket at the last funeral she attended.

"You're right." She holds up a finger. "I've got something else that might work. Hang on." And she disappears into the bathroom again.

I lie back on the bed, staring up at the ceiling, wondering what it would take to get her to stay here with me tonight where I can keep her all to myself. It's selfish, I know, because it's not like I can offer her anything besides friendship—at least not for a while. My hope is that Drew will see me settling down and feel more comfortable about me dating Lucy. Is it too much to ask that she not kiss, date, or flirt with other men until that time?

Yes.

So that's why I'm helping her get ready for her date. If I can't be the one to take her out, I want to spend time with her up until the moment she leaves the house. Thing is, I'm more than a little scared that Lucy is going to find someone before I can toss my hat in the ring. What if she goes out tonight with this guy and they hit it off? There's a very real chance that, by sitting on her bed right now and helping her approve outfits like one of her girlfriends, I've inadvertently solidified my friend-zone status, and every man knows that's a hard hole to climb back out of.

"Okay! It's a little bold, but what do you think?" Lucy says, opening the door.

I shoot back up to a seated position and immediately grimace. "Ah, no. Take it off; you're burning my eyes out." I hold up my arm to shield myself from the light her floor-length dress is emitting.

She laughs, stepping forward to yank my arm down. "Stop it! You're being dramatic."

"No . . . *that*," I say, pointing to the bright-yellow dress, "is dramatic. Where did you even find something like this? And why does it go all the way down to the floor?" I reach out and run the scratchy-shiny fabric between my thumb and index finger. In the process, the backs of my knuckles brush against her thigh through the fabric. Heat rushes through me, and I look up to see Lucy staring down at me with her signature wide eyes.

"I—" She shakes her head lightly and steps out of reach. "It's called a maxi dress, and I got it from one of those Instagram influencer ads. It looked cute on the model . . . but I'll admit it's a little bright on me with my auburn hair." Her whole demeanor deflates. "You know what? This is ridiculous. I'm going to call Ethan and cancel. I can't go to a fancy restaurant looking like the sun ate a carrot and sprouted hair."

"Yeah, but a pretty sun who ate a carrot. And on the plus side, the restaurant will save money on electricity when you're able to light it with the power of your dress."

Lucy gives me a mocking smile, then sighs dramatically. She looks so downcast now, and my soppy-lovesick heart aches at the sight. Suddenly, I will do anything for her. Absolutely anything to make her smile. I will reenact every movie montage I've ever seen where the friend takes the heroine shopping, and we will max out my credit card until we find the perfect dress that makes the special music turn on and warm lighting appear.

Levi runs back into the room with super speed, looking like that little boy in *The Incredibles*. He's clutching the coveted dinosaur pants. "See!" he says, holding them up super close to my face with the biggest smile I've ever seen.

Lucy sits down beside me, and the mattress sinks with her weight. My arm presses against her, and I feel like a boy again. The smallest touches from Lucy feel monumental, like I'm touching a woman for the first time.

I take the pants from Levi and hold them up for inspection. "These. Are. The. Coolest."

Levi beams. "I told you!!" He says it like we just confirmed a great conspiracy. "My mom can order you some too, if you want. Then we can all match."

I freeze, dinosaur fabric clutched in my hand, and stare at Levi. Because when looking at his big round blue eyes that perfectly match his mother's, I turn into ooey-gooey mush. I want this. I want a life like this. No, not a life like it—*this* one, specifically.

Levi blinks up at me with those hopeful eyes, and my first thought is to say *Hell yeah, I'll match you, buddy*. Then I remember he's a child, and Lucy probably doesn't want me cursing around her four-year-old, so I clamp down on that and nod. "I'd definitely be down for matching. Are you too young to watch *Jurassic Park*?"

He scrunches up his face. "Yeah. It's for big kids," he says like a responsible adult, and I can't help but reach out to ruffle the top of his hair. He's cute—something I've never before in my life thought about a kid. He's also very busy. Not even one second later, he's taking his dino pants with him and running out of the room. Do all kids move this much?

"Okayyyyy, well, I'm glad you two have your fashion emergencies all sorted, because mine definitely isn't important or anything." Lucy shoots up off the bed and goes to her nightstand to pick up her phone. "I'm canceling. Clearly, it was too last minute. I shouldn't have even said yes in the first place. I looked desperate. No one wants to look desperate . . ."

She keeps blabbering on like she does when she's nervous, and as much as it hurts me to do it, I stand up and take the phone out of her hand. "You're going on this date, Lucy." *Even if it kills me.* She deserves to go out and have a good time.

I go to her closet next, taking matters into my own hands. Personally, I love that her whole wardrobe is made up of jeans and tees. She wears them better than anyone else I've ever seen, that's for sure. But tonight, she needs something dressy that makes her feel more like a woman than a mom.

I push past almost all of her clothes, nearly losing hope, before I spot something red in the back. My body feels oddly tingly as I make contact with the soft fabric and remove it from the hanger, holding it up. Holy crap, this is hot. It's a short cocktail dress in a deep red that makes my heart race.

"*That* one?!" Lucy asks, coming to stand beside me. "I didn't get this one out because I haven't worn it since I had Levi, and I doubt it will even fit me anymore. And also, it's a little . . . sultry for a first date, don't you think?"

Okay, yes, it's a *little* sultry. But for the most part, it's just a good-looking dress. I think it's ridiculously sweet that Lucy considers this dress to be too much for a first date. For reasons I can't even pinpoint, it makes me like her more. Lucy is real—what you see is what you get. Which is why it is full-on torture helping her pick out a dress that is going to catch another dude's eye.

"I gotta see it on you before I can cast my official vote."

She gives me a skeptical grin because she's on to me. She knows I just want to see her in this dress. Snatching it out of my hand, she's marching it with her into the bathroom. After shutting the door, I hear the sound of a zipper and resist groaning at the mental picture forming in my head.

I turn away from the door and busy myself with snooping around Lucy's room. It's messy but not gross. There are clothes on the floor and a few cups half full of water on the bedside table. I like it. It's comfy. Lived in.

"Did you know this was my room before you moved in?" I yell to Lucy through the door.

"I guess that makes sense. I knew you were the old roommate, but before now I never thought about that this would have been your room."

I pick up a picture of her and Levi with their faces smooshed together making silly expressions and smile. "Yeah. Does that bird still squawk every morning at seven?"

I'm just about to open the drawer of her bedside table and take a peek when I hear the door to the bathroom squeak open. When I turn around, I fist my hands at my sides just to keep from reaching out for her. *Shit.* I change my mind . . . that dress *is* too sultry for a first date.

My eyes skim from her sparkling blue eyes and rosy cheeks, down the length (the short length) of her dress. The red fabric stretches across her body and hugs every one of her feminine curves before landing a few inches above her knees. It's not risqué on its own, but wrapped tightly around Lucy, it's downright intoxicating.

She clears her throat, and I force my eyes up to hers. She's wearing an unsure smile that boggles my mind. How does she not see how gorgeous she is?

Her nose scrunches, and she gives me a wobbly frown. "It's too much, isn't it?" Her hands run nervously along the fabric, and she looks down. "It's too tight. My pre-baby body didn't have the hips I do now." She says *hips* like they're a bad thing. Like it's the worst thing in the world when women have tantalizing curves—perfect for someone to run their hands all over (me . . . that someone needs to be me). She does a little half turn, letting me catch a glimpse of her back, and I notice that the zipper is still down.

Lucy continues to rattle off reasons she thinks she looks like puke. ". . . and the hem is too short. Maybe all the added inches to my waist have sort of made the bottom hike up a little bit, you know? And I think the color clashes with my hairwaitwhatare-youdoing?" The last of her words all run together as I put my hands on her shoulders and spin her to face away from me.

The back of her dress is open, revealing a tempting amount of skin and the black strap of her bra. I pick up her auburn hair and push it all to one shoulder, watch her take in a deep breath, not letting it out. Moving probably more slowly than is needed, I grab the delicate zipper and begin to lift it, skimming the back of my hand against her soft, warm skin as I go. Every slight touch feels so charged I'm afraid my fingers are leaving blisters in their wake.

My pulse hammers out the words *you idiot you'll never be the same* as my hand glides up the small dip in her lower back.

Lucy's head tilts down and to the side, as if she's trying to sneak a peek at my reaction. I get the feeling this is a vulnerable moment for her. She's standing stock-still, as if every single one of her senses is laser focused on me and my reaction to her.

I swallow when my knuckles trip over the black lace of her bra. I can't help but smile because I like knowing this secret: Lucy wears a sexy bra under what she calls mom clothes. It's like she's been desperately trying to hide behind a comfortable façade, but inside she's still a woman who wants to feel attractive and desired. She wants to feel those things but is afraid to show it. If I could, I'd make Lucy feel both of those things without her ever having to voice it.

But I can't . . . because her brother will hunt me down and make sure I'm never given the opportunity to do it again.

Once the zipper reaches the top, I fasten the tiny clasp at her neck, tension wrapping like a cord around every muscle in my body, restraining me from turning this into something *more*. I want to dip my head down and kiss a line up the side of her exposed neck. I want to breathe in her sweet, warm scent and let it fill my lungs for the rest of the night.

I clear my throat to dislodge my words as I sweep her hair back again. "You should wear this dress tonight. You look amazing." Even to my own ears, my voice sounds strained and gravelly.

Lucy slowly turns to face me, and her eyes sweep slowly over my features. She's searching for *the* answer . . . the answer to why the air feels warm between us, why my pupils are dilated, why my voice sounds like sandpaper and I'm slowly backing away from her.

I remind myself that I'm retreating for tonight only. Not forever. Just for now.

Drew will come around, and when he does, I'm coming after Lucy.

"Where are you going?" she asks with lifted eyebrows, and I grab my hat from the bed and put it back on, making a beeline for the door.

"Sorry, I just remembered I . . . have a thing."

"Oh. Okay. Yeah . . . sure. You have a thing—totally fine. Well, thanks for coming to fly a kite today. Levi loved it. Oh, and thanks for the oil change. Now I have you to thank when my car doesn't burst into flames."

Wait, wait, wait. She's rambling—something I've come to know means she's hiding her feelings. I take quick stock of my actions and realize they look bad. I spent the entire day with Lucy and her son (which was a big thing for her, letting me into Levi's life) and then I see her in a dress that makes her feel uncomfortable and bolt with a weak excuse.

Nah, I'm not going to act like an asshole right now.

I pause my journey to the door and backtrack to Lucy. I stop just in front of her and smile warmly, putting my hands on her upper arms, and lean down to kiss her cheek. *It was a friendly kiss, Drew, sheesh.*

"Thank you for today. It was the best day I've had in a long time." I want to kiss her right on her full mouth, but I refrain and let go of her instead. "You look gorgeous, Lucy. Enjoy your date tonight."

She gives me a belated, whispered *Thank you* on my way out. In the living room, I find Levi, tongue sticking out the side of his mouth as he tries to fit two tiny Lego pieces together, now wearing his amazing dino pants. I give him a fist bump and tell him he's the best freaking kite flier I've ever seen. His jaw drops on the word *freaking*, and I think I might have just taught him something new that Lucy won't like. What can I say? I'm new to this. Hopefully, I'll get the chance to learn.

Once I'm in my car, I make a quick call.

"Hey, Rachel, you up for going to dinner tonight around seven at Thistle?"

CHAPTER 19

Lucy

O kay, why did I let Cooper talk me into this dress? I'm racing up the sidewalk toward the restaurant, wearing my old red dress that feels about two sizes too small for me now, my boobs bouncing up and down, threatening to burst from the scooped neckline, and tripping over the much-too-high heels strapped to my feet. Did I mention I haven't worn heels in at least four years?

Yeah. Terrible idea.

I think I was still buzzing from whatever that moment with Cooper was when I left the house. One good look at me, however, and Ethan is going to get the wrong idea. Now, granted, I haven't worn anything other than some sort of T-shirt and jeans or leggings combo in the last several years, so I might be exaggerating, but I don't think so.

I step inside the fancy restaurant feeling like the PG-13 version of Cinderella—if her boobs were pushed up to her throat and her dress was threatening to burst at the seams. Seriously, if I make one wrong move, this whole thing is going to explode like a con-

fetti cannon. It was a good thing Cooper zipped me up in it, because I never would have been able to achieve it on my own. I'm
already planning on cutting myself out of it when I get home.

"Lucy?" a male voice sounds from behind me, and I turn to find
a good-looking man, with nice white teeth and all his hair, smiling
at me. He looks very businessy in his navy suit and tie, but that's
not a bad thing. In fact, he looks great—like, if I'd never met Cooper, this guy would probably make me turn my head if I passed
him in the grocery store.

Ugh. And there's the problem. Cooper . . . he's infiltrated my
mind. Weaseled his *Baywatch* body and dazzling smile into my
subconscious and bench-pressed the standard I used to measure
men against.

"Yes, and you must be Ethan?" I say, extending my hand in his
direction.

He takes it, and his smile deepens as he does a brief, polite scan
of my body. *Do not blush, Lucy.* This dress is too tight to add any
extra heat.

"Wow," says Ethan, with a tone of reverence I was not expecting. He reestablishes eye contact with me and shakes his head
lightly. "You look gorgeous." He says it in a way that has me standing a little taller. Maybe this dress doesn't look so obscene on me
after all.

"Thank you. It's surprising that I'm not six foot and burly like
my brother, right?"

He takes on a sheepish look. "I wasn't going to bring it up, but
I'll admit I was a little nervous when he mentioned I should ask
out his sister without showing me a picture. You never know how
closely siblings will resemble one another."

We both chuckle lightly at this, and I'm surprised by how
quickly first date etiquette returns to me. *Ha ha, why yes, Ethan, I*

am sophisticated and definitely did not eat a string cheese and fruit snacks on the way over here.

A moment later, the hostess calls our name and takes us to our table. I notice that Ethan places his hand on my lower back to guide me. It's a little touchy-feely for a first date, but I don't hate it. It actually feels kind of nice to be wanted.

Too bad my mind rushes back to feeling Cooper's rough hand glide up my spine, causing goosebumps to erupt down my arms. I shiver a little, and Ethan notices.

"Are you cold? Do you need my jacket?" he asks as we take our seats.

"No, I'm okay, thank you. Just a . . . little draft." I laugh nervously and pick up my menu. I'm only a hundred and twenty seconds into this date and already I need a reprieve from acting normal. Normal is exhausting.

Also, I need to get Cooper out of my head. No more thoughts of that man or his abs or how sweet he looked with Levi up on his shoulders flying a kite. Since Cooper was not the one to ask me out on a date tonight, he's got to go.

Except . . . is that . . . ? Surely not.

"Are you freaking kidding me?" I say, noticing the man behind Ethan as he walks through the front doors of the restaurant with a hot little brunette on his arm.

"What?" Ethan asks, looking up with a furrowed brow.

Ah shoot, I didn't mean to say it out loud. I quickly cover my tracks and gesture toward the menu with an overly bright smile. "A burger! *So* excited they have a burger on the menu. I thought this might be one of those snooty restaurants that only has"—it's at this moment I realize I'm being rude and quickly change my conversational track—"amazing food that will ruin me for all other foods in the future." I give a weak laugh and deeply regret who I am as a person. I also track Cooper and his movements like I'm Jason Bourne and my target has arrived.

Ethan is nice, though, and chuckles softly, ignoring my odd outburst and returning his gaze to his own menu. "I hear you. I barely eat anything grown-up these days. It seems like all my daughter ever wants is chicken nuggets and mac and cheese."

I should be so excited to be talking with Ethan about our kids and boxed pasta. I imagine most men don't want to discuss child menus with their dates, so I should be savoring this moment and whipping out stories of the month when Levi refused to eat anything other than strawberry yogurt. The judgment from his pediatrician was *strong*. Instead, I have the distinct feeling of wanting to tell him to hush it up so I can focus on reading Cooper's lips as he talks to his date across the room. They're laughing about something. Ugh. What could possibly be so funny that she needs to lean across the table and touch his arm? Nothing.

Here's the thing: Cooper knew I was coming here tonight. *And* he knew what time. So, what the *actual hell* is he doing over there with that woman? At first, I think he doesn't even remember I'm supposed to be here tonight; then, without even turning his head, his eyes cut directly to me, and he winks. *He freaking winks*. Like he knew I was sitting here the whole time. Like he sought me out through the window before he even walked in.

He holds my gaze for two breaths, gives a quiet smirk as his head tilts to the side and his gaze drops to my bare legs, and then slowly turns his eyes back to his date. I note, with both pride and confusion, that his smile fades when he looks at her.

"Lucy?" Ethan asks, like maybe he's already said my name a few times. Oh shoot. I bet he did.

"Oh! Yep. That's me. Sorry." I smile and shrug. "I thought I saw som . . ." My sentence trails off when I notice my phone light up on the table. I always have it where I can see it in case my mom needs to get ahold of me about Levi. *This* is not my mom.

I quickly pick up my phone. "Sorry, let me just check this really quick. Could be my sitter." It's not. I'm a liar.

COOPER: Hi.

I cut my eyes to the side briefly and can see that Cooper isn't even looking at his phone anymore. What's his angle?

LUCY: Hi? What do you think you're doing?

I set my phone down again and attempt to dive back into my date. Any responses from Cooper will just have to wait.

"So, tell me about yourself, Ethan." I sound way too excited to hear about his life, like I'm overcompensating for wishing I was sitting across the restaurant instead. I hope he doesn't pick up on that.

"Well, I'm sure you put two and two together and realized I'm *divorced*"—he whispers it dramatically like he knows it's a dirty word—"and I have a daughter named Emily. I love my job at the hospital, and I prefer summer over winter. Blue is my favorite color." I don't love that this is beginning to feel like a round of speed dating. And maybe I'm being unfair by judging our lack of chemistry too quickly, but this whole thing is feeling forced in a bad way. "What about you?"

"As you know, my name is Lucy. I have a four-year-old son named Levi"—*Why am I doing the speed-dating thing now? Oh well, I've committed*—"and I prefer cake to ice cream."

He laughs like this is the funniest thing he's ever heard. A loud shocking laugh that makes my shoulders jump. Thankfully, a moment later, Ethan gets a phone call from *his* sitter and says he has to take it.

My phone buzzes immediately.

I try to keep my gaze appropriately fixed on my date and *not* on that screen. My eyes are watering because I've taken it to the next level and won't blink either. *Must not look away. Prepare to ask this man questions about his daughter's sleeping habits, or daytime activities, or . . . oh, screw it.*

COOPER: You look too hot for him. Is he a snooze fest?

LUCY: Stop it! What are you doing here??? And who's the model? She seems nice.

COOPER: Careful, you sound a little jealous. And she's not a model. She's a lawyer, if you must know.

LUCY: But models as a side job, right? I can see her amazing boobs from all the way over here.

COOPER: I can see your amazing boobs from all the way over here, does that mean you model on the side?

I gasp and look up to find Cooper smiling at his water glass.

Ethan hangs up with an apologetic smile. The waitress then comes to the table at that exact moment, and I'm given five more seconds to respond while Ethan puts in his order, and then I mentally commit to put my phone away after I hit Send.

LUCY: It's different. I have mom boobs. These babies are unpredictable, and you never know how they will react to sudden movements. Hers are so pretty and perky I'm worried your eye might get poked out if she leans forward an inch.

There. I replied, and now I will enjoy my date with this nice, normal guy Drew approves of. Is it a bad sign that we've spent most of the ten minutes we've been here on our phones?

Ethan smiles, glances down at my phone in my hand, and looks back up to my face. "Everything okay?"

"Definitely. Just . . . the sitter needing advice on how to get Levi to bed." *Yep, I'm the worst.*

"Gosh," he says, leaning back in his chair and unbuttoning the top of his suit jacket. "I do not miss those days—the sleepless nights and all that. I swear it gets easier, though. Just hang in there."

Geez—he's so ridiculously nice and I am so ridiculously bored. I know he's trying to be relatable and understanding, but so far we've done nothing but stare at our phones and comment on our children. I wanted to feel like a woman tonight—not a mom.

Did I squeeze into this dress and spend too long applying eyeliner so we could talk about the kids we are trying to get away from for a night? Is this my future? And I know I'm not being fair. He's a super-nice guy, and being sweet to appeal to the parental side of me. Problem is, I feel like we've already been married for five years—and not in a good way. I need some spark, some tension, some . . .

Cooper is calling.

Why is Cooper calling?!

In an incriminating movement, I jerk my phone off the table before Ethan can see the shirtless picture Cooper apparently assigned as his caller ID in my phone. When did he do that? And how did I miss it happening?

"I'm sorry," I say to Ethan, looking deeply apologetic. "I need to take this."

Poor Ethan. He's so sweet. "Of course! Take your time," he

says, wrongly assuming this is my sitter calling me. Someone needs to lock me up in bad-date jail.

I swipe open my phone and hold it to my ear, angling myself slightly away from the table. "Hello?"

"Why do you always do that?" Cooper says, like it's the most normal thing to interrupt my date like this and launch right into a private conversation.

I fumble with my silverware and sneak a glance at Ethan with a polite smile. "Do what?"

"Talk down about yourself. I can't take it anymore. You're beautiful, Lucy, and you've got a great body that doesn't need constant prefacing that you think it's flawed. And you know what else?" *He's really fired up.* "Being a mom doesn't make you less appealing. You're the whole package."

My face is bloodred now—basically, the same color as my dress—as I scan my eyes across the restaurant until I spot Cooper, standing in the hallway that leads to the bathrooms. He's staring right at me.

I can't have this conversation with him right now. I shouldn't even be talking to him. And if Ethan knew I was talking to another man on our date, he'd be out of here so fast I wouldn't even be able to say his name. Which . . . maybe wouldn't be the worst thing in the world? *Yes, it would, and I'm a terrible person.*

"That's okay," I say in a fake happy tone while narrowing my eyes at Cooper. "Just give him an extra sip of water and I'm sure he'll go right to sleep."

Cooper frowns momentarily before he realizes what I'm doing. "Ohhhh. He thinks you're on the phone with your sitter? Okay, I can have some fun with this. What color underwear do you have on?"

"*Yep. No problem. See you later.*" And I hang up quickly.

Ethan frowns at my bonkers smile. "She can't get him to bed?"

"Nope, sure can't. Will you excuse me a minute? I need to use the restroom." I'm already standing and barreling toward the hallway.

Cooper is still standing there, leaning against the wall and smirking at me like he knew even before I did that I'd be meeting him back here. I push him farther down the hall, and his eyebrows lift. Shoot, he looks so sexy tonight in this black button-down and slate-gray dress pants. *He* doesn't look businessy. He just looks impeccable.

"What is your aim here, Cooper? Is this a prank? *Hm? Is it?*" I ask, backing him against the wall and jabbing my finger into his chest.

He breaks the unspoken friendship rules and reaches out to run a hand from my shoulder down my arm. "No, it's not a prank."

"Then what are you doing?"

"I don't know," he says, his hand so tender on my skin.

"What do you mean you don't know?"

He shrugs, giving me an adorable, unsure, tilted smile. "I guess I'm just here as a friend to look out for you . . . since Drew isn't in town. Be around if you needed a quick exit."

I narrow my eyes, every inch of my skin aware of how his hand is still holding my wrist. "As a friend . . . to look out for me," I repeat, having trouble getting that explanation to match up with his actions.

"Yeah. And then I saw how bored you looked and thought I'd spice up your night a little. Play around. I wanted you to have some fun."

"So, you were just playing around when you said all of that on the phone? About my . . . well, you know."

"*No.*" His face goes serious. "What I said on the phone was just me being honest."

"Oh . . ." I don't know what to do with this information. Cooper is touching me tenderly, but he's not making any moves to take us past friendship. I want to ask if this is a product of the bro code, but once again I'm scared. Maybe he's just a touchy-feely guy. *Wait*—isn't he here on a date? *The scoundrel, sneaking off to hold another woman's wrist in a darkened hallway!*

I pull my hand away. "And how do you think your date would feel if she knew you snuck off to talk about my great body?"

He shrugs one shoulder. "I imagine she's fine with it since we're not on a date. Just old friends hanging out. Besides, she knows I came back here to call you. She thinks you're very pretty, by the way."

"Oh . . ." That's an unexpected turn of events. "Well then, I hope you two have a very nice time together."

"No you don't," he says as his smile grows into something so devious my toes curl. I'm no match for that smile. I need to get out of here before I push him into one of those bathroom stalls and become *really* good friends with him.

I begin backing away slowly. Carefully. "Quit doing all . . . this." I wiggle my fingers in his general direction.

He stuffs his hands in his pockets. "All what?"

"You know." I let my eyes rake over him one last greedy time.

"Fine, I'll try."

"No, you won't."

"You're right. Better put your phone in your purse if you don't want to blush all night. Your inbox is about to see some real action."

"You wouldn't."

His grin says, *Wanna bet?*

I turn away and attempt to cool my skin when Cooper calls out to me one more time. "Luce." I pause, and my skin flushes at hearing my nickname on his lips. "Be confident tonight and have fun. You're an amazing woman, and he's lucky to be out with you."

If that's true, then why aren't you out with me?

What. A. Bust.

As far as getting-back-in-the-game dates go, that one had to be the worst. Cooper came in like a shot of tequila, all smooth, crisp, and enticing, and wrecked my system. I couldn't focus the rest of the night. Cooper was right when he said my message inbox would get some action. Except, instead of making me blush, I mainly had to try very hard not to laugh. Ethan, though—*darling Ethan*—luckily wasn't even fazed by my lack of attention. I think he has his own version of Cooper somewhere out in the world too, because he was just as distracted. We both agreed to get the check as soon as socially acceptable and parted as barely acquaintances (but I know all of his daughter's favorite foods, so that's something).

If only I knew if Cooper is actually into me and is just staying away for the sake of respect for my brother, I'd talk to Drew about it and tell him to back off because I'm a grown woman who is capable of making her own decisions. I mentally fight my brother with sophisticated arguments while pulling on my dinosaur PJ pants and an oversized shirt I got at the planetarium that says *I'm stellar!* I wrap my hair in a bun on the top of my head, take out my contacts, and put on my glasses. After brushing my teeth, I plop down on the couch, happy to overindulge in a night of binge-watching something romantic.

Two minutes into streaming my favorite Turkish romance

(don't knock it till you try it), the doorbell rings. In moments like these, I still feel like a child, unsure of whether I should get the door or not. It's late. I'm not expecting anyone, and sadly, I didn't order any food. There's a fifty/fifty chance a murderer is on the other side of that door, waiting to make me the next *Dateline* story.

I do that thing where you put the TV on mute and hunker down, trying to trick whoever is at the door that they were only hearing things before and you're not really home. Wait . . . but then will they just break in? I've lived without my parents for several years now, but I'm still not good at it.

My phone suddenly rings and makes me jump out of my skin. I frown at the caller ID flashing Cooper's abs at me and wonder if I actually drifted off to sleep. This feels a lot like a dream, where there are too many moving components and eerie feelings to fully process what's going on. I bet a clown will walk through that door next and go make himself some lasagna in the kitchen. Sadly, that's a recurring dream I have.

"Cooper?"

"I'm at your door. Will you come let me in before this old lady staring from her porch calls the cops on me? Oh God, her phone is to her ear. I think it's happening."

I let out a deep breath and toss the blankets off my lap. "You scared me! What are you doing here? It's so late."

"Let me in and you'll see." Why do I feel like he's going to be dressed like Magic Mike on the other side of this door? *One can only hope.*

I open the door to Cooper, still dressed in his nice clothes from dinner, but he's unbuttoned one extra button and untucked his shirt. One hand is pressing his phone to his ear, the other holding up a bottle of wine. "Post-bad-date sustenance."

Yeah, more like late-night bad decision waiting to happen.

CHAPTER 20

Cooper

Lucy's gaze bounces from the bottle of wine in my hand to my eyes, and she swallows. I start to feel ridiculous still holding up the wine, and also a little concerned she might turn me away. It sounds egotistical, but I haven't been used to women keeping me at arm's length or turning me away this past year. The fact that she doesn't throw the door wide open and start undressing before I've made it across the threshold is refreshing—sort of.

Finally, she steps aside and gestures for me to come in, but her eyes are skeptical. She's going to keep me on a short leash until she knows what I'm about.

When I walk into the living room, I notice the house is completely dark except for the glow of the TV. I look at my watch; it's only ten thirty. But, yeah, I guess that's actually pretty late to be ringing the doorbell of a home with a sleeping child inside. Shoot, now I feel terrible.

"I didn't wake up Levi, did I?" I ask, turning back around to follow Lucy into the kitchen after she takes the wine from my hands.

She chuckles quietly. "No. He's with my mom tonight. And even if he wasn't, he sleeps like a rock. I imagine I'll have to dump cold water on him when he's a teenager."

Oh, so Levi's not here. And neither is Drew. So that means . . . we're alone in here?

Now I'm contemplating the wisdom of this late-night adventure as I track Lucy moving around her kitchen. Her bun is an enormous mess of auburn waves, her shirt is so big it's nearly falling off her shoulder, and she's wearing thick-rimmed glasses. And don't forget the famous dinosaur sleep pants. She's so freaking adorable I almost can't handle it.

"I can feel you judging my outfit," she says as she pours red wine into two stemless wineglasses.

"Not judging." I move to stand closer to her. "Admiring."

She quirks her mouth into a skeptical grin and leans a hip against the counter. I watch her lips make contact with the glass as she takes a slow sip. "You're so full of lines."

I hold up a hand in the universal sign of scout's honor. "I've never given you a single line. Only honesty."

She's looking for a way to call my bluff. Vast, deep blue eyes search mine, then shift to my mouth, looking for any signs of a teasing smile. Back up to my eyes. She takes another sip and tips her chin toward her shoulder. "Okay, then maybe I'll wear this little number to my next date if you think it's attractive."

Her words are a cheap shot to my gut. "Next? Are you going out with Ethan again?" From where I sat, it looked like both of them would have rather been at the dentist. Maybe I was wrong?

"God, no. I think I have more chemistry with this glass of wine than Ethan. But I had two more of Drew's friends text me tonight asking if I'd like to go out sometime, so I can only imagine how many of them he gave my number to. I'm worried he's trying to rival eHarmony."

I clench my teeth. So, it's not that Drew is against Lucy dating one of his friends; it's strictly *me* he doesn't want his sister going out with. Cool. That feels great and not at all messed up.

"You okay?" Lucy asks when she notices the storm cloud that has settled over my head.

"Yeeeeep," I say, drawing out the word a little too long before taking a deep drink of wine and letting it warm my chest. How am I going to watch Lucy go on more dates? Whatever. I'll have to worry about that later because, right now, I'm here alone with Lucy. *Me.* Not Ethan. Not any of the other guys. *Me.*

And apparently when I get jealous I turn into a caveman. *Me get Lucy.*

She watches me with an amused, calculating look, letting me know I must be openly displaying more of my jealousy than I realize. Sometimes, I can't handle her eyes on me like this. It makes me want to fidget, and I've never been a fidgeter before. I reach up and flick one of her unruly locks of hair, tossing her my best attempt at a relaxed grin just so she doesn't look too hard and find all my flaws and insecurities. "What are we watching tonight, Marshall?"

Her eyebrows rise, making her glasses shift a little on her face. "You want to watch with me? It's a Turkish romance. I doubt you'd be into it."

"Try me."

And that's how I wound up on Lucy's couch, drinking wine and watching a sappy show until the early hours of the morning. At some point during the night (I think after her second or third glass), Lucy's legs ended up draped across my lap. They are still there now, and I have one hand on her foot and the other covering her shin. The side of her face is sort of smooshed against the couch cushion, and we both angrily groan when, once again, the show cuts off with the main couple's lips hovering a hair's breadth away from each other.

"*Why do they keep doing this to me?!*" Lucy says with overly dramatic, slurring words, shoving her whole face into the cushion and sloshing a tiny bit of wine onto her T-shirt. I've lost count of how many glasses she's had now, and her raised blood-alcohol level is showing.

I laugh and tighten my grip on her foot, liking how freely I get to touch her when it's just us. "Should we start another one and see if they finally kiss?"

Lucy's head pops up and her glasses are askew, eyes a little glazed. I right the frames on her face and can't help the sappy smile I feel on my mouth. I can't remember the last time I felt this comfortable and happy. Is this why all my friends with girlfriends and wives always disappear? I thought it was because their women wouldn't let them go out anymore. Turns out, it's that the men don't want to leave.

"No. They're never going to kiss. This show is one nevvvvver-ending tension torture device." Her words stick in a few places, but she finally manages to get it all out. And then her gaze swings toward the TV, smile slowly fading. "'Sides, it's not good to watch stuff like this."

"Why not?" Lucy sets her wineglass precariously on the arm of the couch and then reaches up, tugging her hair free of her bun. Wild auburn locks fall down around her shoulders, and I stare in amazement at how beautiful she is even when she's in this state. But it's not just Lucy's skin, hair, and eyes that contribute to her beauty. It's every smile, every laugh, every little thing she does for her son and did for me when I was sick. It's all of it. I meant it when I said I thought Lucy was the complete package. She's too good to be true.

She gathers her hair and pulls it to the side, sectioning off three pieces and stumbling over her own clunky hand coordination, attempting to braid it. She's doing a poor job and has very clearly tipped over into I've-had-too-much-land. "Because it's not real. In life, the guy doesn't wait a hundred years for the most romantic moment to kiss the girl. He sleeps with her right away, gets her pregnant, and leaves her sorry ass with a baby."

The vessels of my heart constrict at the sight of Lucy. A brokenhearted woman is bad enough, but a brokenhearted woman who's a little drunk, slurring, and spilling her wine as she tries to balance the glass and tame her hair . . . it's too much. She looks like a wounded baby bird, and all I want to do is scoop her up, take her home, and protect her until her wings heal.

First, I take Lucy's wine from the armrest and place it on the coffee table because she's had enough. Then I scoot a little closer and move her hands so I can pick up where she left off. Her eyes meet mine, and with an overly dramatic breathy flair, she says, "You know how to braid?!"

I laugh and continue to move my hands through her soft locks, overlapping strands and moving slowly as I go. Being this close to Lucy and keeping things strictly friendly is the equivalent of jumping off a roof with the hopes of defying gravity. "I have several female cousins. Any time we would get together for the holidays, they would teach me stuff like how to braid hair and paint nails."

"And you wanted to learn?"

I give her a half smile. "Around age thirteen, I realized if I knew how to braid hair, I'd be a hit at summer camp. And everyone knows summer camp is where teenage dreams are made."

"And were you? A hit?"

I meet her eyes and wag my eyebrows playfully. "I definitely made some dreams come true."

Lucy laughs and shoves my arm. I pluck her hair tie from her fingers and wrap it around the end of the braid. When I look back at her face, I find her watching me closely, head leaning against the couch, legs still draped over my lap. "Jamanji was an ass."

A laugh shoots from my mouth, and I lay my head back against the cushion, eyes level with Lucy's. "Who?"

"The woman you loved," she says with a slur.

"*Janie.*"

She frowns and shakes her head a little. "No, I'm Lucy."

"No—not you, drunky. My ex's name is Janie."

"Ohhhhh. Yeah, that's what I said." Lucy shrugs her bare shoulder, drawing my eyes to the sharp line of her collarbone and velvety skin. I reach over to pull her T-shirt back up to cover her.

A soft smile tugs the corner of her mouth, and the next thing I know, Lucy is running her finger across my eyebrows. "You have pretty eyes," she tells me in a dreamy voice.

I'm trying not to laugh at her, but it's difficult. "Thank you. So do you."

"But yours make me want to go to Tahiti. I have a screensaver that looks like your eyes." I think she's trying to tell me she has a screensaver with a body of water from Tahiti on it, not that she has an up-close photo of my eyeball, but I've been wrong in life before. "Jackie is a spud for giving up your Tahiti eyes." She places the warm palm of her hand on my now scruffy jaw and looks deep into my eyes. "I wouldn't have given them up. I would have said yes."

My mouth opens, but I'm not sure why, because it's not as if I have any words to let out. I don't know what to say, what I should say . . . what she'll remember in the morning of her own words or of my reply. Luckily, she doesn't even seem to want an answer.

Instead, she smiles and shuts her eyes, letting her hand slowly sink down my shoulder and then arm, stopping to land on my biceps. I notice her dark lashes fanning across her cheekbones, her delicate nose and soft silky skin, thinking how sweet and innocent she looks.

That is, right until she squeezes my biceps and says, "You know what I think about sometimes?" Her eyes pop open and meet mine, looking a little wild all of a sudden. "S-E-X." She spells it like that somehow makes it less sexual.

I expel a breath like someone just punched me in the lungs. "What?" I ask with a jarred laugh.

She jolts upright and adjusts her glasses, swaying a little to the side. "You know . . . *intercourse*." She whispers the word this time.

"Yeah, no, I can spell. I knew what you meant the first time. I'm just trying to figure out why we're talking about it right now, out of nowhere."

"Because," she says in a dramatic tone that could rival the greatest stars on Broadway, "did you know it's been over four"—she holds up three fingers—"years since I've been with anyone?"

I'm sure my eyes are sixteen inches around. I didn't see this coming (although I really should have). "No, I didn't realize that. But there's nothing wrong with it." I'd also be lying if I didn't admit it makes me slightly happy to know she and Grim Tim didn't sleep together. Which is a double standard and completely unfair of me, I realize.

She makes an exaggerated *pshhhhhh* sound, and her lips flap a little in the process. "It's for the birds!"

My senses tingle. I know where this conversation is headed, and I've got to slow this thing down before she steamrolls right over the point of no return.

Gently slipping out from under Lucy's legs, I stand and pick up our half-empty wineglasses, then carry them into the kitchen. "I think we're good on the wine for tonight, yeah? I better be headed home." I'm not actually leaving here tonight, but I don't think telling her I plan to sleep on her couch would be such a good idea.

Lucy is up now too, a woman on a mission as she blocks the kitchen doorway. That wine has fully soaked into her bloodstream and emboldened her in a way she will not look back on fondly tomorrow. I want to stop her before she can embarrass herself, because I know what it feels like to make decisions under a warm fuzzy wine blanket, and believe me, it does not feel so warm and fuzzy when the sun comes up.

"Orrrrrrr," she says with her attempt at a seductive smile. I love that she's not good at it. "You could stay here tonight. With me. In my bed."

Oh, someone make it stop. Not because I don't want to do what she's suggesting. Believe me, on any other night, with a fully sober Lucy, I'd be so down for it. But I can't let her say these things tonight, because I know for a fact that if she were sober, she would not be saying them. It's clear that Lucy values intimacy as more than just an act, and I will absolutely honor that.

"You know, Lucy . . ." I walk closer and put my hands on both of her shoulders to gently turn her around and walk her toward her bedroom (so I can make sure she safely makes it there and no other reason). "I've got a really early morning at work tomorrow. I better go back—"

She hits the brakes and whirls around to face me. Her finger suddenly runs a trail down the side of my neck. "But you know what I'm suggesting, right?" She tips her head almost aggressively toward her room.

"Yeah. I think I get the gist."

"Nothing serious. No commitments or anything, of course." I know she's not meaning to cut me with her words, but she is. Each word is razor sharp and tears right through me. Does she really think she's suggesting something I would want, or would find enticing? "You think I'm too sweet for it, *but I'm not.*" Her words are growing more and more impassioned.

I turn Lucy back around and start pushing her the rest of the way to her room.

She misinterprets. "*Oh!* Did it work? Are we going to do it now?"

I shake my head as I spin her around and sit her down on her bed. "No. You're going to go to sleep in this bed alone. That's what's happening tonight."

Her shoulders sink, and she pouts. "Whyyyyy? You don't like me?"

I sink down to my knees and look her directly in the eyes, brushing her hair behind her ear and noting how fragile and vulnerable she looks right now. "We're not doing this tonight because, one, you're drunk, and I don't take advantage of intoxicated women. Two, I refuse to be your onetime booty call, Lucy. Not now, not ever."

She giggles, and I can practically see wine bubbling out of her pores. "*Booty.*"

"Uh-huh," I say, coaxing her to lie down while I pull her covers up over her. "Yep, *booty* is a hilarious word. Thaaaaat's it, let's get you to sleep there, killer."

"Cooper?" Lucy peeks one eye open, comforter pulled up around her head like a cocoon, and I wonder if this is how she sleeps every night. She wiggles one finger out of the face hole she's created and wiggles it, gesturing for me to get closer.

I lean in, unable to keep the grin off my face.

When I get close enough, she whispers, "*I'm drunk.*"

I nod and lean forward to kiss her forehead. "You're a cute drunk, though."

She passes out immediately and is snoring before I can close her bedroom door behind me.

I go back into the living room and turn off the TV, put the empty bottle of wine in the trash, and then curl up on the couch, tugging the blanket over me. Lucy overindulged tonight and deserves to have someone here to look after her and keep her safe while she lets loose (and sleeps it off). I set my alarm for 5:30 A.M., planning to be out of here before she wakes up.

CHAPTER 21

Lucy

"Morning, pumpkin! Levi is watching cartoons upstairs, and—oh, you look rough," says Mom after she opens the front door for me.

I grunt as I step into her house, feeling my brain knock against my skull with every slight movement. I deserve it, though. I deserve every punishment the world wants to throw at me today, because I, Lucy Marshall, got drunk last night and made a complete fool of myself.

Yes, I remember it all in crystal-clear, humiliating Technicolor. The moment I groped Cooper's biceps. The moment I tried to cage him into the kitchen. And last, but definitely not least, the moment I tried to get him to sleep with me.

I cringe every time I remember the words falling out of my mouth. So sure. So confident. *So embarrassing.* Thank the stars above nothing happened and Cooper is a good guy, but I think we can all safely say he's going to stay as far away from me as he can now. Any ambiguity or mystery I might have had concerning my feelings for him are gone. Last night, I might as well have been dancing around, holding a glittery poster board above my head that read, I LOVE YOU, COOPER! LET'S GET MARRIED AND I'LL HAVE ALL YOUR BABIES!

I turn around and face my mom. "I've never asked too much of you, Mom, but today I need you to run me over with your car."

She curls her lips inward, making a kooky smile, and pats the side of my arm. "Did someone make a bad decision last night on her date?"

I cover my face with my hands. "No. Someone tried to, but the man wouldn't let her because she was sloppy drunk." I spread my fingers just enough to peek out.

She looks like she wants to burst out laughing but is composing herself for my benefit. "Well . . . that . . . sounds like you got your first date out of the way with a bang." I wait for her to finish because I know what's coming. "Or . . . I guess without one."

She can't contain her laughter anymore, and I shake my head. "Where did you learn to talk like that?"

"Oh please. I've been this way since long before you were even born. I just waited to use my foul language until you were tucked into your Minnie Mouse sheets at night. Now, come on, I'll pour you a cup of coffee and you can lament."

I trail behind my mom, slowly processing her words. There is a magical time in life when your parent shifts to being your friend, and I've entered it. I love that my mom doesn't filter her language around me anymore. I love that she makes inappropriate jokes. If you had told me in high school that my mother even knew what the word *bang* meant, I would have laughed in your face. But here she is, pouring me coffee for my hangover and proving you don't have to stop being yourself in life just because you have a kid—you just have to edit things for a bit.

"Okay, *ma'am*"—that's our longtime nickname for each other—"Levi is busy upstairs being a TV zombie, and your father is cleaning out the garage, so spill your guts."

"Okay, prepare yourself. It's not a pretty story."

"If I wanted a pretty story, I'd go read a fairy tale. Now quit stalling."

After making her promise not to tell Drew, I tell my mom everything from beginning to end, leaving out no details and laying my shame out on the table for her to stare at and judge. She doesn't, though. She pats my hand and smiles softly. "Oh, hon."

"Terrible, huh?"

"No." Her navy eyes look deep into mine. "Sounds beautiful to me."

I gape at her. "Which part? When I threw myself at a man, or when he rejected me?"

She shakes her head lightly. "You know what you're doing, right?" I give her a dumbfounded look because I truly don't know what she's talking about. "You're keeping yourself blindfolded on purpose. We both know that boy likes you, the clear evidence being that he followed you to the restaurant and flirted with you the whole time you were on a date. And we know he's a good man because he put your sorry butt in bed last night and didn't let you make a bigger fool out of yourself—both signs he cares about you."

I pull my hand from hers and lean back in my chair. "Any good guy would have done that."

"Rip that blindfold off, honey! No man is going to crash your date, sexy-text you all night to make you laugh, and then show up at your house with a bottle of wine after if he's not interested. Now, if you don't admit to me right now that he likes you, I'm going to slap you upside the head."

"You're kinda violent in the mornings."

She turns her head and eyes me from the side, a grin hovering on her mouth. "Don't sidestep me, *ma'am*. Admit he has feelings for you."

"Quit being so domineering, *ma'am*."

"Admit it."

I sigh and drop my forehead onto the table. "I don't want to get my hopes up. I've aimed too high before. What if I do it again and he's only being sweet to me because I'm Drew's sister?"

"No, baby. Your inflection is all wrong—he's *only* being sweet to you because you're Drew's sister. I think he'd like to be a lot less sweet with you, if you know what I mean, but your brother has probably put the fear of God in him."

I pop my head up and whisper like it's a revelation: "The bro code."

"Yep. Exactly." She sits back in her seat, a smug smile blooming.

Maybe she's right. Actually, no, I *know* she's right. There's something there between Cooper and me, and it's time to uncover what it is. And even if not, what's a little more humiliation?

In the next moment, Levi barrels into the room and throws his arms around my neck. "Hi, buddy! I missed you!" I smash my lips into his chubby cheeks before he can wiggle away.

"Mom! Grammy got me a new kite!" He's jumping up and down and doing one of those kid dances that's more wiggle and fist pumping than actual dancing. "Can we take it to the park?"

For us, Mondays are like a weekend. Saturday is one of the busiest days at the salon, so I'm always working, but Mondays are for me and Levi. "Yes! Let's do it. And we can stop for donuts on the way." His jaw drops. I am a superhero in his eyes now. "But I need Grammy to come too and sit with you in the car while I make a quick pit stop."

I look at my mom and smirk, because Operation Rip the Blindfold Off is about to go down.

I'm in Cooper's office building, and I'm completely freaking out. One quick Google search of Hampton Creative and Cooper James, and I easily found the address, helpful parking directions, and what floor he works on. Now, standing in the elevator as it carries me up to the third floor, I feel like I'm going to faint. You'd think I was on one of those hellevator rides that suddenly drops out from under you by the way my stomach is twisting and contorting.

My mom is hanging out in the car with Levi, both sugaring themselves up on donuts, and I'm about to deliver myself on a silver platter to a man who very possibly doesn't want the meal I'm offering. Right before the elevator dings its arrival, I consider mashing the emergency button and bringing this whole bad idea to a halt.

The doors open, and I swallow, adjusting the box of donuts I brought for Cooper under my arm. These aren't a kind offering, if that's what you're thinking. My plan if he rejects me is to open the box and rain donuts down on his head as a distraction tactic while I make a break for the exit.

Oh my gosh, this office is gorgeous. I feel like I accidentally went up too many floors and rose all the way into heaven. Everything is white and sparkly and modern, with floor-to-ceiling windows and a gorgeous, expansive view of the city.

"Can I help you?" asks a kind-looking young woman, who I think looks like her name would be Olivia or Heather, from behind the reception desk, and suddenly it's too real. What am I doing here?

I step forward. "Any chance I'm in the wrong building and Cooper James doesn't actually work here?"

She beams too brightly for my anxious state. "No, you have the right place!" She's reaching for her phone. "I'll call him and tell him you're here to see him. What's your—" She pauses with wide eyes when I reach across the counter, grab the phone, and slam it down on the hook. She is just as frightened by my actions as I am.

"I am so sorry," I say quickly. "I didn't plan to do that. It just happened. Please don't call security. Truth is, I'm about to go declare my feelings for Cooper, and my nerves are just a tiny bit on edge."

Her mouth opens in sort of an awestruck way, and she shakes her head. I think she's about to push a secret button under her desk to call the police when her hand juts out and takes hold of mine. "That man is so gorgeous." She presses her lips together and gives me a nod of solidarity. "I wish you the best of luck."

"Thank you," I whisper, like we're two soldiers in opposing armies who just formed a friendship on the battlefield and declared a private truce. I set the donut box on the counter and lift the lid. "You get a donut because you're the most understanding human I've ever met."

She wiggles her fingers over the sugary selection and finally plucks a chocolate sprinkle. It's a solid choice and only confirms my suspicion that we would be great friends.

"Are you ready?" She asks it like she's about to undo the latch on an aircraft and push me out.

I take in a slow, deep breath and nod. "Let's do this, Olivia."

"My name is Ashley."

CHAPTER 22

Lucy

Have you ever had one of those experiences where your life flashes before your eyes and you see all the exact moments you would do over and the ones you'd never change? That's happening to me now as Ashley lays a brief knock on Cooper's office door. We hear "Come in," then the montage starts rolling in my mind.

I see myself in my early twenties, feeling lonely, watching all my friends coupling up and getting married, and me, still working my butt off in a salon and spending my days off reading. Then, I get invited to a pretty wild birthday party at a friend's house. Brent catches my eye from across the room, and I feel a spark. He's the cool guy, should probably be wearing sunglasses and a leather jacket, but instead he's in a T-shirt and jeans. He raises his glass to me, and I look behind me because I'm not sure it's directed at me. He comes over and flirts like I've never experienced firsthand. I'm completely swept up in him and his dark, mysterious eyes and feel ready to dash off to Vegas. He doesn't want to go to Vegas; he wants to go back to my place. We do. We sleep together, and there's no cuddling. He zips up and takes off without leaving his number, completely over me. Done.

Six weeks later, I'm holding a little stick with two pink lines, and I don't even know the phone number of the man who got me pregnant. I search his name on Facebook and message him. He doesn't reply for several days, so I panic and send him the words *I'm freaking pregnant. Call me.*

He does. Makes it clear that he'll help with the child if I decide to keep it but doesn't want a relationship with me. I have false hopes, though. Over the next nine months they get crushed, and reality sets in as Brent goes out with woman after woman, and I'm swollen and alone on my couch.

The next memory is me crying on the bathroom floor while my brother holds me. I'm sure I've ruined my life and I'll never be happy again, but he quietly reassures me I will.

And then my mom is holding my hand while the nurse puts a baby in the crook of my arm, and I sigh a breath of relief because I freaking did it. I birthed this child, and it was the hardest thing I've ever done, but I did it! *Me.* And I love this little squish ball more than anything. He's worth all the pain.

More memories of Christmases where I should feel lonely but I don't because Levi and I are making cookies with Uncle Drew and decorating the tree with my mom and dad. There's a vague nagging feeling that says someone is missing, but it's not overwhelming.

I remember all of this as the door opens to Cooper's office, and I realize if I was strong enough to get through all of that, I can face the world's hottest man and tell him I'm gone for him without throwing up on his feet. *I hope.*

Ashley steps out of the way and lets me walk past her into the office. She winks as she closes the door, and now I'm alone—shut inside a lion's den.

"Lucy," Cooper says in a happy tone from behind his desk. He closes his laptop and stands, and I'm momentarily stunned because I thought Boat Cooper, Car Mechanic Cooper, and Park Day Cooper were all attractive, but Bossman Cooper is so sexy I think my legs are going to give out.

He scoots his chair away from the desk and shifts to the side, letting me get the full effect of him in a nicely pressed, form-fitting dark-gray suit and tie, hair tousled and waving into perfection with a lock dancing down over his brow. He has a black leather watch on his wrist and dress shoes that match, and with the huge wall of glass behind him, it looks like he is the king of this city. They should name it Cooperville.

"How are you?" he asks with a confused but pleased smile. As he gets closer, I can smell his cologne. Oh lordy, it smells warm and smooth and like I want to dive inside it and swim around all day long.

"I'm good. Well, no, actually, I'm terrible. I mean . . . I *feel* terrible. Physically. Not emotionally. Although, I don't feel so great emotionally either."

"Lucy!" Cooper stops in front of me with his incomparable masculinity on full display as his large hands wrap around both of my biceps with nothing but tenderness. "Breathe." I do, in and out through my nose in a way any yogi would be proud of. "I'm glad you came by."

"You are?"

His mouth tugs up on one side. "Of course. I was afraid you might get weird or try to avoid me after last night."

"Ha! Me? Get weird? Preposterous." That's officially the first time I've ever said the word *preposterous* in my life.

He chuckles softly then lets go of my arms to take a step back, gesturing for me to sit in one of the chairs facing his desk. "Good. Well, welcome to my office. Have a seat and make yourself comfortable."

I glance to the chair, then back at Cooper, knowing I better not sit down and get comfortable. If I do, I'll never tell him what I came here to say. I'll end up settling in and asking him a hundred questions about his fancy title of . . . I squint at the name plaque on his desk, trying to remember what it is he does again: senior brand manager. *Right.* He really is a boss. Remembering this does nothing to help my nerves. Okay, I need to spit it out before I chicken out, pull the fire alarm, and race out of this building.

"Cooper, we need to talk." I set the box of donuts down on his desk and snap my eyes up to him sharply. I'm determined now, like a burly man sitting down to a pie-eating contest at the fair. I want to crack my knuckles. "I asked you to sleep with me last night."

He blinks, and his smile turns amused. "I remember."

"And you turned me down."

He leans back and settles himself against his desk, crossing his arms. "Because you were drunk."

His answer gives me hope. "Only because I was drunk?"

I watch his blue-green eyes narrow, like we're in a game of chess and he's trying to think ahead to my next move. "What is it you really want to know, Lucy?" Not fair. He just wiped all the chess pieces off the board.

I lick my lips—out of nerves, not sensuality—and force myself to meet his gaze like a grown-up. "Cooper . . . I . . . am sort of, kind of having feelings for you, and I want to know if maybe you're having them for me too." I abruptly pick up the donut box again and extend it to him. "Donut?"

CHAPTER 23

Cooper

Lucy shifts the donut box toward me and opens the lid like she's showing me a rare selection of antique jewels rather than sprinkles and glazed dough. Her hands are shaking too. I can see the box vibrating and her cheeks turning that familiar rosy red. She's also wearing her glasses again today, and the whole girl-next-door look with the cutoff shorts and sunshine-yellow tee she's wearing is killing me.

She just admitted to having feelings for me—which, let's be honest, I've known since the beginning of our friendship, or at least knew she was attracted to me—but I have no idea why she's shaking like a leaf over there, because I'm pretty sure my attraction has been apparent too.

I take the box of donuts from her hands and toss it onto my desk. Her eyes watch them go like that box was the last ship that could have carried her off a deserted island. "I rubbed your feet last night," I say matter-of-factly.

Her lips part in shock. And then her brow crumples in confusion. She expels a breath. "I'll be honest, I have no idea what to do with that statement."

I laugh and take a small step closer to her even though I should be putting the desk between us right now. "I'm trying to say I have feelings for you too. I kind of thought it was obvious when I tenderly rubbed your feet while we watched a romantic show and drank wine together until late into the night."

She blinks a few times. "I just thought you did that sort of thing with a lot of women."

I stare at Lucy for a moment, trying to decide if she's serious or not. She is. She's dead serious. I shouldn't, but I reach out and wrap my arms around her, pulling her in tightly to my chest. I hold her close and want to squeeze her because sometimes this woman is just so innocent and unaware of how desirable she is that I can't take it. She's going to give me diabetes she's so sweet. Every cell in my body aches for her.

"No, Lucy, I don't do that for a lot of women—or any women, for that matter. I did it because I like you. A lot."

She slowly wraps her arms around my waist like she's not entirely sure what's happening right now. "Umm . . . okay. So, if we both really like each other, why are we hugging like we're parting after summer camp instead of making out on your desk right now?"

"Because we're not going to make out today."

"We're not?"

"Nope." And this is the part that sucks. I pull away enough to look down at her. Her glasses are sitting an inch to the right, so I shift them back onto her nose.

Her brow is pinched, and if it's possible for a person to have sad cartoon puppy eyes, Lucy does. "Can I ask why not? Because the making-out option sounds like a win to me."

I smile and lean back against my desk, keeping a firm hand on Lucy's lower back, taking her with me. Her hips lean into mine, and her soft eyes drop to my mouth. One of her eyebrows lifts the tiniest bit, and a dreamy smile tugs at the corners of her lips. Her thoughts are practically projected above her head. She's imagining it—playing out every detail of what kissing me right now would be like—and I want more than anything to bring that fantasy to life.

I clear my throat and roll my shoulders back. "Because I promised your brother I wouldn't."

Lucy's eyes shoot up to mine, and her mouth falls open. She stares at me for approximately three seconds until my words fully register, and her body goes rigid. "I knew it! Ugh. You chauvinistic men, talking behind my back and deciding my life without me." She uses her hands to push off of my chest and gain some space, but I don't let her. Instead, I lean forward and grab her hips, pulling her back to me. She lands up against me with an *oof,* and I smile down at her, making her frown deepen. "No, don't smolder at me like that. I'm pissed at you and Drew right now."

"Me? Why are you upset at me?"

Her deep-blue eyes bounce back and forth between mine, angry fire flashing from her irises, threatening to spark out and singe me. I've seen Lucy embarrassed, comfortable, nervous, and flirtatious, but *this* is new, and I'd be lying if I didn't admit that it's sexy as hell. "You made the promise to my brother before talking to me first. This is the twenty-first century, Cooper. You should have told *me* you were interested first, and then *we* could have talked to Drew together. You can't just make decisions for a woman anymore—not unless you're dressed up in a hot, 1800s gentleman's outfit with a cravat and waistcoat . . . then I might make an exception."

I tighten my grip on her waist, feeling heat rise up from my toes and surge through my veins. "Was that a flirt?"

She narrows her eyes. "No, because I'm angry at you, remember? I don't even want to kiss you anymore." I'm holding her too tight for her to move away, so she crosses her arms over her chest instead. "Moment is over. Sorry, but you missed the boat, buddy. No Lucy for you."

"Really?" I pull her in tighter. There's no distance between us now. All of me is touching all of her, and everyone in the office can probably see what's happening, but I don't care. Far from it. In fact, my thumb slips under the hem of her shirt, and I glide it back and forth across her warm skin. "Well, that's tough, but I understand."

Her lashes flutter a little, and she looks down to where my thumb has journeyed into uncharted territory. "Well," she says, her voice a little breathy, "let's say, hypothetically, you didn't miss your boat . . . what are your travel plans for the future?"

I give her a little *eh* shrug and withdraw my hand, releasing her and standing up to retreat back to my side of the desk. Predictably—and just as I hoped—she grabs the lapels of my jacket and pulls me back in place. *Yeah. I like this new side of her.*

"Cooper. Please. I can't handle your sexy games. I want to be cool and suave like you, but my kneecaps are melting underneath me, and I don't know how to act around you. Do I pin you against the wall and force you to kiss me"—*Yes, always that option*—"or do I grab my box of donuts and leave? I haven't watched enough heated teen Netflix movies to know what to do in this situation!" She's shaking me a bit via my jacket, and just like every time I'm around Lucy, I can barely contain my laughter. But with that feeling of happiness comes a healthy dose of reality too.

I cover Lucy's hands with mine and stare down into her eyes, looking like one of those sappy fools I usually want to punch in the face due to how queasy they make me feel, but I can't help it. This woman, her sweetness, her odd quirks . . . they've turned me into some kind of vanilla pudding you're embarrassed to pull out at lunch. "Lucy, I want so much more with you . . . but I can't give you anything besides friendship right now."

"Because of Drew?"

I nod. "Because of Drew. I know it seems like I'm picking him over you, but that's not the case. He's nervous about the prospect of us because . . . well, he has a little reason to be. He hasn't ever seen me commit to anyone, and he knows you and Levi need a good man in your life who won't let you down."

"But—"

I put my finger on her lips. "It sounds absurd, but Drew's friendship is really important to me, Luce. Although he makes me want to slam my head against the wall sometimes, he feels like my brother in a lot of ways. I need his approval where you're concerned—which I do believe he'll give to me with time. But if I pursued a relationship with you right after he asked me not to, he would not react well. Imagine how much strain that would put on me and you right from the beginning?"

She lets out a sad little whimper and drops her forehead on my chest. "Yeah, you're right. That would suck. I can't even take it when Drew is upset at me for eating all of his Lucky Charms. Why do we have to love him so much?"

I wrap both of my arms tightly around Lucy, allowing myself this one last moment of intimacy with her before I force us back into the friend zone. "I know. He somehow has bigger puppy eyes than you do."

"It's because he used to practice them in the mirror as a kid. Got him better Christmas presents."

"Figures."

Lucy turns her face so her cheek is pressed up against my collarbone, and I can feel her breath on my neck. I know she's not trying to seduce me, but consider me fully seduced. With every hot exhalation against my skin, I feel my resolve slipping.

"So, what are you proposing we do?" Did she nuzzle in closer? Her lips definitely grazed my skin as she spoke.

I shut my eyes tight, forcing myself to think straight and tune out the pleas of my body. "I think we both have to agree that a relationship between us is off-limits for now. Strictly friends—at least until Drew gets home and we can both talk to him together about how we're feeling."

"What if he's never okay with it?"

"Then we'll become Romeo and Juliet."

"They both die in the end."

"Yeah, what's your point?"

Lucy laughs and puts her arms around me to squeeze me like a lemon. She and I stand here for another minute, her locked in my arms and our hips pressed together in a more-than-friendly way, both savoring what we know has to be the last form of contact between us for a while. At first, I think she's crying with all the sniffling sounds coming from her. Then I realize what she's actually doing.

I pull away enough to look down at her. "Lucy, are you smelling me?"

Her eyes are shut, and she smiles, not the least bit ashamed. "Yeah. It's weird, I know. But you smell like a cologne ad, and I think it makes my brain cells morph into new hormones. Can I just loosen your shirt and run my hands up your back real quick?"

I sputter a laugh and grab Lucy's now-wandering hand to pin it to my chest. She grins up at me, eyes sparkling, and now I can add *mischievous* to my list of favorite expressions from her. "You're going to be trouble, aren't you?"

"Tempting, dangerous trouble," she says, and I think the effect might have been stronger if all that eyebrow wagging she just did hadn't made her glasses sink down her nose an inch. Still, I want to kiss her. I want to take her bottom lip in my mouth and taste it.

"Yeah, you gotta go," I say, abruptly releasing her and turning to run my hand through my hair because *that* can't happen until after things are settled with Drew. Everyone knows how difficult *just friends* is once you've both established feelings. It's all happy times until one kisses the other and it breaks every boundary you've created. There's no going back after lips touch. The ground shatters, and you fall. I'll fall.

I hear her soft, pleased chuckle at knowing she successfully got under my skin, followed by the door to my office opening. "Sorry to interrupt, Mr. James, but your next meeting is here. Dr. Peterson."

I expel a breath, not quite ready to tear myself away from Lucy and jump back into work mode. "Thanks, Ashley. You can go ahead and send him in."

It's only after Ashley has left that I realize Lucy looks like someone just stole her purse and kicked her in the stomach. "Whoa, what's wrong?"

Her nostrils flare, and her jaw flinches. "Did she just say Dr. Peterson?"

"Yeah . . . he's one of my clients, a doctor who's working on re-branding his new private practice."

Lucy whimpers and looks like she's going to drop to the floor from sudden loss of feeling in her legs. "*Cooper!* Please tell me his first name is not—"

"Brent." It's only after I've said it out loud that I realize who he is.

Lucy begins gathering her purse and donut box as quickly as possible. "I have to go! Right now. I don't want to see him today. I have to prepare myself before a face-to-face with Brent because he always has this way of making me feel small, and clunky, and like a puddle of muddy water. I don't want to see him."

But when she turns around, we both spot him through the glass wall, approaching the office behind Ashley.

Lucy's shoulders sag in defeat, and my heart tugs for her. I know she doesn't have feelings for this guy. I think he just reminds her of that time in her life when she was made to feel like she wasn't enough for someone.

An idea forms in my mind, and suddenly my pulse is jumping in my neck. They say bad decisions are made on a whim, but I think what I'm planning to do next is the best decision of my life.

"Do you want to make Brent feel jealous today?"

She looks at me skeptically. "I'm not sure that's possible," she says slowly, sensing danger.

"If you want to find out, follow my lead."

As Ashley opens my office door, I grab Lucy around the waist, haul her up to my chest until I can feel every one of her curves pressing into me, and drop my head down, kissing her directly on those lips I've been dreaming about since I met her.

So much for not crossing that boundary. I can practically hear the ground beneath me cracking.

CHAPTER 24

Lucy

Did I just teleport into an alternate reality? Sure feels like it, because not two minutes ago Cooper was telling me we could only be friends. And now . . . well, this does *not* feel like friends.

It does, however, feel like warm lips, a strong body, and all kinds of hot and bothered mixed into one as he hungrily caresses my mouth. I decide not to care (*Ha!* Just kidding. It's actually that I can't form a thought coherent enough to resemble caring) and wrap my arms around Cooper's neck. He drags in a deep breath through his nose, and I relish the way his hands are biting into my back like he can't get me close enough.

Usually, kisses have a buildup, a soft-to-intense pliable rhythm that feels a lot like swimming in the ocean, floating over the waves one by one. Not this one. Cooper's kiss is devouring as if he's been dying for me. We tilt and slant, allowing our connection to some-how grow deeper. I'm not in the ocean; I'm on a roller coaster, and it's just crested the first drop. When I taste mint on his lips, my world goes fuzzy around the edges and fire tornadoes spin in my stomach. His hands blaze a trail from my lower back up to my jaw so he can cradle my face, and I drop my hands to wrap around his waist. He smells like cologne today—nothing intense, just professional and clean and attractive. I tunnel in on this kiss—our lips, our breath, his scent—and I lock my arms tightly around him. I'm not sure what is happening between us right now, but I'm willing to do it all day.

Cooper begins to slow the kiss, his lips softer and more yielding than before, and I refrain from whimpering like a sad puppy. *But then* his hands slide from my lower back to drop into the back pockets of my jean shorts, and now I'm the coolest girl in school. My head is spinning because I feel like we just zoomed from zero to one hundred in a blink. Even in all the time I dated Grim Tim, we *never* kissed like that. My heart never wanted to beat out of my chest like it does right now.

It's then that a throat clears, and I remember we're not alone. I think Cooper remembered the whole time, though. I rip my mouth away from him, and he smiles slowly before pulling his hands out of my pockets and turning to Ashley and Brent standing at the door, mouths gaping and eyes blinking. I'm sure I look a lot like them, but Cooper is the hot guy from *The Breakfast Club* and doesn't give a crap about things like public indecency.

Ashley finds her voice first. "I'm so sorry, Mr. James. I didn't realize you two . . . weren't finished yet." She and I both cringe at her unfortunate word choice.

Cooper lightly clears his throat on a chuckle. "No, I apologize. Lucy was just getting ready to leave, and the goodbye kind of got away from us." He looks over at me and winks. I wish I could focus on this moment to figure out what's happening, but instead all I can do is stare at Cooper's mouth and think, *That mouth was just on my mouth. How can I make it happen again?*

"Lucy?" Brent's voice has me peeling my eyes from Cooper's lips. "What—I didn't realize you . . ." He can't find the words to explain what he just saw. *You and me both, buddy.*

"Hi, Brent." I raise my hand stiffly, then lower it back down in the most awkward wave anyone has ever seen. Looked more like I should have been holding a traffic sign or introducing myself to extraterrestrials.

Cooper steps closer and puts his big, fantastic, possessive hand on my hip, holding me close to his side. It wraps around my entire hip bone as he grips me. "How do you know my girlfriend, Dr. Peterson?"

Hearing the word *girlfriend* makes me nearly choke on my own tongue. He asked his question so convincingly, like he had no idea in the world that Brent, once upon a time, ripped out my heart and stomped on it. He also added that special inflection men do on *girlfriend* (we'll get to freaking out over that word in a minute) that conveys a territorial caveman warning. Next, he'll get out a giant club and start waving it around.

Brent lets out a small, incredulous laugh. "She's . . . well, Lucy is . . . that is, Levi is my son. I'm assuming you know who Levi is?"

Cooper should be in a movie. The shocked expression on his face is so believable I want to laugh. I love being on this side of the curtain. "No way. You're *that* Brent? What are the odds?"

"Slim, I'd say," Brent says, a hardness to his voice I don't recognize. Is he . . . jealous? No. Never. Not Brent. "Lucy, I didn't realize you were dating anyone."

I shrug and smile, afraid to say much because my acting skills don't come anywhere close to Cooper's, and we all know it. "Just sort of happened. We met through Drew." It's best to stick as closely to the facts as possible when lying.

This moment is so thick with awkward tension I'm afraid we're going to need someone with a rope to pull us out. Poor Ashley; she feels it too and is unsure what to do. I raise my hand and tap a knuckle against Cooper's chest while hitching my head a little toward the door. Somehow, he speaks my silent language and understands me. "Oh, Ashley, you can go. Thank you."

She's relieved to exit this *Jerry Springer* episode and scurries out the door. Brent does not look happy that Cooper and I do not have to use words to communicate. Would it be too gloaty if I did a little *nana-nana-boo-boo* dance and stuck my tongue out at him? I'm not even into Brent anymore, wouldn't date the man if he begged me to. It's just that it feels the tiniest bit amazing to see a jealous expression on his face—the man who found me undesirable except for when he was using me. And yes, I realize it's super unhealthy. *I'll work on it tomorrow.*

"Come in and have a seat," Cooper says, gesturing toward his office chairs. "I'll walk Lucy out to her car and then we can get down to business." We're moving toward the door now, and Cooper looks like my bodyguard, escorting me away so the fans don't get too handsy. I need some sunglasses and a big floppy hat.

Brent steps into our path. "I can walk her out. It'll give me a chance to get caught up on this relationship between you guys." Oh no. *No, no, no.* I'll spill my guts with the truth that Cooper and I aren't really a couple yet, and this jealousy-inducing charade will backfire, making me look even more pathetic.

I look up in time to see Cooper's easy smile and tipped eyebrows, silently asking me what I want to do.

"I'll call you later and catch you up to speed, Brent. I'd like Cooper to walk me out." The strength and finality in my voice tickles my own spine.

Brent takes in a breath through his nose and lets it out while nodding slowly, thoughtfully. "Sure. I guess." He's not quite ready to let me go yet, though, and he turns his attention square on me. "So, where's Levi if you're here?"

Okay, *hello,* I do not care for the accusing tone he's using. He does realize I've spent nearly every single day with our son since I birthed him four years ago, right? That I've sacrificed absolutely everything to love my child well? He doesn't get to talk to me like that.

I speak through lightly clenched teeth. "He's with my mom, and after this she and I are taking him to fly his favorite kite at the park. Have you ever flown a kite with him before, Brent?" Yeah, no one was expecting that jab to come out there at the end, least of all me. I've never said anything like it to him before, and honestly, it's not totally warranted. Brent is a good dad when he has Levi. He's attentive, caring, fun, and never fails to be there if Levi asks him to. It's strictly me Brent strings along, ignores, uses, leaves, rinse-and-repeats. I'm just taking my years of frustrated rejection out on him in the form of questions about kites.

"Yes," he says, sounding both confused and amused by my intended sting. "Several times, actually. Don't you remember I took him to that kite festival a few months back too?"

"Oh . . . right." I'm a popped water balloon, confidence spilling out all over the place. "Good. Yeah, he loved that festival. Okayyyyy, well, I better be going. I'll call you later, Brent." I tuck my tail between my legs and speed toward the door so fast I'm sure my feet look like roadrunner-sized dust circles.

"Wait, Lucy, what are you guys doing tomorrow night? Maybe we could all go out to dinner—you two and me and Tanya—so I can get to know Cooper better? Since it seems he's going to be in your life and Levi's." Brent gives me a meaningful look this time, say-ing, *You have no choice.*

I don't have a choice, because I have insisted on going out to dinner with him and every single one of his girlfriends before I would allow Levi to stay with him for the weekend. I was never comfortable with the idea of my son spending time with some random woman, so it helped to at least get a sense of them over dinner first. Now he's throwing my rule back in my face. But . . . I guess it makes sense. I can't really fault him for it.

Except for the tiny detail that Cooper and I are not actually together and, just five minutes ago, were making a pact to remain strictly friends until Drew is on board.

"Umm, well, I think Cooper has—"

"I'm free," Cooper cuts in unhelpfully, then turns to look down at me. "Maybe we could ask your mom if she's free to come over and stay with Levi?"

Careful, Cooper. Your paternal instincts are showing, and it's super attractive.

"Sure. Okay." I look to Brent and smile. "I'll text you with de-tails."

"Don't worry about it. I'll make reservations somewhere and send you the info," says Brent, and I want to stomp on his toes because I know he's only doing this because he assumes I would make reservations at Chuck E. Cheese.

We finally give awkward goodbyes, and Cooper tells Brent he'll be right back, his hand landing on the small of my back, guid-ing me all the way to the elevator. He has to guide me because I'm not conscious anymore. My brain is lost in a fog of what just hap-pened, everything zooming past me as we walk like we're moving at warp speed.

We get in the elevator, and the moment the door closes Cooper lets go of me. That snaps me out of my trance, and I turn my eyes to him.

He's frowning as he leans back against the elevator rail. "Will you be mad if I say I hate that guy?"

A laugh shoots from me. "No. But *hate* feels like a strong word."

"It's not strong enough." His jaws clench. "He's so condescending to you. And what was that shit with the reservation about? You deserve so much better than that. You're the mother of his child for God sakes."

"Brent always thinks he's the most important, wonderful person in the room." It's why I was originally drawn to him. And ultimately why I'm repulsed by him now.

Cooper has a face for fighting. "I'm sorry I kissed you back there too. I shouldn't have."

My heart sinks. "You regret it?"

His eyes dart to me and his expression softens. "No—that's not what I meant. I just . . . I asked if you wanted to make him jealous, but that was immature of me to put it on you, because *I* was the one who wanted to make him jealous. You deserve better than how I treated you too."

I can't help the smile clawing at my lips. "Maybe you're right, but you don't hear me complaining about it."

His mouth tics ever so slightly in the corners as we continue to stare at each other—steeped in a moment of shared desire. Suddenly, this elevator is a sauna, and my clothes are going to catch fire.

It feels strange having him all the way over there when we were just pressed together like a peanut butter and jelly sandwich. Cooper reads my thoughts. "I have to stay over here."

"Why?"

"So I don't pick up where we left off in my office."

Every nerve ending in my body tingles. "Right. That would be terrible. Very bad. Us kissing is a very bad thing."

He smiles as the elevator door opens, but frankly, I'm annoyed at its timing because I was just about to try to work my feminine wiles one last time. He gestures for me to go out ahead of him, and then when I do, he swoops in behind me, leaning down like a spy whispering a top-secret message in my ear as we walk. "It's going to be the hardest thing I've done in my life to resist you, but I will, because I want to get this right. When Drew gets home, we'll talk to him."

I swallow and barely manage to keep moving. "But what about tomorrow night? You agreed to go on a double date as my boy-friend."

He nods with a slight grimace. "Yeah. Probably shouldn't have said yes. It was a knee-jerk reaction to that asshole and the posses-sive vibes he was giving off." He runs a hand through his hair, look-ing out over the street and then back to me. "Okay, tomorrow night we get a break from our off-limits rule—but only when Brent is present. All other times, no touching. Deal?"

I let my smile curve my lips, feeling more empowered from the leftover heat of our make-out session. "Deal. I think we better seal it with a kiss."

He shakes his head slowly at me. "Trouble."

He's right. For the first time in too many years, I finally feel like a little bit of trouble—in the best way possible.

CHAPTER 25

Lucy

"What underwear do you have on?" Jessie asks as I put the finishing touches on my soft-pink lipstick. Her question makes me jump, smearing it a little in the corner. *Great, now I look like a toddler.*

I look to where she's leaning against the bathroom doorframe and huff out an annoyed breath. "Wonderful. Now I have to fix this." Or maybe I should just take off the lipstick altogether? I'm not really a lipstick girl. I'm more of a swipe-on-some-mint-lip-balm-and-call-it-a-day kind of a person.

"Not my fault you're jumpy about your undies."

I rip off a piece of tissue and dab the corner of my mouth. "I'm not jumpy about my undies. I'm just jumpy in general. But to answer your question, don't worry, I'm wearing something new, cute, and lacy under this dress."

"Change it," she barks, making my shoulders jump again.

Jessie is here because she's quickly become my BFF in the cheesiest *Baby-Sitters Club* sense of the word, and also because she's going to stay here with Levi while I'm gone. Don't worry, I'm not one of those terrible friends who begs her pregnant, miserable friend to watch their kid while they go have a good time. The dinner reservation is for 7:30, when I knew Levi would already be asleep (which he is currently), and I stocked my pantry with a wide selection of chocolate, candy, and potato chips. I bought a leopard-print Snuggie and tied a bow around it for her to find when she goes to the couch, and I also started a seven-day free trial of HBO so she can watch whatever movie she wants—basically, I'm a saint.

"Huh? Change what?"

"The lace. Get rid of it and replace it with something scratchy and old. Period panties would be preferable if you have any—and I know you do because it's a universal truth. Bonus points if the elastic is worn out." She turns around and goes to my dresser, rummaging through the top drawer, which everyone knows is designated for intimates.

I watch, slightly horrified at the intense set of her shoulders as she dives into my underwear like she's searching for weird buried treasure. "Stop that! Are you seriously searching for gross old underwear?"

"Yes. Why would you think I'm joking?"

I go snatch away the *especially* unfavorable panties she has found and is brandishing like a victory flag. Her scary eyes tell me she might go plant them in Cooper's front yard or something. "I can barely tolerate looking at these horrible things as it is. Why in the hell would I want Cooper to see them?! I don't even think married people who've been together for decades like for their partners to see them in something like this horror show."

"Exactly." Jessie rips the panties back from my hand. This is a strange game of hot potato. "Do you have an old bra to pair with these? Something tan with a wire poking out and a gaping cup, maybe?"

"Ugh, just stop," I say, closing the drawer and only narrowly pausing for Jessie to extract her fingers. She deserves to have them chopped off for being the worst wingwoman in the history of wingwomen. "I'm not sure where you took your seduction classes, but I think you should get your money back."

Jessie crosses her arms over her little baby bump and lifts a taunting eyebrow—no smile anywhere to be found. "I'm not your wingwoman tonight. I'm your wing clipper."

"Oooh, how very Tinker Bell villain of you."

"Lucy, you need to put your boundaries in place right now. If you're not intending to sleep with Cooper tonight—and I don't think you are, because you're afraid to stand up to your brother— then you need to wear the most unappealing thing you can think of to act as a deterrent."

My shoulders sink. "First, I'm not afraid to stand up to my brother. Cooper and I both agreed we didn't want to get off to a rocky start with this relationship, so we're waiting until the idea grows on Drew."

Jessie has not been thrilled about our decision ever since I called her squealing and blabbering about it last night. "It shouldn't have to grow on Drew. It's none of his business."

"It is his business. I'm his sister, and Cooper is his best friend. Our choice is going to affect him." Even as I say the words, though, they don't feel quite right. It's bothered me ever since Cooper mentioned that Drew made this choice for me without my knowledge . . . like I couldn't be trusted to make my own good decision. It also bothers me that Drew doesn't see that Cooper *is* a good decision. I don't know. I've never been upset at Drew on this level before, never questioned his intentions toward me, so part of me wants to take these uncomfortable feelings and bury them somewhere until I know what to do with them.

Another part of me, however—the side that's learning to come out of hiding and go for the things I want—that part wants to tell my brother to stick his "good intentions" where the sun don't shine and let me live my life. I think I would if it didn't seem important to Cooper to gain Drew's blessing. So, for now, I go along with the off-limits rule.

Jessie presses her lips together and shakes her head. "My pregnancy hormones are raging too much to have a conversation with you where you stick up for your brother's bad choices."

"You're grumpy and need some chocolate."

She narrows her eyes into slits. "No. I. Don't. And I'm not grumpy." She looks to the side, grinding her teeth into dust before she looks back to me. "But if I did happen to want chocolate, where would I find it?"

I bite down on my smile because I'm afraid she might punch me if she sees it. Pregnancy hormones should never be underestimated. "Top shelf in the pantry."

She rolls her eyes because she's now a teenager who's committed to being annoyed with her parent even though they are doing something cool. "Okay. I probably won't even want it, though."

"Uh huh." I step forward to yank my period panties out of her hand one final time, then pull open the top drawer of my dresser, digging for my saggy, disintegrating, pathetic excuse for a bra. "You go and *don't* eat that chocolate while I go change into my chastity belt."

CHAPTER 26

Cooper

I'm almost to Lucy's house when my phone rings. I answer it over my truck's speaker without bothering to look at the caller ID because I know who's calling. "Hey, beautiful, I'm almost to your place. Traffic was terrible." Did I just call her beautiful? Was that weird? I've never been the guy to call women by little pet names like that, but it just kind of slipped out. What's happening to me?

"Awwwww, hello to you too, handsome."

Annnnnd I should have looked at the caller ID.

"Drew. I thought you were someone else." *Your sister.*

He chuckles. "I got that vibe. I mean, we both know I'm good-looking, but out of the two of us, you're definitely the beautiful one."

"Well, that's just not true. Your eyelashes are longer."

"You have nice cheekbones, though."

"Eh—they're okay. Your teeth are straighter. And they're so white."

"Thanks for noticing," he says, sounding genuinely grateful. "Wait . . . should we just get married?"

"Probably."

"This conversation has taken a turn somewhere."

Speaking of turns, I'm about to pull into Drew's driveway to secretly pick up his sister and take her on a fake date that will be entirely too real to me and lie to him about the whole thing. I'm a great friend. "What were you calling about? And how are you even calling me right now? Aren't you in a remote part of Costa Rica?"

"Yep. I have trouble getting service in my own bathroom back home, but Costa Rica's got me three bars." There's some commotion in the background, and I hear someone ask Drew about checking vitals on a patient. "I gotta go in just a second. We've been nonstop here. I just wanted to check and see if you've seen Lucy at all this week?"

"Why would I have seen Lucy?" *Whoa there, Cooper, let's take that defensiveness down a notch.*

I can hear the quizzical smile in Drew's voice when he says, "Relax, man, I wasn't trying to accuse you. I just haven't heard from her in a few days, and she hasn't returned my emails, so I was checking if you've seen her around at all?"

Damn, I'm a bad friend.

After tonight, though, I'm buckling back down. Lucy and I will take a major step back from each other until I get everything settled with Drew. I'll help her show off a little in front of her baby daddy, and then it's back to friends only.

"Yeah, I mean, I'd be happy to drive by your place right now and make sure everything looks all right if you want." In fact, the door to the house is opening, and Lucy steps out, allowing me to confirm that, yeah . . . everything's looking real good.

"I thought you were on your way to pick up your date?" Drew asks.

"Oh yeah, I am. Your place is kind of . . . in the neighborhood, so it's cool." Ah, shit. I'm becoming a worse liar as I get older.

"You all right? You sound a bit weird all of a sudden."

By *weird* he means I'm breathing heavy and slowly losing my mind at the sight of Lucy in a little black dress. Must be new. This one definitely wasn't in her closet the other day. I gotta get off this phone before he somehow assesses my blood pressure over the line. "Yeah, I'm good. Listen, I gotta go, man. Don't worry, I'll watch out for Lucy." *Won't take my freaking eyes off her for one second.*

Her blue gaze meets mine through the windshield right as the wind catches her long auburn curls. She's wearing black flats tonight instead of heels, but her curves still sway with every step. Now that I know what those curves feel like under my hands, they are twice as attractive.

She opens the door, and I put my finger to my lips to keep Lucy quiet just before Drew says, "Cool, man. Thanks for looking out for her."

Yeah, yeah, yeah. I flip him the mental bird because he's completely ruining my night of justified betrayal by dumping a load of sentimental crap on me. I'm no longer thinking about Drew, though, because Lucy steps up into my truck and the hem of her dress hitches up a few inches when she settles onto the bench.

"Yep, super-good friend over here. Talk to you later, Drew." I hang up and let out a long, exaggerated groan as my head drops back against the headrest. I roll it side to side and find a concerned-looking Lucy as she tilts her face to the same angle as mine.

"Hi," she says simply.

"Hi." I grin and take her in completely (just once) from head to toe. My eyes take a nice slow perusal inch by inch, and I'm not proud of it, but I whimper like a sad dog that's begging for a treat it can't have. "You look gorgeous."

When my gaze reaches her face again, Lucy's lips are slightly parted, and her eyes are . . . you guessed it, wide. She snaps her mouth shut, swallows, and then proclaims, "I'm wearing hideous underwear."

And this, ladies and gentlemen, is one of the reasons I'm falling for Lucy.

"Not going to help, but I applaud your efforts. Let's do this, Marshall."

CHAPTER 27

Lucy

Do you know what's awkward? Me and Cooper.

We both sit stiff as boards and don't say more than two words at a time for our entire twenty-minute drive.

"Good day?"

"Yep."

"Levi good?"

"Yep. You?"

"Mm-hmm."

His knuckles are white from where he's gripping the steering wheel. I think maybe he's upset at me, or having second thoughts about this fake date, until we speed into the parking lot and Cooper all but jumps out while the tires are still rolling. He flings my door open, reaches in, unbuckles me, and then tugs me out. I squeal, trying to keep up with him as he puts his hand on my lower back and propels me toward the restaurant. "Cooper! What are you doing?"

He doesn't answer, only barrels us through the front doors. The moment they close behind us, he grabs my hand and yanks me into a somewhat secluded corner of the waiting area. He puts his hands on my jaw, backing me against the wall. "There," he says with a mischievous grin. "We're officially on our fake date. The off-limits rule is suspended, and for the next two hours you're all mine."

I suck in a breath as Cooper dips his head and lays a hot kiss on the base of my neck, making sparks fly across my skin. "*Cooper!* We're in a restaurant."

He stacks another kiss above the last, making himself a little trail up my neck. "You smell incredible. How do you always smell like this? Sweet and soft and like berries . . . or . . . I can't figure it out."

"People are staring!" I say in a whisper-hiss, but I feel my desire to care losing the fight as Cooper's hand slowly glides from my shoulder down to my fingers, where mine and his intertwine.

"Good. It'll really sell this relationship to Trent."

I chuckle as his skin brushes across my jaw. "You mean Brent?"

"Sure." Cooper rounds my jaw with kisses, and I melt into his strong body. "You look beautiful, Lucy," he says, pulling away enough to look me in the eyes.

My heart flips in my chest, and I didn't realize how much I needed to feel this way until Cooper came along. Didn't realize how much I had dimmed my light, forgotten to do things for myself, fallen into a contented slumber where all I worried about was if Levi was smiling and safe. Don't get me wrong, those two things are—and will always be—the most important to me. But somewhere along the way, I forgot that I could be Levi's mom *and* still be a woman. They say if a plane starts to go down, adults need to pull on their masks first so they can then take care of the children. I had forgotten to pull my mask on. And until Cooper came along, I didn't realize my oxygen was running out.

Now I'm breathing again and realizing I can be both Lucy the woman and Levi's mom.

I feel like I'm waking up from a long sleep. Or no . . . like I'm growing into something new. Because I'm not the same woman I was before I had Levi; I'm stronger, warmer, *fluffier,* and wiser. And I think it's okay that I'm changing—good, even. Because the old Lucy would have been too afraid of rejection to initiate a kiss in front of a restaurant of people. The new Lucy, however, rises up on her tiptoes, grabs the front of Cooper's shirt, and plants her lips firmly on his with abandon.

I feel Cooper smile against my mouth as his hands slide around my back and pull me in tight. I wrap my arms around his neck and sink into our kiss, even daring to lightly taste his bottom lip. A quiet groan sounds from the back of his throat, and I'm no longer worried about the world around us. Neither is he. We're like that sappy newlywed couple you can't bear to be around and want to unfriend on social media. I love it.

Kissing Cooper feels so good it makes me irrational. Like I want to run out and have someone make us matching airbrush T-shirts with our couple name on them. *Luper* or *Coocy.* Choices, choices. I'll make an Instagram poll and have my twenty followers decide for me.

"Is this all you guys do?" Brent says from somewhere behind Cooper, sounding disgusted with a capital *D.*

I extract my lips from Cooper and pry my eyes open, taking in his lopsided smile, and honestly, I want to dive right back in. Maybe if I ignore Brent, he'll just go away?

Cooper leans forward and kisses my forehead briefly before turning to face Brent and his girlfriend, Tanya. "Pretty much. It's tough to be around Lucy and not kiss her." Does he really mean that? It's not just part of the fake-date act, right? I hope he and I are on the same page that this is a *fake* fake date and that I'm taking to heart every little thing he says; otherwise, I'm going to be crushed when this is all over.

Brent clearly has no idea what to do with that statement because he's never once felt that way about me, so he turns the conversation to Tanya and introduces his runway-model girlfriend to Cooper. Just kidding, she's not a model. She's actually a bioengineer who *looks* like a model, so you can imagine how hard it is for me to feel incredible in this moment. *Should have worn the lace.* Luckily, I really like Tanya. She's sweet and has always been kind to me.

After awkward introductions, the hostess takes us to our table with Brent and Tanya leading the way. I'm trying hard to stay positive and affirming toward my body while being faced with Tanya's firm booty swaying in front of me, and I would say I do a moderately good job of it. I'm in the middle of mentally telling myself that even though her beauty is different than mine, it doesn't mean mine is less than hers when Cooper's hand slips behind me, and before I can register what's happening, he lightly pinches my left butt cheek. I gasp and look up at him with wide eyes, my melancholy from a moment ago erased and laughter buzzing through me.

Cooper gives me the most overly innocent eyes and helpless shrug I've ever seen. "It's what I'd do if we were really together. Got to stay in character."

I can't hold it in. I laugh and lean into him, wrapping both of my arms around his biceps, walking like this the rest of the way to the table. He kisses the top of my head with a smile on his mouth, and I can't help but wish this moment could be permanent.

Maybe it can be.

I want to kill Brent. My hands are itching to wrap around his neck because of how frustrating and terrible he's been to me all night. First, he asked how Cooper and I met, and when Cooper told him the story of me jumping off the cliff, Brent made an obnoxious comment, insinuating I must have been drunk, because I would never do something fun like that. Then he tried to act like a buddy-buddy man's man with Cooper and nudged him across the table, asking him if he'd seen my *usual look* yet. He insinuated heavily that the way I look tonight is nothing close to how I look on a daily basis. Cooper—bless him—responded, saying he was actually disappointed I didn't wear my dinosaur pants tonight. I wanted to put my hands in his hair and kiss him into oblivion.

The dinner proceeded just like that, with lots more tiny little digs at me from Brent that felt so out of place I almost couldn't believe it was happening. He never treats me like this—putting me down in front of other people. He and I truly have always been like two platonic-friendish people raising a kid together, so the hostility he's shown me this evening makes no sense. It feels intentional and personal.

"So, Cooper, I know we're already briefly acquainted through work, but tell me more about yourself outside the work world," Brent says like he actually cares while dabbing the corner of his mouth with his napkin. I try to hide an eye roll, because I know he doesn't care about Cooper. I've proved myself able to make good choices where Levi is concerned over these past four years, so he's not really doing this out of a need to know that Levi is safe. I think this is his way of getting revenge because I'm the one who doesn't trust him to make good choices about what company he keeps.

"Sure," says Cooper, with an easy smile that makes my insides melt. He drapes his hand over the back of my chair and rubs a soft line up and down the back of my neck while keeping his attention focused on Brent. My world is spinning. "What do you want to know?"

"What do you like to do for fun?" Brent's eyes follow Cooper's hand as it tenderly caresses my neck, and then something odd happens. He lifts his arm and wraps it around Tanya's shoulders. Am I imagining things, or does that seem a little competitive?

"In the summer, I like to wakeboard"—*Ah! I know this!*—"and the rest of the time I'm pretty easy. I like to read, watch movies, maybe go hiking occasionally."

"Hiking," Brent scoffs. "Good luck getting Lucy to do anything outdoorsy with you." I frown at Brent because it's annoying that he's acting like he knows me when he doesn't, and also that he's trying to make me look bad in front of Cooper.

"I'd actually love to go hiking with you."

"Yeah? I'll take you any time you want, Luce."

Brent snorts again, and I have no idea where this is coming from, but let me tell you, I'm sick of it. "Sorry, I'm just not buying it."

Cooper's hand falls from my neck to rest on my thigh. It's not meant to be seductive; it's comforting. His glare across the table, however, is terrifying. "Well, it's a good thing it's none of your business then, isn't it?"

Brent frowns and leans forward to rest his elbows on the table. "As long as you're around my kid, you and the mother of my child's business becomes my business." He did *not* just say that. Someone, hold my earrings! This man suddenly trying to act like he is devoted to Levi rather than an occasional part of his life is really getting on my nerves.

"So, what's this really about, man?" asks Cooper, his voice calm but with an edge to it that has me covering his hand where it rests on my leg. Cooper is tall with a powerful build, and I've never thought of it as dangerous before. But with that sharpness aimed at Brent, I see he is not a man you'd want to mess with.

"Excuse me?" Brent shoots back, adding his own taunting inflection.

Tanya interjects by waving the drinks menu in the middle of the table like a flag. "Who wants another drink? I'm thinking maybe a white wine this time? What about you, Lucy? Cocktail?" She gives me a happy smile, and—*sweet darling*—she really thinks that's going to distract the guys from whatever is boiling between them.

"I'm just wondering why you seem to be shooting down everything Lucy has said tonight. Seems odd to me for a man who's never been in a relationship with her to pretend he knows her so well."

I tug on Cooper's sleeve a little, trying to figure out how to stop this train that has clearly left the station. I'm afraid I'm going to have to throw my body in front of it—and not in a sexy way.

Brent rolls his shoulders a little and nods toward me. "I just think this whole thing is *odd*. One minute Lucy's single and living with Drew, and the next you two are all over each other anywhere I turn. I'm making sure whatever this is you guys have going on is healthy and that Levi is not going to get hurt in the mix." On the surface, that sounds true and noble. But it's in his eyes that you see his words are a front. I am all for Brent wanting to get to know any man I'm seriously dating so he can feel comfortable with Levi being around him too. Even if it is a little unconventional, it's always worked for us. But what I can't stand for is his insinuation that I would put my child in an unhealthy situation and that Brent should be the judge of it—especially in such a public way.

"No, that's not it. Lucy would never put anyone in Levi's life that isn't good for him and you know it." Cooper's smile is cunning and sort of tingles my spine. "We both know why you're acting like a dick tonight, and it has nothing to do with your concern for Lucy or Levi."

Brent's eyebrows fly up, and he looks to me like I should be his backup. When he sees I'm not coming to his defense, he sinks back in his chair and steeples his fingers in front of him. "Well, by all means, tell me, since you seem to know already."

Cooper's smile falls, and now his face looks like beautiful stone. His eyes flare as he locks them on Brent. "If I had to guess, I'd say you've always kept Lucy as your backup option." I wince at Cooper's words, feeling the uncomfortable truth in them. "She was having your child, but you weren't ready to commit, so you tossed her to the back burner. But it seems like you try to keep a spark of hope alive in Lucy so when you're ready to settle down, she'll be there."

Is Cooper right? His words are alcohol on a wound I didn't know I had. Did Brent think I was only back-burner material? Somehow, that feels worse than him just *not* having feelings for me.

Cooper leans forward slightly and smiles, looking more like a feral animal baring its fangs than a person giving a friendly greeting. "But here's problem number one." Cooper holds up a finger, sarcastic smile still in place. "You're a selfish ass, too arrogant to believe Lucy stopped wanting you a long time ago." Another finger pops up. "Number two, you weren't counting on me coming along and seeing that a woman like Lucy is not plan B. She's the one you work your ass off to try to come even *close* to deserving and still know at the end of the day she's only with you because you're *lucky*. Like it or not, I'm here for Lucy as long as she'll let me be in her life, so you need to knock it off with the rude comments. As for Levi, you sure as hell better believe I'm going to take care of him." Cooper's head tilts slightly to the side after his breathtaking monologue, and he turns remorseful eyes to me. "Uh . . . sorry about the language, Luce. I'm working on it so it doesn't slip around Levi so much. I'll get better."

A laugh bubbles out of me, closely followed by a few tears I really wish weren't leaking out of my eyes, because no one has ever stuck up for me in that way. I also find it absurdly endearing that, after all that, Cooper is worried I care about his mild language.

I lean forward and lay a soft kiss on his lips, pulling away only far enough to hover my mouth over his and whisper, "You're the one who taught him *freaking*, aren't you?"

"Maybe. Maybe not," he whispers back, and I wonder if maybe there's a supply closet or something he and I can slip away to. It's fair game, right? We're still technically just "faking it."

Brent plops his napkin down on his plate. "Well, this is definitely the weirdest and most awkward dinner I've ever had, and it's safe to say we won't be working together on rebranding anymore." I think we all silently acknowledge that he is not defending himself against Cooper's accusations right now. "Maybe you could have waited to make that speech until after the check came? Could have stormed out on a powerful note and made more of an impact."

"Nah," Cooper says, settling back and resting his hand on my knee. "We don't have anywhere to be." He looks at me from the corner of his eye, and we speak our secret language again. When we leave this date, the no-touching rule falls back into place.

Would it be weird if I sat in his lap in the middle of this restaurant? Yeah . . . I might still do it anyway.

After our *fake* date, Cooper drops me back off at my house. Neither of us touched the other the entire ride home, each the epitome of decorum. It was complete torture, but I'm willing to go along with it because it's important to Cooper to wait until we talk to Drew.

I step into the dark house and immediately find a little leopard blob sunk into the couch, feet propped up on a pillow on the coffee table, a halo of junk food scattered around her body.

"Hi there," I say, leaning over the back of the couch to make eye contact with Jessie.

Her dark eyes pop up at me from beneath her Snuggie fort. "I ate it all." Her voice is flat. "Every bit. Like a hundred thousand calories, and I couldn't stop myself." Her voice shakes on the last two words, and now I realize she's not being funny.

I rush around the side of the couch and push through all the wrappers and sharp chip crumbs to cuddle in beside her. She lifts a corner of her Snuggie and lets me inside. It's warm and cozy, and exactly what I need.

"Well, good. Because I got it all just for you to eat and enjoy. You're pregnant—it's one of the few perks."

She sniffles. "That's the problem. I don't want to be pregnant anymore. I don't even know if I want to be a mom. Have I made a terrible mistake?"

I've been in Jessie's exact shoes, and I know how she's feeling. Which is why I don't pounce on her statement with fear or judgment. I don't try to convince her to take those words back with my own placating ones. Whatever she needs to feel right now is valid, and I want her to know it.

I put my hand on her belly because I remember how much I wished someone would sit beside me and love my belly bump—just share in the joy of it. "It *is* scary. What else are you feeling?"

Jessie's eyes shut tight like she's trying so hard to keep her tears locked inside. "My butt's getting lumpy, and I don't love that."

"Ugh, it's the worst. The dimples get real. Mine were like craters."

"And I'm getting stretch marks on my boobs."

"We call those *tiger stripes,* babe. Get the terminology right."

Jessie spills out a laugh, and together we shake on the couch. I feel the baby kick against my hand, and Jessie does too. Her smile dips into a frown. "This wasn't the plan. When I read the pregnancy test, I was excited. Not the least bit hesitant. The problem is it never crossed my mind I'd have to do it alone at that point. I thought . . . we were going to be a family."

"And he doesn't want to be?"

She shakes her head no.

I rub a little circle on her still-small baby bump. "Well—with or without him, you're not alone anymore. You have me, and I'll be here for you every step of the way if you'll let me. And just because the *unfortunate sperm donor* isn't in the picture doesn't mean you're any less of a family."

"Thank you, Lucy." Jessie sniffs. "And thank you for not promising me I'll find someone someday, or this will all be worth it in the end, or any of that other crap. I hate when people say those things. It all feels so fake and empty."

I roll my head to the side to look at Jessie. "I've seen too many of life's twists and turns to make promises of sunshine and butterflies . . . but I can promise to hold your hand no matter what comes at you next." She smiles and I add, "Well, that is if I don't, like, die tomorrow or something."

She can't believe I just said that. "I don't know what to do with you sometimes."

"People rarely do. Now, did you save me *any* candy?"

"You might be able to find a Skittle wedged under one of my boobs."

I grimace. "I'm sure that would be a real treat for someone, but it's just not doing it for me."

"Fair enough. How did your night go?"

I unzip the side of my dress so my body can breathe and pull my legs up underneath me. My skin pops out like a can of biscuits when you first crack it open and the dough tries to jump out.

"It was one for the books, but here are a few highlights: Cooper is an excellent kisser. He also called Brent out for keeping me as his 'back-burner option.' Brent did not deny it. And after sitting silent for nearly fifteen minutes, Tanya abruptly broke up with Brent when it finally sank in how much of a butthead her boyfriend is."

"Ooooh, I love public breakups. Did you film it?"

"No, I couldn't get my phone out in time."

"Amateur."

"And then!"

"There's more?" I knew Jessie would eat this up.

"Much more. Brent left right after Tanya, but Cooper and I stayed and enjoyed the last bit of our fake date. Then, when we left, Brent was waiting outside for me."

"No!"

"Yes. He asked to speak with me privately, and of course, Cooper was fine with it because he's the best. But when Brent got me alone, he said Cooper was right, and he hadn't realized it, but he had always been keeping me in the back of his mind as the woman he would settle down with when he was ready. And that he thinks he's finally ready."

"Flattering."

"Exactly. He tried to kiss me too, but I did that amazing move where you turn your face to the side and he only gets the cheek."

"Savage!" Jessie is perched up on her knees now, listening intently. I'm happy my trainwreck of a life is giving her joy. I'm so giving.

"I got to tell him that I might have been waiting for him at one point, but not anymore. That I want someone who can see my worth from the start and he'd missed his chance. It would have been such an empowering moment."

"Would have been?"

"Yeah, at the end of my speech, my decrepit bra gave up its will to live, and the fastener broke, giving these mom boobs the freedom to let themselves out the bottom of the cups like a dam breaking. It was quite the sight. Looked like I had two sets of boobs."

Jessie's mouth is wide open now, and she shakes her head, just now realizing I'm no longer wearing a bra. "How?! How do these things happen to you?"

"I'm special."

Jessie matches my smirk. "Cooper definitely thinks so . . . is that a hickey?! Weren't you not allowed to touch outside of the restaurant?"

Now I'm smiling like the Grinch. "Yeah. The restaurant got dinner *and* a show."

Jessie and I both laugh, and it feels so good. Good to have a friend. Good to be home late. Good to know I'll wake up in the morning to my favorite little boy and make pancakes. Everything feels good right now. How did I hold myself back from this for so long? I was trying to force myself into a picture of who I thought I should be, and it was suffocating. Now I'm here, I'm growing, breathing, and I might not be the exact image of what motherhood should be, but I am full of messy happiness, and that's enough for me.

Jessie and I end up talking until way too late in the night for her to drive home. She stays over, and when Levi wakes up in the morning and busts into the living room, diving into my arms for my favorite morning snuggle session, Jessie gets to see it all, and I'm glad. This—a picture of what will be—is far more encouraging than any speech I could have given her. She stays for pancakes, and Levi starts calling her Aunt Jessie before breakfast is even on the table.

I disappear for a few minutes to shower, and when I go into my room, I find my phone lit up with a text message on my nightstand.

COOPER: Just thought I'd let you know my pantry is empty.

I frown, wondering if he sent me this by mistake.

COOPER: So I'm going to the grocery store today after work.
COOPER: The one on the corner of 8th.
COOPER: Probably around 6. So . . . yeah. If you have an emergency, don't come by my house at that time to find me . . . because I'll be at the grocery store . . . on 8th.

I bite down on a smile, thinking the off-limits rule might be a little fun after all.

LUCY: Shoot, would you look at that? I just ran out of milk. I definitely need milk for Levi's cereal tomorrow. Looks like I have to go to the grocery store later.

CHAPTER 28

Cooper

I have never felt like more of a creeper in my life than I do now, pushing my empty cart down every grocery store aisle, eyes hunting for a woman and her son. The lady with the high ponytail and yoga pants is seconds away from calling security. Well, I am too, because she keeps pushing her cart down every aisle I'm headed toward, and it's starting to really annoy me. For someone who doesn't want to be stalked, she sure is doing a poor job of trying to avoid it.

I speed-race my cart to the end of the aisle and loop around to choose a different one from high-ponytail lady—but would you look at that? She did the same thing. Now we're headed straight for each other, and I realize this person is a little strange. Almost looks like she *wants* to be stalked.

Where is Lucy? I've been cruising this place for twenty minutes with an empty cart, and I don't know how much longer I can do this without getting arrested.

I approach Ponytail with a soft face and my most non-creepy

I'm-not-a-murderer demeanor, hoping to just quickly sail right by her. I can't, though, because at the last second she jerks and knocks her cart into mine bumper-car style. It's so unexpected and jarring that my knee-jerk reaction is to throw my hands out in front of me and apologize for a mistake *I didn't make.*

"I'm so sorry! I don't know how that happened." But I do know. I want to point an accusing finger at the woman and yell *She did it!* because I'm a little afraid this is going to be a second mark against me in this grocery store—lurking and then causing a scene. One more strike and I'll be kicked out. Then I'll be forced to man up and go see Lucy at her house instead of a grocery store where we "accidentally" bump into each other. Yeah, it's a wimpy move, making her see me in public places like this, but I don't trust myself with her alone. And if I want to keep everything above board until Drew gets home, this is my only option.

Anyway, Ponytail is doing something strange now.

"Hi," she purrs while running a delicate finger along the front of my cart. I strangle a laugh in my throat because never have I ever had anyone come on to me via metal grocery cart before. "I know you've been trying to get up the courage to talk to me for a few aisles now"—*oh please no*—"so I thought I'd take matters into my own hands. I'm Kate."

As I watch Ponytail Kate subtly lick her lips, it becomes clear I'm not dealing with a normal person. She should be alerting an attendant about me, not fondling my grocery cart. And let me be clear, even if I wasn't into Lucy, I'd still be getting the hell away from this woman as fast as possible.

"Uh, sorry. I think you misinterpreted. I'm just—" My statement is cut off when something—or someone—rams into my legs from behind.

"We found you!"

Huh?

I look down to find two chubby little arms wrapped tightly around my legs, followed by the sexiest hands I've ever seen slowly sliding around my abs and up to my chest. *What is happening to the women in this grocery store?!*

"Hi, babe," says Lucy—*oh thank God, it's Lucy*—peeking her twinkling eyes around my shoulder to grin up at me. "Making friends?" she asks, squeezing in tighter before wedging herself up under my arm to face Ponytail, one arm wrapped possessively around my waist with my arm draped over her. She's doing that thing where she plays with my fingers dangling over her shoulder, and I have the strongest urge to tell her this is the hottest thing I've ever experienced in a grocery store.

"Oh uh—" Ponytail looks between me and Lucy and then down at Levi. "Sorry. Oh gosh—I didn't realize . . . I thought you were coming on to me." *Did she really, though?*

I bend down to pick Levi up and put him on my shoulders. He laughs as I stand to my full height and wrap my arm around Lucy's shoulder again. "Nope. I've just been looking for these two all along."

Lucy's playful smile dims into something meaningful as she looks up at me, trying to see if I buried a hidden meaning inside my statement, Hallmark style.

I did.

"Okay, well . . ." Ponytail looks mildly annoyed. Like she's offended at the prospect of me having a family. "I guess I'll go then?"

It's alarming that she phrased it as a question.

"Buh-bye," Lucy says with a catty squinty smile.

Ponytail Kate pushes by us, and Lucy whips around to me with wide eyes. "Be honest—how often does this happen to you?"

"Children running up and randomly bear-hugging my leg? This would be a first."

"No, I meant how often do women try to pick you up in the bread aisle?"

I shrug like a player. "Not my fault I'm a *snack*," I say, making her laugh and jab me in the ribs. "But seriously, this is the first time. Did you see her scary eyes? I'm worried to find out what she would have done to me if I let her take me home." I shiver playfully.

Lucy's shoulders relax. "Good. For a minute there I was worried you would be upset I interrupted." She tries to pass her statement off as a funny *ha-ha* moment by chuckling, but it has an undertone of insecurity to it that I can hear from a mile away.

"Luce, I'm here for you—and eggs, but mainly you." I grin and bend down, holding tight to Levi's legs so he doesn't topple off while I kiss Lucy's cheek. *Just her cheek; this is totally acceptable behavior.* I watch her face turn my favorite shade of rosy, and she presses her lips together, hiding her smile.

"Okay, well then, let's go get you those eggs."

And then, without thinking, we abandon my empty cart, and I walk beside Lucy, Levi on my shoulders and her pushing a cart. She grabs a loaf of bread and tosses it inside the basket, and I do too. Levi leans to grab a bag of donuts from the top shelf, but I do a quick lunge. He laughs, and now it's a game as I'm lunging up and down the aisle, quads burning and cheeks aching from too much smiling. I look like a cheeseball, one of those poor fools you frown and shake your head at for losing all his game when he chooses to lower himself to physical comedy for the sake of his kid.

Here's what I never saw before, though: those *poor fools* don't give a shit about their game because they don't need it. If their partners are looking at them like Lucy is looking at me, they're not having any trouble in *that* department.

We carry on through the grocery store, checking items off her paper list and seeing if they correspond with the mound of coupons clutched in Lucy's rainbow-nail-polished hand, and I honestly can't believe I'm enjoying this. I am, though. I've never felt more content, and I'm wondering if everyone out there getting ready to go bar crawling tonight knows how lit the grocery store can be.

As Lucy walks close to me, her arm brushing against mine and her smile dimpling as she tells me about the intimacy advice the old lady who got a perm today gave her, I want to pin her up against the canned soups and try out some of the suggestions Lucy's relaying to me via spelling so Levi doesn't learn new things. And I would—I'm not afraid of PDA—except Levi is on my shoulders, so I have to behave. It's good she brought Levi.

He tugs my right ear to signal which direction I'm supposed to turn, and Lucy slips her hand into mine. I should probably be focused on my own grocery shopping, but I can't because I'm mesmerized by Lucy's soft skin. She's running her thumb up and down the side of mine, and I'm dying inside. How can that tiny touch spark so much inside me?

I'm seconds away from telling her we need to get out of here. Go home. Put Levi to bed. The groceries can rot in the car for all I care. I'll replace them all in the morning, whatever. I just need Lucy.

"I need to pee," Levi says from above my head, which is honestly a nice dose of reality.

"Whatever you do, bud, please hold it until I set you down."

Lucy laughs beside me because she can see the sudden horror on my face. I may be getting better at the whole being-around-a-kid thing, but I'm not ready to be peed on yet. Not sure I ever will be.

"Come on, buddy, I'll take you," Lucy says, helping Levi down off my shoulders.

"Mom," Levi says in what I would describe as a courtroom voice, "Grammy lets me go in by myself when it's just one bathroom. I can do it," he says, pleading his case effectively, I would say.

Lucy and I both look toward the bathroom and note that it is a single-stall room. She looks to me for some reason—like she wants my opinion. Like my voice in this situation matters. And, somewhat strangely, I do not take this lightly. It feels big. *Don't screw this up, Cooper.*

"Let me go in and make sure it's not gross first."

"Oh," says Lucy, looking surprised. She wasn't expecting that answer, and I wonder if it was weird. What exactly am I supposed to be looking for in here anyway? I don't know . . . but just to be safe, I rip off a few paper towels and do a quick wipe-down because, apparently, becoming a parent also turns you into a janitor.

"There," I say, opening the door like Superman, fresh from saving the whole freaking world rather than wiping some pee off a toilet seat. "All clear, bud. Have at it, and don't forget to wash your hands."

I nod. Levi nods. We're just two men taking care of business—nothing to see here.

Levi shuts the door (and locks it, which is a little frightening), and I turn around to find Lucy staring at me with a quizzical smile that makes my stomach flip.

"What?" I ask with my own questioning grin.

She shakes her head. "When I first met you . . . I just never would have guessed you'd be like this." She gestures toward the bathroom door.

"Like what?"

She inhales a deep breath and pulls her shoulders up toward her ears. "Soft. Sweet. I mean, I knew you had all the other qualities I like in a man—sexy, handsome, a big flirt, exciting . . ."

"No, no, go on. I like hearing how sexy you think I am."

She tries to swat my arm, but I catch her hand and pull her up to me. *Finally.* I've got Lucy in my arms, and it's the best I've felt all day. I shouldn't be holding her, but I can't help it.

She tilts her head up to me and pulls her arms up between our chests, letting me fully hold her, right here—outside the men's bathroom. "I just didn't think you could have it all. I thought there would be a catch somewhere, some glaring flaw hiding beneath the surface."

I squint dramatically. "Well, you haven't seen my collection of Russian nesting dolls yet."

"Is it impossible for you to be serious?"

"Nearly, yes."

"Cooper," she says, her voice dropping a notch and taking on a more sultry tone that has my heart rate ramping up. "I like us together." Her finger inches up to trace a line over my collarbone, her eyes tracking the movements like she's studying and memorizing every small trip her finger takes.

I know I don't have long before Levi comes out of that bathroom, so I grab Lucy's hips and swing her around so her back presses up against the wall. My hand cups her jaw as my other sweeps around her lower back. I don't know if I dip my head down or if she rises up onto her tiptoes, but what I do know is, in the next moment, my mouth is slanted over Lucy's. Most kisses start soft and mount into something hungry—this one is consuming from the start. Her tongue sweeps my mouth and I return the favor. Drinking her in and unable to get enough.

We're kissing like two teenagers trying to perfect the process when the handle of the bathroom door jiggles. Lucy and I break apart like a KitKat bar. She flings herself across the small hallway and leans against the wall, while I turn a half circle, not sure where to go until I realize we're adults and don't have to hide.

Levi opens the door, smiling ear to ear, pride beaming from his chubby little cheeks, and steps out. "Told you I could do it," he says to Lucy, whose face is flushed and lips are swollen from *me*. I wonder if my cheeks are beaming with as much pride as Levi's are.

She laughs, catching my eye briefly and giving me a rueful grin before putting her hands on Levi's shoulders and guiding him back toward our full cart. "Never doubted you for a second, buddy."

I stay in the hallway for a moment longer, watching Lucy and Levi walk out together and feeling something snap into place in my head: *I will do anything to be in their life.* And another thought directly follows that one: *I'm so glad Janie refused me.*

. . . and also: *Lucy's butt looks so good in those jeans.*

I jog to catch them, run up behind Levi, and pick him up by the armpits so I can make a *rawr* sound and swing him up onto my shoulders. I didn't even know I knew how to make that noise and definitely didn't plan to. It just sort of came naturally, which is surprising. Once he's laughing and settled on my shoulders, I nudge Lucy with my hip, pushing her out of the way so I can steer the cart. She wraps her arm around my biceps, and now we're one happy family. It's odd how you can know someone for such a short period of time and yet feel like you've always been there with them. That's how being with Lucy and Levi makes me feel.

Lucy lets go of me briefly to grab a bag of apples off a produce shelf, then Levi suddenly shouts, "UNCLE DREW!"

Lucy and I both freeze, slowly make eye contact, then look up to find Drew holding a shopping basket a ways down the aisle and staring blankly at us.

Okay, so maybe the grocery store wasn't the best meeting place, and I'm definitely the worst friend in the world.

CHAPTER 29

Lucy

"Drew," I say, resisting the urge to shove Cooper as far away from me as possible. "You're home early."

"Yeah. A guy from our team had a family emergency, so the trip got cut short and we had to fly back early. Then one of my bags was lost at the airport, so I stopped in to buy more deodorant and toothpaste before going home." I know that look on his face. He's processing—unhappily. His eyes shift from me to Levi up on Cooper's shoulders, then fall down to Cooper, where they land with an angry scowl.

Feeling this surge of protection for Cooper, I hurry to say, "Oh bummer! About your bags, not you coming home early. That's a good thing! We've missed you. Uncle Drew is back, *yay!*" From the corner of my eye, I see Cooper mouthing *stop* and realize I'm rambling. Shoot. Drew will see right through that. "So anyway, Levi and I were just doing some shopping and bumped into Cooper. Funny, right?" Is he buying my fake calm smile? Probably not, but I'm trying to sell it like I'm on QVC. *And here we have a lovely new lie in the intriguing shade of blushing! Order now before the truth comes out and everyone's lives are miserable!*

I look up at Cooper, who is also frowning now. Super. We're the Frowny Bunch.

"Looks a lot like you're shopping together," Drew says, only mildly less uncomfortable than he was a moment ago. "Where's Cooper's cart?" Who asks a question like that? A skeptical person, that's who.

Cooper opens his mouth, and I can see honesty all over his sweet face. It's killing him to lie to Drew about us, and he probably thinks I want him to come clean and put us first. He'd be wrong. I know how much Drew means to Cooper, and I won't be the reason their relationship is severed. We had a plan to ease Drew into the idea of this relationship, and we're going to stick to it.

I step forward and pull on my no-big-deal face, giving a lazy wave of my hand. "Oh, he had one at some point, but then Levi wanted to ride on his shoulders, so he ditched it, and we combined our carts. Want to join us? There's totally room for your stuff to pile in here too!" *Okay, take it down a notch, Lucy. No one is this excited about grocery shopping.* Someone from this store franchise should be filming me right now and turning it into a commercial, because apparently I love shopping for groceries more than anything in the world and want everyone to join me.

It works, though, because Drew buys it. He finally closes the gap and steps into our space, and Levi leans forward to jump into his arms. "Hey, buddy! I missed you!"

"I WENT INTO THE BATHROOM BY MYSELF!" Levi announces at the top of his lungs.

Drew laughs and high fives him, and while they are distracted, Cooper and I take that moment to give each other a look. My expression says *Be cool.* His seems to be trying to convey an entire conversation in one intensely lifted eyebrow as his head twitches toward Drew. I think he's telling me we should come clean.

No, I mouth back. *Not yet.*

He can't read lips, though. He gives a squinty frown while looking at my lips, then shakes his head. *What?*

"So," Drew says, setting Levi down, making Cooper and me snap our expressions back into easy-breezy-nothing-to-see-here mode. "Are you guys almost done here? Let's grab a pizza or something to bake when we get home. Coop, you want to come back to the house and hang out for a bit?" Is it just me or does he seem suspicious? Have his eyes always slanted like that?

This feels like a trap.

One Cooper will see from a mile away. No way will he take the bait.

"Sure, sounds good."

Or maybe he will.

Dinner was not ideal.

Cooper and I stayed on far ends of any room we were occupying at the same time and barely made eye contact. Eight times I had to interrupt Levi so he wouldn't accidentally spill the beans about me and Cooper, and no sooner did he finish his last bite than I whisked him out of the kitchen and into the bathroom for a bath. I think I left half of my pizza abandoned, but who cares? (I care. It was delicious, and I will definitely sneak out to the kitchen in the middle of the night to eat the leftovers from the fridge.)

I'm in the middle of pulling Levi's jammies down over his head when Cooper speaks from the doorway, making me jump six miles into the air. "I'm headed out."

I clutch my heart and expel a heavy breath like you do when you've just narrowly escaped death. "Geez, you scared me."

His smile is soft as his muscular shoulder leans against the doorframe. He's wearing his baseball cap facing forward, and it drops shadows on his face, only adding to the romantic vibes he's putting out.

"Where's Drew?" I ask.

"In the shower."

"Oh, okay. Well . . ." This is awkward. I don't know how to act around him now. "Be safe driving home."

"I will." He never breaks eye contact and doesn't appear to be making any moves to leave. I think we are going to sit here all night, staring at each other and building this tension between us until Levi speaks up.

"Mom, can we read *Red Truck* tonight?" He's already all the way across the room, grabbing the book and racing back to me.

"Yeah, let's read it!" I stand up and move to the rocking chair, where I pull Levi into my lap. I take a deep inhalation of his freshly washed hair; I love the way clean children smell like hopes and dreams. Once he's settled, I look up and realize Cooper is still standing in that same place, arms folded, soft smile tilting the side of his mouth. "I thought you were leaving," I say softly, suddenly nervous to have an audience for my nightly routine with my son.

"I am." He nods toward me. "Go ahead."

I try to tune Cooper out as I read to Levi, but it's impossible. His presence is as unobtrusive as a bonfire in an enclosed room. I'm aware of his every move, breath, gaze. But something odd happens the longer I read: I settle in and feel comfortable. Levi and I laugh and tease and tickle, and somehow Cooper being here feels normal.

I think maybe Levi forgot Cooper is still watching until I tuck him in and he says, "Can Coop come say good night?"

I chuckle. "Did you just call him Coop?"

Levi nods, and Cooper is already rounding the bed. "Yeah, of course he did. All my best friends call me Coop." He leans over the bed and brushes some of Levi's hair out of his face before tucking in the covers all around him like a burrito. How did he know Levi likes that?

"Then why do I call you Cooper?" I ask with a hand on my hip.

He tilts his head to look at me with a sideways grin. "Because I've never thought of you as just my friend."

Mmmm, good answer.

Cooper finishes tucking Levi in and telling him good night. I give my son one more kiss, then turn out the lights. I step out into the hallway, shutting the door to Levi's room behind me and coming face to chest with Cooper. His eyes are kindling as he stares down at me, and I hate that my first reaction is looking side to side to make sure Drew isn't around. This isn't wrong, and I shouldn't have to hide. I know this; I just don't know how to go about fixing it.

"Lucy, you are . . ." He breathes out like he can't find the words. "I loved watching you put him to bed." He picks up my hand and presses it to his chest. "Do you feel that? My heart is going mushy. You're turning me into a sap, and I don't know what to do about it. It's weird."

"I felt the same way when I first held Levi." I shake my head at the memory. "I was fully prepared to hate him and resent him for ruining my life. But imagine my surprise when, suddenly, my life felt full and wonderful with him in my arms. Kids have this way of making you want to rip your hair out one minute, then snuggle them up and never let them go the next."

Cooper's smile is soft and nostalgic, thoughtful in a way I hadn't seen from him yet. He pushes some hair from my face. "Do you think you'll want to have more kids?"

My eyebrows rise, and my heart skips. I can now feel the blood whooshing through my veins. "Umm . . . yeah. I guess I do. But not alone again. Ideally, I'll be married next time—to a man who will get me Cheetos when I'm craving them at midnight and help with diaper duty."

He grins. "You just want a Cheetos runner?"

"*Mm-hmm*." My eyes drop to Cooper's mouth, and one side curls up slightly. He lightly brushes his fingers against mine before he leans down and whispers, "I better go before Drew gets out of the shower." His warm lips press into my cheek for only a fraction of a second before he pulls away. "Leave your window open tonight."

"What? Why?" I ask Cooper's fantastic retreating back. He looks too good in navy T-shirts.

He shrugs those big shoulders. "Going to be a nice night."

CHAPTER 30

Lucy

I'm lying in bed with my window open, feeling like a kid waiting to see if Santa shows up. But that's ridiculous, right? Cooper is not going to come through my window. That would be insane. I don't even have a tree or a lattice or anything for him to climb up. So, unless he's Peter Pan and can fly me off to Neverland, I don't think he's going to show up tonight. Maybe he really did just want me to enjoy the nice weather.

Or—

Wait . . . was that a sound? That was definitely a sound.

I shoot up in bed and clutch my covers against my chest. It's dark in my room, the only light coming from the moon, and suddenly I'm terrified. The boogie monster definitely exists, and he's about to climb through my window.

Ah! There's a shadow looming now, and if I pee this bed I will never forgive myself. "Cooper?" I whisper angrily. "That better be you! I swear if it's not and whoever is coming into my room right now is an ax murderer who kills me in this bed, I'm going to come back and haunt you in terrifying ways until the day you die!"

Cooper's familiar low-rolling chuckle washes over my skin and goosebumps surface. There's something about hearing that chuckle in the dead of night with limited visibility that makes my body go tingly. "You got lucky this time. The ax was too heavy to carry up the ladder, so I left it in the truck." Cooper puts a long leg over the windowsill and ducks his head through. Now he's in my room, and I can't catch my breath.

"You brought a ladder?!" I guess it's a good thing my room is at the back of the house, where no one will see it.

"A freaking tall one. Not gonna lie, scared me a little climbing up it."

A pack of wild horses are all stampeding through my chest. That's normal, right? I'm not dying?

Cooper gently closes the window, and now we're trapped in here together. I'm not wearing enough clothes. My T-shirt and sleep shorts are too flimsy; I can feel the breeze blowing through them. And Cooper is walking toward my bed. Oh gosh, he's walking toward my bed!

I force myself to swallow that lump in my throat as I watch his masculine silhouette approach. I scoot to the far side of the bed, but it's only a puny little queen-sized mattress, so when Cooper and his big body sit down on the side, I roll toward him like a marble.

"What are you doing here?" I whisper, pressing my back up against the headboard.

I can hear the smile in his voice when he says, "You wouldn't spend any time with me tonight in front of Drew. I wanted to talk to you more."

"So you're just here to talk?"

"Mm-hmm," he says, leaning forward and pressing a soft, slow kiss to my lips.

This isn't talking.

Cooper grabs my ankles and tugs me down so my head slides from my headboard to my pillow. He then climbs on the bed and hovers over me, elbows on either side of my face. Even in the dark, I can see his beautiful smile.

"You should see how wide your eyes are right now," he says, a chuckle in his voice. He leans on one elbow so he can run his thumb across my cheekbone. "I don't know how you open them that wide. You're like an owl."

I'm basically a wooden board. My arms are superglued to my sides, and my back is rigid. I don't move. I don't breathe. I'm afraid if I do, Cooper will vanish into thin air, and I'll realize this was all a glorious dream.

"Cooper . . ."

"Lucy . . ."

He dips his head down and kisses right below my earlobe. My shoulders melt, and I sigh. His lips are warm, and his body is heavy, and I feel so safe. There's nowhere—not a single place—I'd rather be than here with this man.

Tentatively, I move my hands up his arms and over his shoulder muscles. I feel every dent and ridge and can't believe I get to be touching him. Cooper's arm slides under my back to curl me up close to him as his kisses move up my jaw to my mouth. He hovers there, his lips brushing tender warm sparks across mine. His restraint is unearthly, a paradox. The tight hold of his arm coiling around me is the polar opposite of the light touch of his mouth.

I breathe deep, smelling Cooper and letting his scent wrap around me. It's his freshly showered, manly smell—the one where he should be starring in a commercial, standing in a towel, chest glistening with moisture in a locker room, holding up a green bodywash bottle and getting paid a million dollars to do it.

"Are you smelling me again?" he asks, lips tickling mine as he speaks.

"Busted."

He takes his lips away from mine to bury his head in my neck, and I hear him breathe in audibly. "Mmmm. I finally figured it out," he says as he lays a warm kiss on my collarbone.

"Figured what out?"

"What you smell like." He pauses and breathes in one more time. "Froot Loops." I strangle a laugh in my throat and can feel my smile touching both of my ears. "It's Froot Loops, isn't it? All this time I thought it was a perfume, but you just eat a lot of cereal, don't you?"

"I had a bowl about ten minutes ago." I'm using all of my strength to hold in my laugh so I don't wake the whole house.

"Mm-hmm, thought so." He sounds like he's smiling too.

He leans down and kisses me again, but this time it's not quite as gentle. It's just a little *more*. He pulls away and pauses, staring down at me. So I lift up off my pillow and kiss him—a little bit *more*. It's a tantalizing back-and-forth game of one-upping the other opponent . . . until it's not a game anymore, and Cooper's mouth is slanted over mine, and we're lost in this deep kiss. It's passion like I don't think I've ever experienced, and yet, it's still just kissing. His arm is still firmly wrapped around me, and his other hand is woven deep in my hair, but he's not exploring.

Does he know how much I appreciate this? I feel safe. I feel out of control—but also still *very* in control. Cooper knows my history, knows I haven't slept with anyone since Levi was born, and he's so gentle with my heart it's making me ache. Many men would be rushing this, pushing me forward toward an end goal that's selfish and fleeting. Cooper is set to *low and slow.* To have a man who's so sexy and powerful be nothing but tender and patient is intoxicating. I wish I could send this moment back in time to my younger self, when I was hopeless and thinking the world is made up of nothing but selfish pigs, and whisper, *Just hold on, there's a good one out there.*

I run my hands up Cooper's corded back into his hair. He makes a sound that strikes a match inside me, and now I don't think we'll be doing much talking tonight. Our kisses turn hungry, and I think the world outside could be burning down and I wouldn't notice. Somehow, between breathless kisses, Cooper's shirt comes off. (Because I took it off him.) I run my hands over his shoulders and biceps, dying a little at how electrified I feel from touching him.

I am tuned in to nothing but Cooper and his hands and his lips and his breath. His fingers move an inch toward my stomach, and my abdomen clenches. A thought hits me like a cannonball, and I peel my lips away from Cooper's.

Sensing my sudden distress, he stops and pulls back. "What's wrong? Moving too fast?"

"I'm a mom, Cooper."

He's silent for a second, needing to process this abrupt change in . . . everything, then he lets out a short, breathy laugh. "Yes, Lucy, I know this." His big hand comes up to cradle my face. "I'm perfectly aware of your motherliness."

"No, I mean . . . I have a *mom* body. Seriously. It's not the same as when I was a twentysomething."

"You're a twentysomething right now," he says as a counter-point.

"It's different." I'm not deterred from trying to talk him out of this, though. "My stomach has this squishiness to it that I can never ever get rid of no matter how many sit-ups I do, and my boobs are definitely not perky like they used to be—" My voice is shaking, chin wobbling. I'm completely ruining this romantic moment, but I can't help it. The words are pouring out, and I can't stop them. "I feel like nothing about me is the same as it used to be before I had him. I have stretch marks all over my stomach and thighs and—"

Cooper cuts me off with a simple yet forceful kiss. "Lucy." He says my name but nothing else. Instead, his hand moves slowly from my face to my navel, where he tenderly rolls up the bottom hem of my T-shirt to expose just my stomach. My breath is frozen in my lungs as I watch Cooper lay his warm palm flat across my abdomen and spread his fingers from farthest rib to farthest rib. Even in the dark, I can make out the way his eyes are staring down at me, and I want so badly to hide, to pretend none of what I said is true and just keep my clothes on for the rest of my life. But when his thumb runs delicately across my deepest stretch mark and he smiles, I relax—I rest.

He rolls my shirt back down before hovering over me again, pinning me in so he can look me right in the eyes. "You are beautiful, Lucy. Everything about you." He gives me a slow, lingering kiss. "Sexy." *Kiss.* "Feminine." *Kiss.* "Strong." *Kiss.* "Everything I could ever hope for."

Tears are rolling down my cheeks, and Cooper kisses them. I bury my head in his neck and let his weight and words soothe me, not realizing until tonight just how insecure I really am. He rolls over to his back and pulls me onto his chest. His hand strokes my hair, and another tear rolls down my face. For the last four years, I have been soothing Levi, tending to his needs, sacrificing my own desires and comforts so I can make sure his are met. But tonight . . . I am the one who is comforted.

He doesn't say anything else, and I don't either, because I'm not even sure what to say. Everything feels too weak, and I'm afraid if I say what my heart is really feeling, I'll scare him away. Instead, I run my hand slowly up Cooper's chest until it settles on his jaw. I play with my favorite lock of hair that flips up at the nape of his neck and smile before settling my head in the crook of his shoulder. I close my eyes, feeling the warmth of his skin against my face and listening to his quiet, steady breaths. He's good for me, and I think I'm good for him.

I don't know how long we lie here together, my arm wrapped tightly around Cooper's chest and his hand gently stroking my hair away from my face, but it's bliss. Eventually, as I'm drifting off to sleep, I think, *I'm never letting him go.*

The sun wakes me early the next morning, and I squint my eyes open, taking in the large man-arm draped over my shoulder. I kiss it and smile against his tan skin, the hairs of his arm tickling my lips.

Cooper takes in a stirring deep breath as I roll over to look at him. Because everyone knows morning breath is a beast, I bunch up the sheets and pull them over my mouth before saying good morning.

He gives me the most adorable scrunched-nose smile and cracks an eye open. His hair is sticking up in all directions, and his bare chest is on display for all to see. Well, not all—just me. Only I get to see it, because even though we don't have an official title yet, Cooper is mine—all mine—and I refuse to share. "Morning, beautiful."

My smile beams because it's cheesy lines like this that get me. I want to gather up as many as I can and dress myself in them each day, strolling all over town and flaunting them so everyone can see. Flowery words are wonderful when they're genuine.

"Is this real?" I ask Cooper, snuggling into his chest and feeling heat radiating off his skin like he's made of the earth's core. My shirt is uncomfortably twisted around me, and I don't know how Cooper senses it, but he does. His hand reaches behind me and tugs it down so it's sitting correctly again. It's the little things like this he does that turn me inside out.

"I hope so," he says in a sleepy, gravelly voice. I can't help but smile and kiss his chest.

"You've got to climb out of this tower soon, Rapunzel," I say, snuggling deeper into him.

His chuckle rumbles in his chest, and he kisses my hair before resting his chin on my head. "You're not making a very compelling case for me leaving."

"I know." I wrap my arms around him and bear-hug him. "But you really do have to go. Levi will be up soon, and he does not knock before he busts in here."

He groans and rolls over onto me playfully so he can bury his face in my neck. I can barely breathe with his weight on me like this, but to say I love it would be an understatement.

"So tired," he grumbles. "Just want to sleep here with you all day."

I intertwine my hands in his hair. "You. Have. To. Go," I say between wheezing breaths. "And I have to go to work."

He half growls, half grunts, then moves back over onto his back, popping his hands behind his head and letting his smile slant as he stares at me. With my room full of wonderful, *wonderful* light, I'm able to see every defined ab, oblique, pectoral, and biceps. I'm staring like muscle inspecting is my new full-time job, and my voice takes on a zombie-like quality. "Oh good gracious, you need to put on a shirt."

His pearly white smile turns cocky. "Yeah? You like what you're seeing?"

I poke him in the side. "Why do you always take on an Italian accent when you're trying to come on to me?"

"Don't act like you don't like it." He reaches for me and tugs me up to him so he can try to convince me to let him stay with neck kisses. It would probably be highly seductive if he wasn't saying the only Italian words he knows in between kisses. *Spaghetti. Fettuccini. Parmesan.*

I'm laughing and trying to push away from him half-heartedly. "Stop it—you're just making me hungry."

"*Lasagna,*" he says in his deepest bedroom voice.

I can't stop laughing. "You are so weird, but I love you anyway." No sooner do the words leave my mouth than I realize what I've just said.

I freeze.

Cooper freezes.

His grip on my wrist loosens, and his eyes slowly cut down to me. "What did you just say?"

"Huh? Oh. Nothing. Said nothing. Did nothing. Nothing, nothing, nothing." I'm squirming now, trying to free myself from his grip and impending embarrassment because it's *way* too soon to be saying things like *I love you.*

Because I'm a nimble little ninja, I wiggle away from him and dart out of the bed, racing toward the bathroom, ready to lock myself in for the rest of my life. But if I'm a ninja, Cooper is a panther. He shoots up and has his arms around my waist before I can take five steps. He tosses me back onto the bed and pins his forearms on either side of me. His eyes are twinkling dangerously. "Say it again."

"No."

"Why?"

I grimace. "Because it's embarrassing to say it first."

"Say it." His voice is dark and passionate, and it matches the look in his exotic blue eyes.

I sigh, morning breath forgotten, and hold his gaze. Time to be brave. "I said . . . I love you. Because I mean it. I didn't mean to fall in love with you so quickly, and it's completely fine if you don't feel the same way because it's way too soon to be saying things like that, but—"

"Lucy, I absolutely love you. No question about it." He doesn't smile yet, and my eyes eat up every bit of his serious expression. "I think it's probably unhealthy, but since the day I met you, you're all I think about, and I'm helpless to do anything about it." His lips finally form a sideways smile, and his eyes crinkle in the corners, like he knows all of this is ridiculous but doesn't care either. "I love you. And Levi. I want to be in your life as much as you'll let me."

My eyes are welling up, and I wish I wasn't the kind of person who cried when both happy and sad. I put my hands on either side of Cooper's face as he bends down to kiss me, moving straight past soft and tender to passionate and adoring. Our lips part, and the sheets start twisting, but I put the brakes on again because I do not want to have to explain any of this to Levi.

"Okay, okay, yeah," Cooper says, sitting up to rest his elbow on his bent knee and run his hand through his hair.

I shake my head at the sight of pure masculine perfection, silently cursing him for making it so difficult to say goodbye. "Okay, time to sneak back down that ladder now."

His eyes catch mine, looking serious and calculating in a way that makes my heart skip. "I don't want to." He sighs deeply and shakes his head, falling back against the pillow to scrape both of his hands through his hair. "I don't want to go, Luce. I don't want to hide us. I don't want to acclimate Drew to the idea of us before we tell him." He rolls his head to look at me—dark lashes framing ocean eyes, bronze skin a stark contrast against my white comforter. "It feels a little crazy to do that, doesn't it? I mean, we're the ones who know what's best for us." I can see more thoughts running behind Cooper's eyes than just the ones he's voicing. A plan is being set in motion, and for some reason it's making my palms sweat.

"Well, yes . . . I agree that it doesn't feel right, but—wait, what are you doing?" I ask, watching Cooper rise from the bed with a determination in his shoulders.

"It's not right that he decided this for us. I'm not sneaking back out that window."

"Then what are you doing?"

"I'm staying here and having pancakes with you and Levi, because contrary to what Drew thinks, I am capable of commitment, and I do trust myself with this. I'm all in with you and Levi." He extends his arm and points a finger at me like he's a star quarterback and I'm going to be the one catching the ball. "And you and I start now."

"Umm! Like *now,* now?!" I hop from the bed and trail after Cooper, who is headed for the door. "Wait, wait, wait! Shouldn't we think about this for a minute?! Form a nice plan? Maybe have you go put on a button-down shirt and arrive with flowers—for Drew, of course—and then we can all talk about it over breakfast? *Oh gosh, Cooper, at least put a shirt on!*" All my protesting is pointless.

I'm trying to grab his belt loops to hold him back, but he's just dragging me along like a barefoot skier.

He throws the door open with gusto, his sinewy muscles rippling with the movement. Cooper pauses for only half a second to listen for any signs of Drew until we both hear the sound of water running in the kitchen. He gives one distinct nod, then starts heading for the stairs. I'm taking them in rapid succession right behind him while frantically whisper-yelling, "Cooper! *Cooper!* Stop. This is not going to go over like you're hoping. *Gahhhhh,* please go slower. Come back to bed. *Let's make love!*"

Not the slightest pause.

I guess this is really happening.

CHAPTER 31

Cooper

"Drew," I call out before I even make it to the kitchen, because I'm just itching for a fight now.

I hear Lucy groan behind me and offer up some prayers of protection as we round the corner.

Quickly taking in my surroundings, I stop in the threshold, and Lucy bumps hard into my back. "*Ouch.* Brake lights next time." She puts her hands on the outsides of my biceps and peeks around me like a little baby bear.

The coffeepot is in Drew's hand, hovering unpoured over his mug, jaw hard and flexing. There's a moment where we both do nothing but stare at each other, and if my adrenaline wasn't pumping through me in unhealthy quantities, I'd probably regret my decision. Drew takes me in from head to barefoot toes and the word *angry* writes itself in a thought bubble above him.

"Drew," I say, making the first attempt at conversation. "We need to ta—"

"What are you doing in my house right now?" Oh, that is *not* a happy tone.

"That's what I want to—"

"And where is your freaking shirt? And your socks. And your shoes."

He's not actually worried about my socks and shoes; he's just wanting to point out that I'm far too naked to be in his home right now with his baby sister holding on to me.

Lucy squeezes my biceps, and it gives me the courage I need. "I spent the night here last night."

Drew's nostrils flare, and he swallows dangerously. I want him to set down that mug. I think it's about to shatter under his white-knuckled grip. "You slept with my sister?"

Thankfully, he turns and sets down the mug and coffeepot—except now his hands are free to strangle me.

"Not in the way you're suggesting, but I will sleep with your sister in the way you're suggesting at some point."

Lucy's fingers bite into my arm. "Not helpful," she hisses at me.

"I told you to stay away from her," Drew says, his voice somehow getting closer even though he's staying put.

Lucy pushes around me this time. "Okay, enough of your macho talk. I'm my own woman, Drew, and you can't tell men to stay away from me like you own me."

"Luce." My tone is soft and pleading, begging her to let me deal with Drew. Her sharp blue eyes cut to me and melt. She gives me a single nod before I turn my gaze back to my friend.

"What was that?" He has scary eyes bouncing between me and Lucy, and he wiggles his finger between us. "That little silent communication. What was that? Because to me, that looked an awful lot like two people who have been talking about something for a long time."

I nod. "That's exactly what it was. Look, I'm sorry I went behind your back, and I tried as hard as I could to not see her, but—"

"But you did what Cooper does best and did exactly what you wanted."

"Drew!" Lucy says in a warning.

I point at Drew. "*That*—why do you say stuff like that about me? Dude, you've known me one year. You've barely scratched the surface of who I am, and yet you're acting like you've known me my whole life. Why did you just shut me down when I first approached you about Lucy? We could have talked. I could have told you I went through a really hard breakup before I moved here, had a long-term, serious relationship and wanted her to marry me. I have a whole life I lived before I met you, but for some reason you've been content to just know me in the now and let that be enough."

Drew isn't swayed. He folds his arms like a defiant child. I think he'll stomp a foot next. "I do know you. I lived with you, remember? I saw the parade of women you brought through here—"

"Hardly a parade, okay? Let's be accurate with our insults."

"*Don't* be funny with me right now. I am not laughing."

"I'm not trying to be funny, Drew. I'm trying to get you to see that I'm not the guy you have built up in your head. Yeah, I dated a lot, but that doesn't mean I didn't *want* something more serious."

Drew scoffs with a scary smile. "Bullshit. You may think you've changed and want something stable, but Lucy doesn't get to be your test subject. She and Levi deserve the best—not to be your next trial to see if you can be a family man or not."

Maybe a month ago, I would have believed him. Because here's the thing about people you admire speaking into your life: sometimes you trust their opinion of yourself more than your own. But just because they say it doesn't make it true, and I'm done letting him tell me who I am.

"You're wrong, and I'm asking you to try to see me differently."

Drew scrapes his hand across his jaw and shakes his head. I look to Lucy, and she must see the weakness behind my armor, because she smiles and comes to wrap her arm around my middle, burrowing up under my arm. Every touch from her feels like home, and it gives me courage to push forward.

"I love your sister, Drew, and I love your nephew. I know this all comes as a shock because you haven't been around to see our time together, but—"

"Enough." Drew holds up a hand and looks between Lucy and me with an expression of disgust that I don't feel is warranted. "I don't support this, and I'm pissed that you did this behind my back."

"Well, I could say the same to you," Lucy says to Drew, a wobble in her voice that cuts me.

He shakes his head slowly at her. "You're making a bad choice again." Lucy sucks in a sharp breath through her nose, and I know she's trying not to cry. I pull her in closer. "And you . . . I have nothing left to say to you." Drew's feet pound the floor as he storms past us, knocking into my shoulder as he yanks his keys off the counter and leaves the kitchen. A second later, the front door slams behind him, making both my shoulders and Lucy's jump.

We both stand frozen, staring at the spot where Drew just stood, holding on to each other, speechless. My thumb glides slowly up and down her arm, and her fingers squeeze my hip. I know Drew isn't right about me. I know he isn't right about Lucy making a bad choice. And yet . . . his words burrow under my skin and tell me maybe I'm the one who's wrong. Maybe he sees some glaring fault in me that I can't.

Maybe Lucy and Levi would be better without me . . .

"Well, that didn't go the way I hoped," I say, finally breaking the silence and trying to drown out my own insecure thoughts.

"You should have just taken me up on having sex."

"Is that option still on the table?"

Lucy pinches my side, and I squirm, trying to get away from her torture. She turns her face to kiss me square on my chest, then peels herself away, going to the coffeepot and pouring us both a cup. "Can you get the pancake mix out of the pantry?" she asks over her shoulder. Her hair is hanging long down her back in loose, beautiful, wild waves, and her T-shirt is askew, showing an extra inch of her collarbone. Maybe it's just Drew's voice still ringing in my ears, but I can't help the feeling that I don't deserve to be here.

"You still want me to stay for breakfast?"

Lucy pauses and turns around to lean back against the counter, a sweet smile settled over her mouth. "Cooper James, I love you, and nothing my ignorant brother says will change that. I know you better than he does, and I want nothing more than for you to stay and eat pancakes with me and Levi this morning. Please don't go." She holds out her arms, and I gladly step into them because now I'm a man addicted to Lucy's touch.

"I don't want to come between you guys."

She sighs. "Sometimes confrontation is necessary, and clearly this one was. I think it's okay that we're asking for Drew to see us differently. He's used to knowing each of us a certain way, and we've both changed, grown out of who we used to be, and he's trying to hold us in a box we don't fit in anymore. I'm sure it's going to be uncomfortable for a bit, but he'll come around."

"And if he doesn't?"

"Apparently, you don't know Drew very well either. He will. He just has to throw a tantrum first."

I lean away so I can take Lucy's face in my hands. "Have I told you I love you?"

She grins. "Are we going to be that annoying couple who says it every five seconds now?"

"Oh yeah. I can see myself becoming very clingy."

She lets out a groan. "Insufferable. Are you going to call me a hundred times a day?"

I pick her up and set her on the counter so I can kiss that patch of her shoulder that's peeking out of her shirt. "A hundred and one."

"Gross. You're not going to call me *babe,* are you?" She tilts her neck and taps a finger to it, showing me exactly where she wants me to go next.

I grin and do as I'm told, laying a warm, lingering kiss right above her finger. "Oh yeah, baby."

"*Baby?!* Oh, that's worse. I don't know if I can allow that." Her voice is trailing off as I nip at her earlobe.

I feel her shoulders melt as I hover my mouth over her ear and whisper, "I'll call you anything you want me to, Lucy."

"Oh goodness." Her tone has me scooping her up off the counter and carrying her out of the kitchen. She kisses my neck as I carry her to the stairs, her room my destination.

Until . . .

"PANCAKE DAY!!!" Levi shouts from the top of the stairs.

I pause in my tracks and shut my eyes in a tight, pained squint because I've never been more upset to hear those words in my entire life. Lucy laughs and strokes the back of my head, then whispers, "Welcome to parenthood."

CHAPTER 32

Lucy

"Do you want to come over and watch something sappy with me tonight?" Jessie asks as I'm cleaning up my station and getting ready to head out of work for the day.

"I would, but I'm headed over to—"

"*Cooper's house!* I know, I know; it's what you do every day now."

I puff out a breath. "I'm not that bad."

"Oh yes you are, but I don't blame you. I'd be the same way if I had a fine man loving on me like Cooper is with you." Jessie's gaze drops, a familiar forlorn look creeping in. She must sense I'm about to console her, though, because she abruptly holds up her hand. "Nope. I'm good. Don't need a pep talk today. Maybe tomorrow, but today I'm okay."

Nice try. I pull her in for a hug anyway.

It's been three weeks since I started "officially" dating Cooper, and yeah, now that I think about it, I guess we've been pretty inseparable. I should probably worry about how obsessed I am with him, or how attached Levi has become, but I'm not. He fits. It just feels right between us in a way I didn't know was possible.

"So you're going over to Cooper's to—"

"*Put together furniture,*" I hurry and interject before she says something blunt that will make me blush. Jessie and Cooper are the worst—especially when they team up. It seems like their life's mission is to turn my cheeks into raspberries.

"Mm-hmm. That's an innuendo if I've ever heard one."

I laugh as I stuff my freshly sanitized scissors back into their case. "This time, it's really not. We ordered a bunch of furniture for his house last week, and he got a big shipment of it today. We're going to order pizza and put it all together."

"And thennnnn get to the good stuff, right?" Her eyes are sparkling, and her eyebrows are wagging. "Right? I'm right, aren't I? What bra are you wearing?" She's reaching for my shirt like she's going to take a peek.

I swat her hand away and jump back. "Stop that! You're so nosy."

"I'm living vicariously."

"Well, knock it off, you creepy preggo."

She shrugs and rolls her eyes.

I sling my purse over my shoulder and pull out my phone, refreshing my messages again, like *that* will change anything. Are phone glitches still a thing?

"Still no word from Drew?"

I pull my lips to the side and shake my head. "Nope."

Unfortunately, he has not come around to the idea of me and Cooper yet. In fact, he's been straight-up avoiding me. We live in the same house, but I barely ever see him. He's been working like a maniac, picking up extra shifts so he doesn't have to face me. I'd almost swear he moved out because, despite me staying up late and waking up early, I never see him. The only evidence I've found of him living with me is when I almost dunked myself in the toilet two nights ago because he never puts the seat back down.

"What a big baby," she says, shaking her head with disgust marking her mouth. If there's one thing that's certain in this world, it's that Jessie hates my brother. It's awkward, and I try to avoid the conversation as much as possible because her pregnancy hormones scare me sometimes.

"I know, he is acting like one."

"I think my child will come out more mature than your brother."

"Most likely."

"I should buy him a big diaper for Christmas."

"Yep! Sounds good!"

"You're doing that thing where you're backing away from me while I talk."

"Nooooo. Not me." My back bumps into the glass door, and Jessie crosses her arms and flattens her smile. I flash her all of my pearly whites and blow her a kiss. "Love you! I promise I'll let you rant about my brother who you've never officially met tomorrow!"

"Have fun tonight." She rubs her belly dramatically. "And remember to always be safe!"

I'm still laughing about Jessie's comment as I make my way to my car and get in. I drive all the way to Cooper's house with a cheesy smile, feeling the need to sing Christmas tunes even though it's nowhere near Christmas. Christmas tunes make me happy, so I do it anyway.

When I arrive, my phone rings. "Hey, Mom! I just made it to Cooper's house and should be at your place in about two—"

"Honey." Something about the way my mom's voice sounds as she cuts me off has an immediate panic shooting through my veins. "I need you to meet us at the hospital."

I don't even know what's wrong yet and tears are welling in my eyes. "What happened? Is it Levi?"

At that moment, I see Cooper step outside, still wearing his nice work clothes: a button-down dress shirt, slacks, and dress shoes. The bright smile stretching across his face does not fit the words that are coming out of my mother's mouth.

"I'm sure everything is going to be okay, but Levi is having really bad lower abdomen pain, and he just started throwing up. We're on our way to the ER now to have him assessed."

Cooper opens my car door, and I can't even look at him. My mind is frantically running to dark and scary places. "Have you called his pediatrician yet?"

The shake in my voice has Cooper crouching down beside me and putting his hand on my leg. "Yes, about an hour ago. I thought it was just a stomachache, so I didn't want to worry you, but Dr. Daren said to take him in if it progressed, so that's what we're doing." My mom's voice sounds calm, and I know if Levi had to be with anyone during something like this, my parents are the perfect people. Still, I'm terrified.

"Okay, I'll be right there."

The moment I hang up, Cooper asks, "What's wrong? What happened?"

"My parents are taking Levi to the hospital. He's having severe stomach pain. I need to go. I need to get to the hospital." Tears are streaming down my cheeks as I numbly put my hand on the steering wheel, suddenly feeling a thousand miles away from my baby and like I won't get there in time.

Cooper softly peels my hands from the wheel and guides my

chin to look at him. "Let me drive, Lucy. Everything's going to be okay."

I swallow and let him help me out of the driver's seat, then I rush around to the passenger side and get in. My hands are shaking as he starts the car, and I can't get the buckle to snap into the buckle thing. I try to slam it in five times. Six. Seven!

"*Gah!* It won't go! The freaking buckle thing won't buckle!" I'm frantically trying to jam it in, and if I look insane, Cooper doesn't say anything. He leans over, takes the buckle from my hand, and slowly clicks it in place before taking my hand and interlacing our fingers. His eyes lock with mine, and my chin wobbles, tears streaming down my cheeks like waterfalls.

"It's okay. I'm going to get you to the hospital, and everything is going to be okay." It's a brave promise on his part, but I cling to it like I'm dangling off a cliff and those words are my only lifeline. Cooper kisses my knuckles before putting the car in drive and breaking every speed limit on the way to the hospital, and I'm more thankful now than ever that I have him. Otherwise, I would have definitely rammed into the back of the snail in front of us driving two miles an hour on the interstate.

Miraculously, Cooper doesn't even threaten to break up with me when I roll down the window as we pass said snail and stick my head out, yelling, "The gas pedal is on the right!" I do regret flipping that lady the bird, but it was her fault for getting between a mama bear and her cub.

Whew, what a night.

Several hours after arriving at the hospital, I'm sitting beside my child, who's hooked up to an IV and sleeping, still under the effects of anesthesia after having his appendix removed. Yep, my four-year-old had appendicitis tonight. I almost can't believe it. For some reason, I thought that was like an old man's disease. Turns out, it most commonly affects kids, and I *hate* that my kid is one of them. But it's over now, and he's sleeping peacefully as I stroke his hair.

My mom has had a series of meltdowns, the poor thing. She feels so guilty for not calling me as soon as the pain started. She didn't want to disturb me if it ended up just being gas, but then everything escalated quickly, and she realized what was going on. I've hugged her at least a hundred times tonight and reassured her that I won't be taking her grandma license away, because honestly, I would have done the same thing in her shoes. Kids have five thousand aches and pains a day. It's hard to know when things are serious or not, so I don't fault her for waiting to call me. I'm just thankful we were here in Nashville and around my family when this happened.

Beyond the obvious reasons—like the man walking into the hospital room right now with a gigantic coffee for me—I'm glad I came home. Not everyone has the ability to live near their family in a healthy way, and I feel beyond thankful that I do. This is where I belong. Making it on my own is overrated when I have a family like mine.

Speaking of . . .

"Have you heard from Drew yet?" I ask, looking up and taking the Styrofoam cup from Cooper.

He shakes his head. "Not yet, but your mom is still trying him."

I can't believe Drew isn't here for this. It makes me so angry I want to stomp the ground, Hulk style. He can throw a tantrum about Cooper and me all he wants, but to make Levi pay for it is inexcusable. If he ever shows up, I will wait until he has hugged and kissed his nephew (and hopefully showered him with lots of amazing gifts) and then I will *murder* my brother.

"You have terrifying eyes right now," Cooper says, retaking the seat he's been occupying beside me all night. He wraps his hand around mine, and I feel my blood pressure lower to less of a cardiac arrest zone.

I look at my little boy sleeping peacefully in the hospital bed, and my heart squeezes. "I'm so angry at Drew. He should be here."

Cooper squeezes my hand, then drops it so he can scoop my feet up into his lap and rub them. "Don't worry about Drew right now. Levi's safe and taken care of, and that's all that matters. I'll kick Drew's butt later."

I turn my eyes to Cooper and his handsome disheveled hair, his big calloused hands tenderly massaging the arches of my feet. The immature part of me wants to stick my tongue out at Drew and say *Told you we're good together,* but the other part of me doesn't give a crap what Drew thinks, because I'm so happy I could burst.

Cooper's long lashes fan out as he stares at my feet, his movements pausing and his broad chest expanding with a deep breath like he's taking his first relaxed inhalation of the night. Which he probably is . . . because Cooper has been my rock tonight. He got me to the hospital, made sure everyone had everything they needed, ran home to pack me an extra set of clothes when we found out Levi would be going into surgery, and held me in the waiting room while fear of the worst gripped me and I cried. He called Jessie and told her everything while asking her to cancel all my appointments for the week. He's been busy, and I'm just realizing that not once tonight did I feel that familiar ache of wishing someone was with me to help carry the load.

There he is, my very own pack mule. Okay, admittedly, that's not the most flattering comparison, so I decide to keep it to my-self. Instead, I trace a line with my eyes down the slope of his nose, over the silhouette of his pillow-soft lips, and across the scruff of his strong jaw. He doesn't have to be here, but he is.

Cooper's head swivels to me, catching me red-handed as I stare at him like a piece of meat I'm weighing at the market. *Busted.* He gives me his signature smirk, the one that makes women everywhere swoon, needing resuscitation when they see it. The one with the boy-next-door dimple in the corner and bad-boy eyes that make you want to run home and break up with your oh-so-average boyfriend.

"What are you thinking about right now?"

"If I have a Sharpie in my purse so I can write my name across your forehead."

He grunts a laugh and continues rubbing my feet. "You're in-sane."

I scoff. "Puh-lease. Don't think I've been too consumed by my worry to not notice the way Nurse Jessica keeps giving you bed-room eyes."

"Bedroom eyes?" he asks with one eyebrow lifted in confusion.

"Yeah, you know? These." I slightly curve my lips and lift my eyebrows, tilting my head softly. I hold the pose for way too long, waiting for him to recognize the look, until I realize his mouth is twitching and he's trying to hold back a smile. Ugh. I'm so gull-ible. Of course he knows what bedroom eyes are.

I release my incredible expression and punch his arm. "You do know what bedroom eyes are!"

He jerks his arm up to his chest to defend himself against my attack. "Yes, but I wanted to see your attempt at them. You looked like a bad imitation of the Cheshire Cat."

I gasp dramatically. "Take that back. I looked like a sex kitten!"

He buries his head in the crook of his arm while I knock him out with my otherworldly strong punches. He's laughing as he says, "More like someone who just ate something nasty and is trying to keep on a polite smile until they can spit it out."

I rip my feet away and shoot up out of my chair so I can stand in front of him and purple-nurple him. He doesn't let me. He wraps his arms around my thighs and rear end to pull me up close to him. "I love your bedroom eyes."

I squint an eye and run my hand through his blond waves. Gosh, he has really fantastic hair. Such a shame to have natural highlights like this wasted on a man.

"You're just trying to butter me up to avoid my incredibly intense punishment."

"You have the strength of a baby. Levi could arm-wrestle you and win."

"Such a charmer," I say, pushing my hands firmly through his hair so his face has to tilt up at me. I bend and drop my head to lay a soft, polite kiss on his lips. "Thank you for being here today."

His arms coil tighter around me, contracting like a boa. "Always. I'll be here *always*."

"That's quite a promise."

"Mm-hmm," he hums in a self-assured way that leaves no room for argument and makes my belly fill with heat.

Somewhere in the middle of him kissing me, the door to the hospital room opens and in steps Drew, holding an obscene number of balloons.

CHAPTER 33

Cooper

I'm kissing Lucy's neck, then suddenly she pulls away and pushes her open hand onto my face, shoving me back. "Ow—what was that?!"

"Drew!" Lucy says by way of greeting, and I drop my arms from where they were wrapped around her.

I turn my head to find Drew standing motionless in the doorway, eyes bouncing from me to Lucy to Levi asleep on the bed and back to me. I think there's going to be a big fight. I set my shoulders and prepare for battle, then Drew sighs and steps in farther. "I'm sorry."

Neither Lucy nor I expected that—not after three weeks of silence and then not hearing from him once over the past few hours of Levi's surgery. So we both stay quiet, stunned.

Drew runs the free hand that's not clutching enough balloons to carry a small child into space through his hair. He then takes three big, fast steps forward, shoves the balloons into my hands, and grabs Lucy to pull her in for a bear hug. "I'm so sorry, Luce. I've been the worst."

"I'm glad you can see it too," she says, stiff in his arms, not yet ready to reciprocate the hug. He doesn't seem to care, though, just holds her tighter.

"I would have been here sooner, but my phone was in my locker at the hospital while I was attending a birth, and then when I was finally able to check it, it was dead. I didn't have my charger, so I didn't realize Levi was in the hospital until I showed up at home to your friend I've never met before ready to fight me in my driveway."

Lucy pulls away to look at him. "Jessie?"

"Yeah, she was there to confront me. And let me tell you, she's scary. This was definitely the first time I've ever had a pregnant woman threaten to use her baby bump as a weapon."

"Oh my gosh. I love her."

His face screws up. "Really? Can't say I'm a big fan. And she seemed to really hate me."

Lucy laughs. "Yeah, she does *not* like you."

"That was definitely communicated." He pauses for a moment, and his face turns serious. "But she was right about a few things. I shouldn't have reacted the way I did."

"No, you shouldn't have," I say, standing and inserting myself into the conversation. I can see that Lucy is wavering and her arms are itching to give in and hug Drew, but I'm not there yet. He pissed me off, treating Lucy the way he did these past few weeks.

Drew lets go of Lucy and turns to face me. He looks remorseful, but I'm ready to fight him anyway. We're about the same height, so it would be a fair match. "I know. I'm sorry. It started with good intentions of protecting Lucy and Levi, and then . . ." He shrugs like he's embarrassed. "I might have gotten my pride hurt a little that you went behind my back. In the beginning, I really was worried that you didn't have it in you to commit, but then I think I started to worry more about what would happen if you guys split. Then, admittedly—and thanks to Jessie for so violently pointing this out to me—I don't think I liked the idea of losing my wingman to my sister. No offense, Luce."

"Lots of offense taken," Lucy says in a dry tone that makes my lips twitch.

I stare at Drew for a heavy minute, because my feelings are twisting together. Anger is fusing with understanding, and the large part of me that hates confrontation is ready to just move on. If he sees the error in his ways, I'm good with that. Sometimes men need time to process, so I'll let it go. "Cool," I say, reaching out to do a bro-high-five-hug thing. Our hands clasp, and our shoulders bump against each other, and we're good now. Water under the bridge.

We pull apart to find Lucy standing directly beside us, hands on her hips, eyes blazing. "That's it?! After everything we've all gone through, y'all are just going to do whatever that was and move on?"

Drew and I both look at each other and shrug. "Yeah," we say in unison.

Lucy is not okay with this. She folds her arms and stomps a foot defiantly. It makes me smile and want to do something silly like pick her up and spin her around. Drew moves first, though. Lucy must know what's coming, because her eyes widen and she turns like she's going to bolt out of this room, but he catches her first, bending down to wrap his arms around her thighs and flipping her upside down. Some change falls out of her pockets and clangs against the ground.

"Ugh. Put me down, you big jerk! You're such a nincompoop. I bet you're going to steal my change next and run out of here."

"Say you forgive me," Drew says with a big grin.

The tips of Lucy's hair are brushing against the floor, and she folds her arms. She'll stay like this all day if she has to. She will pass out in this pose before she gives in to him. "Never. You said mean things to me."

"I'm sorry, Lucy. Really. It was a bad move, and I won't do it again. And I don't think you're making a bad decision with your life. I wish I had never said that. But I'm so tired of fighting with you. I miss talking to you."

"What happens when you tell me not to eat the pie on Thanksgiving and I do anyway? Are you going to freeze me out again?"

"No," he says, indulging her and speaking in his most serious tone. "I'll respect your decision to eat the pie."

Her arms soften a smidge—maybe because she's about to pass out. "And you need to apologize to Cooper for insinuating that he's a sleazeball, incapable of becoming a family man."

Drew's eyes rise to mine, and I raise my eyebrows like a snooty teenage girl waiting for her due apology. "My darling Cooper, please accept my sincerest apologies for doubting your character. I will never do it again. But also . . . if you leave my sister, I will beat you into dust."

"Fair. I accept."

Drew looks back down to Lucy. "There, see? We made up. Will you forgive me now, Luce?"

"Yes. But only on the condition that you owe me ten nights of babysitting."

He chuckles and turns his eyes to Levi. "Deal. I've missed that kid. Is he mad at me?"

"Nah," I say, all too happy to rub a little salt in his wound. "He's had me."

Drew's eyes slowly cut to mine, but there's humor there underneath the tough façade—also maybe a little gratitude. He gives me a silent nod, and that small gesture feels loaded with more meaning than any words ever could. I nod back. It's settled. I'm officially welcomed into the family.

"Hey, guys," Lucy says from her inverted position. "Is the room starting to get darker to you?"

Lucy doesn't pass out, but she does wobble adorably when Drew sets her back on her feet. I wrap my arm around her shoulders, pull her back against my chest, and kiss the side of her face. It feels good to be openly affectionate like this in front of Drew. His gaze definitely still hitches on us for a fraction of a second, but he forces a smile and turns to Levi.

He takes my seat beside the bed and offers to do a shift sitting with the kid until Brent gets here in a little bit, so I can take Lucy to get some food. She never ate dinner, and I know she's starving but unwilling to leave Levi. Now, with Drew here, she finally lets me guide her out of the room. In the cafeteria, we find Lucy's parents and end up spending a whole hour laughing and getting to know one another over Jell-O and nasty plastic-wrapped turkey sandwiches because the kitchen is closed.

Despite the less-than-mediocre food, it's good. Her parents are hilarious, just like her and Drew. Claire takes my hand from across the table and thanks me for being so good to her daughter—which makes Lucy's cheeks turn my favorite shade of raspberry sorbet. Then her dad leans back so Claire can't see him and mouths, *Respect my daughter . . . or else,* which is terrifying on so many levels, and I will definitely have a nightmare about it tonight.

After the frightening threat, Drew calls to say Brent is there, and Levi is awake and asking for us. Us—as in me and Lucy. It's the wildest thing, going from a life of bachelorhood and late-night drinking to having a four-year-old in a tiny hospital gown wrap me around his finger and ask me to sing him "The Itsy Bitsy Spider" eighteen times and me doing it gladly.

Around midnight, after Brent went home with a promise to come back in the morning and then take the overnight shift tomorrow, I look across the hospital bed where Levi is asleep holding my hand, to Lucy who is passed out, legs curled up in the seat with her, wearing one of my sweatshirts that pretty much swallows her whole. It's a sight I don't think I'll ever forget and certainly never want to.

CHAPTER 34

Lucy

It's been a few days since Levi's surgery, and thankfully, he is recovering quickly. I have barely left the house since we got home from the hospital, but since he's feeling more like himself today, I left him with Drew and headed for Cooper's house to finally put together his new furniture.

"Hellooooo," I call out as I struggle to shove the front door open. It feels like a sumo wrestler is on the other side, and when I get through, I see why.

My eyes widen at the enormous wall of brown furniture boxes piled up all around the entryway, and I can't help but feel a little guilty at the sight. Did I really order this much stuff for him? Felt like a lot less in the online cart.

"LUCY!" Cooper yells from somewhere past the cardboard tower. "You got some 'splainin' to do!"

Ladies and gentlemen, if you are looking for Cooper's fault, I have found it. He uses this *I Love Lucy* joke more times than anyone ever should. I forgive him his faults, though, when his handsome face peeks up over the row of boxes and I can tell he's not wearing a shirt. Suddenly, I'm in a ninja warrior competition and scaling these boxes because *I will win my prize*.

I crest the top of the tower and spot Cooper on the other side. He's wearing black gym shorts slung low on his waist and no shirt. He is sort of a nudist, I've learned. If he's home, that shirt is coming off.

He takes my hand and guides me down off the box wall, and I land in his arms. He smiles down at me, nose to nose, and then his eyes drop to my mouth. That—the moment where his gaze settles on exactly what it is he's after—never fails to make my stomach leap. The freshly showered, damp-hair look he has going on doesn't hurt either.

"Hi," he says in this low, delicious, grumbly way. "How long do we have until you have to get back?"

"A few hours."

He lifts an eyebrow, his smile turning devilish. Maybe Jessie was right about how little furniture we would actually end up putting together. "Hmm, well, we're going to have to get to it, because we have *a lot* of work to do in the bedroom."

Cooper bends down and hauls me up over his shoulder like a brute. I love it. I especially love the view of his back as he carries me through his living room and down the hall. My stomach is buzzing with nerves, and I'm anticipating a lovely evening—until Cooper finally sets me down and makes a sweeping gesture toward the frightening number of boxes stacked against the walls in his room.

That's when I remember the extent of my late-night shopping spree. Cooper told me he was ready to commit to furniture but wanted me to pick it all out for him. The gesture was not lost on me since he once told me he would wait until he'd found the woman he wanted to marry to make all the big purchases, and oh boy did I! I don't think he meant to buy everything for the house at once, but that's on him. He should have been more specific.

I make a hissing sound and turn my eyes to a glowering Cooper. He folds his arms, which is really unfair of him because it makes his biceps bulge out and the sexy veins in his forearms pop, but judging by the look on his face, it would be ill-advised to touch him at this moment. Or maybe it would be the *perfect* time to touch him?

"So . . . just to be clear, you *actually* meant we have work to do back here?" I say, pouting.

He shakes his head slowly like a disappointed parent. "I thought you were ordering a few things for each room."

"Well, it started that way." I take a step away from his grumpy look and bump into a box. "But then I saw a lamp I thought you would really love and would go great with your wall color . . . which then reminded me that you didn't have a bedside table, so naturally I had to order you one."

"Naturally. So where does the . . ." He trails off to read the tall slender box in front of him. ". . . *faux fiddle leaf fig with matte blush planter* come into play?"

I widen my eyes like he's a chump for not seeing the answer on his own. "Once we get the new drapes hung on this side and put your new dresser over here, that corner would have looked ridiculously bare." I put my hands on my hips and lift an eyebrow. "You don't want to look ridiculous, do you?"

"Tell me now, woman—are you a compulsive shopper?"

"No, but I just couldn't stand how empty it was in here—and I already know you make tons of money, so you're not hurting from the extra expense. I hated the thought of you living in here all by yourself with no furniture or things to make it a home. Don't be mad. Are you mad?"

He takes a step closer. And then another. His hands drop to his sides, and his head tilts as he takes yet another step forward. His hand flexes like the sexiest scene ever filmed (aka the Darcy hand flex from *Pride and Prejudice* . . . you know what I'm talking about) and the room heats to eighty million degrees. My skin is ready to melt off my bones from the intense look he's giving me.

When he gets close enough to touch me, he stops. I can feel the heat rolling off his chiseled chest like waves, and I imagine if I were wearing thermal goggles he would look like a ball of fire. I want to place my hand in the center of his abs and burn.

He leans down, and I tilt my head back, exposing my neck, ready for my favorite trail of kisses. Instead, his lips brush, soft as a paintbrush, all the way up my neck, barely touching, so he can whisper against my ear, "Until all of this is put together, no kisses for you, Miss Shopaholic."

My mouth falls open as I watch Cooper's retreating back. "Ugh! You're kidding, right?"

He smirks at me over his shoulder. "Afraid not. You order, you assemble. Get to work, Bob the Builder."

"But where are you going?"

"To put together my new dining room table and *eight* matching chairs for my imaginary giant family."

"WHICH YOU LOVE, RIGHT?!" I yell because Cooper has already left the room.

Frankly, I think he's being ungrateful of my very thorough design services. Then again, as I look around the room and sigh, this does look like a lot.

An hour later Cooper comes to find me. I'm lying on the floor, holding my phone above my head, watching TikTok dance videos, and when I spot him I chuck it across the room and pretend to be tinkering with something under the bed. "*Ah*—there we go. Much better."

He stands above me. "Whatcha doing?"

I slap my hand against the bottom of the bed. "Oh, you know, just tending to a few other things while I'm here. I noticed your bed screws were loose, so I thought I'd give them a little tightening."

"With your bare hands?"

"Don't be jealous of my strength."

He glances around the room. "Lucy, it's been an hour."

"And?"

"You put together the lamp."

"It was difficult to screw the shade on."

He bends down to wrap his hands around my ankles and slide me out from under the bed, a knowing smirk on his mouth. "You're not going to put anything together, are you?"

"No, I am! I really am. I just got distracted." I crack my knuckles. "I'm ready to get down to business so I can get those kisses. Here, hand me a Jerry."

Cooper's eyebrows rise quizzically. "A what?"

"A Jerry. You know, one of those little doohickeys they include with the furniture so you can tighten the bolts up." I'm miming the gesture of screwing something in, and Cooper is looking at me, dumbfounded. How is he not getting this? "You know, it's a right angle. It looks like a flat star on each end?"

Cooper rubs the back of his neck, and I have made a *poor* choice not getting this stuff built because, honestly, he looks so good it hurts. Dang those distracting TikTok videos. "Do you . . . do you mean an Allen key?"

"What's an Allen key?"

He bends down (hello, fantastic backside) and picks up the exact tool I was talking about. "Allen key."

"Ohhh, is that what it is? Yeah, I call it a Jerry."

He frowns, looking torn between amusement and horror. "Why?"

I shrug. "Because I can never remember Allen."

"But you can remember the name Jerry?"

"Mm-hmm. Why are you laughing like that? Seriously . . . do you really need to double over so dramatically? Oh, you're going to slap your thigh now. Okay, yeah, laugh it up, Mister Chuckles. *Lucy doesn't know the names of tools because she's not Mrs. Fixit!* Hardie-har-har."

Cooper finally controls his laughter enough to come over and help me up off the ground. His arms go around me, and he hugs me tightly to him. "Lucy, you're the craziest person I've ever met."

"Rude."

"I love you." He cups my jaw, and his lips crash into mine. Just like that, he caved on his own no-kissing rule. I knew this would happen, which is why I didn't take the furniture assembling too seriously. Cooper always tries to withhold physical affection from me when he wants me to do something, and it never works. It does the opposite. It makes him twice as passionate when he gives in, but I'm impressed, because an hour is definitely the longest he's made it.

"Would you say yes if I asked you to marry me?" he says in a gruff voice with an intoxicating smile.

I freeze and meet his gaze. "Are you seriously asking me?"

"Maybe. Give me your answer first and I'll tell you." The way his eyes are twinkling almost has me complying. It's very difficult to not give in to Cooper right away.

"That's not how it works."

"Allen keys are also not called Jerrys."

"That's different . . . those are tools. This is you asking for me to mix my life with yours in a permanent way."

He grins and drops his hands away. "We don't do anything the normal way. So tell me—would you say yes?"

My breath constricts in my lungs, but I have to be honest with him. "I don't think I could. We've only been seeing each other for, like, two months." I say it casually like I don't know exactly how long and I'm not the kind of girl to tick off every single day on the calendar and mentally celebrate things like week-iversaries. "And some of those days, we weren't even official! Imagine what people would say if we got married. They would think we're delusional. You haven't even known me long enough to really decide if you want to spend every day for the rest of your life with me. We need more time together so you can realize I stick my stray hairs to the shower wall so they don't go down the drain and then forget to clean them off."

It's terrible that I'm not saying yes right away, especially given the fact that his last relationship ended because his girlfriend didn't want to marry him. But it's not that I don't want to marry him—it's that I'm scared to. Scared he'll get tired of me.

I'm preparing for a fight or for Cooper's shoulders to sag and him to walk away, Charlie Brown style. He doesn't, because like he said, we're not normal, and that's mainly because he's an extraordinary man. He does, however, do something unexpected.

Cooper smiles, scoops me up, carries me through the house and out the back door, marches to the pool, and dumps me in without so much as pausing.

I come up, gasping for air, mouth wide open and disbelieving as I stare up at him grinning from ear to ear beside the pool. I swear, if his freaking abs didn't look so incredible, I would break up with his sorry butt right now. "What was that for?!"

Cooper dives in next and surfaces beside me, eyes dark as the night he first brought me out here to his pool. Seeing that look has me sucking in a sharp breath. Cooper's strong shoulders hover above the water as he swims closer, grabs my hips, and picks me up to wrap my legs around his waist. He smiles and kisses me softly, and I feel disoriented. What's happening right now? Should I be mad? Because that's definitely not the feeling I'm experiencing.

"Lucy," he says, pushing my wet hair from my face as I cling to him like a little koala. "In this pool is when I first decided I wanted to spend forever with you. I knew it perfectly then, and I know it perfectly now. You are unique and a little strange at times, and I love that about you. I don't need more time, but it's okay if you do. I'll wait for you until you're ready, but I just wanted you to know I've been crazy about you from day one."

I sniffle and wipe my eyes. "These aren't tears," I say, shaky voice betraying my lie. "It's just water from the pool dripping off of my lashes." Cooper wipes away the "water" with his thumbs. I stare into his eyes and feel what I know is unusual but also completely *right* settle over me. Sometimes life is kooky and happens out of order. Sometimes it's a roller coaster, and you can either buckle down and hold on or throw your hands up and scream your heart out as you soar around the loop-de-loop. Honestly, I think both reactions are necessary, but for this particular loop, I'm throwing my hands up.

"I love you, Cooper. Let's get married."

And I'll tell you one thing: we will *not* be assembling any furniture tonight.

EPILOGUE

Lucy

Cooper and I got married. Like married, married. Ring-on-my-finger, marriage-certificate, move-all-my-stuff-into-his-house-and-sleep-in-*our*-bed-every-single-night kind of married. Want to hear something even crazier? We tied the knot a month after he proposed in the pool. I'm still shaking my head at it because I know we're completely loony to have done this. But who cares, right? We're happy loons, and we knew what we wanted, so we went for it.

We had the most romantic small wedding in a vineyard a little outside of Nashville. Even in my wildest dreams it couldn't have been more perfect. We then took a weeklong honeymoon at a beautiful resort in the Caribbean. Seven full days with just Cooper was . . . well, I'm blushing just thinking of it.

But we're home now, and tonight we're having a family movie night wearing our matching dinosaur PJ pants (you better believe Cooper has some now). If everyone wasn't gagging enough at our whirlwind romance, they definitely will when they see this picture of us in our matching jammies on social media.

We're here on the couch, snuggled up with Levi, and putting down some new roots as a family. The strangest thing about all of this, though, is that it *doesn't* feel strange to think of Cooper as a part of our family. His long arm is resting across the back of the couch so he can still run a finger across my collarbone while Levi lies between us, and it feels like this is how it was always supposed to be. Natural. *Right.*

Levi starts snoring with his head in my lap, and Cooper throws his head back with an exaggerated *Finnnallly.*

"Whoa," I say, eyes wide as I watch him pop up from the couch and begin scooping Levi into his arms. "Where is this sudden angst coming from?"

"I love this kid to the moon and back, but he takes way too long to fall asleep." Cooper is hightailing it down the hallway toward Levi's room. (Cooper had dinosaur wallpaper put up before Levi moved in to surprise him, and I've never shed more tears in my life.)

I'm chuckling quietly as I follow behind Cooper and his speed-racer body, just narrowly managing to get Levi's door open before Cooper rams right through it like the Kool-Aid man. He sets Levi on his bed and tucks him in, creating a little Levi-burrito with the covers, but I feel like I'm watching it all happen on 2x speed. I didn't even realize Cooper was capable of moving this fast.

Finally, he whips around, grabs my hand, and tugs me out of the room, closing the door behind him, then hauling me like a trailer hitched to his truck, bobbing in the wind, as he races us toward our room. I'm laughing so hard I can barely keep up.

"Move those short legs faster, woman!"

"I can't! They're not used to exercise. Why are we running?!"

Cooper pulls me into our room and shuts and locks the door behind him. He turns around, an animal who has just caught its prey. He points toward the closed door, stalking toward me in precise movements. "That child could wake up demanding water or comfort after a bad dream at any moment." It's adorable how quickly he's caught on to the parenting life. "And I intend to make complete use of our alone time."

Not wasting a second, Cooper grabs my hips and tosses me back onto the bed. I'm still laughing even though I know I shouldn't. He tells me the same thing as he starts kissing my neck. "This is serious. You're my wife, but that cute, bossy little guy keeps me from touching you all day. I have to make up for lost time." His warm calloused hands run up and down my sides, sending a familiar thrill up my spine. His mouth presses against mine, and no sooner am I able to taste his lips than my phone begins buzzing angrily on my bedside table. Cooper's head sinks onto my shoulder in despair, and he groans. *Poor Cooper.*

"You're going to want to answer that, aren't you?" he says, dismay blanketing his voice.

"Could be an emergency."

He sighs dramatically and scoots over to sit with his back against the headboard. "Go on. I'll wait."

I give him a quick peck on the lips and answer my phone. "Hey—"

"*You have to help me!*" Jessie cuts me off, voice frantic like she's just outrun a serial killer.

"Jessie, what's wrong?! Is it the baby? Are you okay???"

Cooper sits forward, mimicking my concerned expression.

"NO! MY GRANDADDY IS COMING!" She says it so loud I have to hold my phone away from my ear to protect my eardrums.

Once Cooper and I both register her words, we relax. He rolls his eyes and stands, grumbling something inaudible that I imagine is not very kind-spirited toward Jessie. "I'm going to go lock up the house. Tell Jessie I hate her and she's never allowed to call at night again."

Jessie heard all of that. "Oh, he sounds grumpy. Did I interrupt sexy times in the James household?"

"Please, never call it that again. And yes, you did. It's very likely he will hold this against you for the rest of your life."

"What a pouty little man-baby." Jessie has no sympathy for men. I wonder if she's always been this way or if it's just residual anger against the man who left her. Which is valid anger, I might add. "But seriously, you've got to help me."

"Because your grandaddy is coming to town? I don't see the problem. I thought you guys were really close. He raised you, right?"

"Yes, and yes. But that's exactly why I'm in so much trouble!"

"Why? Is he mad at you for getting pregnant or something?"

There's a suspiciously long pause. "Not exactly."

"Jessie . . . please tell me you haven't been hiding your pregnancy from him."

"Don't be ridiculous. Of course he knows I'm pregnant! How in the world would I be able to hide that? No. He just . . . thinks I'm engaged."

"*What!* And *that* is easy to hide?"

She groans loudly. "I know! It wasn't a great plan, but I've been making up excuses all through the pregnancy of why my fiancé could never come with me to visit, and I thought maybe I could eventually say he got hit by a bus and died or something."

"Breaking up would probably be an easier lie . . ."

"But then he surprised me and said he'll be here in the morning and can't wait to meet my fiancé! That little sneak is trying to pull a fast one on me! And *who am I going to get engaged to before tomorrow?!*"

The scary part is, I think she's serious. I wouldn't put it past her to be hunting the aisles of Target right now, looking for a clean-shaven man in the bodywash section. He might actually say yes because Jessie is drop-dead gorgeous, pregnant or not pregnant.

"No one. You're going to woman up, face your grandaddy, and tell him the truth."

Complete silence settles heavy on the line for four beats before we both break out in laughter and she asks, "So what's the real plan?"

"Well, obviously I have an idea, but you're not going to like it."

"Tell me. I'll do anything."

I screw up my face like she can see me through the phone and say the one name I know makes her skin crawl. "Drew."

"No." Apparently, she didn't even need to think that over.

"He's your only option, Jessie. And even though you think he's a pigheaded jerk, he's actually a sweetie and would help you if you asked." She's quiet . . . deep in thought. "Or you could just tell your grandaddy you broke up with your fiancé and then this whole problem is solved."

"No!" Her no is even more forceful this time. "I just . . . I can't do that. I want for him to think I'm engaged."

"Why?"

"Because I do. Don't worry about it." That's odd, but I don't push it because if I've learned anything about Jessie, it's that she doesn't like to talk about personal problems until she's ready.

"Okay. Then we're back to Drew."

She whimpers. "Do I have to marry him?"

"No. In fact, I think you shouldn't since you generally hate him, but I think he could stand in as your fake fiancé for a few days until you decide to kill him off." I pause briefly and then add, "Just so we're clear, I mean *pretend* to kill him off."

"Such a party pooper. Breaking up is probably better, though, so I don't have to stage a fake funeral too. That might get expensive." I'm worried money is her only reason for thinking a fake funeral would be a bad idea.

After one last long, dramatic groan fit for a war movie, Jessie concedes. "Okay. Fine. You're right; he's my only option. Can you call Drew and beg him to meet me at my place tomorrow morning at eight? I can't do it without showing my disgust."

I roll my eyes. "You're going to have to be nicer to him if you want him to really help you."

"Gosh, I wish I could drink. It would make this all so much easier. But, okay, tell him I promise not to hurt his itty-bitty fragile feelings if he helps me."

"Not gonna say that."

"Whatever you think is best."

The sound of the bedroom door shutting makes me jump. My gaze bounces up to Cooper, standing in front of the closed door, moonlight reflecting off his chest and abs and an I-mean-business look on his face. I hurry to get rid of Jessie. "Yep, I'll work it all out, gotta go, *bye*!"

I end the call and pretend to chuck my phone across the room with all my might (but really, I gently tuck it away in my bedside table drawer). I look back up, and Cooper's eyes sparkle with anticipation.

"I'm done sharing you tonight." He advances into the room until he's close enough to plant his hands on either side of me. "You're all mine now."

Well, if he insists . . .

BONUS EPILOGUE

Two weeks prior (The Wedding Day)

Cooper

I take one last glance out the window at the sprawling vineyard. Everything is golden right now, warmly lit by the sun, and making this moment—the biggest moment of my life—feel like something out of a movie. It was Lucy's idea to get married here, and I'll never forget the look on her face when she told me about it. *Okay, don't freak out,* she had started with her signature nervousness showing all over her pretty face. *But the one place where I've always dreamed of getting married had a cancellation. It's this perfect little vineyard over beautiful hills about an hour outside of Nashville. But here's the catch . . . the date of the cancellation is next month. If we don't take it, we'll have to wait a year. Which is completely fine if you want a long engagement since we're already being ridiculous by getting engaged so quickly but—*

I cut her off with a kiss. *Book it. I would marry you tomorrow if that were an option.*

I still find it funny she thought there was even a chance I'd say no to her. Not only have I never been more sure of something in my life, but my soul is tied to Lucy in a way I can't explain. Why would I ever want to wait a single day to marry the person I breathe for? Society says we've lost it—we're out of our minds to marry this soon. And maybe we are. But who gives a shit what people think when we're this happy? Lucy and Levi have so easily wrapped me around their fingers and I'm content to remain that way for the rest of my life.

Speaking of Levi, when I glance at myself in the mirror, tugging at the collar of my tuxedo, Levi does the same to his little suit. He's been getting ready with me and Drew (Lucy and I are keeping the wedding really small, which means our wedding party is comprised of Drew and Jessie only) and continues to look up at me with eyes that someone should only look at their greatest hero with. I don't deserve that look, but I'll strive every damn day to be worthy of it.

"Nervous, buddy?" I ask Levi, meeting his gaze in the mirror. He's going to be walking Lucy down the aisle today because she wanted him to know how important he is to her, and so he knows that I'm not just marrying Lucy—we're becoming a family.

"I don't want to make Mom trip," Levi says with sweet, wide eyes that make him look exactly like his mom.

"If it helps you feel better, I'm nervous about tripping too." I turn to him and drop onto one knee to help adjust his tiny dinosaur-print bow tie. *God, this kid is cute.* I'm so excited to watch him grow up. He has a dad, and I'm not trying to upstage that role, but I love Levi more than I thought possible, and I will always make sure he knows I'm here for him in any way he needs during the years to come.

"You're nervous too?"

"Oh yeah. But the good news is, every single person out there loves us both. Even if we mess up in front of them, it'll be just fine."

When we were making the guest list, Lucy and I decided we wanted it to be intimate. She's not comfortable being the center of attention, and I didn't want to force her into a stressful situation on a day that was supposed to bring her nothing but joy. There's only about fifty people out there waiting for us, and it's perfect.

Levi's smile is a mix of excitement and nervousness. It's also contagious because suddenly my stomach turns over and I'm hit with the very real thought that my life is about to completely change. *And I can't wait.* His face says he's thinking the exact same thing—just maybe in a less aware sort of way. We're in this together, both trying to look relaxed and confident.

Today, Lucy is going to walk down the aisle with Levi holding her hand, and I get to be on the receiving end of both of them. *How the hell did I get this lucky?*

Drew pops his head into the room. "You two ready? The ceremony is about to start."

Levi sucks in a nervous breath and bounces on his feet, looking like he might pee his pants.

"You good?" I ask him, not sure if I'm already failing at this parental gig and I should give him a better pep talk or what. "Do you need to go to the bathroom?"

Levi shakes his head.

"Do you need a high five?"

He shakes his head again.

I glance over my shoulder briefly at Drew and he just grins lightly, completely unwilling to help me out, even though he probably knows exactly what Levi needs. *Jerk.*

I take in Levi's nervous face once again and soften. "What about a hug?"

This time Levi nods and he falls face first into my arms, burying his little face against my shoulder. I wrap my arms around him and squeeze, holding on until he's ready to let go. "Thanks for letting me marry your mom, Levi. I promise I'll always take care of her. And you."

Because he's a four-year-old, his response to this heartfelt sentiment is a simple "Okay."

"All right, let's go, big guy," says Drew, holding his hand out for Levi. "Your mom's ready for you to walk her down the aisle. Coop, we'll see you out there."

I'm standing at the front of the ceremony under an enormous flower arch, waiting for Lucy. I tap the side of my thigh in rhythm with the strumming guitar, trying not to look as nervous as I feel while watching Jessie and Drew walk down the aisle together toward their spots up here at the front. Not nervous because I'm getting married, though. Nervous because Jessie and Drew can't be trusted to exist within a six-foot radius of each other because one of them is liable to wind up murdered. Even now, I can tell by the look on Drew's face that Jessie is probably squeezing his arm with hers as hard as possible. He whispers something to her that has a scowl as cold as ice forming over her mouth.

I breathe a sigh of relief when they part ways and Drew takes up his spot behind me. Finally, the music changes, announcing Lucy's arrival. My heart is a stampede as I wait for that first glimpse of her. We haven't seen each other in twenty-four hours, and I'm starved for the sight of her. Heads turn and everyone stands, letting me know she's there. I'm irrationally jealous of every single person at this ceremony getting to see my soon-to-be wife before me. And then, a flash of white emerges from around the trees and there she is. Emotions slam me in the stomach. *God, she's beautiful. Gorgeous.*

She looks like an ethereal nymph, stepping right out of a story as she makes her way down the aisle in a glittering, gauzy wedding dress with her auburn hair waving down her back and wildflowers pinned through her hair. She's clutching a bouquet in one hand and Levi's hand in the other. The setting sun is at my back, lighting her up with a golden glow that leaves me breathless. And because Lucy is truly incredible, she grins down at Levi—making sure he feels important even though this is her wedding day.

I don't deserve this woman.

A flood of panicked thoughts hit me in succession, one after another. Why did she choose me? How am I ever going to deserve her? Will I be able to love her like she needs to be loved?

But when she gets closer and her eyes lock with mine, a quieting certainty washes over me. We are meant for each other. Lucy is mine, and I am hers, and I will spend every single one of my days making sure she knows just how hopelessly devoted I am to her. And with every step she takes toward me, I feel my heart and breath settle. I just want her in my arms. I want her forever.

When she gets close, she mouths *hi,* like we're casually meeting on any old day. The gesture is so *Lucy* that it makes my eyes well. Does she know she has me in a choke hold? That she could tell me to jump into a volcano for her and I'd do it?

I mouth *I love you* while holding her gaze. Finally, when she makes it to the front, I step forward and take her hand from Levi. But not before giving him a hug and a high five and telling him what a great job he did, bringing his mom down the aisle.

"I didn't trip!" he whispers, eyes lighting up like fireworks.

"You did great, buddy."

He gives Lucy a kiss on her cheek and then runs over to Drew. I bring Lucy with me to stand underneath the canopy of flowers overlooking the rolling hills of the vineyard. And yeah, there's family and friends sitting out there watching us, but as far as I'm concerned, it's only me and Lucy now. Her full lips tremble with a smile and she's blinking a thousand times. It'll be a miracle if we make it through this thing without sobbing.

"You okay?" I whisper quickly, and for some reason that question makes her laugh, easing the tension in my chest.

"I'm so good. Are you having second thoughts? Now's your chance to tell me. I'll let you run off into the sunset with no hard feelings if you do." She pauses. "Actually, that's a lie. I will be upset. Probably for a while. But I'll likely get over it in time. You shouldn't let that stop you, though, if you need to—"

As much as I love to listen to her blabber about literally anything, I cut her off because I don't want her to think there's even the slightest hesitation on my part. "Lucy, there is nothing else in this world I would rather do than marry you. You're stuck with me now."

"Thank goodness," she breathes out, briefly shutting her eyes. Her eyelids sparkle in the light, and I have never felt more captivated by a person. My gaze roams her face and collarbones, down to the low dipping neckline of her dress. She is absolutely perfect.

Lucy squeezes my hand and I look back up to her eyes. "Caught you," she whispers with a twinkle.

The officiant steps closer and bends her head toward us. "Are you ready?"

We both blurt the word *yes* maybe a little too loudly because everyone gathered laughs.

The officiant gives her intro speech, having written it after spending some time with Lucy and me and learning our story. It's simple and real, explaining how our love story started like a wild-fire, leaped into the unknown, and ended up here as a family. And then Lucy begins the vows.

"Cooper, I promise to love you with all my heart, mind, body, and soul. I promise to love you with all I've got, today and every day after," Lucy says, her voice cracking over half of the words. The force of her promise hits me in the deepest, fleshiest part of my heart. *She's mine.*

I run my thumb up and down her wrist. "Lucy," I start, my voice miraculously steady despite my swirling emotions. "From the moment I met you, my world changed. You brought color into my life and furniture I never knew I needed into my house." We both chuckle. "I promise to love you fiercely and wholly. To give you all of me and hold nothing back for the rest of our lives."

Her eyes glimmer with tears as I continue. "I promise to stand by your side, no matter what life throws at us. I promise to love Levi with that same ferocity, and to provide a home filled with laughter and warmth. I'm so honored to be your husband."

Everything happens in a blur after the vows. We exchange rings, are pronounced man and wife, and I get to kiss my bride. In every wedding I've been to, everyone rushes this moment or makes a joke of it. But I want to start this marriage off with letting Lucy know I will cherish every damn second I get with her. Every time our lips touch. Every night I get to share her bed and make love to her. I want her to feel it all in this kiss.

I step closer, slide my hand up her arm, and settle it against her jaw, looking in her shimmering eyes and hoping she can see every-thing that stirs inside me for her.

"My wife," I say in an awed whisper before dipping my head and pressing my lips to hers. Cheers and applause erupt around us, but I'm not done yet, and neither is Lucy. Our lips push and pull against each other, and Lucy quickly goes up on her tiptoes, looping her arms around my neck. I cinch my forearms tightly around her waist, hugging her and feeling every inch of her glorious body press into mine as we kiss the hell out of each other. We finally pull apart when we hear Levi whisper to Drew, "Ew. They're kissing a really long time."

The outdoor reception is a mix of wild and heartfelt. Of course Jessie stands up and gives a toast that has Lucy bawling her eyes out (and only I catch it, but she definitely flips Drew the bird behind her back as she walks away from the mic). And then Drew gives a toast that *ahem* might have made me tear up a little too. After that, I don't think any of us stop laughing and dancing until it's time to close everything down.

Levi is passed out on Lucy's mom's lap, and we wake him up gently to give him hugs before our send-off. Lucy promises him we'll call him every day and that he's going to have a blast with Grammy and Grandpa while we're gone. Levi, however, is back to sleep before she's even finished talking, and it's clear she's having a harder time leaving him than he is with her leaving for a week.

Lucy didn't want to have the classic send-off where everyone shouts and throws things at us, so instead of making a huge to-do, I steal her hand and pull her quietly away with me into the night.

"Cooper!" Lucy whispers as she picks up the front of her dress so she can keep up with my pace. "We can't just leave without saying bye to everyone, though!"

"Why not? It's our wedding. We can do what we want."

She's struggling with her dress too much to keep up, so I pick her up and carry her toward the parking lot, heel-toeing it as quickly as I can with a woman in my arms and dress draping to the ground that I have to avoid ripping. I'm out of breath and sweating when we're only halfway there and Lucy notices.

"Parking lot's a little farther away than you thought, isn't it?"

"Yep," I say, shamefully struggling as I continue carrying her. When did they put so many damn hills in here?

"Wish you'd had Drew drive us in the golf cart, huh?" Her eyes are glittering, cheeks flushed, and her hair is a little sweaty around her temples from the humidity and dancing. She's never looked more beautiful.

"Listen here, wife," I say, setting her on her feet and then putting my hand to her abdomen to back her up against a tree. "We've only been married a few hours and you're already being a smart ass?" I say, making sure the tender affection in my voice shines through.

"I've trapped you. Now you'll see my true colors." She angles her face up, resting her head back against the tree to look at me; and I press my lips to the curve of her neck.

"Yes, please," I say before running my tongue against her throat, drawing a sweet, soft moan from her. I kiss my way up her neck to her mouth, and just before I capture it again, Lucy takes my face in her hands, forcing me to look her in the eyes.

"Cooper James."

"Yes, Lucy James?"

"I need you to know something very, very important."

I place my palm flat on the tree behind her head, brushing my lips over hers as I say, "I'm ready. What is it?"

The grin she gives me lights a flame down my spine. "Tonight . . . I am wearing fantastic underwear."

ACKNOWLEDGMENTS

Every book is an immense labor of love, and my books wouldn't be nearly as good without the incredible team that helps me every step of the way!

Thank you to my alpha and beta readers (Ashley, Brittni, Kari, Summer, and Kirsten)! You ladies are all gems and so sweet to read my story and help me make it better!

Thank you to my original lovely editors! Caitlin and Jenn! Ah— I'm so lucky to have such brilliant women working on my book and taking great care of it. Thanks for helping me feel good about sending this thing out into the world! And thank you to my current editorial team at Dell who has brought this book into your publishing house as a rerelease and made it so special!

My bookstagram friends!! You make book launches so fun. You have no idea how much your support means to me and helps my career! You guys are a blessing <3.

And to my family, thank you for your constant love and support :).

READ ON FOR AN EXCERPT FROM

THE TEMPORARY ROOMIE

BY SARAH ADAMS

CHAPTER 1

Jessie

The line rings three times before Lucy answers. "Hey, Jes—"

"HE DIDN'T SHOW!" I immediately yell at my best friend.

Lucy chuckles. She's lucky she's not anywhere near me right now, or I'd pinch her in the tender spot under her arm for taking this so lightly. "Who didn't show? Your grandaddy or my brother?"

"DREW. YOUR OBNOXIOUS BROTHER!"

"QUIT YELLING!" Lucy yells back.

"I can't!"

"Why not?!"

"Because I'm fired up! This is Drew's way of getting back at me for hating him so much. He agreed to help me today, *planning* to stand me up and make me look like a fool in front of my grandaddy. I bet he's walking into the sunset with a devious smile, wearing a white linen suit right now."

"M'kay, first, it's still morning. And second, you really don't know him at all."

I frown. "You don't think he'd wear a white linen suit? I'm positive he—"

"No. What I mean is I'm sure he has a good excuse, because last night when I called and asked him to help you, he didn't even hesitate before saying yes. Have you tried calling him this morning?"

"Ha! Have I tried calling him?! Only fifteen times. It went to voicemail all of those times. I'm sorry to inform you, Lucy, but your brother is a class-A jerk, and I was right not to trust him."

What I don't admit to Lucy is that this is my own fault for ever letting myself rely on a man who would love nothing more than to ruin my life. I can't really blame him, though, because the feeling is mutual. Believe me, if there was literally anyone else in the world I could ask to pose as my fake fiancé, I would. I even asked a random guy in the grocery store last night, but oddly enough, he said no. Actually, it wasn't so much *no* as it was him speed walking away from me clutching his bottle of mustard. I was forced to rely on Drew because I was out of time and options, and that's a terrifying place to be in life.

Last night, my grandaddy (the man who raised me) called to let me know he was surprising me and coming for a weekend visit in the morning (which is now). I would normally be ecstatic about a chance to see my favorite human in the world, but that is *not* the case when I'm about to be found out as a big fat pregnant liar. *Liar, liar, maternity pants on fire!*

I didn't even have a good reason to lie to my grandaddy—he's never made me feel like I needed to be someone I'm not in order to have his love. But for some reason, when I had to call and tell him I was pregnant, I panicked and said I was also getting married.

Now, in all fairness, I also thought I *would* be getting married. I was naïvely convinced my boyfriend at the time had gone on the road with his band because he needed some time to process this big development in his life, and then he'd be back. I thought he needed to throw a little (read: huge, mega, horribly mean) tantrum over this sudden change in his life plan and then he would boomerang right back to me. Breaking news: he didn't. Some boomerangs don't circle back, apparently.

My ex-boyfriend, Jonathan, bolted just like my dad did, and now, after several long months, I've finally come to terms with the fact that he's not coming back. (Jonathan, not my dad. I lost any hope of that man returning when I was still drinking out of a sippy cup.)

So, when I called my grandaddy and told him he'd soon be getting a great-grandchild, I also might have mentioned that I was getting married. Since the word *delusional* is not very pretty, we'll say it was hope that drove me to tell that lie—hope that my life wouldn't be following the same path as my mom's, since that one clearly didn't turn out well.

Surprisingly, I've maintained this lie pretty well up until now. I've gone home to Kentucky to visit my grandaddy several times since announcing my impending nuptials . . . but unfortunately, my dear, *dear* wonderful fiancé was always too busy with work to be able to come along. *The work of a prestigious lawyer waits for no man!* (And yeah, I have no idea why I also turned Jonathan into a lawyer. I think at that point, some part of me must have known he was never coming back.) Anyway, it was all fine and dandy until the surprise trip my grandaddy sprung on me last night.

Then Lucy talked me into faking a relationship with her brother, to whom I dream of feeding laxatives via a surprise coffee delivery to his office. Drew, the physical embodiment of how a person feels when they are assigned jury duty. But wait, there's more!

Drew is:

- The human version of a popcorn kernel stuck in your teeth.
- The man so boring he eats celery for dessert.
- The only person in the world with whom it would be more pleasing to run barefoot over a trail of pointy Legos than have a thirty-second conversation.

In case anyone is still confused, I absolutely can't stand Dr. Stuck-up Marshall.

I pull back the curtains again and stare out at my driveway like a peeping Tom. If Drew pulls in right now, he'll see my face pressed up against the glass, with a squished piggy nose and death-glare eyes, and he'll keel over at the sight of it. I'm forced to let the curtain fall again when a mom pushing her toddler in a stroller sees me and looks like she might call the cops.

"Jessie, I'm sure Drew has a good explanation. I know you're determined to hate him, but I promise he's one of the good ones."

"No. My grandaddy is the only good single man left in the world—and if those old grannies at bingo were smart, they'd snatch him up. So, no . . . I do not believe Drew is one of the good ones, and I'm certain he did this on purpose. He's mad at me for throwing the bag of diapers in his face, and this is his retaliation."

"What diapers? No—you know what? I don't want to know. At least tell me what happened when your grandaddy showed up and Drew wasn't there."

Crickets. I don't say a word, and I'm hoping Lucy will think the line went dead and give up and go about her day.

"Jessieeee." She drags out my name like she just found out I ate all the cookies from the cookie jar. "What happened when he showed up?"

I sigh dramatically. "He didn't, okay? He called me this morning saying he woke up to a flat tire and had to have his car towed to a mechanic. He said he'd have to take a rain check on the visit."

"Oh my gosh! Then why in the world are you so upset with Drew? You didn't even need him!"

I blink. "Because *he* didn't know that! I never told him because I wanted to see if he'd show or not. And he didn't, so HA!"

"You are unbelievable." I know Lucy is shaking her head right now. "This hate needs to stop. You both act like babies, and I can't handle it anymore. Also, you need to tell your grandaddy the truth."

"I already did," I murmur under my breath.

"What was that?" She's being so pious now.

"I said I already told him I don't have a fiancé. Well, actually, he guessed it. He asked to reschedule for next weekend, and when I told him I thought Jonathan would be out of town that weekend, and the weekend after that, and the weekend after that, he told me he already knew and had pretty much guessed since the beginning that there was no fiancé. I guess it was suspicious that Jonathan hasn't been around at the same time as my grandaddy even one time in seven months." Duly noted: I need to fabricate better lies in the future.

Actually, I feel a tad bit silly now for ever making it such a big deal in the first place. I thought he was so proud of me because I was getting married, starting a family, following the path of the typical American dream. But get this—he's just proud of me for being me. He doesn't care a bit that I don't have a husband; he's just happy he gets to see me become a mom. At that statement, my heart swelled to the size of Texas. Once again, my grandaddy has proven that no one will be able to top his goodness.

"That's amazing, Jessie! So now all that's left is forgiving Drew."

Forgiving Drew? Over my dead body. "Oh, honey, this animosity has only just begun."

"Very mature." I can hear the eye roll in her tone. "Tell you what . . . why don't you go eat some pickles like you love, and I'll try to get ahold of Drew to find out what's going on? And then maybe we can circle back around to the forgiving each other thing."

"Bleh—no to both. My cravings have moved on to Flamin' Hot Cheetos now."

"You know, it really makes me mad that you eat whatever you want all the time and barely look pregnant. I was an elephant at your stage of pregnancy."

I know, people! I'm small for a woman in her third trimester. I get it. Everyone mentions it all the time, and it makes me feel terrible. They all look at me like I'm starving myself and my poor child will never be healthy or go to the Olympics because of me! I'm just petite, okay?! My doctor even offered to write me a note to keep in my purse that states my child is measuring perfectly and my size is more than acceptable for a healthy pregnancy. Fine, maybe I had to beg and plead (and sob) for her to write it, but it doesn't matter—that slip of paper is laminated in my purse, so every humiliating tear I shed was worth it. That old lady at the grocery store had to totally eat her words when I whipped it out and flashed it in front of her smug, know-it-all face.

When I don't respond, Lucy asks, "Jessie? Are you okay?"

I'm trying to hide it, but I can't. I let out a sharp sniffle and swipe the tear from my cheek because I'm extra sensitive about my size. And basically anything and everything all the time.

"Oh no, are you crying?"

"No."

"Yes, you are."

"No, I'm not," I say through very obvious tears. "I never cry."

"Mm-hmm."

"Crying is for suckers." My voice is cracking and wobbling because of my rude pregnancy.

"Oh, hon," Lucy says, with nothing but fondness in her tone.

"What?" I ask, going to the bathroom to rip off a piece of toilet paper and blot my eyes before my mascara has a chance to run.

I don't know what comes over me these days. One minute I'm completely fine, and the next I'm watching an erectile dysfunction commercial and weeping because it's so freaking sweet that that couple holds hands while soaking in their side-by-side bathtubs! And don't even get me started on the dog food commercials full of puppies.

"Only two more months," she says, knowing how completely over pregnancy I am. She knows it because I text it to her first thing every single morning. Combine that with my hatred of her brother, and it's really a miracle she hasn't blocked me from her life yet. A terrible thought hits me: Maybe she's only my friend because I'm her boss? I'm the owner of Honeysuckle Salon, where Lucy works, but surely she's not friends with me for that reason . . . *Gah,* now I'm crying more. This is ridiculous. Drew! I need to keep thinking about Drew so I can channel all my emotions toward hatred instead of weeping.

"It still feels so far away," I say, unsuccessfully pushing away my emotions. "Two months might as well be an eternity as long as I have insomnia and this baby continues to kick me in the ribs."

"He'll be out soon enough."

"He?" I ask, like maybe Lucy performed a secret ultrasound I don't know about and determined the sex of my baby before I did.

"Or she."

"But you said *he* first. Do you think it's a boy?" I could end this guessing game by just asking my doctor, but I'm not ready to know yet.

Lucy doesn't get a chance to answer that question. "Oh, it's him! Drew is beeping in on the other line. I'll call you back with what he says."

"Don't bother."

"Do you at least want me to have him call you?"

"Nope," I say, closing the toilet seat lid and sitting down. "He wouldn't get through because I already blocked his number. Well, I blocked it after sending him a lovely little message I'm sure he enjoyed." It was cathartic, and I don't regret it no matter how disappointed in me Lucy will be.

She sighs deeply. Poor thing is weary to her bones of all this fighting. "Okay, well, I'll call you back in a few minutes and *not* tell you what he says." She'll tell me. Lucy can't keep things to herself. It's physically impossible for her.

"Okay. Hey, Luce? You're beautiful and I love you!"

"Mm-hmm," she murmurs before saying she loves me back, because Lucy is so sweet that she's incapable of not returning affection, and then she hangs up.

I let my shoulders slump and stare at the plain blue wall in front of me, anxious to not allow the feeling of loneliness to creep up on me too close. Then a loud boom followed by a hissing noise under the sink makes me jump out of my skin. I rush to the vanity and drop down to my knees, and before really thinking about it I fling open the cabinets. *Water.* Water sprays from under the sink like an open fire hydrant, soaking my face, body, and bathroom in a harsh, stinging deluge.

Wonderful. Just wonderful.

ABOUT THE AUTHOR

SARAH ADAMS is the author of *The Rule Book, Practice Makes Perfect, When in Rome,* and *The Cheat Sheet.* Born and raised in Nashville, Tennessee, she loves her family and warm days. Sarah has dreamed of being a writer since she was a girl but finally wrote her first novel when her daughters were napping and she no longer had any excuses to put it off. Sarah is a coffee addict, a British history nerd, a mom of two daughters, married to her best friend, and an indecisive introvert. Her hope is to write stories that make readers laugh, maybe even cry—but always leave them happier than when they started reading.

authorsarahadams.com
Instagram: @authorsarahadams

ABOUT THE TYPE

This book was set in Hoefler Text, a typeface designed in 1991 by Jonathan Hoefler (b. 1970). One of the earlier typefaces created at the beginning of the digital age specifically for use on computers, it was among the first to offer features previously found only in the finest typography, such as dedicated old-style figures and small caps. Thus it offers modern style based on the classic tradition.